Eleanor Goymer spent many ye
Originally from London, Eleano
where she is a publishing consultai..
or writing Eleanor likes to spend her time musing on ..
the US is not like London.

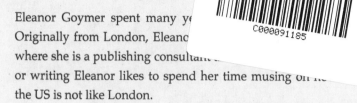

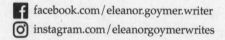

facebook.com/eleanor.goymer.writer
instagram.com/eleanorgoymerwrites

THE FALLBACK

ELEANOR GOYMER

One More Chapter
a division of HarperCollins*Publishers* Ltd
1 London Bridge Street
London SE1 9GF
www.harpercollins.co.uk
HarperCollins*Publishers*
Macken House, 39/40 Mayor Street Upper,
Dublin 1, D01 C9W8

This paperback edition 2024
1
First published in Great Britain in ebook format
by HarperCollins*Publishers* 2024
Copyright © Eleanor Goymer 2024
Eleanor Goymer asserts the moral right to be identified
as the author of this work

A catalogue record of this book is available from the British Library
ISBN: 978-0-00-865657-7

This novel is entirely a work of fiction. The names, characters and incidents
portrayed in it are the work of the author's imagination. Any resemblance to actual
persons, living or dead, events or localities is entirely coincidental.

Printed and bound in the UK using 100% Renewable Electricity
by CPI Group (UK) Ltd

Playlist

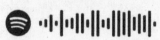

The Night We Met - Lord Huron ♥
Sofia - Clairo ♥
Scott Street - Phoebe Bridgers ♥
cardigan - Taylor Swift ♥
I miss you, I'm sorry - Gracie Abrams ♥
lacy - Olivia Rodrigo ♥
Little Bit Louder - Mimi Webb ♥
Two Ghosts - Harry Styles ♥
'tis the damn season - Taylor Swift ♥
Used To Be Young - Miley Cyrus ♥
making the bed - Olivia Rodrigo ♥
Beautiful Things - Benson Boone ♥
Again - Noah Cyrus ♥
Homesick - Noah Kahan, Sam Fender ♥
Mess It Up - Gracie Abrams ♥
Remember That Night? - Sara Kays ♥
Heaven - Niall Horan ♥
see you later - Jenna Raine ♥
The Archer - Taylor Swift ♥
Want You Back - HAIM ♥
Margaret - Lana Del Rey, Bleachers ♥
Till Forever Falls Apart - Ashe, FINNEAS ♥
invisible string - Taylor Swift ♥

For Charlie

Prologue

THEN

Rosie nervously patted the pockets in her black cargo pants, confirming once more that she had her phone in one of them and her Oyster card in the other. She wondered how long it would take her to get used to carrying a train ticket with her at all times. Probably about as long as it would take to get served a drink in this pub by the looks of it. She adjusted the strap on her rucksack, easing the weight a little between her shoulders, and looked meaningfully along the length of the bar, which was sticky and littered with damp beer towels. It was hardly a bustling pub, but the barman looked like he had all the time in the world and didn't mean to spend it serving anyone a drink.

Rosie took out her phone and checked it, hoping she hadn't got the wrong pub. He had said 4pm, hadn't he? She looked up at the clock on the wall above the bar to double check; it was yellowed with age and cigarette smoke, and she couldn't be sure it was accurate, but it agreed with her phone and therefore he was already six minutes late.

Six minutes wasn't long, but it was long enough when you didn't know the city, were wondering if you were even in the right pub *and* you were waiting to meet a potential flatmate. Rosie tried once again to catch the barman's eye but he either hadn't noticed her yet or was now deliberately ignoring her. Rosie suspected the latter and decided there and then she needed to work on her drink-ordering skills if she was ever going to make London her home.

'Are you Rosie?' Rosie turned and looked up. She hadn't noticed him walk up the stairs and into the pub, but she knew at once he must be Mitch – and not just because he knew her name. He just had such a 'Mitch' feel to him. If you'd asked Rosie five minutes before what that meant she wouldn't have been able to tell you. But now she could. She looked up at him, at Mitch, and she already felt like she knew him.

'Hi,' Rosie replied, taking her hand out of her pocket and holding it out to shake his, noticing how tall he was. And then immediately she worried that this wasn't the accepted form of greeting for a flatmate interview. This was her first time except for student living. But Mitch grinned and scratched his ear and then grabbed her hand, shaking it firmly.

'Sorry I'm late,' he said, 'I never leave enough time to get across town.' Rosie said nothing because she was too busy looking at the slight dimple on his left cheek that his smile created.

'You're not late, don't worry,' she said, quickly realising she was staring, she looked at her watch as a means to look away, but Mitch caught her doing it and grimaced, obviously misinterpreting her look.

'I am, and I'm sorry. My mum would kill me. She'd tell me it's terrible manners to suggest a meeting place and time and then not be there at least five minutes early. I should have suggested somewhere near the flat, but this place is close to the lab and easy

2

to find if you don't know the area.' If Rosie hadn't already fallen for his smile and the dimple-crease thing he had going on, then she was definitely falling for his attention to manners and promptness. Maybe less keen on his devotion to his mum, but she would see how that one played out.

Mitch waved his hand at the barman and to Rosie's astonishment the barman made his way over. She gaped. What magic power was this and how could she learn it? She made a note to ask him about this if she passed the flatmate interview.

'What can I get you?' Mitch smiled down at her. 'Do you drink beer?' Rosie nodded slightly non-committally – it wasn't her drink of choice but she wasn't convinced ordering a glass of wine in this pub would result in a positive experience.

'London Pride is good if you like bitter, but actually the house lager is OK despite being one of the cheapest pints in town.'

'Is that why you chose this place?' Rosie joked and immediately wished she hadn't when she saw the crestfallen look on his face. 'Sorry,' she said swiftly, 'now I'm being rude.'

'It's fine,' Mitch said, recovering quickly. 'Although I confess I had hoped you would think I was a really generous flatmate when I offered to buy you a drink. But now I've told you how cheap this place is, you're just going to think I'm a cheapskate.' He grinned sheepishly. 'I'm such an idiot. Always saying the wrong thing.'

Rosie hoped he would carry on saying the wrong thing if it made him seem this sweet and endearing – and if it meant he would talk about them being flatmates again. Yes, he *was* cute and he did seem *really* sweet, but she was also really *really* hoping he'd offer her his spare room because she was fast out of other options.

Mitch nodded in the direction of the barman who was starting to look like he might pour a pint of the cheap beer over the pair of them unless they ordered something smartish.

'I'll have a pint of the lager then,' Rosie said quickly, not wanting to risk losing the attention of the barman or getting a beer tipped on her, 'if you recommend it.'

Mitch put his hand on her arm, which sent a jolt of electricity up it – and not the good kind. 'Sorry!' he yelped, snatching his hand back. 'Cheap carpets in these places, always give me an electric shock.' And then seeing the stormy look on the barman's face, he said quickly, 'Two pints of lager please,' pointing at the beer pump which Rosie noticed was lacking any kind of sign. Mitch pulled a face at Rosie as soon as the barman's back was turned which made her want to laugh out loud.

Mitch picked up the two pints and ushered Rosie to a table in the far corner of the pub, where they could escape the evil glances of the barman.

'Whoops,' he said as he put one of the drinks carefully down in front of her and then pulled a beermat from the far side of the table to put under his. 'I'm now worried I might not be able to come back in here. I've called both the beer and the carpet cheap and I'm fairly sure he's not going to forgive me. Which is annoying because this is a good pub to have up your sleeve if you're ever in Covent Garden and everywhere else is packed full of tourists.'

Rosie looked dubiously down at the 'cheap' carpet and back at her rucksack.

'Here, let me take it,' said Mitch, seeing the look of concern on her face. 'I know, I definitely wouldn't risk putting it on the floor either,' he continued and then looked quickly over his shoulder to check that the already offended barman was out of earshot. He leaned over and lifted the rucksack out of Rosie's arms and then put it down on a chair next to the table.

'Wow,' he exclaimed, 'have you got everything you own in here?' Rosie felt her face begin to go red.

She grimaced. 'Not everything. But everything I need for a

while,' she conceded, looking down at the table to avoid looking at him. She picked up her pint of beer and took a big swig. Although she wasn't an expert, Mitch was right, this wasn't a bad pint.

She glanced up to see that Mitch was looking at her curiously. 'When did you say you were supposed to start work?'

Rosie suspected that this was the moment Mitch was going to think she was totally bonkers, speedily finish his pint and hastily make an excuse to leave, before he even had to tell her that his spare room was taken.

'Uh... Tomorrow,' she admitted and slowly raised her eyes to look across the table at him. To her surprise his face broke into a grin.

'That's hilarious,' he said.

'It is?' Rosie asked in confusion.

'Yeah, I mean, what was your plan?'

Rosie shook her head, not understanding him.

'If I hadn't offered you the room? What were you going to do?' he asked, not unkindly.

'Actually, I hoped you'd inevitably fall for my wit and charm so no risk there,' she joked shyly. 'But I guess if that had failed, I'd have gone back to my brother's flat and begged to stay on his and his girlfriend's sofa for a few more days till I found something else.' Mitch laughed loudly at her reply and his cheek dimpled once more.

'But Jasmine – that's my brother's girlfriend – doesn't really approve of people staying on their sofa. She says sofas are for sitting on, not for sleeping on. I've been living at my mum's this summer, but it's too far to commute in each day so I...' Rosie paused, she realised she was rambling.

'Wait, hold on a minute,' she continued. 'You said what would I do if you hadn't offered me your room? Does that mean...' she said a little more tentatively. 'Does that mean you *are* offering me your spare room?'

Mitch shrugged his shoulders. 'Sure, I mean that's if you still want it after I've brought you to the grottiest pub in town.' Rosie's cheeks flushed again, this time with excitement and she looked around the pub, taking in the sticky carpet, the yellow flocked wallpaper and the two old boys propping up the bar. She grinned across the table at Mitch. 'It's not the worst place I've ever been in but, wow, I mean are you sure about the room? You don't know me, we've only just met.'

Mitch nodded sagely in agreement. 'True, but you don't know me either and you seem OK with sharing a flat with me so I guess either we're both insane or excellent judges of character. And anyway,' he continued, 'we're going to be working in the same lab. Rachel says you're a genius and I worry she'd fire me if she heard I hadn't offered you my spare room.'

Rosie didn't know whether to be more excited by the offer of a spare room or the praise from Professor Rachel Leas, the head of department at the university and the person who would be overseeing Rosie's PhD. Rachel was one of the most eminent virologists in the country, so to be called a genius by her was both a source of pride and of terror. If Rosie wasn't already worried about living up to expectations she was now.

'You've met her, right?' asked Mitch. 'Rachel?'

'Yes of course!' exclaimed Rosie. 'But only at my interview. What's she like to work for?' she asked, nervously twisting her fingers together.

'Brilliant but terrifying, which reminds me.' Mitch looked at his watch. 'I need to be in the lab later today.' He looked thoughtful for a moment and pushed his hair out of his eyes. Rosie had noticed that he seemed to do this quite often and she rather liked this tic of his. She tried not to stare as he did it. She was already borderline obsessed with his dimple and she didn't need something else to stare at. 'I was thinking we could take your stuff back to the flat now,' he said, 'but then I really need to go check on this experiment or Rachel might have me killed.'

'You mean, go to the flat today?' Rosie asked in surprise.

'Yeah.' Mitch paused. 'I mean unless you wanted to annoy your brother's girlfriend a bit more?'

Rosie thought for a moment; she was in London, a city where she knew no one except her brother Chris and his girlfriend Jasmine. Both of whom she loved but was fully aware she was overstaying her welcome with. And now she knew Mitch, who had brought her to (allegedly) the worst pub in London and who she'd met not ten minutes ago. But he seemed funny and kind and genuine. And he worked in the same lab as her, so the chances that he was a mass murderer were negligible. She took her chances.

'I think I've annoyed them both enough.' She bit her lip and looked Mitch straight in the eye. 'How about I come to the lab with you and then we can both go back to the flat later?'

Mitch's face lit up. 'Brilliant! Great idea.' He picked his beer up and raised it to Rosie. She picked hers up too.

'To new flatmates?' she asked.

'To new friends,' he smiled. They both took a drink. 'Can I ask what your original plan was?' Mitch asked, straightening up the beer mat and putting his beer back down.

'My original plan?' Rosie asked.

'Yeah, I'm guessing you had an original plan which didn't involve sleeping on your brother's sofa or moving in with a man you'd never met before?'

Rosie looked down at the table, suddenly fascinated by the aged beer marks indelibly printed on the dark wood polish. She tried to ignore the pricking sensation behind her eyes. Mitch seemed lovely, perhaps dangerously lovely for a new flatmate. *Park that thought for another time.* But that didn't mean she wanted to cry in front of him, at least not the first time they met. No one wanted to offer up their spare room to a heartbroken, crying mess.

'Was it a guy?' he probed. 'Actually, you don't have to tell me, that's incredibly rude of me to ask.' He waved his hands as if dismissing the question from the room.

'Not really,' Rosie shrugged her shoulders. 'You've just offered me your spare room, I think you're allowed to ask why I don't have another choice.' She took a deep breath and willed her eyes not to leak. 'I was supposed to be moving in with my boyfriend, ex-boyfriend now. But then he moved to America instead, so I'm out of options. Apart from my brother's sofa.'

'Wow,' Mitch exclaimed. 'Instead of moving in with you, he moved to America? What does he know that I don't?! I'm joking!' he said quickly, scared of putting his foot in it again, but Rosie forgave him by smiling back at his joke.

'Yeah, it was a pretty drastic get out of jail card to play,' she agreed.

Mitch reached across the table and grabbed her hand. 'Seriously though, whatever happened, I think he's an idiot.'

Rosie looked up from his hand in surprise. 'I'm going to say this again: you don't know me!'

'Professor Rachel thinks you're a genius, you've forgiven me for taking you to the Worst Pub in London (trademarked)—' he saluted in the general direction of the barman '—and you just seem like a really nice, funny person. So yeah,' he shrugged, 'I think he's an idiot.'

'Thanks,' Rosie said, feeling a sense of relief and wellbeing course through her for the first time in days. 'And thanks for offering me your room. I know it looks like I'm only interested because everything else went wrong.' Rosie flapped her hand in the air between them indicating broken hearts, shattered dreams and homelessness. 'And that I don't have other options.' Realising she could be dangerously close to talking Mitch out of his kind offer she quickly shut up.

Mitch sat back in his chair and stretched his arms above his head. 'No problem,' he said as Rosie tried hard not to notice the inch or so of flat stomach he had inadvertently showed her. 'I think it'll be fun, don't you?' Rosie nodded, worried that if she spoke it would come out as a squeal.

'I'm very happy to be your Plan B.' He grinned as he said it. Rosie started to protest but he continued, 'Or your fallback, whatever you want to call me. And I can't wait to show you around London, but we should get going if we don't want to risk the wrath of Rachel.'

They tussled over Rosie's rucksack for a few seconds before Rosie gave up and grudgingly allowed Mitch to carry it for her. He turned and waved at the barman as they made their way to the steps. The barman nodded grumpily and went back to whatever it was he was doing before. Rachel turned and looked back at the pub and smiled; grotty though it was, she was excited to start her London life.

'Which part of Rachel's team do you work in?' she asked as Mitch shouldered the door leading out to the Strand. Streams of people walked past in every direction and Rosie braced herself for the rush of commuters and tourists which she would need to get used to.

'Antivirals,' he said as he held the door open for her. She looked up at him in surprise as she walked past him out into the street.

'You're kidding! Me too!' she exclaimed.

Mitch looked down at her and grinned, his blue eyes sparkling with amusement. 'Yep, I might have had another incentive to offer you my spare room,' he admitted. 'I thought it couldn't hurt to have a genius as a flatmate who just happens to share my area of research.'

Rosie laughed and jokingly swiped at his arm. 'Now I feel like I'm doing *you* the favour!'

'I think you just might be,' he agreed and grabbed her hand, pulling her out into the London street.

And just like that, Rosie and Mitch were flatmates.

Chapter One

NOW

Rosie tipped her head back and enjoyed the feel of the sun on her face. She put to the back of her mind the fact it would bring her hated freckles out. It was UK sunshine after all, hardly tropical. She stretched her feet out under the table as she waited for Mitch to come back from the bar and silently congratulated herself on the purchase of her new sandals. They were both cute and comfortable, and made her realise she desperately needed to paint her toenails. She sighed. There was always something beauty-related to do, she wondered how other people had the time to keep up their grooming habits so effortlessly.

She spotted Mitch coming out of the back of the pub, carrying two drinks and picking his way through the beer garden towards her. She could tell just from the way he was walking that he was miserable about something. That and the fact he had summoned her to an emergency drink before dinner with his mum that evening. But despite his gloomy look, her heart still squeezed tightly when she saw him – in a completely friendzone manner, of course.

Mitch arrived with a face like a black cloud and hooked his foot through the legs of the chair opposite Rosie, pulling it out so he could sit down. He plonked a wine glass in front of her and a pint of beer in front of him and said 'They didn't have a French Sauvignon so I got you a Pinot Grigio. Hope that's OK.' The tone of his voice told Rosie that it better bloody be OK, because he wasn't in the mood to be questioned on his choice of drink.

'Thanks,' she said, and quickly pulled her feet back towards her under the table as Mitch's boots caught her ankle. 'I don't know how you wear those things in the summer,' she said, pointing under the table at the black Chelsea boots Mitch had on. He glanced down as if he had forgotten what was on his feet and shrugged.

'What would you prefer I wear? Sandals and socks? Yeah that's a good look,' he grumbled. 'Not that it matters what I look like now, anyway.'

'All right,' Rosie took a deep breath. 'Tell me. What's up? Why the urgent meeting? Why couldn't we meet at your mum's as usual.'

'Tessa dumped me,' he moaned and flopped back into his seat in a dramatic fashion.

Rosie watched him. Her heart wanted to sympathise but her head was telling her not to indulge him. Poor Mitch. Not again. He claimed he had lost count of the number of times his heart had been broken, but Rosie knew that it was him that did the breaking. Mitch was the one that would end a relationship like a shot as soon as real life popped the romantic bubble.

Pulling herself back into the moment, she tried to picture Tessa, thinking this might help her in offering support. Was she the one with the curly hair who made a peculiar noise when she laughed? Or no, perhaps the one Mitch met at a work party? Giving up, she settled on composing her features into what she hoped was a compassionate face.

'I had a really good feeling about Tessa but it turned out she didn't feel the same.' Mitch sighed deeply. Rosie half expected him to swoon dramatically but instead he reached for his beer and took a long drink. He hunched his shoulders and Rosie could see he was tense. Maybe he'd actually been serious about Tessa, and if that was the case she felt a sense of guilty relief that it was over.

'I'm sorry Mitch, I know you really liked her.' Rosie reached across the table to give his hand a quick squeeze but he grabbed hold of her hand and held it tight.

'I don't know Rosie, sometimes I wonder if I'll ever meet "The One".' He gazed at Rosie earnestly. 'Don't you feel like we're running out of time?'

Rosie tried unsuccessfully to pull her hand away. 'Hmm, not really.' She pulled harder and Mitch reluctantly let go. 'I'm sure it's only a matter of time before you meet someone amazing,' she said in a distinctly unconvincing tone. Mitch glanced over at her, evidently unconvinced too.

'Did Tessa give you any reason why she ended it?' Rosie asked cautiously.

Mitch sighed. 'She said she could tell I wasn't ready to settle down.'

Rosie's forehead wrinkled in confusion. 'I thought you had a good feeling about her? What made her think that?'

'Oh, well she found out I had been messaging someone else on a different dating app... What?' he said defensively, seeing the look on Rosie's face. 'We never had the exclusive conversation, OK?'

Rosie couldn't bring herself to shout at him; actually, she felt like laughing.

'I don't know Rosie, it's just really got me down this time.' Rosie pushed her uncharitable thoughts to the side and tried to concentrate.

'I know I don't have a great track record of committing to relationships,' he said, 'but I'm starting to feel that I'm getting something wrong, that I'm not meeting the right people. That maybe I'm missing something.'

Rosie picked her glass up, trying to think of something to say that wasn't too judgemental but was also constructive. If Mitch really did want to meet someone then he needed to stop messaging other girls while he was already seeing one, was what she wanted to say. But she knew he already knew that. And she knew that he knew that if he had met the right girl, he wouldn't be doing that. And to be honest with herself, she dreaded the day when he did meet the right girl.

She took a long drink of her wine, thankful that Mitch knew her well enough to order her second-choice wine when her first choice was unavailable. The wine was cool and refreshing and Rosie savoured the tartness of it. She looked past Mitch, back to the wisteria-covered wall of the pub. It was long past flowering but still covered much of the back of it. The beer garden was relatively empty for a sunny Sunday afternoon. Evidently, the residents of West London had decamped to their villas in Italy, or country houses in the Cotswolds for the summer.

Rosie thought enviously of that way of life – where one could just leave on a whim for your weekend place. Or leave London entirely for the summer, leaving the smog and humidity behind. But if she was to be stuck in her middle-class existence, without the hope of regular exotic escapes then this wasn't so bad: a quiet pub garden in the sunshine with her best friend. Her broken-hearted best friend, she was reminded, as Mitch let out another dramatic sigh.

'I feel like being single is so much harder for me than it is for you,' Mitch said.

Rosie rolled her eyes in exasperation. 'How do you figure that out?' she protested.

This was such a well-worn conversation between the two of them that Rosie could barely be bothered to contradict him anymore. Maybe Mitch actually had a point. Dating was difficult enough if you were doing it half-heartedly. It must be even harder if you took it as seriously as Mitch did. And yet, Mitch never seemed to have any problems finding dates, even starting relationships. It was when those relationships reached the point of discussions about the future that they faltered for him.

'Because I'm always meeting the wrong women and you never seem to meet the wrong men!' Mitch exclaimed, crossing and uncrossing his long legs.

Rosie looked across the table at him and narrowed her eyes. 'You don't think that it might have something to do with the fact that I never meet any men in the first place?' she snipped, taking a glug of her wine.

There was a silence. 'Look,' Rosie said in what she hoped was a more conciliatory tone, 'I know you're heartbroken right now and also I don't really feel like arguing, but you have to admit that you have more luck than I do in actually *finding* people to go on dates with.'

Mitch shrugged, his dark hair flopping across his eyes. Rosie watched the familiar movement. She liked it when he didn't add product to it; something that only happened when he was in the throes of a break-up. Rosie liked his more natural look, preferred it when he didn't style it. Not that she would ever tell him, because that would make it look like she actually *thought* about how he did his hair. She pursed her lips and took another sip of her wine. And she definitely *didn't* think about that, she told herself sternly.

Ever since she had known Mitch, well over ten years now, he'd had a plan. First it was a two-year plan, to get out of academic life alive. Then it turned into a five-year plan, getting enough promotions to have his own flat. But his overarching plan had never changed in all the time Rosie had known him, and despite everything, he had never stopped believing it would happen. Mitch was certain that at some point he would meet someone, they would fall madly in love, get settled, get married and have babies together. Rosie had lost track of the number of times he had told her how important marriage and children were to him. It was actually rather sweet, if it wasn't being permanently forced down one's throat.

And if one didn't find it too irritating how his everyday decisions didn't exactly tally up to his long-term goals. Mitch seemed incapable of commitment and had never yet stayed with the same girl longer than a few weeks. But he was constantly falling in love.

Rosie had always viewed Mitch's plan in a rather detached manner, as something that might work for other people, but maybe not for her. While she was sure she would enjoy the part of meeting someone and falling madly in love, she had never focused on marriage, and was largely ambivalent on the subject of children. Something she tended to keep to herself, because people got weird when faced with a thirty-something woman who wasn't desperate to procreate. She certainly didn't understand the allure that babies held for Mitch who was always first in line to hold any baby that visited the office and was on speed dial for babysitting duties for several of their friends.

'Anyway,' he said with a sigh, 'I wanted to tell you all this before we got to my mum's because she's going to kill me when she hears about Tessa. So I was wondering...' He gave Rosie his best beseeching look. 'If we could try and steer clear of the subject of my love life tonight?'

Rosie broke into laughter. Sunday evening dinners at Jackie's were a regular occurrence in both Rosie's and Mitch's calendars. Mitch had been going back to his mum's for a Sunday dinner ever since he moved out and, back when he and Rosie were flatmates, Jackie would insist Rosie went, too. Now Rosie would go every so often, just enough to keep Jackie happy and plenty enough to know that the chance of keeping Jackie off the subject of Mitch's love life was impossible.

Jackie had been a single mum after Mitch's dad walked out when he was a baby. She doted on Mitch and was as fiercely protective of him as she was exasperated by his continued failure to find a girlfriend and settle down, regularly complaining about Mitch's single status. Rosie just knew that Mitch wouldn't hear the end of it if his mum found out that he'd been dumped by Tessa, and that the reason for it was because he was messaging other girls.

'What's it worth?' She poked his knee under the table with her unpolished toes.

'I'll get you another glass of wine?' he offered.

Rosie shook her head. 'Not good enough. Keeping your mum off the subject of your love life for an entire evening is a tall order. You need to come up with something better to reward me with.'

Mitch reached under the table and grabbed her foot in his hand. 'Mitch!' she shrieked, twisting her leg to try and get her foot free but he held it fast.

'I'm sorry,' he said. 'Were you trying to blackmail me?'

'Please don't tickle me,' she begged. This was a definite downside to having a best friend who knew the real reason she had to paint her own toenails. 'Mitch!' she said more insistently.

He tweaked her little toe and then carefully put her foot back down. 'Sorry Rosie.' He grinned. 'What was that you were saying? I think you were agreeing not to tell my mum about Tessa, right?'

'Right,' agreed Rosie scowling across the table at him and trying to ignore the butterflies that seemed to be having a party in her stomach.

'Oh, and your toenails need painting by the way.' Mitch gave her a wink which just encouraged the butterflies to party harder. She shot daggers back at him.

Mitch laughed at the expression on her face and then looked down at his watch. 'Mum's not expecting us for another hour so you have time to distract me from my heartache.' He leaned lazily back and stretched which made the rickety wooden chair creak with protest at his tall frame. 'What's been going on in your world?'

'Not much,' Rosie began, irritated by how quickly he seemed to have got over Tessa. It wasn't that she cared who he was seeing, he went through them at a rate of knots after all, it was the amount of energy she was expected to expend offering him sympathy when it all went wrong due to something stupid he had done.

Mitch looked at her expectantly and she realised he was waiting for more. 'Erm…' She wracked her brain for anything interesting to say and came up lacking.

'Work is the usual. I've got a new post doc starting next week,' she said, 'which might shake things up a bit. Not like that!' She swatted him across the table when she noticed the smirk on his face. 'I meant that it's always funny to see how the rest of the team react when a new person starts. Some of them will start posturing and others will fall apart at the prospect of any kind of competition. You remember what it's like, how fragile scientists' egos are.'

Mitch rolled his eyes. 'Don't remind me. I still have the occasional anxiety dream.' He shuddered.

'Anyway, this new post doc has written some really interesting papers so I'm excited to see what he can do if we give him some proper lab space and funding,' Rosie said.

'I couldn't care less about his research,' Mitch replied, propping his chin up on his hands and staring dreamily into Rosie's eyes. 'Tell me the important stuff: Is he hot? Is he single? Is he straight?!' Rosie threw a beer mat at him.

'Ow!' he protested. 'I'm really not interested in his academic credentials, I want to know whether he's going to be your one!' he said teasingly and ducked as she pretended to throw another mat at him.

'Oh please,' Rosie said, 'I've told you before I never meet anyone through work – and don't even start on this post doc, he's far too young.'

'Well what about *outside* work Rosie, you know there is a big wide world out here.'

'Really? Random people don't meet in a bar when they're in their thirties.' Mitch raised his eyebrow. 'OK,' she conceded, 'You might, but I don't.' She gesticulated around the beer garden at the people on offer, and Mitch looked around and then shrugged his shoulders in agreement.

'And I'm giving up with online dating. It's too much admin with too little...' She paused. 'Actually cancel that, with *zero* return.'

Not all of this was strictly true: yes, scientific research was not an obvious place to happen upon romance, and it was true that once she turned thirty, Rosie had stopped speaking to men in bars – not that she did a whole lot of that in her twenties, but there was at least the possibility that she *might*. However, her position on dating apps was not entirely honest. In reality, she had deleted most of her profiles months ago. At the time she told herself it was while she got through a busy patch at work, but work had been quiet for weeks now and her profiles remained dormant.

Her reluctance to reactivate them was a result of several factors. Firstly, she hated the chat one had to go through just to try to work out whether someone was worth meeting. Secondly, she begrudged the amount of time she felt she needed to devote to going through messages when she could be doing something much more interesting. And finally, it was the ultimate disappointment she had felt each and every time she finally went on a date. Rosie knew she wasn't going to meet the man of her dreams on one of these apps, so what was the point?

Mitch looked at her with a painfully soulful expression. 'But you can't just give up Rosie, the next person you swipe right on could be the one!'

Rosie tried to hide her smile. Mitch, ever the optimist, the eternal romantic, was always convinced that the next person he met not only could be the one but *would* be the one. This was one of the reasons she loved him so much and one of the reasons their friendship really worked. It wasn't that Rosie was a pessimist but her pragmatic approach to life and problems always appeared to be a glass half empty next to Mitch's overflowing cup.

It was this that had drawn her to Mitch in the first place. That and the fact she was desperate for somewhere to live in London, fresh out of university, floundering in heartbreak. Completely spontaneously, Mitch had recently taken on the lease of a beautiful mansion block apartment just moments from Hyde Park. He had met the owner at a party, charmed them immediately and when they had asked if he would be interested in renting the place while they 'went traveling to find themselves' during a delayed mid-life crisis, Mitch had jumped at the chance, never bothering to find out how much the rent would be and whether he could afford it.

He couldn't afford it, which was why he was so desperate to find another PhD student who would be willing to share the one-bed space. All of this was very Mitch, as Rosie would soon discover. But she got the bedroom and she didn't much mind if Mitch turned what was supposed to be the sitting room into a bedroom for himself. And the result was perfect in two ways; firstly, they could both afford to live in this amazing place and secondly, they became best friends.

Rosie had hoped from their first meeting, all those years ago, in that grotty pub off the Strand (which Mitch seemed strangely nostalgic about and which they still went to when Covent Garden was heaving with tourists), that they would become friends. She had been so nervous about the move, about the job, about being in London single and friendless, but Mitch's easy manner and charm had made the conversion to London life seamless. Mitch just presumed everyone would be his friend so he didn't think twice about including Rosie in all his plans. And now, almost all of her London friends were people she had met through Mitch.

That flatshare, and indeed working together, may have been a distant memory, but their friendship had endured. Mitch had swiftly moved on from academia, almost before the ink was dry on his PhD certificate. A certificate that it had been touch and go if he would ever receive. Mitch always told people that the only reason he had got it in the end was because of Rosie. And Rosie, being terrified of being drawn into a plagiarism scandal, would play it down entirely and change the subject swiftly anytime it came up.

Mitch was eminently more suited to the life he had gone on to as a journalist. As science correspondent on one of the national newspapers he could still claim he was using his science background, but Rosie knew that what he really relished was his role in breaking stories and being the one with all the connections.

He was king of the roost, even if that roost was situated in the somewhat niche world of academia and science.

Mitch met new people through his work all the time: scientists, other journalists and a steady stream of new government officials. He had a strict policy never to mix work and pleasure. It was strict more in his referencing of it rather than in observation. Rosie had lost count of the number of times he had become romantically entangled with people he had met through work. Normally with hilarious (for Rosie) and sometimes disastrous (for Mitch) consequences. But he wasn't selfish, it wasn't just *his* romantic life he considered, he was always trying to pair Rosie off with people. She had never forgiven him for the humiliating episode where she had finally agreed to meet his colleague for a coffee only to realise that the man in question was using this as a fishing exercise to find out more about Mitch.

'I honestly didn't know he was interested in me!' Mitch had protested loudly. But the incident had put a dampener on her trust in Mitch's judgement of suitable men. Ever since, Rosie had refused to meet anyone Mitch had suggested.

'We should get going,' Rosie said, drinking the rest of her glass of wine and nudging Mitch's beer towards him. 'Your mum won't forgive you if you're late.'

Mitch downed his pint and stood up. 'Promise you won't tell her?' he asked.

Rosie nodded. 'But you know the chances of her not finding out are slim to none?'

'Come on,' he said and pulled Rosie's arm through his, 'let's get the interrogation over with.'

Jackie still lived in the two-bedroom flat in Chiswick that Mitch had grown up in. It was just a couple of streets back from the river and Mitch made Rosie walk the scenic route, which she didn't mind. The Thames always looked beautiful in the sun, especially if you didn't lean over the railings and notice the mud and the rats down below.

'Mitch will do the washing up, won't you Mitch?' Jackie said, pulling Rosie to sit back down. Reluctantly, Mitch began to pile the plates up and then shot Rosie a murderous glance as he left the room. Rosie knew that this wasn't because he was annoyed about having to do the washing up but more because he didn't trust Rosie not to tell his mum about Tessa while he wasn't in the room to defend himself. Actually, it was more that he didn't trust his mum not to break down Rosie's defenses and sniff out the story.

Jackie leaned forward and rubbed her right knee. 'How is it feeling?' Rosie asked with concern. Jackie had never been quite the same after she was hit by a drunk driver last year. Mitch and Rosie had been on holiday in Italy when they heard the news, and the memory of that phone call still made Rosie feel shaky. Mostly Jackie didn't complain about it, but every so often Rosie would notice that she was walking with her stick more regularly, or that she needed to sit down a little more often. Rosie glanced at the corner of the dining room and saw that Jackie had propped her stick there.

'I'm fine love, honestly. It just twinges every now and again. Don't tell Mitch though, I know how he worries.' Rosie knew that Mitch saw everything and would already have noticed that Jackie was more tired than usual. But she was happy to pretend to Jackie that she would keep her secret; one secret for Jackie and one for Mitch, she thought as she smiled and nodded.

'Tell me what's going on with Mitch and that girl Tessa?' Jackie said, causing Rosie to start with alarm. There was no getting anything past Jackie, she might be in pain and tired but she had

23

some sort of sixth sense when it came to Mitch. 'They've split up, haven't they?' Jackie asked.

Rosie pulled a face. 'I promised I wouldn't say anything,' she said.

Jackie threw her hands up in exasperation. 'Honestly...' She was about to start a rant about Mitch's love life and then saw the look of concern on Rosie's face. 'Don't worry,' she patted Rosie's hand kindly, 'I won't tell him you said anything. You didn't really, I guessed. Anyway, it's hardly a surprise. It's not like he's got a great track record with these things.' She sighed. 'What do you think he's waiting for?'

'What do you mean?' asked Rosie, hoping they could finish this conversation before Mitch got back. In fact, if they could wrap it up quickly she could be putting her coat on and saying her goodbyes by the time he walked back in.

'In a girl?' Jackie asked. 'What do you think he's waiting for? It's not like he hasn't dated enough different women.' Jackie paused, 'surely he should know what he likes and doesn't by now?'

Rosie shrugged, unwilling to speculate on what Mitch may or may not be looking for in a girl. This was the sort of conversation that made her squirm and then look in the mirror later, searching for any similarities.

'I'm not really sure Jackie, maybe he just hasn't met the right one yet?' Rosie said optimistically, hoping to shut down this conversation.

'Maybe...' Jackie said, sounding unconvinced.

At that moment Mitch came back in and put paid to Rosie's plans of a quick escape. 'Done,' he said, holding up his damp hands which he was drying with a towel. 'What did I miss?'

'Oh nothing,' Rosie said nonchalantly at exactly the moment Jackie said, 'I hear you and Tessa split up.'

Mitch turned to Rosie and gave her a furious look. 'You promised!'

'I didn't say anything!' protested Rosie.

'She didn't,' agreed Jackie, 'I guessed.'

Mitch groaned. 'But I didn't tell her why!' Rosie said pleadingly and then realised her mistake.

'You know what we should do?' Mitch had evidently forgiven Rosie as he had gallantly insisted on walking her to the tube despite the fact that he was staying over at his mum's that night.

'No, what?' Rosie stopped at the edge of the road and waited for a car to pass. Lost in his thoughts Mitch almost walked straight out into the road and she quickly grabbed his arm and pulled him back. This could be a metaphor for their friendship Rosie thought, her cautiously watching and planning, Mitch striding out without thinking.

'We need some kind of incentive,' he continued.

'Sorry what?' Rosie asked, pulling Mitch across the road now that there was a break in the traffic.

'All our friends are pairing off. If we're not careful we'll be the last two singles left. Maybe we both need some kind of deadline.'

He stopped abruptly on the pavement, causing a couple walking behind to almost crash into them. The woman gave Mitch a dirty look which he didn't notice at all. A grin started to spread across his face.

'A deadline that is really going to spur us on this time.'

The glint in Mitch's eye alarmed Rosie; she was used to his enthusiastic schemes but there was something wilder to his look than normal.

'What do you suggest?' she tentatively enquired, trying to pull him in the direction of the tube. This sounded like the kind of conversation that could go on for hours and result in her missing the last tube home and ending up on the night bus – not OK on any night of the week, but especially not on a Sunday.

'Well, it's got to be something drastic,' he said, allowing himself to be propelled in the correct direction. 'Maybe something that neither of us have ever considered before,' he continued.

'Does it?' asked Rosie nervously.

'Yep,' said Mitch definitively. 'And of course, we'd have to agree that neither of us could back out of it. We need to shake things up!'

Rosie really was feeling anxious now, both about the plan and the tube. Mitch had slowed to a snail's pace. She had no idea what Mitch was going to suggest but she was convinced it wouldn't be something she was comfortable with.

'Mitch, what are you thinking?' she demanded as they finally arrived in front of the tube station. It was still busy for a late Sunday evening, people eking out their last few hours of freedom before the working week began. Rosie watched from out of the corner of her eye as a group of drunk teenagers vaulted the ticket barriers, hoping they wouldn't be on the same train as her.

She turned her attention back to Mitch. If he was going to come up with some harebrained scheme she needed to know what it was sooner rather than later so she could plan around it. Make a contingency. Or make her excuses.

'I don't know, I don't know,' he replied tersely. 'It will come to me, I'm starting to get an idea.'

Neither of them said anything for a minute and then he gripped her arms and grinned down at her before pulling her into a goodbye hug.

'Leave it with me,' he said gleefully then he turned to walk back down the road. 'I'll have it all worked out by the end of the week.' He looked back at her and waved.

Rosie watched him go and sighed. She hated saying goodbye to Mitch, but sometimes she hated his crazy plans more. She reached into her pocket where she always kept her bank card as Mitch turned the corner and disappeared. He sounded more serious than she had anticipated, and she wasn't sure she liked the sound of it.

Chapter Two

While Mitch might have willingly left behind the world of academia and research, Rosie was happily entrenched in it. And she loved it. All that order and methodology. There was nothing like the process of setting up an experiment to take your mind off things you couldn't control, like emotions, or your best friend's madcap schemes.

Not one for crowding her desk with personal effects, Rosie was still sufficiently proud of gaining her doctorate to have a laminated photo of her receiving it in her desk drawer. The drawer was locked, and the photo was under a couple of notebooks. But when she was feeling unsure of herself, or needed a boost, she would unlock the drawer and look at it, remembering the moment the photo was taken before locking it back up again and getting on with her day. Weird yes, but absolutely necessary when a month long experiment had just gone to hell.

Rosie had been one of the fastest students to gain her PhD, putting in crazy hours to get the results she needed and then tackling her writing up as a seasoned climber might think about plotting an Everest ascent. Pulling all-nighters was not Rosie's style, instead she foreswore socialising and weekend fun and did her write up in record time. Much to Mitch's annoyance both professionally and personally. The latter because he was bored of the hours he spent trying to persuade her away from her computer, only for her to ignore him and write up yet another chapter.

Rachel, her supervising professor, had been suitably impressed, although not surprised, and had quickly offered Rosie a post-doc position at the university. It wasn't long before Rosie was asked to set up a lab under Rachel's mentorship. Their area of virology was well funded and Rosie was lead author on several important papers and was regularly asked for comment by journalists if these made the news. Mitch loved the fact she always gave him first and often exclusive comment.

Rosie was now senior enough to be in charge not just of PhD students, but a number of post docs, too; something that caused her to become breathless with anxiety if she thought about it too long. She relished the research she did; to the outside observer it might not seem so important but Rosie knew that some of the experiments her lab ran had real impact in the world. One of the trials she had been working on resulted in a new drug which was now used in the treatment of previously hard-to-treat viruses and was heralded as a breakthrough. Her mum kept newspaper cuttings on that one but Rosie drew the line at adding those to her desk drawer.

Rosie felt an incredible sense of pride in her work and deep down she knew she was good at it, too. Not just in the lab but in the other varied roles she filled. Rosie actually enjoyed the challenge of writing grant applications, something most other research scientists dreaded, it was important to Rachel to keep the funding coming and it was important to Rosie to keep in Rachel's good books.

On a more prosaic level she also loved where her lab was based. Right in the heart of London, nestled in between the beautiful squares of Bloomsbury. It was in a modern building that on paper would seem completely at odds with its neighbours, but when you stumbled across it, it fitted perfectly in with the Georgian architecture.

Unlike most Londoners, Rosie loved walking to work in the morning through the throngs of tourists that gathered in that part of London at all times of year and at all times of day and night. There was always a sense of anticipation amongst them; the excitement of seeing beautiful London landmarks for the first time, feeding off their energy. Perhaps it was because she had only moved to London as an adult but she still shared that feeling of excitement with them. Except on rainy days when they would cluster around the tube entrance with their umbrellas and wheelie suitcases blocking the entrances and just getting in the way.

Right now, Rosie was fulfilling another of her important roles, that of office confidante to her longtime colleague and friend Nadia. Nadia also worked under Rachel but in a slightly different area of virology, and she and Rosie regularly met to talk about work but mainly to gossip over whether Rachel was in a good or a bad mood. The latest news on Rachel's love life was a constant source of considerable interest.

Rachel remained as terrifying to Rosie as she had been when she started her PhD. Despite the esteem that Rachel obviously had for Rosie, she wouldn't cut her any slack if she thought Rosie had made a mistake or wasn't performing to the standards of excellence she expected in her team. Rachel was effortlessly chic, her work wardrobe was simple and stylish and when she donned her lab coat she wore it as a fashion accessory.

'You heard that her and the Vice Chancellor are no longer a thing?' Nadia asked Rosie.

'I didn't know they *were* a thing!' Rosie exclaimed and immediately grimaced. The VC was at least sixty-five and looked as if he could stand in as an extra Hogwarts professor at a moment's notice. 'I thought she was with that musician that we went to see that time at the Scala?'

Nadia frowned at Rosie, 'That was ages ago.'

The lab had heard rumours that Rachel was dating this hot twenty-something female singer-songwriter and had gone en masse to see her in concert, hoping to catch a glimpse of who had captured the heart of their professor. But the outing had been short-lived when Rachel was spotted in the crowd, wearing tight leather trousers and a distressed (obviously vintage) Ramones T-shirt and they had issued the abort mission signal and made a quick exit before they were seen or had heard a single song. Rosie still had palpitations when she thought about how close they were to getting caught that night.

But the musician made more sense than the aging VC. Rachel's tastes were certainly eclectic, which was why everyone in the lab so eagerly followed her love life.

Rosie and Nadia had taken a while to get used to one another when Nadia had first arrived, because for a long time Nadia had seemed disorganised and scatty to Rosie. But weeks and months of Nadia coordinating tea breaks and offering cookies had finally won Rosie over. And now, Rosie recognised that Nadia was neither disorganised nor scatty but simply permanently preoccupied either with gossip about their boss or with whatever she happened to be working on at the time. Nadia *was* quite simply a genius and Rosie had lost count of the number of times she had turned to her for advice on a trial that was going wrong or a drug result not going the way she had anticipated.

Over the years Nadia had become even more preoccupied, first when she acquired a boyfriend – Nico, who was now her husband – and then latterly when the two of them became parents. Now Nadia's brilliant brain was as likely to be filled with school schedules, parents' evenings and planning the weekly food shop, as it was to be dreaming up a cure for the common cold.

Honestly, Rosie didn't know how she did it. Nadia raced around at a hundred miles an hour, leaving a wake of dropped Post-it Notes and scattered pen lids behind her. Yet she never messed up her experiments and rarely forgot to pick her kids up. And over time Nadia had also managed to master the technique of appearing to be interested in Rosie's life when Rosie strongly suspected she was thinking of the next stage in her latest clinical trial, or whether she had enough fish fingers in the freezer for the kids' tea.

Right now, uncharacteristically, Nadia was not in motion, she was sat in Rosie's office leisurely sipping her coffee. Rosie tried to subtly nudge the mouse on her desk to see what the time was. It was lovely that Nadia was taking a breather but it would have been nice if she had checked in with Rosie to see if they could coordinate their time for headspace. Rosie had some results she needed to go check on and if she left it too long they would be completely unusable. She sent up a silent prayer to a deity she rarely believed in that one of her students would realise the time crunch and do it for her, if they weren't too busy sleeping off their weekend hangovers.

Nadia took a long sip of her coffee and pulled absentmindedly at the sleeve on her misshapen cardigan. If Rachel was poised, then Nadia was her absolute opposite; tiny and curly-haired, she moved through life as if it was out to attack her. Except for now, when she seemed happy to spend most of her morning in Rosie's office chatting.

'Aren't you in the lab today?' Rosie asked hopefully.

'I was,' Nadia responded languidly, 'but I swapped my slot when I saw who had reserved the next bench to me.'

Rosie raised her eyebrows quizzically.

'Handsy Pete.'

'Oh, god. Yes, good thing you swapped,' Rosie said shuddering.

Handsy Pete was one of the less desirable colleagues in their lab. Apparently, it was OK to make sexually suggestive comments to colleagues if your publication list was as long as Pete's. Rosie had voted for the moniker Pervert Pete, finding something rather pleasing in the alliteration, but she had been vetoed by Nadia, amongst others, who felt 'Handsy' was less confrontational than Pervert, should Pete ever find out about his nickname. Sometimes Rosie despaired that the #MeToo spotlight had completely missed the dingy corner that scientific academia occupied.

'So funding looks like it might be fucked for next year,' Nadia announced dramatically. 'If these politicians carry on in this manner, this country will have a major brain drain on its hands.'

Rosie nodded sagely. She wrote the funding applications and took credit when they were fulfilled but she never followed the ins and outs of whether they were or not, that's what Rachel was for. But Rosie knew how seriously Nadia took the political aspect of their work, and frankly, Rosie was too scared to admit that she didn't really understand how it all worked – where the money came from and how the government allocated the funds it had. So far, she had got the money she needed when she needed it and had been happy to accept Rachel's praise for doing so.

'But anyway,' Nadia said, her face brightening, 'let's not discuss that shitshow. Tell me about your weekend? I'm sure it was far more entertaining than mine. Unless you went to a school fete and ferried your kids across town to their piano lessons, which they hate and never practise for but that Nico feels they ought to have because he had a terribly deprived childhood and was never allowed to play an instrument.'

Nadia pretended to play a tiny violin which made Rosie laugh.

Nadia grinned, 'Did you see Mitch?' she asked.

Mitch loved Nadia, he loved the way she handled life and work in a completely haphazard yet ultimately successful way. He often suggested Rosie could relax and be a little more Nadia which irritated Rosie no end. Despite his rejection of the world of academia he still knew what made for a brilliant scientist and he held Nadia in the highest esteem.

Nadia in turn seemed to find Mitch an amusing distraction at parties and tolerated him when she came across him in everyday life because of the special place he held in Rosie's heart.

'Yep,' confirmed Rosie, 'he's reeling from his latest break-up and convinced that he needs to do something fast before he is left on the shelf forever.'

Nadia laughed loudly. 'Remind me how old he is?'

'He's the same age as me,' Rosie replied tartly. 'Thirty-four. Which is hardly being left on the shelf age.' Rosie straightened her top and sat up a little taller.

Nadia grinned at Rosie's uptight reaction and took another sip of her coffee. 'What sort of thing do you think he has in mind?' she asked.

'He hasn't told me yet,' Rosie replied. She thought back to their conversation on the walk to the tube and felt a shudder of intrigue flit through her.

'He said he's working on a plan and will tell me at the end of the week.' Rosie looked at Nadia and shrugged her shoulders. 'To be honest I'm a little nervous,' she admitted. 'Whatever he's thinking about he's implied he wants me to be a part of it.'

Nadia looked at her, quizzically raising her eyebrow. Rosie sighed, wondering just how much of their conversation she should relay to Nadia.

'Mitch is convinced I've given up on dating and that I need some kind of incentive to get back out there and meet "The One".' Rosie leaned back in her chair and stretched her arms above her head. It seemed to Rosie that Nadia was in no hurry to get going this morning so if she could get one of her students to check on those results she may as well tell her all about Mitch. She fired off a quick message and saw a notification that her most dedicated post doc had read it. She immediately relaxed.

Nadia stopped picking at the holes in her cardigan and looked levelly at Rosie across the desk 'And do you?' she asked.

'I don't know,' Rosie admitted, 'I love my life as it is.' Nadia made no reply. 'I enjoy my work,' Rosie said defensively and gestured to their surroundings, 'I have really good friends, like you and Mitch, it's not like I'm lonely,' she continued. 'Why do I get the feeling you don't agree with me?' she demanded into the ensuing silence. Nadia shrugged and laughed.

'No reason. If you say you're happy, I believe you,' Nadia replied. 'But it does sound a little bit like you're trying to persuade yourself as well as me.'

Rosie poked her tongue out at Nadia. 'And,' she continued, 'at least I get on well enough with my family not to dread seeing them every holiday.'

Nadia pulled a face in response to Rosie's dig. 'They're not *my* family,' she said grumpily.

Now it was Rosie's turn to laugh. 'Well they're as close as!'

Nadia's relationship with Nico's family was strained to say the least. As an only child of unassuming (now retired) academics, Nadia had never understood large and loud families. Or the

35

complex and fraught sibling dynamics between Nico and his many brothers and sisters. Her brain didn't have room for the messy complexities of extended families.

Rosie sympathised, she wasn't sure she could deal with Nico's family if half of Nadia's stories were true. Rosie's family was small and contained just like Nadia's although that was partly because her parents had divorced when Rosie was back in primary school. It was so long ago now that Rosie barely remembered her father living in the same house as them.

Occasionally, on a slow day and if she had nothing better to do than indulge in some introspection, Rosie might poke at this issue, wondering exactly how much her parents' divorce bothered her, and if it really ought to bother her more than it did. On reflection, Rosie concluded that the only lasting impact was a rather ambivalent attitude towards the institution of marriage, and it wasn't as if this made her especially unique.

Rosie suspected that her brother Chris might have dwelt on it more – he had been a few years older than Rosie when their dad had left – and he might have thought about it more since becoming a dad himself, but he and Rosie had never really discussed it, which was their sibling relationship in a nutshell. Their dad, though he remembered birthdays and Christmases was sporadic in his correspondence the rest of the year. Hand on her heart, Rosie couldn't say she really missed him.

But Rosie's mother more than made up for his absence. Susan, an impressive woman, some might say intimidating, had been headteacher of a school with 'distinct challenges.' But Susan turned it around so that by the time she retired it was a school that the middle-class families in the neighbourhood would perform postcode contortions that verged on immoral, if not illegal, to get accepted at. It was even rumoured that several celebrities had tried to bribe Susan to gain access for their offspring. But Susan remained tight-lipped on that matter; she was not someone to care much for the fleeting nature of celebrity.

Susan, now retired, was busier than ever with demands on her time from various committees and projects. This kept her from paying too much close attention to Rosie's love life and Susan had always encouraged Rosie's academic and professional success; though lately, Rosie had been starting to get the feeling that her mother worried that Rosie's drive and ambition might result in her complete lack of interest in providing grandchildren anytime soon. Recently, her mother seemed much more interested in Rosie's life than she had ever been before.

Rosie toyed with her mouse, the computer screen flickering into life, she wanted to double check that her experiment was being attended to. She saw a brief message from her post doc informing her that all was well and she turned back to the conversation.

'Half the issue, Nadia, is that I just can't be bothered,' Rosie confessed. 'I hate online dating,' she grumbled. 'I don't think I've ever had a successful date off the back of it.'

Nadia put her coffee down and threw her hands up in protest. 'What about that guy who really loved the fact you were a scientist?'

Rosie spluttered. 'Do you mean the one who asked me on our first date if I would insist on using Doctor as my title if we ever got married because it might "undermine the dynamics of a traditional marital relationship"?'

'Oh, right.' Nadia grimaced, reclaiming her coffee mug and hiding behind it. 'I'd forgotten that part. So,' she continued in a more upbeat manner, 'what do you think Mitch has in mind?'

Rosie groaned. 'I don't know but it had better not involve

speed dating, double dating, or any extreme sports. I just want him to leave my love life out of his plans. I know he means well,' Rosie insisted, 'I just wish he wasn't so obsessed with us both meeting people and getting married.' She leaned forward and shuffled some papers on her desk, her body language the epitome of diversion. She really didn't want Nadia probing her on why she was so opposed to Mitch meeting someone and getting married.

Nadia said nothing and just raised her eyebrows at Rosie. She pushed her chair back and stood up. 'Got to get going,' she said, making for the door. 'Hey, haven't you got an experiment running?' she asked her. 'Shouldn't you be checking on it?'

Rosie rolled her eyes and looked at her watch; she was sure her post doc would have it covered but if she was fast, maybe she could make it in time just to double-check on things. She followed Nadia to the door, picking up her empty coffee mug and handing it to her friend as she went.

Nadia took the cup and walked out into the corridor. 'I know it's hard when it feels like someone is meddling in your life,' Nadia grabbed Rosie's arm, 'but just remember how long you two have been friends for. And, as you said, he does mean well.'

Rosie nodded and smiled at Nadia who let go of her arm and made her way back down the corridor, tissues falling from her pockets as she searched for her key card. Nadia called back over her shoulder, 'Anyway, keep me posted on Mitch's plan. I am *most* intrigued by what he comes up with.'

Rosie and Mitch. They had become such a stalwart unit in their group of friends that people always thought of them as a pair. If one of them was invited to an event the other went too. And for a number of years people had assumed that there was something going on between the two of them: how could they be *that* close and not be sleeping together? Or friends theorized that something *would* happen just as soon as they got drunk enough. But there wasn't anything going on, and it came to be accepted that they were what they were: just really good friends. And gradually, over the years, people stopped asking, stopped theorizing. Mitch definitely had a type which was very much not Rosie. He seemed to prefer small, extroverted blondes. And Rosie's type was...well, that was harder to determine.

Chapter Three

London had an end of summer feel about it that week. It had been an unusually beautiful summer with long hot spells. The cafes and bars had capitalised on this, setting up tables and chairs outside wherever possible. But the heat that Londoners had been enjoying, now threatened to break over the weekend and, to Rosie, it felt like everyone was trying to make the most of the last of the summer sunshine.

Rosie had always loved this time of year; she got a back-to-school feeling and had a hankering to go and buy new stationery and put on tights again. But tonight, she too planned to enjoy the last of the sunshine and chose to walk to meet Mitch. Not only was she wearing her new sandals but she had even painted her toenails this time. A quick slick of mascara and lipstick in the lab bathroom before she left and she was ready.

Mitch had suggested a bar near his office which she wasn't familiar with. They had their regular haunts, pubs halfway between their flats, a tiny Italian restaurant which they had been going to for years and at which they never bothered to look at the menu. Rosie liked their routines, their favorite places. It made her relationship with Mitch feel special and exclusive. But this place was new to them and Rosie wondered why Mitch had chosen it.

Since her conversation with Nadia, Rosie had tried to put Mitch's plan from her mind. He'd likely forgotten all about it, she told herself. Knowing him, he'd probably met someone new by now and with any luck she could deflect his interest in her love life even if it did mean another painful evening faking interest in yet another new girlfriend. But as she walked to meet him she felt a strange sense of nervousness, his words echoing in her mind about making a change. Perhaps this new venue was all part of his plan?

The bar was tucked away in a courtyard off the busy street. It took Rosie a few minutes of wandering around nearby streets to find it but when she did it was worth it. She took a moment to appreciate how pretty the setting was. A tiny cobbled square, right in the hubbub of the West End, surrounded by Georgian buildings and sheer glass-fronted modern office blocks. The bar itself had a striped awning which arched over several chairs and tables set out in the square. At the one tucked in the corner sat Mitch, nose in a book. Rosie watched him for a moment and thought that if this had been a date this would be her perfect setting, and the perfect way to find a man with whom you would spend the evening. She took a deep breath and walked over. This was not a date she reminded herself, this was Mitch, her *friend*.

'What are you reading?' she asked when she was close enough.

Mitch grinned up at her over the top of his book. 'You can borrow it when I've finished.'

Rosie tipped her head to one side to read the spine and pulled a face. 'You're such a geek,' she said as she pushed his long legs out of the way so she could pull out her chair.

'You don't know what you're missing,' he mused. 'Debut author? Mashup sci-fi thriller? What's not to like?'

'Where should I start?' Rosie loved Mitch's geeky side as much as she disliked his taste in books. It was at such odds with his cool, charming persona. But whereas other people might pretend to have more highbrow taste, Mitch was completely at ease with parading his inner geek.

'I think the last time we both read the same thing was back when we were doing our PhDs and *you* had to read science papers. Bet you can't remember the last time you read one of those,' she teased.

He pouted back at her, his blue eyes glowering at her under his naturally sculpted eyebrows.

'I'll have you know that I spent this afternoon reading a paper on a new and exciting, yet woefully underfunded, form of gene therapy,' he said huffily.

Rosie laughed. 'Alright, alright. But *please* let's not talk about anything work related tonight?'

Mitch's glare cleared. 'Bad week?'

Rosie shrugged. 'Disgruntled post docs wanting more money, delays in grant funding coming in and a useless grad student who messed up the timing on our current trial.' She sighed. 'You know, just the usual.'

'Stop,' declared Mitch, laughing and holding his hands up, 'any more talk like that and you'll make me miss it!'

Rosie smiled at him. They both knew that – professionally speaking, at least – Mitch was just where he needed to be and it was not in a lab with Rosie, running clinical trials.

They had to send the waiter away twice before they even looked at the menu. Eventually Rosie asked Mitch to stop speaking so she could decide what she was ordering before they had to send the poor man away for a third time.

'This is why I like our usual Italian so much,' she moaned, 'I never even have to look at the menu.'

'Oh, stop complaining, we can't always do the same things over and over again.'

Rosie bristled at his choice of words. *Why not?* she wondered. What was wrong with their traditions?

'And, anyway,' he said leaning forward conspiratorially, 'the food here is supposed to be *amazing*. And just look at the setting...' He threw his arms out towards the square.

'Hmm, I suppose so,' replied Rosie, sounding less than convinced.

Eventually she settled on a plate of rigatoni and a cold glass of Sauvignon Blanc. Mitch was right, the food did look delicious and her wine was served at exactly the right temperature. She was happily savouring her first sip when Mitch shifted in his seat.

'So,' he started, sitting forward and staring at her with a determined look. 'My plan.' There was a pause.

'Your plan?' she answered falteringly. She slowly lowered her wine glass back to the table, hoping that perhaps she could deflect whatever was coming by pretending to have forgotten their previous conversation.

'Yes!' he exclaimed. 'The plan I said I was going to work on? To change things for us? To get us to focus on sorting our lives out?'

She looked around at the other people hoping that they were too engrossed in their own conversations to eavesdrop on theirs. 'Erm, Mitch, I'm not really sure I need—'

Mitch interrupted her with a wave of his hand. 'Nonsense, of course you do. We both need this.'

'Do we? Do *I*?' she anxiously asked.

Mitch took a deep breath. 'We've been friends for ages, right?'

'Yes,' she agreed.

'Really good friends, right?'

'Yes,' she agreed again.

'We know everything about each other, right?' Rosie decided at

43

this point that Mitch wasn't really looking for affirmations so she kept quiet. Something told her that whatever Mitch was about to suggest, this would not be the time to confess to her long-held secrets.

'And we both feel it's time to start thinking about settling down.' This was very definitely a statement, not a question. 'But neither of us has met the right person yet.'

Now it was obvious that Mitch was only talking about himself. Rosie could feel her heart beginning to beat even faster.

'I think both of us have been messing about a bit,' he mused, 'not taking this dating thing seriously and...' He paused, giving Rosie a long look across the table. 'Perhaps dismissing people that really we should have given a second chance.'

'You mean breaking up with people because they want you to meet their family,' muttered Rosie under her breath before taking another gulp of wine. Mitch glared at her and she quickly shut up.

'So, as I said before, I think we need an incentive *and* a deadline. And I've come up with something I think could really work, *and*...' Here he paused again for dramatic effect. 'And would solve lots of our problems even if we don't find The One,' he finished in a rush.

He now leaned back in his chair looking extremely pleased with himself. Rosie decided she really didn't like Mitch's plan, and she hadn't even heard it yet.

'And?' she snapped at him. 'What is this magic plan of yours?

'Oh right, sorry.' He sat back forward again. 'Right. The idea is that we both commit to trying to find The One by the time your work Christmas party comes around.'

'OK,' Rosie said slowly, this actually didn't sound too bad.

Mitch pushed on, clearly reading her mind. 'No Rosie, we really commit to doing this. I don't mean pretending to be looking for someone but actually deleting all your dating profiles.' He shot her a meaningful look and she felt herself blushing.

'Yes, yes, I know what you've been doing,' he said, waving his hand perfunctorily across the table at her. 'There's no point pretending that's not the case. You do know I can look you up, don't you? And anyway, I set half those profiles up for you.'

'Have you been logging into my dating profiles?' Rosie spluttered.

'No,' Mitch replied firmly, 'I haven't. Because they don't exist anymore, because *you* deleted them.'

'But you tried, right?' Rosie protested, trying desperately to shift Mitch's focus. He just gave her a dismissive look. She thought about protesting further, but realised the futility of it and decided to keep quiet and hear Mitch out.

'I'm talking about messaging people, being open to different people, not just our usual types. But maybe a good start would be reactivating your profiles?' he said.

Rosie shot him a filthy look which he pretended not to notice. Being open to different types of people was going to be a challenge, as Rosie wasn't sure what her usual type *was*, so how she was supposed to avoid it? Whereas for Mitch it was obvious what his type was and he seemed to find it impossible to avoid.

Mitch continued, 'We need to open our minds a little, give people a second chance when maybe we would have dismissed them on the first date. Perhaps be a little less picky.' He said the last part in a faux whisper which Rosie couldn't help but laugh at.

'I'm not talking about settling down with terrible people,' he insisted in response to her laugh. 'I just mean I feel like *you* – sorry, *we* – sometimes dismiss people before we have even met them. Or —' he looked at her meaningfully '—because they say the wrong thing once on a date.'

'If you're talking about some of my dates,' Rosie declared

loudly, 'I can tell you that it's not just *one* wrong thing they say.' Mitch raised his eyebrow at her. 'I sat through an entire evening where a guy thought he could mansplain immunology to me, just because he once watched a documentary on National Geographic,' she said defensively. 'I can be tolerant, OK, but *my god*,' she huffed.

'OK,' he replied appeasingly. 'You shouldn't have had to listen to him. But you know what I mean?'

Rosie glowered across the table at him. 'And then what?' she uttered confrontationally. 'What happens at Christmas, a whole *four* months from now, if we're not *engaged to be married*?'

Mitch laughed 'Ah,' he said in what Rosie felt was an annoyingly self-satisfied manner. 'That's where this gets interesting. I think if we don't meet anyone by then we should agree to be each other's fallback.'

Rosie felt herself relax immediately. 'Oh, OK sure,' she readily agreed, taking a drink of her wine in relief. She and Mitch always ended up going to her work Christmas party together so really this didn't seem such a bad plan. And if Mitch was dating someone serious by that time then Rosie was sure she could stomach hanging out with her colleagues instead of him for once.

'Sounds good,' she confirmed, raising her glass to him.

Mitch watched her carefully across the table, suddenly seeming nervous. 'No, Rosie, I don't think you understand...' He wavered for a moment, as if weighing up exactly how to say what he planned to say next.

'I don't mean we should just go to the party together. I mean we should be each other's fallback...*in life.*'

Rosie took a gulp of wine, the realisation of what Mitch was suggesting beginning to dawn on her.

'You hear about it all the time,' he continued.

'You do?' Rosie queried.

'Yes! Friends who have been friends for years and when they don't meet someone by a certain age they have an agreement to settle down together and have a baby.'

If they hadn't been in such a public place Rosie would have spat her wine all over the table. It was a testament to her good manners that she didn't. She did however splutter her wine into her napkin and turn a very dark shade of red, putting her glass down with a plonk on the table.

'What?' she eventually managed when she could breathe again. 'I must have misheard you, I thought you said...' She tried to make herself say it with a chuckle just to underline the ridiculousness of her mistake. 'That if we don't bring a date to the Christmas party then we should have a baby together.'

The illogical leap from one fact to the next seemed even more insane when she said it out loud but Mitch's beautiful face split into a grin and he nodded wildly at her.

'Exactly!' he declared triumphantly.

'I'm sorry, what?' Rosie replied. 'That has got to be the weirdest and frankly *stupidest* idea I've ever heard!'

Mitch looked briefly hurt before quickly regaining his stride. 'Why? It's brilliant!'

'Brilliant?' Rosie asked incredulously.

'Yes!' Mitch exclaimed. 'Both of us want to meet someone, both of us want to settle down.'

'Do we?' Rosie asked, bewildered.

Mitch ignored her and ploughed on. 'This is the perfect solution!'

'It is?' asked Rosie.

'Yes!' he exclaimed again. 'We've got four months to really crack this dating business. To stop messing around and to really try to meet The One. And if we don't...'

'If we don't...?' echoed Rosie weakly wondering whether now

was the time to take issue with Mitch's repeated use of 'The One' which made her feel a little sick and mad. But she decided she had bigger issues to address.

'If we don't, we'll have each other, and hopefully a baby!' he declared agreeably, as though he hadn't just turned her life upside down.

Rosie stared at him. The dawning horror of what he was suggesting and just how much he didn't know about her feelings rolled over her. Not just about her dislike for internet dating, not only her lukewarm approach to men over the last few years, but fundamentally misunderstanding *who* and *what* actually made her happy. She picked up her wine glass and took a large swig, giving herself time to think.

'You can't be serious?' she finally said. 'This has got to be one of your jokes, right?'

Rosie looked frantically into Mitch's blue eyes searching for the glint that suggested he was about to start laughing and tell her that he was taking the mickey. But all she saw was a disconcertingly steely look, which suggested he was not only deadly serious about the proposition, he was not going to be easily dissuaded.

She took a deep breath. 'Mitch,' she started in what she hoped was her best calm and measured tone, the tone she used when dealing with hysterical PhD students who thought they were about to fail. Or with her nephews when they were having a very public meltdown and people were beginning to stare. Because it had not escaped Rosie's notice that a few of their fellow restaurant customers were beginning to take an interest in their conversation, no doubt drawn in by Mitch's excited tone, and her previous coughing fit.

'Mitch,' she continued, 'OK, let's just say, for arguments sake, that you're serious.'

Mitch nodded his head eagerly.

'Let's just take a step back and discuss this...this...' She was tempted to say 'madness' but settled instead for 'proposal' as a less inflammatory term. Rosie searched Mitch's face for signs that her reaction was starting to have a dampening effect on his enthusiasm. There were none.

'Right. So, if I can get this straight,' here she lowered her voice, not wanting to give their neighbours the satisfaction of being able to repeat this story to all their friends later on, 'what you're proposing is that if neither of us can find someone to bring to the Christmas party we should have a...a... we should have a baby together?'

Even as she said it, she was again struck by a crazy desire to laugh, by the ludicrousness of what she had just said. Mitch continued to nod enthusiastically.

'A child? An actual child? Together?' She stared at him.

'Yes!' he exclaimed. 'But I also think we need to set some boundaries,' he said seriously, sitting up a little straighter as if it was now time to get down to business.

'Oh, phew,' said Rosie caustically, leaning heavily back in her chair. 'Yes, I really think we might need some *boundaries* if we're going to have an actual real-life baby together!' Her voice rose at the end, sending a frisson of tittering through their fellow customers.

'No, what I mean is...' continued Mitch, seemingly completely oblivious to the wagging ears at the nearby tables. 'What I mean is, we can't just bring *anybody* to the party. It has to be someone we're really *serious* about. Someone that we're actually thinking of spending *the rest of our lives with.*'

'OK, so let's just think about this,' Rosie said, sarcasm dripping from her voice. 'Is there some kind of metric by which we measure whether we're serious enough about this person?' She waved her arms around, refusing to indulge Mitch's use of 'The One' anymore. 'This person that we're bringing to the party? I mean how am I to know, or you to know, whether I am indeed serious enough about this as yet unknown person to avoid what might come next?'

Mitch pulled a face at her. 'You're always so analytical,' he berated her. 'This is love, true love, *The One*, we're talking about. We will know, there will be no hiding it!' he exclaimed in triumph.

If the stakes weren't quite so high, Rosie would have laughed about the innocent enthusiasm Mitch was showing in his belief of true love. As it was, she just felt sick.

'Right,' she said slowly. 'So if we *do* bring someone to the party then we're off the hook?'

Mitch looked blankly at her, 'What do you mean?'

'I mean,' she hissed, 'that the pact is fulfilled and we can forget about having children together.'

Mitch looked wounded. 'But I thought that was one of the best bits?' he said sorrowfully. Rosie looked at him incredulously. 'I mean, we know and love each other, we both want kids and we could share the parenting. I thought it would be brilliant!' His voice tapered off as he saw the look on Rosie's face.

He watched her for a while. 'Rosie,' he said seriously, 'I can't actually think of anyone I'd rather have a child with.' The sincere tone he used did something rather funny to her insides. For a moment she allowed herself to indulge in an alternative reality, where Mitch was declaring his true feelings for her, and not just proposing that she become the vessel through which he could play out his fantasies of fatherhood.

'At least at the moment,' he continued, 'until I meet someone else. But you're always welcome to be my fallback if it all goes wrong.' He grinned innocently at her, completely unaware of the impact of his words.

She honestly didn't know what to say. Both parts of the pact sounded awful to her. First, having to wade back into the mire of online dating, but this time with an added agenda and a deadline in play, and then, if she didn't meet someone, having to navigate this unholy mess of Mitch's creation and his plan of them sharing a baby.

Anything she said right now was going to be the wrong thing. She couldn't risk having this conversation with Mitch. She didn't feel strong enough to tell him just why this whole plan was a disaster from start to finish. If Mitch really hadn't understood why she felt how she did about dating, then this was a bigger conversation than she ever wanted to have with him. And as for the part about parenthood, the whole thing just sounded disastrous.

'Mitch, I think I need some time to think about this. Actually,' she said, looking at her watch, 'I should get going. I've got a lot on at work at the moment.' She thought fleetingly of her failed experiment and how much she would prefer to be in the lab right now sorting that mess out than here sorting out this mess with Mitch.

'OK, sure,' he nodded. 'That's understandable. But you'll think about it?' He looked across the table at her with those eyes and she felt incapable of doing anything other than nodding back in agreement.

Chapter Four

'He suggested *what*?!' Jasmine looked up from the carrots she was aggressively chopping and stared at Rosie.

'I know!' laughed Rosie. 'Completely crazy right!'

In all honesty Rosie didn't feel like laughing at all but she was hoping that sharing the details with her sister-in-law would lessen the burden. Perhaps Jasmine could persuade Rosie that Mitch *must* have been joking and that would be the end of it. But the look on Jasmine's face suggested she found this anything but funny.

Rosie was sat at the huge marble island in the beautifully designed kitchen of her brother Chris and his wife Jasmine. It was Saturday afternoon and Jasmine had rudely removed Rosie from the snug cocoon she had been in, enjoying watching TV with her nephews to 'help with the dinner.'

Jasmine needed no help with this. Jasmine needed very little help with anything. What she needed was for Rosie to sit and have a glass of wine at the island while Jasmine prepped vegetables for the gourmet meal she would effortlessly throw together later. Currently, Rosie was wishing she could crawl back to the space she had recently been occupying in between her nephews and pretend she had never brought this subject up.

'What did you say?' demanded Jasmine, menacingly pointing the knife she was holding at Rosie.

'Well, to be honest, I didn't say much.' Jasmine's aggressive reaction was not the one Rosie had been hoping for. 'It sort of took me by surprise and well, we were in a restaurant, so it was hard to know quite what to say.'

'What?' exploded Jasmine. 'Your best friend propositions you about getting you knocked up and you didn't "know quite what to say"?'

Rosie couldn't work out whether Jasmine was merely perplexed or completely apoplectic. Jasmine was always forthright with her opinions but Rosie really hadn't expected this level of reaction.

'Erm, well I'm sure we will talk about it more fully next time we meet,' Rosie cringed. Just hearing herself say this, she wanted to give herself a slap. No wonder Jasmine was so enraged.

'But you told him no, right?' Again the knife pointed perilously close to Rosie's face. 'I mean you told him to mind his own business and to stop interfering in both your love life and your decision as to whether or not you want kids?'

Rosie wished she had Jasmine's confidence and commitment to her beliefs. Secretly, she wondered whether it was easy to be that confident and committed when you had met and married the love of your life, had two children with them and still had a successful career as a lawyer. All while maintaining the slender figure Jasmine had had since Rosie first knew her. And that elusive art of making anything she wore look chic and expensive.

But this was not a popular opinion and was certainly not one Rosie would ever dare to voice. Especially not the part about the figure and the clothes. Jasmine would frown upon the frivolity of caring about that, not to mention the role that the patriarchy played in putting such pressure on women.

And anyway, Rosie was terrified of Jasmine and mostly just grateful that Jasmine was her friend and was always on her side. Plus, the easy access that she had to Jasmine's wardrobe. Because while they weren't *exactly* the same size, Rosie could certainly make use of some of Jasmine's looser tops. Trousers were a different matter; Rosie was tall yes, but her legs did eventually stop whereas Jasmine's seemed to go on forever. Rosie had never successfully borrowed a pair of Jasmine's trousers, she found herself thinking sadly, and wildly off topic.

'Well, I'm not really sure what I want to be honest,' Rosie said limply, realising that Jasmine was expecting a response about her future and not her musings on trousers. It seemed that no matter how confident Rosie felt in her opinions when she was alone, when she was with Jasmine, her conviction paled beside her sister-in-law's righteous opinions. Jasmine narrowed her eyes slightly but thankfully lowered the knife.

'I thought you didn't want kids?' she questioned.

'I'm not sure I ever said that, did I?' Rosie faltered.

'Well, you've never shown any interest in having them,' Jasmine countered.

'Haven't I?' Rosie felt increasingly bewildered by the turn this conversation seemed to be taking.

Jasmine noticed Rosie's face and tempered her response. 'I just thought that you might have shown more of an interest before now if you were keen to have them.'

Rosie frowned, trying not to take massive offence at what Jasmine seemed to be suggesting. 'I thought I was quite a dutiful aunt?' She nodded towards the sitting room where her two nephews were sitting, still entranced by the cartoon on the TV that she had been so rudely dragged from.

Jasmine floundered uncharacteristically, immediately realising her mistake. 'No, no I didn't mean... You've always been brilliant with the boys!' Jasmine's face flushed. 'You're the best aunt they could hope for! Their favourite aunt!'

Rosie smirked in spite of herself. 'I'm their *only* aunt!' she said dryly, secretly enjoying making the unflappable Jasmine flap. Jasmine smiled and looked distinctly relieved that the tension had been broken.

'I only meant,' Jasmine said, 'that you've never talked about wanting to have kids of your own, and have never seemed that bothered about meeting anyone.'

Rosie stared off into the well-manicured garden behind Jasmine. She had often wondered how Chris and Jasmine had managed to keep the garden so immaculate with two football-obsessed sons. It was probably a combination of fear and expensive football lessons in the local park.

'I'm not really sure how I feel to be honest,' Rosie started. 'I guess I've never felt strongly that I wanted them, but I always thought that one day that might change. That the magical biological clock would kick in and I would wake up knowing that I desperately wanted children. Is that what happened to you?' she teased Jasmine who just shrugged. Rosie thought it was good that her nephews weren't within earshot, because right then Jasmine seemed rather lukewarm on the concept of parenting.

Jasmine eyed her warily. She seemed like she had something to say, but was hesitant. 'I don't want to alarm you,' she began tentatively, 'but if you think you *might* want them someday you might need to get on with the process. You're not, I mean *we're* not' she quickly corrected herself, seeing the look on Rosie's face, 'getting any younger.'

Rosie felt her hackles rise, 'Thanks. Point made,' she snapped. 'Yes, we're both getting on a bit, I get it. But it's fine if *your* ovaries give up the ghost right now,' she retorted, 'you've got your two perfect kids. Meanwhile I am sat here while mine shrivel up and I'm not yet sure if I do want to have kids at all.'

'Rosie!' protested Jasmine, and Rosie noticed a peculiar look on her face. Had she missed something? It was almost a look of yearning. Rosie took a sip of her wine and wriggled a little on her bar stool. This was not a comfortable place in which to undergo this interrogation. Chris and Jasmine were more about style than comfort when it came to designing a house.

'I didn't mean to upset you,' Jasmine said. 'Shall we change the subject? Is it more or less controversial to ask you about dating?'

'What about dating?' said Rosie.

'I mean, maybe Mitch has a point about that?' Jasmine suggested.

Rosie stared in surprise. 'I thought you were on my side! You're supposed to be outraged on my behalf! My love life and my reproductive organs are none of his business. Remember?' she said pointedly.

Jasmine smiled. 'Of course I'm outraged, it's not his job to point any of this out, but I don't think it's so controversial to say that you have been rather, let's say, half-hearted about dating over the last few years?'

While Rosie wasn't exactly enjoying this topic of conversation, especially when she could be laid out on the sofa watching *Lego Star Wars* instead, she was grateful to Jasmine for her discretion. It was not just the last few years that Rosie hadn't shown much interest in dating, the truth be told Rosie had been half-hearted about dating ever since she moved to London.

'We can't all have met the man of our dreams during the first term of university and married him straight after graduation,' she quipped.

'It wasn't straight after graduation, it was after we had both qualified and could afford a party!' Jasmine shot back. Of course that was Jasmine's style, to have it all worked out and coordinated. Don't let true love and passion get in the way of your career ladder and student loan repayments. It was a trait Rosie truly admired.

But Rosie didn't really believe that. She knew how much Jasmine loved her brother, Chris. And after all these years Chris was still just as besotted with Jasmine. Rosie could relate; in all honesty she sometimes felt that if Chris had messed this relationship up, Rosie would have chosen Jasmine over him in the post-break-up-division-of-friends, and not just because of her wardrobe. Rosie was fond of Chris, and obviously they had a shared history in common, but she did wonder how much of her fondness for him was down to his marriage to Jasmine. And Rosie also adored her two nephews, Rory and Joe, despite what Jasmine thought. They had been dutifully supplied at well planned intervals by Jasmine and Chris, and were enough of a distraction that her mum never bothered Rosie too much on the subject of having her own. Until recently.

It wasn't as if Rosie had lived the life of a nun. And it certainly wasn't due to a lack of offers. Although she often felt a little on the stumpy side when she was next to Jasmine, she knew she was attractive. Just perhaps not to the men that she found attractive. Which was an irritation.

Rosie had had a teenage boyfriend who was completely hung up on her for a time. In fact, Matthew had been absolutely dead set on a long-distance relationship when he and Rosie had gone off to separate universities, right up until the point that he slept with his next-door neighbour during freshers' week. The last Rosie had heard, Matthew and said neighbour were married and living in suburbia. And although Rosie had gone through the whole crying-into-her-pillow for a few days, she now felt she had

had a very lucky escape. If marriage in suburbia was Matthew's lifetime ambition then Rosie was pleased not to have been a part of it.

University boyfriends came and went. They normally lasted just as long as it took for the boyfriend to suggest meeting the parents. Perhaps she wasn't so different from Mitch in that regard. And it wasn't because she didn't impress parents; in fact, they normally loved her. But it had given Rosie a glimpse of the future expected of her, which often left her cold.

There was one exception: Connor, who she had started dating during her finals. Connor Ryan was an English student, the yin to her yang in many ways. He was smart, funny and opinionated; a poet at heart. Rosie had adored him. They had spent one glorious and happy summer together. He was her first introduction to the real London, having grown up there. They walked the London parks, went to the Proms at the Royal Albert Hall, careened around Soho late at night after too many drinks. Although she had never admitted this to anyone but Jasmine, *he* was the reason she had applied to do her PhD in London. It was just meant to be.

Except it wasn't. Three weeks before she was due to move to London, Connor accepted his dream job as a trainee journalist and had been immediately posted to Washington to cover the upcoming presidential elections there. Nothing could come close to this for him and she would never have stood in his way. They had had several tearful conversations about the logistics of making it work, but they both knew that it was fated to fail.

THEN

Hyde Park was packed full of picnickers. It was a warm evening and Connor had told Rosie to meet him near the Serpentine Gallery; he said he had something to discuss. It was an in-between time, they had both graduated earlier on that summer and Rosie had the promise of her PhD starting in the autumn. She'd spent the summer waitressing at a pub near her mother's house and any spare time she had up in London, where Connor lived with his parents in a mews house in Belsize Park.

Connor didn't have a job yet. He had the luxury of parents who were keen for him to get the *right* job, not just something to pay the bills, so he had been busy applying for internships at newspapers in London. Nothing had come up yet but Rosie had a feeling that he might have some news and that was why he wanted to meet.

It was hard to see an inch of grass between the rugs thrown out for elaborately planned post-work picnics, and jackets thrown down for impromptu ones. Rosie craned her head looking for the familiar sight of Connor. Eventually she spotted him, standing out amongst the suits and ties. He was waving and laughing at her inability to see him.

'Didn't you see me?' he asked as he pulled her down to the blanket he had laid out on the grass for them and kissed her full on the lips, making her grin with happiness.

'I brought wine,' he said and opened a screw-cap bottle, pouring Rosie a large glass into a plastic cup. Connor was much more of a drinker than she was and could happily spend the evening drinking and talking, having an opinion on everything and never thinking once about food. Rosie would have two glasses and either be all over the place or ravenous.

She accepted the glass and he held his up for a toast. 'What are we drinking to?' she asked, eager to hear what he had to tell her.

'I got the job!' he said, his face splitting into a wide grin.

'Connor that's amazing!' she squealed and launched herself at him, kissing him again. 'I knew you would. What did they say?

59

When does it start? What department will you begin in?' she bombarded him with questions.

'The political desk,' he said, his face beaming with pleasure.

Connor was a poet *and* a political animal, ferociously intelligent and opinionated on everything. Politics was his life blood, he lived and breathed it, and it was the promise of a stint on the political desk at *The Guardian* that he had been hankering for. Rosie had tried to temper his excitement, trying to point out that during his traineeship he would be expected to move around between departments but he never seemed to listen to her. And now she wondered that if they started him off in that department how they would ever manage to move him on to the next. But that wasn't her problem, she was just so pleased that he had got the job. They could start looking for a flat together as they had planned.

'I'm so happy for you.' She squeezed his arm and enjoyed once again the feeling of being here, in London, with her twenties ahead of her and her brilliant boyfriend at her side.

'There's just one thing, though.' Connor's face twisted as he said the words. Rosie felt her stomach lurch, this didn't sound good.

'What?' she asked, both wanting to know and not wanting to know what he was about to say.

'They want me to go to Washington.'

'Washington?' she asked. 'As in, Washington DC? In America?

Connor couldn't help laughing at her confusion. 'Yes, as in DC,' he confirmed.

'Wow, OK, that's great,' she said and then saw the look on his face. 'For how long?' she tentatively asked.

'That's the thing, Rosie.' He grabbed her hand and she looked down as he did so, intuitively aware that her life was about to change but not quite understanding what was about to happen.

'It's not the job I applied for,' Connor said, squeezing her fingers to try and persuade her to look at him.

'Right,' she said, not feeling right at all.

'It's a permanent position in Washington.'

'But...' she started. 'What do you mean permanent? What about London?' What she really meant was what about *us*?

'I'll be shadowing the team covering American politics, learning the ropes, it's a huge opportunity,' he said, ignoring Rosie's question and instead explaining the magnitude of this job offer to his girlfriend who had planned her entire post-university life around him.

Rosie nodded dumbly, staring down at the picnic blanket and willing the tears not to fall on it. Of course she understood; this was momentous, the job of a lifetime, but it was also a job that was breaking her heart.

'I'm sure they'll fly me back, from time to time,' he said eagerly.

Rosie looked up at him, her large eyes wet with tears. 'Did you ask them?'

'Ask them what?'

'About flying you back? About how often they would do it?'

'Well, no,' Connor faltered.

And at that moment Rosie knew, she knew she wasn't going to move in with Connor, that their twenties weren't going to be spent together in London. That all her visions of the future were going to be a little off kilter, not quite what she had imagined. And that the restless soul of Connor was never going to be satisfied if he didn't take the job. That she couldn't be enough to make up for it if he stayed here. And that she couldn't and wouldn't be responsible for crushing his dreams.

'We can make it work, though?' he asked. 'Can't we, Rosie?'

After their emotional farewell at Heathrow, Rosie had done the only thing her logical brain would allow her to do: cut off all contact with Connor and let her bruised heart heal. In time, she told herself, it would never have worked once they both faced the realities of working life; they were just too different.

But every so often, she allowed herself to daydream an alternate reality. One where she hadn't had to go looking for somewhere to stay in London, one where she and Connor had moved in together and started their adult lives at the end of that summer. One where she had never moved in with Mitch, perhaps they were friends from having briefly worked together, but he certainly wasn't the central figure in her life that he had become.

Over the years she had caught fleeting references through mutual friends as to what Connor was up to. It seemed that so far, he had never made it back to the UK, he had moved from assignment to assignment in various places around the globe. She never dug deep enough to find out whether he was married or with someone and she stalwartly refused to have anything to do with him on social media.

NOW

The late afternoon sunshine caught Rosie's eyes and she blinked, realising Jasmine was watching her waiting for a response. Had she just zoned out in a Connor daydream? It had been a long time since she had allowed that to happen.

'You know I'm only joking about your marriage.' Rosie smiled at Jasmine. 'I am eternally grateful that you ensnared my brother and brought the two of us together.' Jasmine glared at her. 'But it is true,' Rosie continued, 'that you've never had to dabble your toes into the murky underworld of online dating. It's just so soulless.'

Jasmine had picked up her vegetable knife again and pointed it at Rosie, 'Never say never,' she said with force. 'When Chris trades me in for the young office graduate, I'll be right behind you on all the apps.' Rosie rolled her eyes, safe in the knowledge that Chris was far too sensible to trade Jasmine in. Or perhaps scared was the correct term, she thought, eyeballing the vegetable knife.

'OK, well until that time comes you can put swiping left or right from your mind,' Rosie replied. 'I, however, need to throw myself into this unless I want to end up co-parenting with Mitch.'

Jasmine grinned cheekily at her. 'So, what's your game plan? Got any new apps to try?'

Rosie sighed. 'I guess I should see if there are any new ones to sign up to, although I'm not sure I can see the point. It's amazing how often you come across the same person on several sites.' She paused. 'Did I tell you about the guy who messaged me on eHarmony and told me he thought we would be perfect together, only to ghost me when I messaged back to tell him that we had been on a date the previous week and he had impolitely told me that I was most definitely not his type?'

Jasmine laughed, 'OK, yeah, I can see you need to be made of stern stuff.'

'No kidding,' replied Rosie. 'It's a jungle out there. You can't take anything personally or you'd spend most of your life curled up in a ball crying.'

Jasmine turned to open the fridge door, leaving it open long enough for Rosie to wonder just how much Jasmine and Chris earned that they had not one bottle of champagne chilling in the fridge but a whole shelf of bottles. And then she felt churlish because she knew she would be offered a glass later.

'I was reading about a dating app the other day,' Jasmine said, her head buried inside the ice box.

'Oh, right, anything good?' Rosie asked, feigning interest.

'It was supposedly a feminist app, women make the first move.'

'That's Bumble.' Rosie laughed. 'So feminist. Because prior to that we were all just sat on our arses waiting for our knights in shining armour to arrive!'

Jasmine laughed loudly. 'That's more like it! Let's smash the patriarchy one dating app at a time.'

'Yeah, except it presupposes that the woman finds a match she likes.' Rosie paused. 'I guess I *would* like to meet someone like-minded though...' she said wistfully, staring into the middle distance past the art-deco pendants which hung over the island. 'Someone who likes reading, food, living in London, hanging out with friends. Maybe another scientist?' she said hopefully.

'Almost sounds like you're describing Mitch,' Jasmine said, jokingly.

'Ha ha!' Rosie laughed a little too loudly. 'I thought we had agreed that I wasn't looking to settle down with Mitch'.

'OK, so not Mitch. Is there a specific dating app for London-based, well-read, foodie scientists?' Jasmine asked.

'If only,' Rosie sighed. 'I'm going to have to take Nadia up on her offer, aren't I?'

'What offer?' Jasmine shot back, suddenly interested.

Nadia and Jasmine had an interesting relationship. Both of them would have died rather than admit it but they were jealous of each other. Both secretly thought they were the only best female friend Rosie needed and that she really didn't have space in her life for the other one.

'Oh, she's always trying to invite me over when her and Nico are hosting some single visiting professor.'

64

'But why don't you ever say yes?' Jasmine asked incredulously.

'Because it's a bit embarrassing, isn't it?' Rosie asked, 'To be so obviously set up like that?'

'Is it?' Jasmine said. 'I'd have thought that being set up with a friend of a friend would be perfect, practically the same as getting together with a friend, and they'd at least figure you have a couple of things in common.'

Rosie felt a little uncomfortable with where Jasmine might head next with this train of thought. 'Maybe I'll think about it,' she said quickly.

'I honestly don't know why you're so against being set up, or dating apps, to be honest,' said Jasmine. 'I think it would be fun to go out with some different people, it's exciting. You never know who you're going to meet!'

'Exactly,' Rosie practically shouted back, 'you never know!'

'But they could be the man of your dreams!' said Jasmine enthusiastically.

'No, they're not going to be. More often than not, it's a complete disappointment from start to finish, and it's a wasted evening when I could be seeing friends or doing something a lot more worthwhile.' Rosie was feeling desperate for this conversation to end. 'And please don't mention "the man of my dreams" again, you're beginning to sound like Mitch,' she grumbled.

Jasmine started to open her mouth to say something. 'No, Jasmine. Please, just leave it. I don't want to talk about it anymore. The chance of meeting the man of my dreams on a dating app are almost completely zero.' Or actually a big fat zero, Rosie felt like saying, because she knew for a fact that even if the man of her dreams did stumble upon her profile he wouldn't swipe right.

At that moment, her two nephews came tearing into the

kitchen. Evidently they had finished watching TV, and it was a matter of absolute urgency that they be fed that very minute. At five and seven, they were still happy to be occasionally cuddled by their aunt, especially if she had food for them, and at that moment she had never been more relieved to be handing out the carrot sticks and crackers that Jasmine had already laid out in tasteful porcelain snack bowls on the island.

Rosie pulled them both into a hug, burying her face in Rory's neck. He still had that sweet babyish smell that Rosie remembered them both having as newborns. She might have been using him to deflect Jasmine's attention but she also genuinely loved his smell and the feel of his still little body enveloped in hers. Perhaps, she thought to herself, perhaps it would be rather lovely to have one of these.

Chapter Five

R osie was in her office, head down, poring over lab reports. It had been a happy moment when she had discovered that not all the data from her recent experiment was redundant. She'd made it just in time after Nadia left her office to oversee her post doc and rescue the results, and while some of those results weren't what she was hoping for, some were OK. Rosie had done a little shimmy of delight and then quickly stopped before one of her colleagues saw her.

For most people, spending an afternoon studying lab reports would constitute mind-numbing boredom, but Rosie was in heaven. She felt calm and in control with pages and pages of numbers in front of her, her office door shut and no one to disturb her.

Rosie had always loved data, finding beauty and patterns in places where other people merely saw columns and numbers. Even as a child she'd loved the order that maths imposed on an otherwise confusing universe. She was sure a psychologist would have a field day with this, but Rosie chose not to think too much about it. She enjoyed it, it made her good at her job and to be honest it was no one else's business.

She was in just such a headspace when there was a knock on her office door. Somewhat startled, she looked up to see Nadia's head poke around the door.

'OK if I come in?' Nadia asked. Rosie looked at her watch, surprised to see how much of the day had passed. Trying not to be irritated at the interruption, she nodded and gestured to Nadia to come in.

'But close the door behind you, if you leave it open I will be inundated with students,' Rosie sighed. 'I think having an open-door policy is the way madness lies.'

Nadia grinned at her. 'Buy yourself a lock, that's what I do.'

Rosie pretended to look scandalised, 'What would Facilities say?!' she joked.

'"Good idea?"' Nadia said with a wink. 'Anyway, I knew you had lab reports in today so I don't suppose you've stopped to eat or drink since you got in this morning?' She held up a large paper bag and two cups of coffee and then dumped them on Rosie's desk, right on top of her lab reports. Rosie carefully eked the papers out from underneath while Nadia plonked herself in a chair opposite. After a moment, Nadia said, 'I've been thinking about Mitch.'

Rosie head snapped up. An added bonus of losing herself in the lab reports was that she hadn't had to think about awkward propositions for several hours. But it would probably have been a more effective strategy if she hadn't told Nadia about it in the first place. Then Rosie could avoid Mitch forever and pretend it had never happened.

When Rosie had told Nadia earlier on in the week, her response had been incredibly muted which was exactly what Rosie had been hoping for. It gave her hope that maybe Jasmine's reaction was over the top and Mitch's plan really was nothing to worry about. Although Rosie had suspected at the time that Nadia just wasn't listening. And the fact she had brought it up now made Rosie worry that Nadia had simply been thinking about it quietly ever since, mulling it over like a scientific puzzle she needed to solve.

'Oh, right,' Rosie attempted casually, quickly taking a sip of her coffee and scalding her mouth in the process.

Nadia pretended to ignore Rosie's false breeziness. 'I've been thinking about his proposal. About you being his fallback,' she said bluntly.

Rosie didn't reply, preferring instead to see where this conversation was going before she had to respond. She pretended to brush non-existent crumbs off her jumper.

'I've been thinking about it most of the week,' continued Nadia, taking a bite of one of the pastries she'd brought. 'And...' she paused, mouth full of croissant, 'I think you should take him up on it.'

This was most definitely not the direction Rosie had expected. For all her external chaos, Nadia was sharp-minded and observant. She would not be making such a suggestion without having really thought things through. For a moment, Rosie simply stared at her and then, aware that her own croissant was inelegantly hovering halfway to her mouth, she lowered it carefully.

'Well, that's an interesting idea,' she said, in exactly the tone that said it was not an interesting idea at all, that in fact it was a completely terrible idea and that they should just go back to their coffees and discuss lab reports and pretend Rosie had never told Nadia about Mitch's proposal in the first place.

Unfortunately, it didn't seem that Rosie had effectively

conveyed this meaning. They eyed each other slightly warily, wondering who was going to speak first.

Eventually Nadia put down her croissant on Rosie's desk and held her hands up placatingly. 'I know, I know, it sounds like I'm crazy, but just hear me out.'

Rosie nodded, indicating that Nadia had her permission to continue.

Nadia started carefully. 'I know we never really talk about serious "life" things. Nico tells me I lack empathy.'

Rosie risked a small smile, just imagining the reaction poor Nico got to this revelation.

'But I've been thinking about things a lot over the past couple of days and I realised that we've never really had the "baby" conversation.'

Rosie raised her eyebrows, wondering if she was about to get propositioned by yet another one of her friends. Nadia saw the look on Rosie's face. 'No, not like that!' she protested. 'You know, the, do you want them, don't you want them. I guess I felt it wasn't any of my business but Nico says this makes me emotionally disengaged and a bad friend.'

'It doesn't!' Rosie said emphatically.

'OK, well I'm just going to come out and say it – I sort of presumed you didn't because you always seem to be busy when I invite you round to mine. Which is fine!' Nadia added quickly. 'Because, to be honest, if I didn't *have* to spend time with my kids I'd probably make excuses too.'

Rosie spluttered at this, 'No!' she exclaimed, horrified that Nadia would misinterpret her reasons for not visiting and think this was about her children, who seemed, on the few brief occasions Rosie *had* met them, as delightfully clever and crazy as their parents. 'No,' she said again, 'it's not that at all.' Rosie looked up at the ceiling, wishing this awkward exchange away. 'It's just that you only ever seem to invite me round when you or Nico are trying to set me up with someone.' She blushed more furiously.

Nadia stared at her, 'Do I?' she said in bafflement, 'Do we? I hadn't ever noticed.'

Rosie looked incredulous. 'Really? You've really never noticed that the only time you invite me round is when there happens to be a single man at your dinner table as well?' Rosie was trying to keep her tone measured but she simply couldn't believe that Nadia hadn't made the connection.

'But...we invited you to our parties,' Nadia said a little desperately.

'Yes, and I've come to those,' Rosie faltered. 'Well, most of those.' She began to mentally run through her head the parties she had missed. 'But I can't remember a time when you've invited me over just to have dinner with the two of you, or for lunch with your family.'

Nadia's face looked distraught. 'I had honestly never noticed. I mean, perhaps now you come to mention it...' She tailed off. 'Was it really that obvious?' Rosie nodded her head.

'Because it wasn't obvious to me,' Nadia shook her head a little sadly, 'but this is probably why Nico says I lack emotional intelligence.'

Seeing the look on her friend's face, Rosie leapt in. 'Of course you don't...but perhaps it would be nice just to be invited to have dinner with you in your home rather than being invited to make up the numbers, or to try and set me up with someone?'

Nadia looked sheepish. 'I'm sorry,' she said, 'now you mention it you're probably right. I hadn't really thought about it before as a set up. We just have a few single male friends, I guess. And it's always nice to have more people around.'

Rosie softened. 'It's OK. But you know, I don't really want to be set up with people all the time.'

'Is it really that bad?' asked Nadia.

Rosie winced. 'Yes,' she nodded. 'It's just so painful and awkward. I end up feeling like the desperate colleague who nobody wants.'

Nadia looked stricken. 'I'm so sorry Rosie. I would never think of you that way. If anything, it's because you're so great and I just want to show you off to people!'

Rosie smiled in spite of herself. 'That's sweet, but really, next time maybe check with me first if there's someone you think I'd want to meet?'

Nadia nodded. 'Of course. And it's just what I was saying before. We never really talk about this stuff so I just presumed you were happy with your life. But subconsciously I must have been keen to marry you off to someone? I am sorry Rosie,' she repeated. 'Forgive me?'

'Of course I forgive you. But I don't understand why you think it's a good idea for me to have Mitch's baby,' Rosie said, half laughing, bringing the topic back around.

'Well,' chuckled Nadia, picking her croissant back up now that the terrible awkwardness seemed to mainly be past. 'I thought that if you *did* want children, then really would it be so bad to have one with your best friend?'

Rosie looked incredulous.

'I've heard about fallback plans,' Nadia continued, 'friends making them with each other. And I've done some research—'

'Of course you have,' said Rosie, rolling her eyes.

'I've done some research' continued Nadia pointedly, ignoring Rosie's interruption, 'and they seem to work in a lot of cases. I mean, you're far more likely to get a fair division of labour if you go into it with a friend rather than through the outdated conventional patriarchal marital system.' Rosie couldn't help but smile, Nadia sounded so much like Jasmine at that moment. Not that she would have told her that.

'And if you didn't want children,' Nadia quickly added, 'maybe this would be a great way of forcing you to finally meet someone and bring them to the Christmas party.'

'Firstly, can we just circle back to the part where you think it would be a good idea for me and Mitch to have a baby together, even supposing I did want a baby.'

'Do you?' challenged Nadia.

'Erm, well, I...' faltered Rosie. 'Jasmine asked me the same question,' she admitted.

'And what was your answer?'

'I said I didn't know.' Rosie looked down at the desk. 'But having thought about it, I guess the answer would be yes,' Nadia's eyes lit up, 'If...' Rosie carried on '...*if* I met the right person and no offence, Nadia, but I'm not sure Mitch is the right person for me to *want* to have a baby with.'

Nadia considered this, then nodded her head in agreement and picked up her coffee.

'Hang on,' she said, putting the cup back down and leaning forward across Rosie's desk. 'Did you just say that you're not sure Mitch is the right person for you to *want* to have a baby with?'

'Yes?' said Rosie, not understanding the point.

'You didn't say that you *didn't* want to have a baby with Mitch.'

Rosie looked stricken. There was a long pause.

'Because there is a big difference between those two statements.' Nadia paused. 'And if you're saying that you don't think it's right that you want to have a baby with Mitch...' Her voice trailed off. A look of understanding and surprise crossed her face. 'Oh,' she said breathlessly, 'oh, gosh, Rosie, I'm sorry I never realised.'

Rosie shrank back in her seat, looking defeated. She exhaled deeply, 'No, of course you wouldn't realise. It's totally stupid.' Recognising that Nadia had finally seen through to the crux of Rosie's dilemma, she put her face in her hands and sighed deeply. 'It's totally ridiculous to be completely hung up on a friend I've known for years who has never shown the slightest interest in me.'

Rosie felt tears pricking her eyes and furiously wiped them away with her fingers. She pushed herself away from her desk and stood up. Turning from Nadia, she stared out of the window down into the London street, unsure if she was looking for inspiration or an escape. There was a long pause, neither of them said anything.

Eventually Rosie turned back to face the room. 'But if we're being honest here, it's also the reason that I haven't found anyone yet.' She looked over at Nadia desperately. 'It's quite hard to date when you've already met your ideal man.' She sighed again. 'And it's even harder when he's your best friend.' She threw her hands up in exasperation. 'So you can see why Mitch suggesting this fallback plan is a complete disaster.'

She met Nadia's gaze; there were tears in her friend's eyes. Rosie realised she didn't think she had ever seen Nadia cry before, or even come close, not even when she had accidentally poured hydrochloric acid into a paper cut on her hand. But before Rosie could think more on the subject, Nadia was round her side of the desk enveloping her in a huge hug. It took Rosie completely by surprise, for someone so short Nadia had a remarkably wide arm span.

'Does he know?' Nadia asked eventually, letting go.

'No!' exclaimed Rosie. 'No one knows. Well, no one apart from you, now. And it has to stay that way.' She looked beseechingly at Nadia.

'Yes,' agreed Nadia, 'of course.'

They both paused for a breath. Nadia stepped back, still holding Rosie's hands in her own and looking at her.

'I suppose I have wondered over the years if there might be more to you and Mitch than just good friends.' Nadia looked into Rosie's eyes. 'But then you both seemed so happy being just friends, and nothing ever happened between you two, did it?' Nadia saw a look pass across Rosie's face, and took a sharp intake of breath. 'Oh, Rosie, no! Something did happen, didn't it? When?'

Rosie shook her head and disentangled her hands from Nadia's, wiping the tears that had been forming in her eyes with the back of one of her hands.

'It was nothing,' she said, 'it was ages ago, soon after we first moved in together.' Nadia waited for her to continue.

'We'd been out for someone's birthday, I can't even remember whose it was now.' She laughed as if that was such a ridiculous thing. 'Mitch had had too much to drink and we ended up kissing.'

There was a long silence. 'And then what?' prompted Nadia.

'Then nothing, literally nothing. He was so drunk. He fell asleep and I went to bed. When I woke up the next day it was as if nothing had happened. I don't think he had any recollection of it happening, and if he did, he never mentioned it.'

'And you never mentioned it, either?' Nadia asked.

'No!' exclaimed Rosie. 'He was my flatmate and my friend, if he wanted to pretend it had never happened then that was probably for the best.'

Nadia looked at her. 'So you've never talked about it?' she asked.

'No!' said Rosie again. 'I was mortified. He was obviously drunk enough to kiss anyone and I just happened to be there. And he was more than happy to forget it or ignore it.' She looked at

Nadia imploringly. 'I was so scared that if I mentioned it and he then remembered it that it might ruin our friendship. He would reject me and I was scared of losing him. And then over the years it never happened again, it never got mentioned; and anyway, I've got to know Mitch's taste in women, and it definitely isn't me.'

Another tear rolled down her cheek. Nadia reached up and brushed it away and hugged Rosie tight again. There was a silence.

'Look at me,' Nadia eventually said, releasing Rosie. 'Nico would be so proud, I'm learning to be all touchy feely!' Rosie laughed at the kindness of her friend and squeezed her back tightly.

THEN

'Come on, let's have one more drink!'

Mitch had his head in the cupboard and was rummaging around to see what alcohol they had in the flat.

'Aha!' he said triumphantly, emerging with a small brown bottle of something and swaying considerably as he did so. 'Whoops.' He staggered into the table and knocked over the chair.

Rosie laughed. 'Mitch, don't you think you've had enough?' she said, righting the chair and plucking the bottle out of Mitch's hands. 'What even is this?' she said, peering at the label.

'No idea!' said Mitch happily. 'It's left over from our flat warming.'

'That was months ago!' she shrieked.

'Rosie,' Mitch said, trying and failing to fix her with a stare. 'It's alcohol, it doesn't go off.'

'I guess,' she said, sounding unconvinced.

Really, Rosie knew she ought to have a large glass of water and a couple of painkillers rather than anything else to drink. She already knew she was going to feel hungover tomorrow. But it was Saturday night, they had been at Mitch's school friend's birthday party. And she didn't want Mitch to think she was a wet blanket. And if she was being completely honest, she didn't want the night to end. She had been having too much fun. It was the first time she had been out with a big group of Mitch's old friends and she had loved it. Mitch had really let his hair down and it had been funny seeing him with them all. She actually felt part of the crew, ribbing him about his clothes, about his taste in music, about his love life.

'So, come on,' Mitch said, 'let's have it in "the sitting room!"' He laughed loudly, even though it really wasn't funny.

The flat they shared had just the one bedroom but they had turned the sitting room into a bedroom for Mitch, and this had become the room they hung out in when they were both at home. It was in a beautiful mansion block not far from the Royal Albert Hall. Rosie sometimes thought back to that terrible afternoon just a stone's throw from her now-flat when Connor had told her the news that he was moving to the US. The girl she was then seemed a million miles away from the life she was now living. She still had to pinch herself to believe she was actually living somewhere so amazing but it did have its drawbacks. They were the youngest inhabitants of the building by several decades and regularly got complaints about any noise they made after 9pm.

'Shh,' Rosie said as they giggled their way through what their landlord referred to as 'a dining hall' but which Mitch used for storing his bike and Rosie kept her cupboard of shoes in.

'Careful!' She raised her voice as Mitch knocked into the bike and sent it crashing to the floor. He lay in a heap giggling and despite her concern over the neighbours she couldn't help but join him in the laughter.

'Look! I didn't spill a drop!' Mitch chuckled, lifting the glass he was already holding steady above his head, despite the fact he was entangled with a bike on the floor.

Rosie rolled her eyes. 'When was the last time you actually used that thing, anyway?' she asked, taking the glass from him and pulling him to his feet with her spare hand.

'Can't remember,' Mitch said, staggering slightly again. 'I got it because I look really hot in lycra.' He raised an eyebrow at her and winked. Or attempted to.

Rosie tried not to think of this image. Ever since they had moved in together she had studiously avoided being anywhere near the bathroom if there was a fleeting chance Mitch might be passing through semi-clad. Imagining him now in lycra was doing nothing to help the unnerving feelings she experienced when she thought of his body. Rosie followed him into his bedroom, where Mitch tried to kick a cushion out of the way and ended up missing by about three feet. Rosie rolled her eyes.

'Just sit down,' she gave him a shove, laughing, 'before you fall down.'

Mitch passed her his glass before collapsing into a semi-prone position on his bed, which doubled as their sofa. Rosie looked at him, wondering if she should just leave him to sleep it off.

'I'm fine!' he assured her. Propping himself up, he took the two glasses from her, putting them on his bedside table and then pulled her down to sit next to him.

'Music?' he asked, pointing a remote control at his stereo. She nodded in agreement. 'So long as you're not rude about it, though,' he said sternly. 'Can't believe you joined in with them all earlier on.'

One of the topics of conversation that evening had been Mitch's suspect taste in music. Whereas all his friends were into cool guitar bands and singer-songwriters, Mitch shamelessly loved the Top 40 and had a long-held passion for Girls Aloud.

Rosie had had to sadly confirm to his friends that it wasn't for show, he really did only listen to pop music when he was at home. He wasn't doing it just to annoy them. A song started and an image of Sarah Harding flashed into Rosie's mind: Mitch had spent one weekend the other month going on and on about her, how cool her peroxide blonde bob was. Rosie self-consciously ran her hand through her own straight dark hair.

'So, what did you think of Camden on a Saturday night?' he asked, reaching across her to pick his glass up. He took a swig and pulled a face.

'Disgusting?' she asked.

'Not at all,' he said, poker-faced, but he gritted his teeth before he took another sip.

'So? Camden? Did you like it?'

Rosie rested her head back against the headboard and thought of the crowded bar they had spent the evening in. It had been loud and dark, full of Mitch's school friends all vying for top attention, shouting to be heard.

'It was crazy,' she admitted. Sipping her drink and pulling exactly the same face as Mitch had just pulled. 'But great.' She smiled. 'I loved it.'

'I'm so pleased!' Mitch said, putting his arm behind her and pulling her into the crook of his arm. 'I loved introducing you to my friends.'

'You did?' she beamed up at him and let herself nestle against him.

'You know Dan thought you were hot,' Mitch said, his eyes heavy.

'He did?' Rosie asked, trying to remember which one Dan was.

Mitch shuffled slightly, his arm slipping down Rosie's back so that their heads become level. 'So,' he asked, suddenly casual. 'What did you think of him?'

'Did he ask you to ask?' Rosie laughed. 'Is this a "my mate fancies your mate" thing?'

'I was just interested,' Mitch replied. 'So you don't think you're ready for the London dating scene, then?' he asked. 'Still thinking about whatshisname? Connor, was it?'

Rosie had filled Mitch in on some of the details about her break-up with Connor but she hadn't wanted to dwell on it too much. She didn't want her new friend thinking she was being pathetic. And if she was being honest, since moving in with Mitch, she really hadn't thought about Connor all that much. She told herself it was because she was busy – new job, new flatmate, new life.

'Not really,' she said, 'just, you know, other things going on.'

'Oh, yeah?' Mitch asked interested. 'Like what?'

'Work mainly, getting settled here, finding my feet.'

Neither of them said anything for a while. 'He's right,' said Mitch suddenly. 'Dan. You are hot, you know.'

'Mitch!' Rosie protested, but grinned nonetheless.

Mitch turned his face towards her, and pulled her chin with his hand so she was facing him. 'Yup,' he said, 'definitely hot.'

Rosie felt a flush creep up her cheeks; they were face to face now, their noses almost touching. She could feel Mitch's breath on her face, it smelt of a mix of mint and the alcohol he had been pouring into his body for the last few hours. Rosie's mind raced. She felt dizzy and confused and suddenly very aware that maybe her breath smelt like all of the alcohol *she* had consumed over that evening.

'Mitch' she said, her voice quavering, 'I'm not sure…'

But whatever it was she was going to tell him she wasn't sure about, it was lost as his lips met hers. They were softer than she had imagined and she felt an electric charge go through her as she quickly thought that this was a terrible idea, before, suddenly, she was kissing him back. All thoughts of whether this was a good or a bad idea forced from her mind by the pure pleasure of kissing Mitch. And then in a split second it was all over. The buzzer at their door sounded loud and sharp, forcing them apart.

Alarmed, Rosie stood up. 'Who is that?' She stared at Mitch, focusing on his lips and subconsciously putting her hand up to touch hers.

'It's probably nothing,' Mitch said. 'Come back here.' He reached for her.

'No, we should answer it, it might be something important this late.'

'I bet it's not!' he called after her as she went out into the hallway, still dazed by the kiss and the sensation of Mitch's lips on hers.

Rosie picked up the intercom phone next to their front door. 'Taxi?' said a voice at the other end of the line.

'Sorry, no,' Rosie replied in confusion. 'No, we didn't order a taxi.'

'Oh, right,' the voice went on. 'Says here "101b"?'

Rosie tried to keep her irritation in check, this happened all the time. 'We're 101c,' she said.

'Sorry! Hope I didn't wake you.' And the line went dead.

Rosie gritted her teeth and replaced the handset, wishing she had listened to Mitch's advice and stayed exactly where she was. She looked at herself in the hallway mirror, ran her hands through her hair and rubbed her finger under her eyes where a little mascara had smudged. She took a deep breath and opened Mitch's door.

'You were right,' she said as she walked in, 'it was—'

She looked down at Mitch lying on his bed, eyes closed, mouth slightly open, absolutely dead to the world. She tiptoed across the room towards him, wondering whether to nudge him awake and then deciding against it. She leaned across him and pulled the blanket on the other side of the bed over him. She took a chance and brushed his hair out of his eyes, something she had been wanting to do ever since she met him. He looked so peaceful, and just so gorgeous. For a moment Rosie couldn't believe that tonight had actually happened. And then her stomach turned because perhaps Mitch wouldn't remember it at all, perhaps for him it would *be* nothing at all. Suddenly feeling all of the drinks she had had that evening, she bent down and turned off the lamp on Mitch's bedside table before creeping out, silently closing the door and going back to her own room, and her own bed, where she lay wide awake and fully dressed, on top of her duvet all night and waited to see what would happen in the morning.

NOW

'So now what?' asked Rosie, 'What am I supposed to do now, Nadia?'

Nadia considered her for a minute. 'Well, you have two options: either you meet someone amazing and totally forget all about being in love with Mitch…' She paused.

'Or?' asked Rosie. 'So far that first one hasn't panned out so well for me.'

'Well,' said Nadia, 'the alternative might be considered unethical.'

'Go on,' prompted Rosie.

'Well, the alternative is that you do nothing and hope Mitch doesn't meet anyone between now and Christmas. And then, come January the first, you plan to get pregnant and keep him to yourself, in a sense, forever.'

Rosie stared at her. 'Yeah,' agreed Nadia, 'it's pretty dastardly, and of course it wouldn't stop him meeting someone at a later date, but at least you know you'd have him in your life forever. Although, of course, as I said, it's completely unethical to do this and not tell him. And I'm sure Nico would have something to say about the fact this thought even occurred to me. So just forget it.' The words kept tumbling out of her. 'Maybe it's better we focus on you meeting someone new, after all... Hey,' she said, suddenly, 'what are you doing Friday? Nico has a new professor visiting from Munich. His name is Tomas. I bet he's hot. You should come for dinner!'

Rosie rolled her eyes.

Chapter Six

*C*ompletely unethical.

Nadia's words followed Rosie around all week, reverberating through her brain like a jackhammer. She felt distinctly uneasy about having admitted her feelings about Mitch to Nadia. What if Nadia stopped thinking of her as the awesome, organised scientist and instead thought of her as the messed-up girl, mooning over her best friend? It was enough to make Rosie never want to participate in a heart-to-heart again.

And she still didn't know what to do about Mitch's proposal. Of course, her first instinct was to reject it outright, but then bloody Nadia had gone and put unethical thoughts into her mind, literally wrenching open the box in which Rosie had carefully compartmentalised her feelings about Mitch, having a rummage around and poring over the contents. Rosie felt sick.

She'd also caught herself staring at passing parents and children, forcing herself to look away before it got too weird. She'd experience an alien yearning to have that parallel relationship in her life, before realising that the harassed parent looked like they were about to completely lose their shit because their darling child wouldn't do something reasonable like stop playing in the traffic. And then parenthood suddenly looked like the worst job in the world. And it was unpaid. At least when Rosie had to do the bits of her job she didn't like, she got paid to do it. Being a parent was the equivalent of the worst, most exploitative internship ever. The kind of role that in the corporate world should be made illegal.

And when Rosie wasn't thinking about babies, she was thinking about Mitch, and not in the baseline way that was normal with best friends that she usually forced her brain to think about him in, but in a distinctly uncomfortable way that often made her blush. Over the years Rosie had come to terms with the fact her feelings were unrequited. She was OK with that. They had an amazing friendship, they spent so much time together, she wouldn't have wanted to jeopardize that. But now Mitch seemed determined to start thinking about settling down, was this going to destroy that friendship?

If he did meet someone and eventually have children, it would be to that person that he would turn instead of to Rosie. Was she ready to let him go? And what if they did decide to have kids together, that would change everything, too. Yes, he would always be a part of her life but with all the perils and pitfalls of parenthood to navigate, would he end up *wanting* to be a part of her life? She sighed as she studied the vegetables in Sainsbury's and wished she had done an online order instead.

As if on cue, her phone rang. Fumbling through her bag she grabbed it just as the name 'Bestest EVER BFF' disappeared from the screen. *Dammit*, she thought as she hit the call button and made a mental note that she really needed to stop giving Mitch access to her phone and allowing him to rename himself. She'd only just worked out how to change the special ringtone that he had given himself after being overcome with embarrassment when Little Mix blared out in the office.

'Sorry,' she said when she heard the phone being picked up, 'I didn't get to you in time.'

'No worries.' Mitch's relaxed tone came through from the other end. 'What are you doing? Are you busy?' he asked.

Rosie looked at her watch, Mitch would be leaving the office about now, either heading to the pub to meet friends or going via the Sainsbury's Local at the end of his road. It was a Thursday so he wouldn't be going to the gym, he hadn't mentioned any work events this week, and if he was out to meet friends there was a good chance she would have been invited to join as well. Was it weird she knew so much about his routine?

Rosie started to panic that perhaps it was. Especially as there was a good chance that he had nothing like that level of interest in Rosie's life. Would he have a clue that she was stood in the same supermarket that she always did at about this time on a Thursday? The possibility that her insight into Mitch's life wasn't reciprocated left her feeling strangely unmoored.

'No, no it's fine,' she said into her phone. 'I was just getting some things from the shop. Sorry, no, you go.' Rosie gestured to the woman beside her that she wasn't waiting for the till.

'What?' said Mitch in confusion.

'No, not you!' she snapped, making the woman jump and consider whether she should do her shopping elsewhere in future. Rosie tried to placate her with a smile and attempted to point at her phone, almost dropping her shopping basket as she did so. The woman did not look convinced.

'I was talking to someone in the shop. I'm in Sainsbury's.'

'So you're staying in tonight?' Mitch asked.

'Mm-hmm.' Rosie picked up some peppers with her spare hand, trying to remember if she had any at home; she thought that she probably didn't. 'What about you?' she asked as she put them into her basket.

'Well, I was just leaving the office,' Mitch said. Rosie could hear the sound of him walking. 'And I was going to stop at the shop on my way home to get some food.' She felt a little sick at how accurate she had been, 'But then I wondered if perhaps you wanted to meet up?' he continued hopefully.

Rosie contemplated the rows of pineapples in front of her and said nothing.

'Rosie? Rosie are you still there?'

'Oh, yeah, no I am. Sorry, you cut out a bit then,' she lied, 'what were you saying?'

'I wondered if you wanted to meet up tonight?' he asked.

'Oh, I'm er, busy tonight,' she said awkwardly, distinctly aware that apart from that time when she was writing up her thesis, this was probably the first time in their entire relationship that she had told Mitch she couldn't meet up. Already his stupid plan was having an impact on their relationship, she thought.

'I thought you said you were staying in tonight?' Mitch sounded confused.

'Yeah, but...' Rosie realised she was sounding panicked. 'I have some stuff to read for work.'

'Oh.' Mitch sounded put out. There was a pause and Rosie held her breath, hoping she had succeeded in putting him off.

'What if I came round and cooked while you read?' he suggested, bouncing back from her knock-back with remarkable speed.

'Well...' Rosie's eyes darted around as if she hoped her local Sainsbury's might offer a well-lit exit from an awkward conversation with a friend. 'I don't have any food!' she announced triumphantly.

There was a long pause. 'I thought you just said you were in Sainsbury's?' Mitch said doubtfully.

'I am! Or I was! But I've just paid and I only bought enough food for one.' She felt bad, she never lied to Mitch and now she didn't seem to be able to help herself, the lies were tripping off her tongue. This was definitely a bad sign.

'No problem!' Mitch said enthusiastically. 'What were you thinking of cooking? I can just pick up some extra on my way to yours!'

Rosie sighed. In her previous life she would have leapt at the chance to have Mitch come over and cook for her, have her best friend to herself, no need to cook, no need to leave the house. In fact, one of the best things about secretly being in love with her best friend was that it never mattered what she looked like. She could go home, tie her hair up and put on some joggers. She was never going to put Mitch off with her appearance because he wasn't interested in the first place.

But this was not like her 'before' life. Something had shifted.

'OK,' she relented, 'I was planning a risotto, just get some extra chicken and we should be fine.' She looked down at the things in her basket. Of course, she could just get the extra chicken now, but then she would have to admit she had been lying.

'Great!' Mitch exclaimed. 'I'll see you in about fifteen minutes.'

Rosie's eyes narrowed. 'Fifteen minutes?' she queried, 'Mitch, where are you?'

'Yep, about that, I was actually halfway round to yours before I called you.'

Rosie smiled despite herself. Frustrating though it was that he had just presumed he could come over to hers, it also meant that he too knew exactly where to find her on a Thursday night.

Five minutes later, she was putting her shopping away. This was one of the things she loved about living in London. At any time of day or night she could walk down her road and buy emergency chocolate or wine. It wasn't as if she had grown up in the sticks, but the charming English village that her mother still lived in had just one parade of shops and most of them closed at 5pm and they certainly didn't open before 11am on a Sunday. If you wanted snacks at night you needed a car, or stronger willpower. Rosie was pleased not to need either.

She checked herself in the mirror in the hallway and ran her fingers through her hair, trying to decide whether she needed blusher or not, and decided against it. What if Mitch noticed and then wondered why she was wearing make-up? And then she might be forced to explain that it was because she now cared whether he found her attractive and that although she *knew* he wasn't interested in her in *that* way, everything had now changed because of *the* conversation. And there wasn't enough wine in the world to cover the fallout from that.

She looked around her flat. It could probably do with a clean but that would have to wait. Probably indefinitely, if they were going to introduce a baby into the surroundings. There would be toys and nappies, food splattered up the walls. What was Mitch thinking? He hated mess. He really wasn't thinking this through, maybe she needed to remind him of just how much mess babies made. Rosie shook her head, she couldn't believe that thought had just popped into her head. She needed to stop imagining cosy (yet messy) domestic scenes of her and Mitch and a faceless baby.

The doorbell rang, shattering Rosie's spiralling nightmare. She felt momentarily grateful that she had made Mitch give her the spare key back when she had needed it for her mum, and so far she hadn't got around to handing it back to him.

'You need to give me my key back,' was the first thing Mitch said when she opened the door. She rolled her eyes at how in sync they were.

'Yes, yes, alright, come in,' she said, hurrying him through the door. She tried not to notice that the walk to her flat had given him an attractively flushed look; on anyone else the slight sheen on their skin from walking fast through the still warm evening air would be off-putting. It was really annoying how little about Mitch she found off-putting.

Mitch busied himself in the kitchen; he unpacked the chicken that he had been instructed to bring and got the things out of Rosie's cupboards that he needed. Rosie felt slightly uncomfortable at how at home he was in her flat. When they'd lived together, this was normal, they would cook for each other all the time, chatting about stuff, discussing Mitch's dreams and ambitions while Rosie kept hers to herself, always worried she might get caught giving her feelings away. But tonight felt awkward, beyond awkward, fingernails down a chalkboard uncomfortable.

'I'm going to get my laptop out,' she said loudly, in the hope that by shouting something, she might dissipate all the feelings she was feeling, 'and get on with my reading.' She made a show of noisily setting out her computer on the kitchen table and plugging the cable in.

'Sure, fine. I'll let you know when it's ready.' Mitch seemed totally oblivious to any of the awkwardness as he hummed to himself as he cooked.

———

'That was great, Mitch, thanks, I couldn't eat another thing, though.' She shook her head as he offered her more risotto.

He beamed at her putting the pan back on the hob, 'See? It *was* worth having me over. You've eaten, you've read and now we can

90

chat.' He leaned over to pick his wine glass up from the table and raised it to her.

Rosie was wondering if she could get away with claiming she needed an early night. She surreptitiously glanced at her watch, it was only 9pm. Mitch would know something was up if she made him leave now.

She braced herself. 'OK, then, let's chat, I'm guessing you want to discuss your proposal?' she asked.

Mitch suddenly looked excited as he pulled his chair out to sit down. 'Are you ready to?' he leaned forward in anticipation. 'I don't want to put any pressure on you.'

Rosie scowled at him. 'I think telling me that I need to find a boyfriend before Christmas or have a baby with you amounts to pressure, don't you?' She arched her eyebrow.

Mitch waved his hand dismissively at her. 'I meant, put pressure on you to discuss terms before you were ready,' he said blithely, completely missing the point. Rosie felt frustrated that he didn't for one moment think that she might say no: no completely, no to the whole damn thing.

'So how do you see this working, exactly?' This came out more aggressively than she had intended.

Mitch grinned, his dimple flashing, 'It's quite simple: we both agree that we will do our best to bring someone we're serious about—' he gave her a meaningful look as he said this, '—to the Christmas party. And if that doesn't happen then we start to look into the options for having a baby together. Because...' He hesitated. 'I guess it takes some planning and research if you're not going to do it the...' He looked awkward and then went a little red '...the usual way.'

For someone so governed by romance Mitch was remarkably prudish. Rosie smiled, despite herself. 'You don't think the old-fashioned way would work?' she teased before noticing a peculiar look cross his face.

'No!' he spluttered, then took a long drink of water as his face went redder and redder. 'I mean, no offence, Rosie, but I don't think that's a good idea.' She wasn't sure what she had expected when she had said this. Mitch to declare his undying love? To tell her that actually, yes, that was a great idea and they should just get down to it. She couldn't really be disappointed, but it still hurt, to be told point-blank that he was definitely not interested, not even to make the baby he so desperately wanted.

The Christmas party Mitch referred to was a thing of legend. Rosie's boss Rachel had been holding it for years, for far longer than either Mitch or Rosie had been on the invite list. Its current venue was in Rachel's beautiful north London townhouse (which went to prove that you could make some money out of a career in science, something that Rosie kept telling herself any time she felt disheartened by the remuneration of academia). But there were rumours that Rachel had been holding the party ever since she'd lived in a bedsit in Hackney, before Hackney became cool and completely unaffordable.

Every year there was a theme; they still talked about the year it was circus-themed. Rosie had never quite worked out whether Rachel had paid the performers to be there or whether she just had very creative and talented friends. And speaking of friends, everyone was encouraged if not ordered to bring friends which was why Mitch still got an invitation and why it was such a landmark in their social calendar.

It was also luxuriously decadent and fun. Everyone would drink too much and say too much, plan their Christmas holidays and discuss their resolutions for the new year. And every year Rosie would have two resolutions – one she would share with the group and then a private one, which so far she had failed at each and every year: to fall out of love with Mitch. So, in a way, it was rather fitting that this would be the pinnacle of their challenge.

Rosie watched Mitch closely. 'Are you really sure about this baby thing?' she asked.

'Yes!' exclaimed Mitch. 'I've always, *always* wanted children.'

A little bitterly, Rosie thought that it might be nice if he had clocked her ambivalence on the subject. Or at least checked with her first.

'I meant,' she started, 'are you sure about it with *me*?'

Mitch looked puzzled for a minute. 'Rosie, you're my best friend. I've known you for years.' He stared earnestly at her. 'I can't imagine anyone better to do this with.'

Rosie felt her heartstrings tug, were there tears prickling her eyes?!

'I mean,' continued Mitch, 'if I don't meet anyone truly hot between now and then!' he grinned at her.

Rosie felt her heart shrink back to its usual size, the tears instantaneously drying up. For a second there she had allowed herself to imagine what it would be like to be the centre of Mitch's world, not just as his friend but as the mother of his child. And then the mirage was rudely snatched away by the hand of a faceless yet irresistibly attractive woman. Was Rosie ready for this new and improved level of heartache?

Mitch didn't seem to notice the rollercoaster of emotions Rosie was suffering, 'So what do you think?' he said, raising his stupidly shapely eyebrow at her. 'Are you in?'

Rosie hesitated, refusing to engage in feelings of jealousy towards Mitch's eyebrows, and then, deciding that as they weren't at the actual insemination stage quite yet, she could always back out, 'Yes. OK. I'm in.'

Completely unethical.

Mitch's absurdly handsome face broke into a smile and he was across Rosie's kitchen in a flash. Rosie allowed herself to enjoy the feeling of being swept up into Mitch's arms, her face pressed against his broad chest, 'Rosie, you're the best! You've made me so happy.' His voice rumbled through her head, right down her body and to parts of her that Mitch couldn't ever know that he reached. And for a second, she allowed herself to relax and pretend that all of this could work out just fine.

Chapter Seven

R osie loved Sundays. She loved the ones she got to stay in bed, the ones she spent the morning enjoying brunch and coffee with friends. She even enjoyed the ones when she had to go into the lab. It was always so gloriously quiet – no students around, no post docs wanting to ask her tricky questions. Rachel would occasionally be there but Rachel had an unwritten rule that Sundays were not the time for small talk (sometimes with Rachel *no time* was for small talk). She would appear in Rosie's office doorway, silently place a cup of coffee on Rosie's desk and then walk back out again. Rosie knew that this was a small act of kindness which meant an awful lot and therefore made it unconscionable for Rosie to ever tell Rachel that she didn't like macchiatos. There were hills to die on and this wasn't hers.

The only other person who sometimes used the lab on a Sunday was Nadia when she was in the middle of a drug trial. Rosie had her suspicions that often Nadia didn't need to be there at all but had used the excuse to duck out of familial obligations and leave Nico in charge of the children. She'd never asked Nadia about this, because she wasn't sure Nadia would take kindly to being outed in such a manner.

But today there was no lab work to be done, no friends to meet and the morning stretched out in front of her. She rolled to her side in bed and opened an eye, wishing that there was someone there to make her a cup of tea so she wouldn't have to leave her extremely comfortable bed. But it would have to be the sort of person who would make the tea just right, and then leave silently afterwards and not expect to perch on her bed and chat. She stretched her arms over her head, yawned, and then caught sight of a new dress hung up over the antique wardrobe that she and Mitch had bought several years ago only to realise afterwards that they had no way of getting it back from Crystal Palace. The van Rosie had eventually had to hire cost more than the wardrobe, and this was what one got from being impulsive and profligate, she had moaned at Mitch later.

'Dammit.' The dress jogged her memory further. 'Mum's birthday.' Susan rarely made any demands on either of her children. She was firmly of the opinion that they should be left to live their own lives and, more importantly, her to live hers. But her birthday was a fixed tradition in the family and ever since Jasmine and Chris had the boys it was understood that Susan's birthday would be celebrated at their house. Lunch was always an elaborate creation chosen by Chris and Jasmine. It would be something adapted from their latest favourite restaurant, with no concessions made for the children. Rory and Joe were expected to eat what the adults ate, which was why they loved it when Rosie would secretly feed them chicken nuggets or fish fingers whenever she babysat, the evidence carefully smuggled in and out without Jasmine ever knowing.

Rosie's contribution to Susan's birthday was the cake.

Sometimes homemade, but this year it would have to be bought. She had used up all baking time this week thinking about having babies with Mitch and buying new dresses to try and distract her from these thoughts. She hoped Jasmine wouldn't disapprove; Jasmine would have been flat-out all week at work and still have found the time to conjure up a gourmet meal for the whole family. Sighing, Rosie pulled herself out of bed; there was to be no lie-in for her this morning. But if she got up now, she could fit in a run before she had to get ready for lunch. Maybe that would help clear her head of Mitch and his nonsense.

The sun was out and the park near Rosie's flat was already busy with early morning joggers. Rosie was not a natural athlete, but so far, at the age of thirty-four, she had managed to get by with the occasional run, plenty of walking and good genes. Idly, she wondered to herself whether that would change if she did have a baby, before berating herself because this run was supposed to banish such thoughts. Without thinking she smoothed her hands over her stomach as she watched a petite woman streak past, pushing one of those jogging buggies that cost about the same as a small car, with two dozing toddlers in it.

Rosie didn't especially enjoy running, what maniac would? But she knew it was good for her, that she ought to do it more and that it was also quite useful for shifting persistently uncomfortable thoughts. Because it was hard to fixate on things when you needed all your concentration just to keep breathing. She looked at her watch, it would have to be a quick run during which she needed to weigh up the pros and cons of admitting to Jasmine that she had agreed to Mitch's proposal. Sighing, she plugged her earbuds in and scrolled to her personally curated, running playlist: if RiRi couldn't fix this then no one could.

Jasmine and Chris lived at the end of the Northern line. Ten years ago, it was the sort of place that Rosie had only heard of in urban myth; people falling asleep on the tube and ending up there in a siding, long after the last tube had left. They had bought the place when Jasmine was pregnant with Joe, eight years ago. Then, it had been a beautiful but completely run-down Victorian villa in a very undesirable part of London. Now it was a show home in a postcode where houses changed hands for millions. Rosie could never work out whether Chris and Jasmine had astonishing foresight or just amazing luck. Either way, she felt they deserved it; they had poured so much money and love into that place, even if Rosie would have preferred them to have installed comfier sofas and places where she felt more at ease leaving a glass of wine.

Rosie bought a cake at the bakery near her flat, because what it lacked in fancy packaging, it made up for in affordability. Unlike the place on the high street near her brother's place where you would need another mortgage to shop. There hadn't been a Northern-line train for about fifteen minutes and so the tube was packed, making for a perilous journey, Rosie hanging on to a rail with one hand and trying to keep from dropping the cake box with the other. Feeling distinctly flustered, she arrived on their doorstep and, keeping the cake box delicately balanced, leaned forward to ring the doorbell. There was a clattering sound from inside, the unmistakable sound of small footsteps running at full pelt. She braced herself.

Rory opened the door – at five years old, he had just become tall enough to reach the catch to unlock it from the inside and was immensely proud of this achievement. He took Rosie in, his little face gazing up at her. Evidently, he had yet to be taught the correct greeting after the front door was opened.

'Granny is in the garden looking for worms,' he told Rosie

solemnly, as if this was an everyday occurrence. Rosie nodded gravely; she knew that there was nothing more insulting to a small child than laughing at whatever it was they were telling you. Unless it was a joke, and then you were expected to laugh whether it was amusing or not.

'I will go and find her just as soon as I put this—' she showed him the cake box '—down in the kitchen. Want to take a look?' she asked. Rory nodded eagerly and she bent down to his level and gingerly opened the cake box just enough so that he could peek in. Rory's eyes grew round.

'Do you think she'll like it?' she asked him in a whisper. He nodded vigorously.

'It has to be our secret,' she told him, putting her finger to her lips. 'But I picked the chocolate one because I knew that it was yours and your brother's favourite.'

Rory nodded again and then put a small sticky hand on her arm. 'It's OK, Auntie Rosie, I think Granny will like chocolate, too.' He then took off at a run past the stairs and down the corridor which led to the open plan kitchen at the back of the house.

Rosie smiled to herself as she stood up. Rory was so sweet and serious. She hoped he would stay that way forever. But she knew it was only a matter of time before he got too big for secret jokes. Already his older brother Joe was frequently out when Rosie came over, more interested in playing with his friends than hanging out with his auntie. Which was only natural and right, she knew. Perhaps if she had one of her own she would feel the same pull of emotions, excited about them growing up but a sense of sadness that they no longer needed her as much.

She shook her head, banishing that thought and pulled herself together just in time to enter the organised chaos of the kitchen.

Jasmine was stood at the hob stirring something that smelled wonderful in a large casserole dish. Chris was re-stringing birthday bunting which had obviously just fallen down. Rosie smiled in recognition; this was the bunting that came out for everyone's birthdays and had done for the last decade. She loved the fact that despite Chris and Jasmine's high-end lifestyle they still had time for those sentimental touches. Rory was trying to help his dad and seemed to be doing anything but. The string was now tangled around his ankles and he had managed to tie a complicated knot around his legs in the brief time since he had left Rosie in the hallway. Impressive, she thought to herself.

Through the bi-fold doors that led out to the garden she could see her mother kneeling on the grass inspecting something that Joe was holding out to her. To her mother's credit she was doing a very good impression of looking extremely interested in whatever it was. Even if she did look rather uncomfortable kneeling in the grass.

'Rosie!' exclaimed Jasmine, noticing her standing there. 'You're here, great, put that down and come and tell me what you think of this sauce.'

Jasmine held out a wooden spoon towards her. 'Your darling brother tells me it has too much basil, but I have told him there is no such thing.'

Rosie shot a glance at Chris who shrugged, still tangled up in the bunting. Rosie smiled at him conspiratorially, they both knew who would win this argument. Rosie carefully placed the cake box on the island and walked quickly over to Jasmine and dutifully tasted the sauce.

'Mmm' she said, 'just perfect.' Jasmine smiled triumphantly, put the spoon down and hugged Rosie.

'Told you so,' she said smugly to Chris over Rosie's head. If

Rosie had been honest there was perhaps a little too much basil, not enough to make it unpleasant but enough to overpower any other flavours. However, this was not an opinion she dared to share with Jasmine.

'How are you?' Chris said, having untangled both himself and Rory and coming over to give Rosie a hug too. Rosie breathed in the familiar scent of him and found herself relaxing.

'Fine, fine. Bit of a nerve-wracking tube journey carrying that thing.' She indicated the cake box.

Chris frowned. 'You should have picked one up at our local place.'

Rosie looked at Jasmine hoping she wasn't going to agree. Jasmine shook her head at Chris and tutted, then she moved swiftly to the island and flipped open the lid of the cake box.

'Rosie this looks delicious,' she said. 'Personally I am delighted you went to *your* bakery, it does *much* better chocolate cake.' Jasmine shot Chris a look which he was completely oblivious to, just as Rosie gave her one of gratitude. Rosie needed to remember that Jasmine wasn't always judgemental, and sometimes, when you were least expecting it, she could be almost compassionate and understanding.

'What are they doing out there?' Rosie asked, pointing out into the garden.

Chris turned his head following her gaze. 'Joe is studying bugs at school so he's taken Mum out there to show off his knowledge.'

Rosie nodded sagely. 'I'll go say hello,' she said. 'You never know, I might learn something. Do you want to come Rory?'

Rory turned his large brown eyes on her and shook his head. 'I promised Mummy I would help.' Rosie looked over his head to Jasmine who pretended to shudder, grinned at Rosie and turned back to the stove.

'Hey, Mum,' Rosie said, stepping out into the garden.

'Hello, darling,' Susan said, straightening up with some degree of difficulty. Rosie noticed this and held her hand out to help her up.

Susan swatted her away. 'I'm quite capable,' she said shortly.

'Yes, Mother.' Rosie grinned. 'Happy Birthday!' She gave Susan a hug. 'I hear Joe is giving you a bug lesson?'

Joe cast a scornful look in her direction. 'It's natural history, yeah?' Rosie could already hear the teenage intonation in the seven-year-old's voice.

'Yes, quite right, darling,' Susan said putting an arm around her eldest grandson. 'And you seem to know an awful lot about it, but perhaps you'd like to tell your aunt now because really I should go and see if I can help your mum and dad with lunch.' She flashed a wicked grin at Rosie as Rosie reluctantly felt herself pulled down to grass level. Susan's aging joints suddenly seemed extremely youthful as she made a fast getaway across the lawn towards the house.

Rosie sat patiently while her precocious nephew lectured her on the life cycle of a ladybird. Every so often she would glance imploringly at the house where the rest of her family were studiously ignoring her. She was regretting coming outside at all. Much as she enjoyed spending time with Joe, she would rather have been inside being offered a glass of wine. She looked on jealously as she saw through the window Chris handing Susan a flute of something sparkling. Just as she was about to lose the will to live, she was rewarded by a shout from Chris.

'Lunch is ready!' he called. 'Joe, you need to wash your hands.'

Joe was about to launch into everything he had ever learned about photosynthesis and Rosie exhaled a secret sigh of relief. She was happy to indulge him, up to a point.

'Can I help?' she asked as she stepped back into the house and headed straight to the sink to wash her hands.

'You can check on Rory's attempts to lay the table,' Chris shouted over the clatter of pans and dishes.

'OK,' she called back. 'Joe! Hands!' she yelled, spotting Joe heading straight towards the cake box with his muddy hands outstretched in front of him. He scowled at her, all brownie points for being the interested auntie immediately vanishing. What a waste.

'Yes, please wash your hands. You, too, Rory,' Jasmine ordered as she lifted the steaming pot from the hob and carried it over to the table.

'And this is very hot. VERY HOT,' she yelled loudly and pointed at her two sons after she had put it down. 'Which means do not touch it.' She swatted Joe's now-almost-clean hand away. 'It does not mean, let's touch it to find out just how hot it is.'

Chris pushed past Rosie carrying another delicious-smelling dish and gestured with his elbow. 'You're over there, Rosie, between Joe and Rory.'

Rosie fixed him with a glare.

'Why am I always on the kids' side?' she muttered.

Chris looked at her in surprise. 'They asked for you there?' he said in bafflement. 'Like they always do. And anyway,' he said putting the dish down, 'you act as a buffer, stops them fighting.' He grinned at Rosie.

Joe took his seat and patted the chair next to him. Rosie smiled at him and tried to ignore the fact that as the childless sibling she was *always* put with the kids. She wondered how the dynamics would change when – *if*, she corrected herself – she ever had kids.

'I wanted you next to me,' said Jasmine, as if she sensed Rosie's thoughts, and she leaned over to put a delicious-smelling basket of bread on the table, 'but the boys insisted.'

Chastened, Rosie smiled at Joe and reached to squeeze the hand of Rory on her other side. She really didn't know what had got into her, she normally loved being at Jasmine and Chris's but today she just felt irritated and out of sorts with everyone. And mainly with herself.

Deciding that food would help, she put a finger to her lips and quickly snuck three rolls out of the bread basket dividing them up between her, Joe and Rory. The boys grinned at her; they would never have got away with this if Auntie Rosie hadn't been there. The aroma of the fresh bread calmed her thoughts and she aggressively smothered Rory's roll in butter, trying to concentrate on the here and now. Not on future events that may or may not involve Mitch.

Lunch was delicious as she knew it would be. The basil in the cannelloni had been tempered with the creamy tomato sauce, and the salad Chris had made had citrusy flavours in it, which cut through the richness of the pasta. Beside her Joe was eagerly mopping up his plate with yet another roll. Rosie watched him eat, while on her other side Rory was being told off for attempting to lick his plate.

'But you normally let me!' he implored of his parents who were shaking their heads sternly. 'Just because Granny is here,' he said grumpily, folding his arms across his tiny chest.

'Oh, don't mind me,' said Susan chirpily. 'It's my birthday, so I give you special dispensation to lick your plate clean.' She winked at Rory as he lifted the plate to his face, Jasmine rolled her eyes in frustration. Rosie smirked to herself; sometimes it was fun to witness the tension between other family members. Especially when she was not involved.

'Are you two finished?' Rosie asked of Joe and Rory. 'Because I need your help.'

She stood to start clearing the plates, shushing both her mother and Jasmine back into their seats. She didn't need to do the same with Chris, who looked like he might be falling asleep.

'Me and the boys have got this.' Joe and Rory followed her eagerly around to the other side of the island, they knew it was cake time. As Rosie cautiously picked the cake out of the box, Joe searched for candles in the kitchen drawer and Rory found the matches – finding them rather too quickly for Rosie's liking, something she might need to warn Jasmine and Chris about.

There was a minor scuffle over who got to light the candles.

'He always gets to do it!' Rory stamped his foot in frustration and anger at being the youngest.

'I do not!' shouted Joe, pushing his little brother.

'OK!' Rosie held her hands up to part the two of them. 'We can split it; you both get to do the same.'

Joe rolled his eyes up to the ceiling, mentally working something out. 'It's an uneven number!' he finally said triumphantly, having remembered how old Susan was.

'Joe, really?' Rosie asked. 'We're not going to put the actual number of candles on the cake. We don't have enough.'

'I can hear you!' Susan called sharply, which cut through the sibling rivalry and Joe and Rory giggled together at hearing Granny get cross.

'Here's what we'll do,' Rosie whispered. 'Four each, OK?' Joe looked like he was about to protest but then thought better of it.

'Any more than that and it would be a fire hazard,' she said more loudly.

'I can *still* hear you!' Susan said again and Rosie grinned at her nephews.

There was a moment of anxiety for Rosie when it looked like Joe's candles would have burned out completely before Rory had finished with his. But finally the cake was ready, and the candles all still burning.

'Ready?' She looked down at both her nephews. They nodded and began singing 'Happy Birthday' together, loudly and completely out of tune. Not that their tunelessness seemed to bother Susan who was smiling away indulgently at her grandsons and did the requisite amount of oohing and aahing over the cake once the candles had been blown out.

'Is this from the bakery near yours?' she asked Rosie, who nodded, pleased that her mother seemed happy. 'Do you remember that Mitch took me there when I locked myself out of your flat?'

'I'd forgotten that!' Rosie smiled. 'I was in the lab, wasn't I, so I didn't have my phone with me. Weren't you waiting in there for hours?'

'Yes!' exclaimed her mother. 'It's a good job I had Mitch's number, I was only ringing him to see if he knew how to get hold of you and he insisted on coming down to sit with me while we waited for you to arrive! He's such a dear.' Susan handed around the slices of cake which were immediately inhaled by Joe and Rory who eagerly put forward their empty plates for a refill.

'How is he?' Susan asked.

Rosie, who was distracted by the amount of cake her nephews seemed to be able to put away, and how quickly, asked, 'Who? Mitch? Oh, fine.' She paused. 'He broke up with his girlfriend so of course he's heartbroken at the moment. Or at least he was last week. But I'm sure he's over it by now,' she said, more sharply than she had intended.

'Poor Mitch,' Susan shook her head. 'He has such a good heart, I just think it's such a shame he hasn't found the right person yet.'

Rosie studied her piece of cake intently, avoiding looking at Jasmine who she could sense was trying to catch her eye. She quickly cut more cake and put it on Susan's plate to stop her mum talking more about Mitch's love life, which admittedly was better than her talking about Rosie's, but still a topic best avoided for the moment.

'Yes, so how *is* Mitch?' Jasmine asked Rosie pointedly as the two of them stood at the sink companionably washing up together.

Chris had fallen asleep in a chair in the sitting room and Susan had been corralled into playing a rowdy game of Hungry Hippos with Rory and Joe. The noise made it hard to hear what Jasmine was saying but it seemed to have absolutely no effect on the snoring Chris.

Jasmine elbowed her. 'What? Sorry, yes I've got it,' Rosie said, taking the Pyrex dish from Jasmine's soapy hands.

'No, not that,' Jasmine said frustratedly. 'I asked you about *Mitch*,' she practically hissed. 'Did you discuss anything with him since, you know...' She tilted her head. 'Since he propositioned you?'

'He did *not* proposition me,' Rosie said vehemently, glancing behind her anxiously to check they were still alone in the kitchen.

'Hmm,' continued Jasmine. 'What would you call it, then? I would call it a proposition,' she mused before Rosie could say anything. 'But let's put semantics aside.' Jasmine waved a soapy rubber gloved hand in the air. 'Have you discussed it at all?'

'Yes,' Rosie reluctantly confirmed, picking up another glass to dry and wondering if she could be excused to go and play Hungry Hippos which would be immeasurably less painful than the inquisition she was about to endure.

'And?' asked Jasmine, barely keeping the excitement from her voice.

'Well, I, er, I sort of agreed to it.' Rosie said,

Jasmine dropped the dish she was wiping into the water with a splash. Bubbles sprayed up all over her beautifully tailored tunic but she didn't bat an eyelid. Rosie's eyes travelled slowly from the splash marks up to Jasmine's face, waiting for the interrogation to unfold. But she was met only with Jasmine's look of surprise.

'Wow!' Jasmine said. 'I was *not* expecting that.'

Rosie carefully tried to mop the marks on Jasmine's top but was pushed away. 'Well, this is certainly going to be interesting,' Jasmine said, continuing to stare at Rosie.

'You think so?' Rosie asked uncertainly, wishing she had a better read on quite what Jasmine was thinking right now.

'Don't you?' Jasmine asked pointedly. 'I'm not sure you've really thought this through.'

'Erm…' Rosie carefully put the glass down that she had been polishing for the last three minutes and wondered whether to drop it on the floor to create a diversion. But she realised it was one of the set that Jasmine had been given when she'd been made partner at her law firm and no matter how much Rosie wished she could change the topic of conversation, this was not worth Jasmine's wrath.

'Rosie, seriously? Do you really understand what you're getting yourself into? Babies aren't something you just decide to have on a whim, with your friend.'

'It's not a whim.'

'Really? Because you didn't seem so sure the other day that you actually wanted a baby. Let alone to go ahead with it with Mitch!'

Rosie said nothing. It was more than a whim, she knew that, but there was a kernel of truth in what Jasmine was saying, which made her squirm with discomfort.

'So, I guess by Christmas we'll either be inviting your new boyfriend to ours or we'll be planning for a baby.' Jasmine raised her eyebrow at Rosie. 'It's going to be quite the year, isn't it?'

Rosie felt herself bristle, she really didn't feel like dealing with Jasmine's judgement right now.

'Look,' she said, 'this is my life, all right? I know what I'm doing.'

'I'm sure you do,' Jasmine said, sounding as if she had zero confidence that Rosie really did know what she was doing, or had indeed thought this through.

'I do' Rosie snapped. 'And this is not some form of vicarious entertainment for you and Chris to enjoy. So you can back off and go back to your box sets and your fancy dinners, OK?'

'Wow, OK?' Jasmine looked shocked by Rosie's outburst, but perhaps not as shocked as Rosie was herself. 'I just want you to think about what this means Rosie, I don't want you to get hurt.'

'Hurt? Who's getting hurt?'

Susan made a surprise appearance in the kitchen. If Rosie and Jasmine hadn't been quite so caught up in their clandestine discussion they would have noticed that the noise of plastic snapping hippos and balls flying off in all directions had ceased. Rosie looked at Jasmine with a pleading look in her eyes, begging her to get her off the hook with her mother.

'Knives!' Jasmine said, turning suddenly and brandishing one at Susan. 'I was warning Rosie to be careful, these ones are sharp.'

'Thanks!' Rosie said rather too loudly and gave Jasmine a grateful look, pleased to be able to move on from their conversation and to smooth things over with Jasmine at the same time.

Rosie carefully took the knife that Jasmine was holding and pretended to dry it carefully before putting it back in the knife rack. Jasmine whipped off her rubber gloves and glided across the kitchen to the kettle.

'Tea, Susan?' she asked, holding up the kettle, 'I was just going to make some.'

'Oh, yes please,' Susan said, 'I'll get the teabags.'

Rosie smiled to herself at Jasmine's inspired move; distract the British grandmother from awkward conversations by handing her a tea pot. She must remember that for the next time her mother arrived in the middle of a private discussion.

Chapter Eight

It was with a sense of relief that Rosie closed the front door to her flat later that evening. Jasmine might have successfully averted Susan's interest for the moment, but it was only a matter of time before Rosie would have to confess what was going on. Either because she was too busy to see her mother due to the sheer number of dates she would be going on. Or because she might eventually be pregnant. Rosie's stomach churned as she leaned back against her front door and shut the world outside.

Instinctively, she checked her phone for messages. It was strange that there had been nothing from Mitch. Normally he was the one who would have reminded her about her mother's birthday lunch, but he had been uncharacteristically quiet. Rosie shook her head as she made her way into her bedroom and peeled off her tights and dress. She stood for a moment contemplating whether to go straight into her pyjamas or to go via lounge pants first.

Lounge pants, she decided as she opened the drawer and found her favourite pair. They were soft and grey and Mitch had bought them for her as the craze for loungewear had taken off.

She had been completely dismissive of them until she tried them on and became an immediate convert. Which was really annoying because Mitch had been so smug about the whole thing.

THEN

'Just try them on, OK?' Mitch grinned as he held out a pair of what Rosie judged to be grey tracksuit bottoms.

'Since when did it become acceptable to wear tracksuits?' Rosie grumbled but grabbed the pair from him and against her better judgement went into the bathroom in Mitch's flat to try them on. She knew Mitch well enough to realise she was not going to hear the end of it until she actually did what he had asked and tried the damn things on.

'You won't regret it!' he called after her and she turned and frowned at him, almost walking straight into the wall as she did so.

'See!' he said in triumph when she eventually came back into his sitting room.

Rosie had been stood in the bathroom for at least ten minutes, turning this way and that, trying to get a sight of her bum in Mitch's tiny bathroom mirror. What was it about men and not having proper-sized mirrors?

'They look great!' he said enthusiastically, standing up to admire her from all angles. Rosie wished he meant *she* looked great, not the lounge pants. 'How do they feel?'

Rosie fixed him with a stare. 'Promise not to make a big deal of this?'

Mitch nodded.

'They feel amazing.' Her expression changed from one of irritation to one of delight. 'Better than amazing, these are like the best trousers I've ever worn!' She paused, running her hands over her thighs. 'But just because you're right on this occasion,' she waved a finger at Mitch, 'it does *not* mean you are always right.'

Mitch laughed and sat down on his sofa, pulling her down with him. 'Promise never to mention it again,' he said and reached for the remote control. 'But I get to pick what we watch tonight.' He turned the TV on. 'Because I'm always right,' he said with a grin.

Rosie swatted him but he caught her hand and pulled her under his shoulder, wrapping his arm around her. Rosie smiled and didn't argue. She was happy where she was, under Mitch's arm, wearing the comfiest trousers she had ever owned.

NOW

Rosie pulled the cord tight on her trousers to stop the onslaught of memories with an overly tight waistband – who could be distracted by cosy memories when it felt like you were slicing your stomach in half? She walked through to her kitchen and bent to open her fridge, thinking food might work as a distraction, but she really couldn't face eating anything and anyway now her trousers were too tight. The chocolate cake earlier was delicious but it was still sitting heavy in her stomach; at least that was what she was blaming her discomfort on and not the acid reflux brought on by being judged by her sister-in-law for contemplating having babies with her best friend in what might be the world's oddest bargain.

Sighing, she slammed the fridge shut and decided a tea would do instead. She glanced at the time on her phone – still nothing from Mitch, and too late for caffeine. Rosie opened a box of peppermint tea, stuck a bag in a mug and leaned against the counter waiting for the kettle to boil. She may as well get on with it; scrolling through her phone, she belatedly remembered that not only had she deleted her profiles from all of the dating apps, she had gone one step further and deleted the apps from her phone, too.

Deciding it would be easier to start from scratch on her laptop, she took the mug over to her table and opened her laptop, letting out what was another overly dramatic sigh for someone who lived alone and was not going to receive her due concern from an audience. This was not how she wanted to spend her Sunday evening. She was tired from all the family time and still grumpy about Jasmine's third-degree scrutiny.

After her mum had interrupted them, Rosie didn't get the chance to be alone with Jasmine again. She wasn't sure if her outburst really was brushed away and they were back properly talking to each other, or just acting polite in front of the rest of the family. Rosie wasn't wild about the fact that she had told Jasmine that she'd agreed to Mitch's proposal, but now that Jasmine knew, and despite the fact she was still cross with her and probably wouldn't like any of her advice, Rosie still craved hearing it.

Irritably, Rosie opened up a new tab on her laptop and looked through her browsing history, wondering exactly how long it had been since she'd been on any dating apps. Sunday evenings were usually reserved for going to the cinema, letting Mitch pick the film, and then teasing him mercilessly about his choice for the rest of the week – his taste in films almost as bad as his taste in music. But also refusing to pick their next film because part of the fun was seeing what hopelessly romantic comedy Mitch would choose next.

Or, if there was nothing on at the cinema, Mitch might come to hers with a bottle of wine and in the mood for mindless TV. She'd lost a summer of evenings one year to *Love Island* before she had finally gone cold turkey and banned Mitch from ever talking of it again.

'Just think of all the things we could have achieved in the time we've spent watching this rubbish,' she had shouted at him, blaming him for their addiction, after yet another housemate drama had left her feeling slightly dirty and used. But Mitch had merely laughed and asked her if she'd like to try *The Bachelorette* instead. Rosie tapped the mousepad on her laptop and wished she was watching reality TV with Mitch instead. Ironically, this was supposed to be fun, or at least the end result was meant to be, but Rosie thought she'd pick a root canal over online dating and scowled at her screen in silent fury. At least at the dentist – or most dentists – you were too numb to be expected to be witty and sparkling or to look years younger than you actually were.

Hinge, Bumble, Match, LetsGetChemical. Rosie peered at her screen, she didn't even remember that last one. She cast her mind back... *Oh.*

THEN

'There!' said Mitch triumphantly, pushing himself back from Rosie's kitchen table and making her fold-up chair squeak in protest. 'Want to look?' he asked.

'What am I looking at?' Rosie walked over, rubbing her hands clean on a tea towel and then resting her elbows on his shoulders. It was her turn to make dinner and she had left Mitch installing an update on her laptop. At least that's what he said he was doing but now looking at the screen, Rosie had a lot of questions.

'What's this?' she asked in surprise.

'LetsGetChemical!' Mitch replied, smiling up at her.

'I *can* read Mitch,' she said. 'What is it and why is it on my computer? Are you shirking your duties? I asked you to update Windows, not scroll through some random website. Hang on...'

Rosie paused and looked closer at the screen. 'Why am I on this?' she turned to look at Mitch.

'Why am I on that site, Mitch?' she asked, a note of panic rising in her voice.

'It's a dating site,' he said, slightly taken aback by her response.

'Oh, Mitch, no,' she groaned. 'Please tell me you haven't signed me up for another dating site.'

'Yup!' he grinned at her. 'What?' he asked, seeing the look on her face.

'I don't want to be on another dating site, Mitch!' she protested. 'They're all a waste of time.'

'No, this one is different!' he said eagerly, pointing at the screen. 'It's for scientists!'

Rosie looked back down at the screen. 'And?'

'And I thought you might find someone more interesting on this one.' He waited for her comprehension which was not forthcoming. 'Rosie, I was listening. I heard you when you told me that you never met anyone interesting on those other dating apps.'

Rosie felt herself flush a little; actually, she barely spent any time on the other dating apps and telling Mitch she couldn't find anyone who shared her interests had been a useful way of getting him off her back.

'So I did some research and apparently this one is really good!' He pointed to the computer screen. 'One of the researchers on the STEM committee was telling me she'd met her boyfriend on there!'

Rosie said nothing, she walked back towards the hob and started stirring the soup she had been making more aggressively than was strictly necessary. When was Mitch going to learn to back off and take his nose out of her love life? Why was he so interested in the first place?

She took a deep breath. 'Mitch, please.' She turned around to face him. 'I know you mean well but you have to back off, OK? Just concentrate on your own love life and stop worrying about mine.' She went back to her soup.

'I don't know why you don't want to give it a go?' Mitch asked in confusion. 'Why aren't you interested in meeting someone?'

There was an awkward silence broken only by the sound of the soup bubbling on the hob.

'Rosie, you can't spend the rest of your life hung up on some guy you met at university.'

Rosie felt her shoulders hunch defensively. At some point over the years it had become easier to use Connor as an excuse, pretend that she was still hung up on him, still too hurt by his abandonment to date anyone seriously.

'You know it's OK to move on, to date again? It's been a long time Rosie, not every guy is out to hurt you, you know. Some of us are good guys.'

Still Rosie said nothing.

'Why won't you ever talk about this, Rosie? I don't know why you won't open up?'

He couldn't keep a note of hurt out of his voice and Rosie knew that she hadn't been fair. She was so dismissive when they talked about dating, shutting him down when he asked her about her love life and instead laughed at the silly events in his. She knew he was always puzzled by her reaction but she couldn't confess the reason behind it. Let him still think she was broken-hearted by Connor, it was just easier that way.

'The soup's ready,' she said, shutting down the topic once again with a dose of guilt and the loud clattering of bowls.

NOW

Rosie really didn't feel like opening LetsGetChemical right now. Maybe save that joyous trip down memory lane for another time she thought, rubbing her forehead with both hands.

She scrolled to Hinge and clicked on the 'Sign In' link. Entering her email address, she almost hit the 'forgotten password' option before she remembered that this had also been one that Mitch had signed her up to. Hazarding a guess, she tapped in 'MitchIsMyHero123#' and then grinned, despite herself, when it opened up her account.

Her profile flashed up in front of her and she winced. There ought to be some kind of algorithm that updated your profile in real time even if you weren't active on the site. She felt a wave of despair wash over herself at being presented with this younger, perkier version of herself, knowing she would need to update her profile before she started using the site again. She was not going to be one of those people who still used the same profile picture for everything, taken approximately ten years beforehand.

She looked at the date of her last log in, almost twelve months ago. Mitch had been right; she really hadn't been putting any effort in. It was her last attempt to put her feelings for Mitch to bed, not that anything had come of it. A few disappointing dates before she cancelled her membership and resigned herself to a life of unrequited love. But could she really have aged that much in twelve months? She shifted a little to the left to look in the mirror hung on her wall and stared appraisingly at her reflection. Yep, frown creases on her forehead, possibly temporary, brought about by current events. Rosie massaged her face, pulling the muscles this way and that. Nope, once she'd massaged out the frown lines, she still looked much the same, no grey in her hair yet and other than her forehead, her face remained relatively unlined. Maybe she just *felt* older, then? Premature aging brought about by making stupid bets with Mitch. They ought to carry a health warning.

Rosie looked back down at her screen and scrutinised her profile picture. It showed her head and most of her upper torso, she was turned a little in profile and was looking back towards the camera. The sun caught the top of her head and allowed the natural highlights in her hair to show through. She was smiling, an easy and genuine smile. And she *was* genuinely happy; it had been taken by Mitch, of course, at the end of the summer the year before when they had gone to Italy for a few days together to make the most of the last of the summer sun.

It had been a blissful few days, despite how it had ended. Mitch had found them this beautiful farmstead to stay on just outside Florence. The food had been amazing and the weather kind. They had spent days just sat by the pool on the farm, reading and eating and occasionally jumping into the pool to cool off and to try to work off some of the food before the next meal. They had taken a day trip into Florence just the once, but both preferred the peace and quiet of the Italian countryside.

Rosie remembered the languid ease of that trip, with none of the awkwardness that had recently crept in between her and Mitch. There had been laughter and chat, stupid teasing and companionable silences. And lots and lots of Italian rosé.

THEN

'Are you *actually* asleep?'

'Mmm, almost.' Rosie rubbed her eyes, pulling herself out of the dozing state she had been in moments before.

'Sorry,' she turned and smiled at Mitch, 'I'm a terrible holiday companion.'

Mitch laughed and put his arm around her, kissing the top of her head as he did so.

'It's OK, I was starting to nod off, too.'

He stretched his legs out in front of him, arching his back slightly and then settling back, allowing Rosie to rest against him again.

'That food was amazing.'

'Mmm...' Rosie agreed, feeling the soporific pull of a full stomach.

'Are you capable of saying anything other than "mmm"?' laughed Mitch. Rosie just smiled happily to herself.

They were sat on a bench on the terrace of the farmstead after yet another amazing meal. This time it was a ravioli dish rich with ricotta and other cheeses and several glasses of a local red wine which was largely responsible for Rosie's sleepy state.

They weren't the only guests but everyone else seemed to have either retired for the evening or made the short walk into the town, looking for more lively entertainment than that provided for on the terrace. But Rosie and Mitch were quite happy where they were. The terrace overlooked the Tuscan countryside and the last rays of sunshine were catching the tall trees in the valley. Sparkling lights in houses had started coming on and the first stars were appearing in the sky above them. If they were on a romantic holiday this would be the perfect moment to kiss, except they weren't, and it wasn't.

'I think this might be the best holiday yet,' Rosie said sleepily, cuddling into Mitch.

Rosie felt him stiffen a little beside her and immediately she was wide awake. Had she said the wrong thing? Had she said too much? She hadn't declared her love for him or anything awful like that, simply said what a great holiday it was. Her thoughts started to spiral and she pulled a little away from him, putting some space between them.

Mitch shifted, moving slightly away from her, too, but turning his body so he was looking at her. He put his foot up on the bench, pulling his knee in under his arm and stared at her.

'Yeah, it is pretty great, isn't it?'

Rosie didn't know what to say, she was sure she hadn't imagined the atmosphere changing between them, but wasn't sure why it had. She'd clearly said something to change things, but she couldn't work out what.

Mitch reached out and put his hand on her shoulder. 'Rosie, I've been meaning to talk to you about something.'

Rosie did her worst fake laugh. 'Huh! Sounds like this could be serious!'

'Rosie can you just listen, OK?'

Rosie nodded.

'It really is a great holiday, and I've loved being here with you,' he said.

This wasn't so bad, Rosie thought to herself, he was just agreeing with what she had said, although it did sound like there was a but coming…

'But…' Mitch paused and took his hand from Rosie's shoulder, twisting back to face out into the valley again so Rosie couldn't see the expression on his face.

But what? she wanted to shout. *But we should never do this again? But I know you're in love with me and this is just getting tragic. But I never want to see you again??* She leaned forward anxiously, her mind already several steps ahead. Planning her escape, wondering how she would ever be able to look Mitch in the face again after the confrontation they were about to have.

'Signor Mitch?' Both of them snapped round immediately, seeing Federico from the farmstead rushing towards them across the terrace. Rosie immediately felt a terrible sensation of vertigo. She knew something bad was about to happen but she was powerless to prevent Federico from telling them what it was. And at the same time, she also had an overwhelming urge to hug Federico for preventing Mitch from telling her some terrible home truths and breaking her heart to boot.

Mitch stood up and Rosie felt the bench rock beneath her.

'Federico? What is it?' Rosie heard the strain in Mitch's voice.

'Signor Mitch, it's a phone call. They say your phone don't work. I don't understand the details but it's about your mother.'

Rosie looked up at Mitch, fearing the worst. His face drained of colour, his mouth was moving but he wasn't saying anything. Rosie was immediately on her feet and by Mitch's side, and she took his hand in hers.

'I think there's been an accident, Signor, you need to come to the telephone now.'

Rosie felt her hand drop, Mitch pulling away from her, running back towards the reception desk and the phone that promised to deliver terrible news. Her stomach plummeted.

And then it was a rush of phone calls, rearranging flights, silent taxi drives to and from airports and for Mitch, a two-day vigil by his mother's hospital bed as she lay in a coma after a drunk teenager had plowed his car into her as she waited to cross the road.

For Rosie it was a period of silent fear. She wanted to be there for Mitch, but there was very little she could do. And always at the back of her mind there was the conversation that Federico had interrupted, the one where Mitch was about to tell her to back off and leave him alone. But he never did, and perhaps her support and friendship during those days and weeks, not to mention her inspired haggling with the airline which got them out of Italy on a flight home within three hours of hearing the news, had made him reconsider his confrontation. Rosie still wondered to this day what exactly Mitch had been about to say.

NOW

Rosie sighed and pulled herself back to the moment. This was why she needed to do something and fast or that friendship she'd been so careful to preserve with Mitch would slip away from her; either because she couldn't get past her feelings for him or because he would fall in love for real and leave her behind.

Rosie looked back down at her computer screen; in the time that her memories had transported her she had received eight notifications already. Five 'likes' on Hinge and three DMs on Match. She allowed herself to experience a small frission of excitement, maybe this would be good for her ego, she thought.

But her ego was quickly deflated as she clicked through the notifications; four of them were definitely from bots, the profile pictures didn't even look real. And of the three messages, two of them asked when she was free to meet, with absolutely no introduction, one of these didn't even say 'Hey!' and the third bypassed even that nicety and asked if she was up for sex.

She put her head down on her table and groaned. This was why she had deleted her profiles. The people out there were just too depressing to deal with, if they were even real people at all. She reached for her phone to message Mitch to complain to him about it all but stopped herself just in time. No, she needed to do this without Mitch's input. There must be somebody out there who could take her mind off him.

She moved on to Tinder expecting the worst. But there was one profile which caught her eye. He actually looked OK, pretty normal. Averagely good-looking enough to be a real person. Encouraged, she read his profile. He was older than her, but not by much. He was in London, and said he was an academic. Rosie held her breath, allowing herself a small hope that she had found that elusive scientist before remembering that she was on Tinder and not LetsGetChemical.

So, it turned out he was an economist at LSE, which Rosie decided she could deal with. She had vague memories of macro/micro terminology but not much more. He also confessed to being a classical music buff. Rosie grimaced – she liked music although classical was definitely not her thing. But she wasn't a complete philistine, she thought, straightening herself up as if her cultural cred might be about to be inspected. She could appreciate classical music; maybe if they got as far as a date she could brush up on her knowledge, play Classic FM for a few evenings. Or just google some useful facts to start the conversation before Graham, as was his name, decided she was a complete savage. And anyway, maybe he didn't know everything about the complex genome classification of viruses. No one could be expected to be an expert on everything.

Rosie could feel her hopes rising even as she struggled with her inferior knowledge on the operas of Puccini. Now she just had to decide how to play it. Presumably he had liked her profile and that was why he was showing up on hers? Should she swipe right now? What if they matched? Should she message him immediately and start up a conversation? Would that be too keen? She checked her watch; it was starting to get late. If they matched and she messaged him now she knew what would happen, he might message back and then she would feel she needed to reply and before she knew it she'd be stuck in a late-night loop of perennial politeness, not daring to log out or send the final message for fear that he would simply move onto the next person on his list.

But then if he was going to be that fickle should she even care?

If that was how he played the dating game then he wasn't right for her, she could just feel it in her bones.

'Rosie!' she reprimanded herself. 'Stop spiralling.'

Rosie picked up her now lukewarm cup of tea and downed it, before remembering it was tea and not a glass of wine. Right, this was what she would do: before she could change her mind and second guess herself she swiped right, logged out of Tinder, shut down her computer and slammed it shut. And then hoped she hadn't done irreparable damage to the screen.

Hopefully he would be able to see she wasn't online and wouldn't automatically presume she was ignoring him should he decide to message her immediately. *Ugh this is exhausting*, she thought as she pushed her chair back and put her empty mug in the sink. Half an hour in and it was already taking up too much of her headspace.

As if to further torment her, her phone began to buzz. Rosie reached for it, seeing 'Mum' flashing on the screen. For a split second she considered rejecting the call but knew she would feel guilty all night if she did this.

'Hey Mum,' she said putting on her best upbeat tone, 'Everything OK?'

'Hi sweetheart,' she heard her mother say down the line, 'I wanted to check in and see how you are feeling?'

Rosie paused. 'Erm, didn't we just spend the day together?' she replied, sounding confused.

'Yes, I do remember,' Susan said dryly, 'but what with all the excitement we didn't get a chance to talk.'

Rosie thought this sounded ominous; her mother's definition of talking was almost always a version of Rosie listening while her mother gave her some unsolicited advice. It didn't happen very often but when it did it was normally surgically accurate and painfully clear.

'By the way, the cake was lovely darling, thank you, I hope you know I appreciate it,' her mother said in a softer tone, and Rosie felt herself relaxing. It was impossible to keep anything from her mother when she played nicely like this. Rosie wondered just how long it would take for Susan to get the whole story out of her about her deal with Mitch. Perhaps if she gave her some of the story it would keep her off her back for a while? Rosie couldn't imagine what her Mum would have to say once she learned the truth, probably something annoyingly supportive and encouraging, which would have Rosie gnashing her teeth in a teenage strop.

'Have you and Mitch had a falling-out?'

'What? No! Why would you think that?' Rosie protested.

'You seemed a bit cross when I mentioned him earlier.'

'Did I?'

Rosie ran through the conversation earlier, perhaps she had sounded more exasperated than she had meant to? Or perhaps her mother was using those superpowers of deduction that mothers seemed to have. She wondered if she would get them, too, and then stopped herself from continuing that train of thought. How her mother had managed to work out something was up was beyond her, but it was obvious that she had. And now Rosie needed to deal with it before her mother worked anything else out.

She sighed. 'Not a falling-out exactly.' Her mother said nothing, irritatingly refusing to fill the silence. 'He thinks I'm not putting enough effort into meeting someone,' she finally said reluctantly.

'Someone?' her mother queried.

'Yes, *someone*, Mother,' snapped Rosie. 'You know, like a boyfriend?' Perhaps telling her mother wasn't such a good idea, this whole conversation was already beyond irksome.

There was a long silence, eventually broken by Susan asking, 'But what do *you* think, darling?'

Rosie felt a lump in her throat. Of course her mother would be kind and understanding; she would absolutely have opinions and good grief you would know about them, but Susan was always only ever interested in what was right for Rosie. It was really annoying at those times when Rosie just wanted to be cross at someone.

'I think maybe he's right,' Rosie finally said in a small voice. 'I don't want to be left behind.'

'What do you mean, darling?' her mother asked softly.

'I don't want to be the last single person standing,' Rosie said, the tightness in her throat growing, making her voice sound high and wobbly. 'If Mitch wants to meet someone he will, he's so great, girls will be queuing up.'

'You know that you're great, too' her mother said, 'just as great as Mitch. But it's about what *you* want, not about keeping up with other people.'

'I know, you're right,' Rosie wailed, the pent-up emotion now fully unleashed in her voice, 'but if he does meet someone and settle down then I'll miss him!'

'I see,' her mother said sagely. Rosie wondered just how much her mother did actually see – probably most of the whole sorry mess. 'You can't make yourself want a partner and children just because that's what society wants.'

'I'm not, Mum!' Rosie said snapped.

'OK,' said Susan, 'but you can't make yourself want what your best friend wants, either.'

'Maybe not,' Rosie replied, 'but what if I end up sad and alone? I don't know whether I do want to settle down and have kids, but I worry that I'll regret it if I don't.'

Susan sighed. 'That's the perennial problem, darling. No one ever feels ready to settle down and have kids but, sometimes, you meet the right person at the right time and everything falls into place.'

There was a long pause. Rosie considered asking her mother the question that had been burned into her brain for so long: what if you had met the right person at the right time but they didn't feel the same way? What were you supposed to do then?

For a moment Rosie wondered if they had been cut off, but then her mother continued, 'And then, sometimes you don't. And you pick yourself up and get on with the life that's been handed to you.'

Not for the first time, Rosie wondered how her mother had actually felt when she and Dad had divorced. Susan always brushed away Rosie's queries with, 'Oh it was a long time ago, darling.' But now that Rosie thought about it, her mum would have been younger than she was now when her dad left, leaving Susan with two small children.

'How did you manage?' Rosie eventually asked.

'What with?' her mother queried, willfully pretending not to understand.

'With us two? With Chris and me, when Dad left?'

'Well, I just did what I had to do, I got up each morning and made sure both of you had what you needed and felt loved,' Susan replied pragmatically.

'But it must have been so hard, on your own,' Rosie pushed. 'Wasn't it difficult?'

Susan sighed. 'When things didn't go as planned, I always found it easiest not to overthink it. I put one foot in front of the other and just kept going, until suddenly, one day, I realised that I wasn't simply keeping going, I was living and that actually the three of us had made a pretty good life together.'

Rosie felt a strange rush of pride in her irritating, opinionated, brilliant, loving mother and realised that if she was going to go ahead with this, with having a baby with Mitch, that actually having her mother in her corner would be invaluable, because Susan had done it on her own as well.

'And anyway, darling, it was all such a long time ago, I barely remember it.'

Rosie rolled her eyes, realising that their heart-to-heart was over.

Chapter Nine

Rosie woke to the sound of her alarm. The September mornings were still light enough that she could see fingers of sunshine filtering around her curtains. She stretched and rolled over to turn off her alarm. Not for much longer would sunlight greet her in the morning. The days were starting to get shorter and before long, the clocks would change and it would be back to dark mornings and dark evenings. She loved seeing daylight at both ends of the working day, but she also savoured the feelings that dark evenings brought: cosy pubs, festivities beginning, London lit up with Christmas lights.

Showered and wrapped in her dressing gown, Rosie poured herself some cereal in her favourite bowl, the one Mitch had brought her back from a long weekend in Prague many years ago, and carried it to her tiny kitchen table. Picking her phone up, last night came flooding back as she was bombarded with notifications. At first, she presumed they must be from Mitch, who she still hadn't heard from, even forgetting to message her to wish her mother a happy birthday from him. But knowing Mitch he had probably sent her mother flowers instead. Rosie made a note to ask her mother next time they spoke.

But she quickly realised the messages weren't from Mitch. Notification after notification came pinging through from the dating apps she had reactivated the night before. Gavin had liked her, Simon had sent her a message, Brandon wanted to know if she was single.

Why would she be on these sites "Brandon" if she wasn't single? But Rosie had lived long enough and experienced enough of the London dating scene to know that what she thought was completely unacceptable in a relationship was, to other people, perfectly normal, sometimes even desirable.

The notifications kept rolling in. For a moment, Rosie watched them scroll down her phone screen before she placed it face down on the table, feeling slightly sick. She couldn't face dealing with them right now and she had to leave for work. At some point she should go through them, just to check that they *were* all offensive before she permanently deleted them. But there were loads of them, how did people do this and hold down a full-time job? Maybe she could hire someone to handle it for her? Mitch would be perfect but getting him more involved would derail the whole purpose of this endeavour.

It was a beautiful morning, the sun was cutting through the early haze with the promise of warmth later on in the day. Rosie hesitated on her doorstep – bus or tube this morning? The tube would be quicker but it would be busy by now. She looked at her watch; she'd never get a seat at this time and she really didn't fancy starting her week in the armpit of a stranger on the Northern line. So she turned left towards the bus stop. It would take longer but so long as she missed one stuffed full of school kids, she should get a seat.

Ten minutes later, and Rosie was happily sat on the upper deck of the bus. She even had a double seat to herself, although she knew that wouldn't last. Breathing deeply, she decided now might be a good time to brave those messages. Hopefully she would be able to unearth any promising ones swiftly and delete the rest.

The first ten were predictable spam, the eleventh was a photo which Rosie feared would now be indelibly imprinted on her mind. She spent the ten minutes it took to get through the traffic lights near Vauxhall Bridge trying to work out if there was a way of reporting a user for sending unsolicited explicit pictures before giving up and hoping someone else would do it. What possessed people to think that strangers would want to see intimate parts of their anatomy? Swiping away a message from Jasmine without reading it – she must remember to message her back later – she went back to Match, hoping not to see any more pictures which would make her sick in her lap. The bus stalled in traffic but Rosie barely noticed, becoming increasingly engrossed in and grossed-out by her fellow humans.

And then there was one message that took her by surprise, actually sounding genuine – in that he could spell, didn't sound like a complete lunatic and hadn't sent her an intimate picture by way of a bizarre flirting ritual. Intrigued, Rosie clicked on his profile only to have her hopes dashed immediately; it was obvious that the man in question was at least twenty years older than her. Rosie realised she really needed to double check she had set an age limit on Match. She gave him credit for putting up a realistic picture and listing his actual age, but not enough credit to countenance dating him. She declined the 'match'.

She almost missed the last message, deleting it along with the rest of the junk. But the name caught her eye; Graham – the academic, classical music enthusiast – had written her a message. The bus pulled in at a stop almost jolting her phone from her hand. She swore quietly under her breath and caught her bag just in time before it fell onto the floor.

A steady stream of people got on, most of them coming straight up the stairs and immediately looking around for spaces to sit. Rosie pulled her bag onto her lap as a man in a suit squeezed into the seat next to her. She looked back at the message from Graham and scanned it quickly, trying to decide whether this was something she could read in her now cramped position or if it should wait until she got to work. That tingle of excitement she had felt last night crept its way back up her spine and she realised that she didn't *want* to wait, maybe this *could* actually be fun.

Graham's message was polite and funny. He seemed like a genuine guy, although Rosie tried to remain sceptical. It was so unlikely to have a real potential match that she needed to remain vigilant about getting carried away. She began composing a reply as she drifted off into thoughts of where they should go on their first date to where he might take her on their second and, before she knew it, they were several months in to a relationship and discussing living arrangements.

She was jerked out of a delightful daydream in which she had just introduced Graham to Mitch, which resulted in Mitch becoming uncontrollably jealous and swearing his undying love for her, by the realisation that the bus had arrived at her stop.

Grabbing her bag and apologising profusely to the man next to her as she inelegantly clambered over him, Rosie ran down the steps of the bus just in time before the driver closed the doors. She took a moment to get her breath back on the pavement before walking the few yards to her work. She also took those moments to have a stern word with herself about wasting time on ridiculous and unrealistic, not to mention unhealthy, daydreams. Getting back on the dating scene was about ridding herself of her infatuation with Mitch, not about trying to make him jealous. *Stupid*, she thought to herself, Mitch would be thrilled if she met someone because he was her best friend, and best friends were always happy for each other's happiness, right? Just like she would be for him if he met someone, right? Right, she told herself as she pushed open the doors to her office building with a determination to set something up with Graham before the day was out. And to really stop getting carried away.

Rosie didn't have a chance to finish her message to Graham since Rachel had called an impromptu emergency meeting to discuss the changes in central funding from the government and how it might impact their department. Rosie sat at the back of Rachel's office as her eyes began to glaze over; none of this would really affect her as most of her funding came from non-government grants but she was a good team-player and tried to take an interest for the sake of her colleagues. Nadia had spent the meeting alternating between chewing her pen and shooting her hand up at every available moment to ask a question. Rosie could tell that Rachel was about ten seconds away from completely losing her patience when the meeting thankfully ended. Rosie planned to grab Nadia straight afterwards and see just how badly she had taken this news when Rachel called her back in.

'Rosie?' Rachel called, looking up from her desk just as Rosie made it to the door. 'Can I have a word?'

Rosie shot Nadia an apologetic look and mouthed, 'Sorry' in her direction. Nadia grimaced and started chewing her pen again as she made her way down the corridor.

'Yes of course.' Rosie turned on her heel.

'Come in,' Rachel beckoned her, 'and close the door.'

Rosie took a moment for this to sink in. Rachel hardly ever had time for a quick word, and if she did, the word was over before the office door was closed. Either this was going to be interesting or Rosie had done something wrong. She wracked her brains trying to think what the latter could be but came up with absolutely nothing.

'Rosie,' Rachel began, leaning back in her chair and folding her neatly manicured hands over her perfectly pressed teal shirt. 'We've been approached about something rather confidential that I need your input on.'

Rosie nodded. 'OK,' she said, silently thankful that so far this didn't seem to be going in the direction of being fired and immediately escorted from the building by security.

'I need your guarantee that you'll keep this to yourself for the moment?'

'Of course.' Rosie nodded again.

'At some point they will probably want us to sign an NDA, but so far they're happy just to take our word for our discretion.'

'Sorry, Rachel, can I ask who you're talking about?' Rosie asked a little nervously.

'BioChem,' Rachel said, a look of steely determination settling on her face.

Rosie swallowed. BioChem were one of the biggest pharma companies in the vaccine and anti-viral area of the market. But they never farmed out their work; they were notoriously secretive and did all their research in-house. This didn't make any sense, why would they approach academics to partner with? They had the in-house expertise, she was sure of it. Plus Rosie would bet that their facilities were far superior to those funded by a university. And then Rosie remembered – Rachel had been at university with BioChem's CEO, the two of them were friends from years back. Possibly more than just friends.

Rosie recalled a conference she had attended soon after she had started in Rachel's lab, a conference which had been funded by BioChem. That was where she had been, sat at the hotel bar late one evening, when she saw Rachel and the CEO coming back from dinner together and then getting in the same lift, and she'd made the connection. Not that there was anything wrong with that. As far as Rosie knew, they had both been single, and anyway getting in the same lift with an old friend was not the same as banging their brains out in a hotel room. Rosie should know that – she'd shared countless lifts with Mitch and thus far no banging had occurred. But this might just explain why BioChem were outsourcing their research.

Rosie caught Rachel's eye and saw that Rachel one-hundred per cent knew where Rosie's brain was going.

'As you know, Brian and I are old friends,' Rachel said, gripping the thorny issue tightly before it became any more uncomfortable for either of them. 'Of course, BioChem normally keep their research in-house but they felt in this instance we had the expertise they needed.'

She pointed at Rosie who blushed.

'Yes,' Rachel confirmed. 'You should feel flattered. They know about you and they're impressed.'

'Wow, OK, thanks, Rachel,' Rosie stumbled, unsure what to say next. It was flattering, sure, but there was a reason Rosie had never dipped her toe into the murky, corporate world of Big Pharma research. Working in academia, Rosie could pretend that nothing she did lined the pockets of pharmaceutical companies, even though she knew this was not strictly true. They were all linked in an unhealthy alliance of money, drugs and power, which made them sound like a cartel. But there would be something different about working directly for a pharmaceutical company.

'This makes you uncomfortable.' It wasn't a question, merely a statement from Rachel which made Rosie even more convinced that Rachel had superpowers and could read her mind.

Rosie made a non-committal sound and pretended to be very interested in her trainers. Which were really good trainers – Vans hi-tops, 1980s style – but not good enough to justify studying instead of engaging with her boss.

Rachel sighed and put her elbows on her desk, gazing across it at Rosie. 'I get it, OK? I've never wanted to work for a big corporation, either, but don't be naive Rosie.'

Rosie felt herself reprimanded and tore her eyes away from her trainers.

'We're all linked,' Rachel continued. 'We might be able to pretend that we're clean and free from any corporate pressure, but the truth is we take money from all sorts of sources and while we might pretend that we can't be held responsible for what pharmaceutical companies do with our results once they're in the public domain, the reality is that what we do here *does* fuel Big Pharma. And we can close our eyes and pretend it's not happening and wait until our funding is cut off entirely. Or we can take their money and put it to good use in our lab.'

Rosie took a deep breath. Rachel was right, of course she was right. So far, Rosie had been able to distance herself from this truth, but it was a truth. None of them were squeaky clean and Rosie had to make peace with this fact and, maybe, in a small way, use what she was given to exercise some power and do some good.

'Of course.' She nodded at Rachel. 'I totally get it. So where do we start and what do you need me to do first?'

Rachel smiled at her, pleased that her philosophical speech seemed to have hit the mark. 'I'm going to give you access to a restricted section in our files. There's a lot of information and correspondence in there that you should read, it will give you all the background you need.'

Rachel turned to her computer and tapped away at the keyboard, Rosie sat awkwardly wondering if she had been dismissed but then Rachel turned back towards her.

'I want you to read through all of this carefully, and once you've done so let me know your thoughts. We can set up a time for a proper meeting to discuss how this is going to work and first steps. OK?'

'OK, sounds good,' Rosie replied.

Rachel turned back to her computer, Rosie stayed put. 'You can go now,' Rachel said, realising Rosie was still sat there.

'Thanks, Rachel,' she said as she walked backwards towards the door, 'I appreciate you bringing me on board with this.'

Rachel looked up at her, as if surprised to see her still in her office. 'I know I can rely on you not to mess this up,' she said sternly. 'And Rosie,' she called, when Rosie was almost out of the door, 'remember that there will be a lot tied up in this. As I said in the meeting this morning, money is getting tighter, this could really help in funding the lab, understood?'

Rosie nodded once more and then crept out into the corridor, silently closing Rachel's door behind her and then leaning against the wall, trying to take all of this in.

———

'I simply don't understand the logic behind it.' Nadia had tracked Rosie down to her office and was determined to make her listen to her much-delayed rant. 'So much for "putting faith in science" as this government is so keen to say.' Nadia ran a hand through her short, curly hair. 'This is going to be disastrous for so many of our trials.' She sat down hard in one of Rosie's chairs.

'I'm sure it will be fine,' Rosie said smoothly, thinking back to her conversation with Rachel and hoping that Nadia would run out of steam quickly so she could get back to the important task of reading the BioChem documents – also known as composing a message to Graham. 'You know, we're *always* getting threatened with funding cuts, and it's always turned out OK so far. We've never had to put a stop to something really important,' she added placatingly.

Nadia shot her an exasperated look. 'It's OK for you,' she said sharply.

Rosie looked bewildered. 'What do you mean?'

'I mean,' said Nadia briskly, 'that you're working at the sexy end of science, the high-profile stuff. You know, results in national newspapers not just obscure science journals.'

Rosie stared at her.

'Your lab will always get funding because it's the kind of science that the average person understands,' Nadia continued. 'Whereas what I do is never going to attract that kind of interest.' She threw her hands up in frustration. 'Despite it being the foundation of what everyone in our field does.'

Rosie felt herself flushing. She had never thought about it like that, she was so used to thinking that Nadia was so much smarter than she was that she had never considered the outside perception of what they both did. Momentarily, she felt elated that Nadia was calling her science 'sexy', before she realised what Nadia was really getting at: that what Rosie did wouldn't be possible without the research that Nadia did before her. Which was true, but Rosie felt there might have been a kinder way to phrase it.

'I hope you're not suggesting that you do what you do because you're smarter than the rest of us?' she shot back. She meant it as a joke but the look on Nadia's face made her think that perhaps Nadia really did think that. Rosie was irritated by Nadia's suggestion but wanted to defuse the situation. 'Come on, Nadia, we both chose our fields. No one forced you to do what you do; you love it, right?'

The fire left Nadia's face. 'Rosie, no, sorry, I didn't mean...' Again she ran her hands through her hair which was beginning to look even more of a mess than usual. 'I'm just worried. If this hits my funding then I won't be able to take on any post docs when the current money runs out. And that means I won't be able to do half the work that I'm doing at the moment.'

She stood up and paced over to the window.

'I'm sorry, I didn't mean to suggest that I'm any smarter than you.' Nadia turned and looked at Rosie. 'You know I think you're one of the cleverest people I know.' She looked imploringly at Rosie. 'You must know that was one of the reasons that I accepted the position here? I'd seen your publications and I wanted to work more closely with you.'

Mollified, Rosie nodded, 'I'm sorry, too. I know you're worried. And you're right, it is much easier to get funding in my area.'

'And I'm also really worried about Nico.' Nadia blurted out.

'What? Why?'

'Because he's lost out on his latest grant application, they gave it to someone else.' Rosie saw the look of resignation on Nadia's face.

'Oh, Nadia, I'm so sorry.'

'And these funding cuts are going to make it even harder for him to access any cash. He's been stressed for months about it all and I am *exhausted* trying to make him feel better all the time when I am worrying just as much as he is.'

Rosie looked at her friend with concern. She hadn't realised that Nadia and Nico had both been worried about their jobs and money. She desperately wanted to tell Nadia about BioChem, that the funding from them would take the pressure off but she also didn't want to jinx it by saying anything before it was confirmed, or face Rachel if and when she found out that it had taken Rosie precisely fifteen minutes to break the oath of confidentiality she had just taken. Rosie walked over to the window and stood next to Nadia, putting her arm around her friend's shoulders.

'I'm so sorry,' she said softly, 'I didn't realise how worried you were.'

They both stood for a moment looking down on the busy London street. It always amazed Rosie that life just went on, even when something awful was happening for one person, someone else was living their best life. The rest of the world carried on.

'I'm here any time you want to talk,' she said, giving Nadia a hug to make up for the huge inadequacy of her offer.

'Thanks,' Nadia replied. 'I know, and I'm sorry for lashing out. Nico will have a field day when I tell him about this conversation.' She grimaced at Rosie. 'You know he's always telling me that I need to think before I speak.'

Rosie smiled sympathetically down at her friend. 'You know that's not true, right?' Nadia gave her a look. 'Well, I mean, you do *sometimes* think.' She gave Nadia a teasing squeeze. 'Hey, do you want to be distracted?' she said next, trying to lighten the mood. Nadia nodded keenly. 'I think I might have matched with someone online!' Rosie said triumphantly.

'Really?' Nadia's eyes immediately lit up. 'Tell me more!'

'Well,' began Rosie, as they both sat back down in their chairs, 'he's an academic. No no…' She waved her hands. 'Before you get too excited, he's not a scientist, he's an economist.'

Nadia shrugged. 'Can't have everything. Where is he based?'

'LSE,' Rosie said excitedly.

'He's smart,' Nadia said, nodding her approval, 'and just around the corner?'

'Yes,' said Rosie, nodding.

'Well, how convenient,' Nadia replied with a grin. 'What else?'

'He loves classical music.'

Nadia looked at her quizzically. 'Well that's going to be interesting given your musical taste.'

'Oh, shut up,' said Rosie, relieved that Nadia was teasing her again.

'So, when are you meeting him?'

'I need to message him back first, calm down!' Rosie said, laughing.

'What are you waiting for?' Nadia screeched. She picked up Rosie's phone from her desk and thrust it across the desk at her, 'Message him now! Let's do this.'

'Er, OK,' said Rosie, taking her phone and swiping away another message from Jasmine asking Rosie if she'd like to go around for dinner at theirs one night that week. Rosie ignored it; she didn't think she could face another interrogation from Jasmine just yet.

'Can I just have a moment to think about what I want to say?' she asked Nadia.

'Yes,' replied Nadia, 'but don't take too long.' She waved a finger at Rosie. 'Hey, do you reckon you've seen him around here? I mean he doesn't work that far away?'

Rosie shook her head. 'I don't recognise him, but I guess it's possible we've been in the same places.'

'How funny that you should match with someone literally next door!' Nadia exclaimed. 'I mean what are the chances? Oh, Rosie,' she said, gleefully clapping her hands together, 'I've got a good feeling about this.'

Rosie put down her phone and laughed. 'Nadia, you do know that Tinder is location-based? So it's not really *that* surprising he works nearby.'

'Oh, all right, cast your shade,' Nadia said crossly. 'I'm just excited for you, what's wrong with that?'

'You're right, you're right!' Rosie said, picking her phone up again. 'What *are* the chances? Maybe you could get one of your statisticians to work it out for me?'

Nadia made a rude gesture at Rosie. 'What does Mitch think?' she asked.

Rosie looked up sharply from her phone. 'I haven't told him,' she said.

'Oh, really?' Nadia said with a small smile. 'Interesting.'

Rosie sighed and put her phone down. 'No, I just haven't spoken to him, OK? Don't make a big thing out of it.'

Nadia looked confused. 'But I thought you two spoke *all* the time.'

'Yeah, we do, normally. Actually, it is a bit odd; I feel like he's gone quiet on me.' She and Nadia looked at each other. 'I'm not really sure what's going on with him, but he hasn't been in touch in days,' Rosie confessed.

Chapter Ten

It was official. Mitch was definitely ignoring her. Either that, or he was dead. Rosie wasn't sure which was preferable. She looked back at her message exchange with him for what felt like the hundredth time that day. She hadn't heard from him since Friday. Nothing on Saturday, which perhaps wasn't so unusual. But it was strange that he hadn't messaged on her mum's birthday (Rosie might have temporarily forgotten about her mum's birthday that morning, but there was no way Mitch would.) And even stranger that he had yet to surface by Monday afternoon.

Sure, there were times when he would be quiet on a Monday because of work, but if they hadn't seen each other all weekend, he would have bombarded her with questions about it and lots of details of what his had been like. Although, come to think of it, Rosie couldn't remember the last time they had gone an entire weekend without seeing each other. She shook her head in confusion. Something didn't feel right, and no amount of secretive data from Rachel and BioChem could fully distract her from this.

When Rosie still hadn't heard from Mitch by the end of the day, and all the messages she had left on his mobile and office phone had gone unanswered, she began to worry. As she pulled on her coat and picked up her bag to go home, she made her decision. Walking down the corridor, she saw the light on in Nadia's office, so, knocking lightly, she opened the door and peered round.

'You're working late,' she said, seeing Nadia bent over her keyboard tapping furiously away. The office was a mess, even more than usual. There were papers piled up against the wall and not for the first time Rosie wondered how Nadia managed to get any work done with all the folders on her desk.

'Everything all right?' she asked.

Nadia stopped typing and looked up at her, blinking as if seeing the light for the first time in hours. 'Yes, I'm just looking into funding,' she said shortly.

'Oh, OK.' Rosie paused. 'What about the kids?'

'Nico is picking them up tonight,' Nadia said, turning back to her computer screen.

Rosie didn't want to disturb her any further. 'Don't work too late, though,' she said encouragingly, 'and let me know if I can do anything.'

Nadia looked back up at her and smiled. 'Thanks, and thanks for earlier.'

Rosie waved at her as if to say 'it's nothing', then turned to go.

'Hey,' called Nadia, 'Any news from Mitch?'

Rosie shook her head. 'Nothing. It's weird. I can't reach him at his office, either. I'm going to go over to his flat now. Maybe he's ill?'

Nadia nodded slowly. 'Maybe,' she agreed. 'Let me know when you find out?'

Rosie nodded.

'And give me an update tomorrow on Graham! I want to know

you've lined up a date!' she shouted at full volume as Rosie closed the door behind her.

Two post-doc students happened to be walking down the corridor just at that moment and turned as they heard Nadia's shout. Rosie grimaced, the last thing she wanted was everyone at work knowing about her love life.

'Night,' she said in what she hoped was a professional and nonchalant manner as she walked past them heading for the exit.

It wasn't a long tube journey from Rosie's work to Mitch's flat, but it did involve two changes of lines and navigating her way through the tourists congregating by the ticket barriers. Rosie tried to stay calm; she was normally sympathetic to their plight as they tried to get their newly purchased Oyster cards to work. But today she was not in the mood. Her anxiety about Mitch had only grown during the day and she was now convinced that something must really be wrong.

She pushed her way between two groups of tourists and apologised over her shoulder as she passed, quickly stepping through the ticket barriers and running down to the platform just in time to see a train pull in. Slightly flustered, she stepped on to the train and saw one seat free. This was a good sign, Rosie thought, perhaps everything would turn out to be fine. Mitch would have forgotten to charge his phone or something. He'd roll his eyes at her concern and then they'd get dinner together, maybe a couple of drinks, too.

Mitch lived in a new-build block of flats in a stupidly trendy part of East London, not far from the Hackney Marshes. On paper, hers and Mitch's flats couldn't have been more different. His was in a modern, architect-designed complex, whereas hers was a converted Victorian terrace. But once inside, their shared taste was evident. A mixture of antique and modern and whatever they had been able to afford at the time.

Rosie stopped outside the building and looked up. Mitch's flat was a corner one, with a view of both the main entrance and the tastefully designed square to the side. He had a balcony overlooking the square, but even from the front Rosie could see the lights on in his flat. So, he must be home she thought to herself. She checked her phone for a final time, there was still nothing, so she pressed his buzzer and nervously tapped her foot as she waited for a reply. She thought back over the number of times she had stood here, never thinking about more than how long it always took Mitch to answer. She waited. The minutes ticked by.

Stepping back, she looked back up. She was sure she could see movement from the lit windows of Mitch's flat. He *must* be in, she thought to herself. Or at least someone was in? Perhaps he had been taken hostage? Perhaps they were just working out their demands right now, he was a journalist, after all. And then she remembered that Mitch was a science correspondent and that anyone stupid enough to kidnap him must have done so by mistake.

Suddenly the front door to the building swung open. Instinctively, Rosie turned wondering if it was Mitch but her heart fell. It wasn't. A girl came rushing through the doorway moving at pace. She was pulling on her coat as she went and flicked her long blonde curls over the collar as she passed Rosie. Pausing for a moment, she looked curiously at Rosie before walking past her out into the evening. Rosie couldn't help but notice the height of her heels and felt a momentary pang of jealousy that this girl could walk in them with ease, before remembering that she much preferred her comfortable hi-tops, in which she didn't have to worry about falling over.

Watching her go, Rosie wondered whether she ought to have taken the opportunity and raced through the open door behind her instead of getting distracted by her shoes, but at that moment the intercom buzzed into life and Mitch's voice echoed out.

'Hello?' he said. 'Rosie?'

She moved swiftly towards the intercom, 'Yeah, hi. What's going on? I've been worried about you.'

There was a pause. 'I'm fine,' came the response.

'Riiiight,' Rosie said, wondering what to do next. Why wasn't he inviting her up? 'Erm, can I come up, then?'

'Oh, right, sure,' Mitch's voice replied. 'Just a sec.'

It was more than a second that Rosie waited for the buzz of the door lock to sound before she could push her way through and into the building. While she stood waiting for the lift she fiddled nervously with the buttons on her coat. There was definitely something going on and she was about to find out what it was.

The door to his flat was ajar when she stepped out of the lift onto his floor, so he'd either propped it open when he had buzzed her in...or... someone had just left Mitch's apartment. Rosie's mind flitted back to the girl she had just seen leaving the building. The one who had looked at her so curiously. Rosie pushed open the door and walked into the flat she knew so well. There was an unfamiliar smell in the air, the scent of a perfume that was definitely not Mitch's. The parts of the jigsaw started to fall into place.

Mitch walked into the hallway just as Rosie realised what was going on.

'Hey!' he said warmly pulling her into a hug. Rosie stood stonily fixed in place.

'Were you really worried?' he said cheekily and turned back into the sitting room. Rosie followed him.

'Yes!' she said. 'I haven't heard from you since Friday, you haven't answered any of my messages *and* you weren't at work today,' she said accusingly. She noticed that Mitch had the grace to look a little ashamed.

'Er, yes,' he said, blushing. She hated it when he blushed, it made her want to reach out and feel the heat in his cheek. 'I took an impromptu day off.'

'Right,' she said, crossing her arms. 'But that doesn't explain why you haven't messaged me back since Friday.'

Mitch looked confused. 'Haven't I?' He bent and picked his phone up from the coffee table. 'Shit. Sorry, Rosie, I didn't realise.'

Rosie felt herself growing even more confused and angry. She glanced around the room. There were two coffee mugs on the table beside where Mitch's phone had been. A blanket which was normally draped artfully over the end of his mid-century sofa was lying pooled on the floor. Looking over the bar which marked off the kitchen area, she could see two plates, two sets of cutlery, two wine glasses. *This* was why he had been ignoring her, he wasn't ill or hurt, he wasn't lying depressed after his last break-up, he had been with someone, *all* weekend by the look of it.

'So how come?' she finally said. 'How come you haven't messaged me back? When was the last time we didn't speak for an entire weekend?'

'I, erm, I'm not sure?' Mitch sounded baffled by her tone.

'Not ever, Mitch,' she said forcefully. 'We *always* talk, we ALWAYS message each other. I was worried about you.' She was veering between shouting and crying. 'And I shouldn't have been, because there was nothing wrong with you. You weren't sick, you weren't hurt, you weren't even sat at home nursing a broken heart, you were with someone *all* weekend, weren't you?'

Mitch looked shocked at her outburst. He hesitated, obviously wondering what the best way to respond was. Eventually he said, 'Yes?' rather warily. 'I met her Friday night and we just kind of clicked.' Despite himself Mitch's eyes lit up. Rosie looked at him, a mixture of hurt and anger on her face.

'She's called Jenny and she's great. We went out for dinner and then drinks, and then she came back here and we spent Saturday together and then...' He tailed off, finally seeing the fury in Rosie's eyes.

'I just met her,' she practically spat. 'Short, blonde, just like the last one, and the one before that, oh and the...should I go on?' Rosie surprised even herself with the vehemence of her words. 'But she's obviously not *great* enough to introduce me to, or perhaps it's the other way around?'

Mitch looked hurt. 'I thought it was too early to introduce her to my friends.'

'But not too early to blow all your friends off and skip work for?' Rosie retorted.

'Hang on, I didn't skip work,' Mitch said, suddenly grappling for his position in this argument. 'I decided to take the day off.'

'And didn't tell me?' Rosie hated herself for having said that, she knew she was starting to sound like the jealous girlfriend. Mitch's expression changed from puzzlement to anger.

'I'm sorry,' he started. 'I didn't realise I had to run all my plans past you first.'

Rosie said nothing but stared at him mutinously. There was a pause.

Mitch softened and reached out to her 'I'm really sorry, Rosie. I didn't mean to worry you.' She jerked her arm out of his reach.

'Yeah, well you did,' she replied.

Mitch sat down on the sofa, his uncharacteristic and momentary flash of anger dissipating immediately. He pushed his hair back from his forehead and looked up at her.

'Rosie, I'm sorry, OK? I got carried away. I just didn't think.'

Rosie watched him warily before she sat down, too, across

from him in the tastefully reupholstered armchair that they had chosen together one weekend away in the Cotswolds. She re-folded her arms across her chest defensively. She knew this wasn't about him not replying to her messages, it was about the fact he had spent the weekend with someone else, and she knew she was in danger of saying something she might regret, but she didn't know how to wrestle all her feelings into submission. She felt like a child, overwhelmed to the point of tantrum.

Mitch continued to watch her with his sincere blue eyes and despite everything, she felt herself begin to thaw. Mitch sensed it, too.

'She's really great Rosie, I think you'd like her,' he said cautiously.

'Yeah, well, it might help if you introduced her,' Rosie said somewhat grumpily.

'I will do,' he said earnestly. 'Soon.'

Rosie harrumphed to herself. 'If it lasts that long,' she said out loud. Mitch looked hurt.

'What?' she said defensively, 'It's not like you have a great track record of long-lasting relationships.'

Mitch straightened up. 'At least I'm trying,' he said, 'unlike you.'

'Actually I've met someone, too,' Rosie blurted out before thinking through the implication of her words. 'He's called Graham and he seems really great as well.' Instantly she regretted telling him.

Mitch hesitated for a moment before he said, 'Rosie! That's great! Tell me about him?'

Rosie shrugged, now desperate to change the subject before she had to admit that she had yet to even arrange a date with Graham. Or that she wasn't so crazy about Mitch's enthusiastic response to her news, she had been hoping for some display of jealousy, rather like the one she had so obviously just put on for him, but she would unpack those feelings later, back in the privacy of her own home.

'No, you tell me – it's probably best you fill me in on everything to do with... I'm sorry, what did you say her name was?' Rosie pretended to forget, despite the fact that the name Jenny was now going to be etched into her mind forever.

'Jenny,' Mitch added.

'Yes, I'd best know everything about Jenny before I have to help you get over her when you break up.' Rosie couldn't resist a dig at Mitch but she tried to do it with a smile and thankfully Mitch laughed at her.

'I don't think you'll have to,' he sounded so confident, 'and for the record she's not that short, and she's nothing like any of the others.'

THEN

'She didn't say anything? No messages at all?'

Mitch shook his head and held out his phone for Rosie to read. 'Look, just says "see you there". And here I am and she's not.' He indicated the empty space at the bar next to him.

'What time did you say?' Rosie said grabbing his phone.

'Seven,' Mitch said sadly.

Rosie looked at her watch: it was eight-fifteen. The girl wasn't coming.

Mitch and Rosie were sat in a bar under the arches of Brixton station. Mitch was supposed to be here with a date, Rosie wasn't supposed to be here at all. But forty-five minutes of anxious texts from Mitch had prompted her to divert and meet him here, offer him moral support *and* make him buy her a cocktail at the same time. She sipped her gimlet appreciatively.

'Thanks for coming, Rosie,' Mitch said, patting her knee as they perched awkwardly on the trendy but incredibly uncomfortable bar stools. He almost lost his balance and lurched towards her. Righting himself, he said, 'I really appreciate it. You didn't cancel anything, did you?'

Rosie shook her head, pushing away all thoughts of her colleagues who she had left drinking in the pub near work.

'It's on my way home, anyway. So, now what?' Rosie asked. 'What's the etiquette? Do you send her angry text messages asking where she is? Threaten to out her for bad dating behaviour?'

'No!' exclaimed Mitch looking horrified. 'Rosie you really need to understand more about how to go about behaving on dating sites.'

Rosie shrugged. 'It's what I'd do.'

'And that might be exactly why I go on dates and you don't.' Mitch said, fixing her with a stern look which was completely undermined as he took a sip of his luridly coloured cocktail. Rosie found it impossible to take any man seriously if they were drinking something that had a plastic flamingo stuck in it.

'Now we're here, maybe this is the time to explain to me once again why you're so against dating?' Mitch said, shifting the flamingo slightly so he could drink more easily.

'We're here to talk about your disastrous love life, not mine,' Rosie said, picking up her far more elegant drink and hiding behind it.

'Hmm, OK. Well anyway, to answer your question: no, I'm not going to shout at her, or publicly shame her. Everyone is fighting their own battle and I'm sure there is a very good reason she's not here.'

Rosie rolled her eyes at him. This was Mitch all over. So good-natured and kind, which was what made him a perfect best friend and terrible at judging who was playing him in the world of dating.

'But, yes,' he continued. 'It is really depressing and sometimes I really do understand why you're not interested in the scene.'

Rosie felt her stomach lurch. Did he truly understand why she wasn't interested in dating...? If so, then tonight was about to take an interesting turn.

'It's soul-destroying and exhausting, and sometimes I wonder whether I'll ever meet anyone right for me. Especially,' Mitch tipped his glass towards hers, causing the plastic flamingo to tilt perilously close to the rim, 'when I'm sat here with you and it's a much more fun way to spend an evening than *any* other dates I have been on recently.'

Rosie felt her vision tunnel, the sounds of the bar echoed in her ears. Was this it, was this the moment to tell him? To finally confess why she didn't want to date, to agree with him that, yes, this was *so much more* enjoyable than any other date she had *ever* been on, too? What was the worst that could happen? He'd laugh at her? He'd look horrified? He would make his excuses and leave and that would be the end of their friendship? But perhaps he wouldn't? She felt herself on top of a tall precipice staring down into uncertainty.

'Mitch?'

Mitch swung round in his chair. Rosie's vision righted itself and she saw stood next to Mitch the future she hadn't wanted to see. It was petite, blonde and wearing vertiginous heels.

'Maxine?' Mitch asked. Rosie immediately saw the way his eyes softened, the way his arm went out to this girl, ushering her into the bubble that had been Rosie's and Mitch's until just now.

'I'm so sorry I'm late,' Maxine gushed. Rosie detected the trace of a northern accent in her voice. 'I completely messed up, I was sat in a bar up the road, swearing at you, thinking you had stood me up.'

Mitch laughed loudly and genuinely. 'And I was sat here doing the same. Not the swearing, though!' he quickly added.

Maxine grinned at him. 'It was only when I checked back through our messages again that I realised I was in the wrong place. I came as quickly as I could, I hoped you'd still be here.'

She put her arm on Mitch's and gazed up at him. Rosie thought she might be sick.

'I'm sorry, you are?'

Rosie realised that Maxine was now addressing her and that her tone had gone from warm and gushing to cold and dismissive. Mitch didn't seem to notice the change.

'Oh, this is just Rosie. She happened to be passing. She's just a friend,' Mitch said.

Rosie hopped off her stool. 'And she's just leaving,' she said, picking up her bag and heading for the door, not even stopping to say a proper goodbye. Mitch could pay for her drink, he at least owed her that. Rosie turned to look back before stepping out into the street, hoping to catch Mitch's eye, to see him smile at her, wave his hand in farewell, but Mitch was animatedly chatting to Maxine, who was already comfortably installed in Rosie's still-warm seat.

Chapter Eleven

NOW

Rosie tugged at her skirt and, not for the first time, regretted her choice of clothes. It was one of her favourite skirts but it was not designed for sitting elegantly on a bar stool and she was beginning to worry that half the patrons could see her knickers. And if they couldn't right now then they surely would when she tried to get off the stool. Because inevitably, at some point, she would have to get down off this wretched stool.

Luckily, nobody seemed to be paying her any attention which was good news in terms of flashing her pants, but not such good news in terms of getting a drink; even the barman who she had tried to flag down three times now without success, was ignoring her. Her drink-ordering skills still needed a lot of work. Rosie looked at her watch again; she had arrived early but it was now looking dangerously as if Graham was going to be late.

They had been messaging for days; first on Tinder and then they had taken the leap of actually exchanging numbers, which made it feel so much more real, and, in the fickle world of online dating, meant they'd practically slept together already. Rosie was excited but nervous to meet him.

Just as the barman came towards her, she felt her phone buzz. Momentarily distracted, she reached into her bag only to see the barman pass her by and start serving the man to her left. Rosie groaned in frustration and looked down at her phone, presuming it would be a message from Graham telling her that he was cancelling. At least he was messaging her, she thought to herself, rather than just ghosting her. But the message wasn't from Graham; it was from Mitch, which she wasn't sure whether to take as a good sign or a bad one.

She and Mitch had reached a sort of uneasy *détente* after their argument at his flat the other evening. Rosie was still really angry (and jealous, if she was being honest) and she was sure that Mitch had been holding her at arm's length ever since, probably confused by her behaviour. She knew that a lot of her excitement about tonight wasn't really about Graham at all, but an attempt to get Mitch out of her head. And, although she would deny this to anyone who dared suggest such a thing, it might also be an attempt to compete with Mitch's new relationship. From the little Mitch had said about Jenny, Rosie could tell it was different this time. And this made her unsettled.

Mitch's message simply said good luck. She had finally admitted to him that she hadn't actually yet met Graham despite what she had said in the heat of the moment in his flat. There were only so many secrets she could keep from Mitch, and in the pecking order of importance, this one fell below her other, bigger secret. His message was short and sweet and it made Rosie smile. He knew her well enough to realise that going on this date was a big deal for her.

Lost in typing a reply, she didn't notice the gap open up at the bar next to her, or the man in the jacket step into it and look sideways at Rosie.

'Rosie?' he said, she looked up slightly startled.

'Hi, er, yes?' she replied, hopping straight off the stool, completely forgetting the constraints of her skirt. As she attempted to straighten it, she dropped her bag on the floor. Immediately the man bent to pick it up and handed it back to her, putting a hand on her arm to steady her as he did so.

'Graham?' she asked. The man smiled.

'Yes!' He looked at her for a moment. 'I promise I wasn't late,' he went on after a pause, 'I'd been looking around the bar for you but couldn't see you because of the crowd.'

Rosie found herself smiling back at him. For the first time ever she had met an individual who was actually better looking in real life than online. There was an awkward moment as they stood rather too close together at the crowded bar.

'I actually booked us a table,' Graham said, gesticulating behind him to the restaurant area, 'but if you'd rather have drinks here, that's fine, of course, whatever you would prefer.'

'No, that would be lovely,' Rosie said, feeling taken aback by this initiative. This was outstanding attention to detail, given that most suggestions from an online date were to go over to theirs 'to watch Netflix' if you were lucky.

'Right,' he said. 'I'll go and find someone to tell us where our table is. Do you want to wait here?' he asked.

Rosie nodded, looking up at him. She watched him move off back through the crowd, he was smartly dressed but not overly formal and she had noticed that she looked up at him. He wasn't too tall but was just tall enough that she could probably get away with heels, if she ever felt like wearing them. Or if they ever even saw each other again after tonight. She tugged at her skirt again anxiously, while she waited for him to come back.

'So, you said you split up with a girlfriend recently?' Rosie asked.

Small talk about London and work had covered the awkward moments of ordering their food and waiting for it to arrive. Rosie had begun to allow herself to relax and ask more probing questions. It was too early in the evening to ask him for his intentions, but this was getting pretty close. Although it wasn't as if he had been hiding the split from his ex, he was the one who had brought her up.

Graham smiled at her a little awkwardly; he had a slightly lopsided smile which, rather than detracting from his looks, added to his charm.

'Not that recently,' he admitted. 'It's about two years since we split up, but it's taken me this long to accept that I'm not going to meet someone the way we met people in our twenties.'

Rosie put her head on one side and asked, 'And how did you go about meeting people in your twenties?'

Graham rewarded her cheekiness with a full grin this time. 'In a bar, with low lighting, too much alcohol and youthful confidence.' Rosie laughed. He was funny as well as good-looking.

'But what about you? Why are you still single?'

Rosie widened her eyes in shock at him. 'You know you're not supposed to ask that question?'

'Why not?' he asked, genuinely interested.

'Because there are two ways to interpret it and neither is good.'

He looked at her waiting for her to explain.

'Think about it,' she said, leaning across the table to take a sip of her water. 'Either you're being corny and asking why someone is single because they're *sooo* amazing. Or you're asking what the hell is wrong with them and could they please point it out so that they can save you the time, make your excuses and leave.'

Graham tipped his head back and laughed, just as the waitress brought over their main courses. The conversation could move on, which was a good thing, because now was not the time to confess that her feelings for her best friend were the real issue keeping her still single.

Graham suggested they stay for another drink after dinner, and Rosie, surprising herself with how much she was enjoying his company, agreed. He found them two seats at the bar, near where Rosie had first been sitting. The crowd at the bar had thinned out a little but it was still busy enough that the stools were pushed close to each other. Rosie contemplated the situation.

'Is everything OK?' Graham asked in concern.

'Yes, yes it's fine.' She paused before she decided to just admit what she was worrying about. 'It's just I'm wearing the wrong skirt.'

Graham looked down at her skirt with confusion. 'I think it's a really nice skirt,' he said in a faltering tone, obviously wondering what the correct response was meant to be.

She laughed loudly; all the wine she had drunk was playing havoc with her volume control. 'I meant, it's hard to get up onto one of these' she patted the bar stool, 'in an elegant way, or without...' she leaned in to whisper to him '...showing everyone my knickers.'

She was definitely drunk. She would *never* talk about knickers to a strange man on a first date.

Graham went a little red but quickly recovered. 'OK, how about I help you up and stand right here so no one else can see your...ahem...knickers?' Softly he put his hand on her elbow and, as elegantly as she could manage, Rosie climbed up on to the stool.

'There,' he said, 'no damage done.' He sat down on his bar stool. Their knees were now touching. Rosie waited for some sensation to register in her body. But there was nothing, maybe the alcohol was mucking up all her senses? Surreptitiously she pinched her arm to see what happened and held back a yelp. Yup, she had definitely felt that, but the touch of Graham's knee on hers, his arm on hers earlier, had precisely zero effect on her. She side-eyed him. He was good-looking, he was funny, he was charming. So what was wrong with her?

'What are you drinking?' he asked as he caught the barman's eye.

'A gin and tonic, please,' she said. Then asked, 'How did you do that?' as soon as the barman had turned away to make their drinks.

'Do what?' Graham asked.

'Get the barman's attention immediately. It never works for me; I'm always stood waiting for ages or until someone comes and helps me out.'

Graham pretended to tip an imaginary cap at her. 'I am at your service, feel free to call me anytime you need help getting a drink.'

Rosie swatted his hand. She was enjoying the sensation of flirting with a man. He smiled at her, evidently enjoying it too. Rosie wondered if she felt the tiniest stirrings of a long-lost sensation tingling inside her as she looked up into Graham's face. He took her hand and she let him. He smiled at her and a queasy sensation of awkwardness washed over her at this intimate gesture. Wondering how long she might have to leave her hand in his, she was saved by the arrival of her drink, which gave her the perfect excuse to let go and reach for her drink. The chilled exterior of the glass cooled her clammy palm.

It was late, the bar had emptied out and Graham had insisted on paying for their evening, before helping Rosie down off the bar stool. She had needed a little more help getting down from the stool than she had needed getting up. On top of the wine and the gin and tonic, she had drunk two cocktails, which she couldn't remember the names of, but which their new best friend, the barman, had assured them they would enjoy. And she had, thank you very much.

She and Graham had chatted, laughed and flirted all evening. Hand-holding awkwardness aside, Rosie couldn't remember the last time she had enjoyed a date like this. But something definitely felt off: despite his charm and humour and the fact he was obviously very good-looking, Rosie felt something was missing. At first, she had put it down to nerves, which she had tried to dispel with a few drinks. And as she struggled to put on her jacket she wondered if she had perhaps gone rather overboard with that. But she was no longer nervous; in fact, if he didn't try to hold her hand, she felt really comfortable in his presence, rather too comfortable. Perhaps that was the issue?

Outside the restaurant, they both stood awkwardly on the pavement. Graham stepped towards her. 'I really enjoyed this evening,' he said holding her arms and looking earnestly down at her.

Rosie shifted from foot to foot, 'Me, too,' she agreed.

'Do you think...' he started '...I mean, would it be OK?' Rosie knew what was coming and instead of feeling excited she felt a sense of dread.

'Can I kiss you?' he finally asked. Rosie said nothing. She didn't want to, really she should speak up, but instead she closed her eyes and hoped to feel differently once he actually kissed her. She tipped her face up towards him and felt his lips on hers. And she felt *something*. Yes! She definitely felt something. Not fireworks exactly. It was nice, she thought, but there wasn't that electric spark she had been craving. Confused, she pulled away and stared up at him.

'Can I see you again?' he asked.

Rosie contemplated this. Could he? She'd enjoyed herself, he seemed nice, did she fancy him? Sort of. Maybe? But she certainly didn't feel swept off her feet. Perhaps that was OK, perhaps this might be a slow burn? She should definitely give him another chance, shouldn't she?

Her phone beeped as her Uber pulled up.

'This is mine,' she said, failing to answer his question or to hide the sound of relief in her voice at the sight of her cab. For a moment Graham looked hurt. Then, pulling himself together, he opened the car door for her and tried again.

'So can I call you?' he asked as she stepped in. She nodded and waved at him as she pulled the car door closed.

'Good night?' the driver asked as he pulled away from the curb. She nodded, hoping this wasn't a chatty Uber driver who would insist on talking all the way home. Luckily he took the hint and went back to listening to his radio.

Rosie rested her head against the cool window. It should have been a good night. It *was* a good night. Graham was almost perfect on paper. Good-looking, clever and charming. Rosie stared out at the London streets, always busy whatever the hour, full of people headed home after a night out. She saw a couple kissing outside the tube station, a group of friends saying loud and emotional farewells and she suddenly felt very alone. What was wrong with her? She had just had a fun night out with a man who was obviously keen to see her again, and all she wanted to do was to go home to her flat and call Mitch. Rosie felt the tears roll down her cheeks as she realised that while Graham might be perfect for someone else, he wasn't perfect for her.

Chapter Twelve

'What's with the sunglasses?' Mitch asked, leaning across the park bench to playfully swat them from Rosie's face.

'It's bright, OK?' she replied and scooted along the bench away from him. If she went much further she would end up falling off the end of it.

'OK,' shrugged Mitch, sounding unconvinced as he looked up at the grey sky.

It was a typical London day. Not wet, just overcast, which suited Rosie's mood perfectly. The sunglasses offered two-fold protection; she was feeling hungover after her night out with Graham. Which wasn't something that happened very often; in fact she couldn't remember the last time she had had a proper hangover, probably over a year ago on that holiday in Italy with Mitch. One too many glasses of rosé and too much sun. Or maybe the Christmas party?

The second purpose of the sunglasses was to stop Mitch seeing her red eyes, which were due to all the crying she had been doing on and off since she got in the cab last night. Rosie kept telling herself to get it together, it wasn't rational to behave like this. But the emotional side of her brain was defiantly ignoring these instructions and instead behaving like a hormonal teenager.

Mitch, in contrast, was behaving like a puppy. The grey London day seemed to have no effect on his mood. It was extremely irritating.

'How did it go? How did it go?' he'd practically panted at her when they met at the entrance to the cafe.

So far she had managed to avoid his questions. He had messaged her first thing this morning demanding they meet for lunch to discuss her date, and Rosie hadn't had the energy to put him off. She had spent the time they were in the queue in the sandwich shop studying the menu to avoid his questions. But now that they were sat on the bench together, she had no other means of deflection.

She mumbled something non-committal under her breath – if it sounded an awful lot like 'sod off' Mitch did a good job of pretending he hadn't heard.

He shuffled up the bench, carefully holding his sandwich in one hand and elbowed her with his other arm.

'So?' he asked again.

'It was *fine*, Mitch.'

'Fine?' he said. 'What does that mean? Fine, as in you want to see him again, or fine as in he's a monster and you never want to see him again? Fine covers a lot of territory, Rosie,' he said, waving his sandwich around. Rosie ducked to avoid the flying lettuce.

'Hang on.' He narrowed his eyes. 'You're eating a bacon sandwich,' he said, staring at it in her lap.

'So?' said Rosie defensively.

'So? You never eat bacon sandwiches unless—' Mitch gasped '—unless you're hungover!' He gaped at her in mock horror. 'Rosie! You got drunk last night!' He could barely keep the glee from his voice. 'Now you *have* to tell me everything.' He swivelled around so he was now looking straight at her.

'I do get drunk,' she said.

'You don't!' he responded with excitement. 'Which means it was either amazing,' he grinned, 'or terrible.' He suddenly gripped her arm in concern.

'I've told you it was fine,' she said through gritted teeth. She realised she was running out of options. 'It was lovely, OK? He was great, really great. But then...'

'Go on,' Mitch said eagerly. 'But then, what?'

'Well, then he kissed me and it wasn't great.'

Mitch groaned. 'Oh no, bad breath? A terrible kisser?' He shook his head sadly. 'But never mind,' he said immediately brightening up, 'we can work on that.'

So many images ran through Rosie's mind. She didn't want to ask him to expand on that idea. 'No, I'm sure he was a great kisser, it's just that I don't think I really fancy him.'

Mitch stared at her blankly, 'But I thought you said he was great.'

'He is,' Rosie said adamantly.

'So, what's wrong with—' Mitch started and for a moment she was sure he was going to finish his sentence with 'you' but he stopped himself just in time.

'I just don't think there was chemistry,' she said sadly.

'Oh,' Mitch was briefly speechless. 'I'm really sorry, Rosie.' He stroked her arm in what she found to be a very distracting manner. 'But you had a fun time, which shows that not all online dates are terrible. And maybe next time you *will* fancy them,' he said encouragingly.

Rosie stared across the park, grateful for her sunglasses, which stopped Mitch seeing her eyes brimming with tears – again. Part of her just wanted to tell him why she didn't fancy Graham, why online dating was so hard, but the rest of her feared her confession would ruin both her day and their friendship. She marvelled at his optimism that she *would* meet someone one day, his sunny outlook was both wonderful and painful and she didn't want to risk not having it in her life.

'How are things with Jenny?' she asked tightly, trying to shake the tears from her voice.

She immediately regretted asking. If she was worried that confessing her feelings might push Mitch away she feared more the effect that the mere mention of Jenny's name had on him. It was like a light lit up inside his face; he was practically glowing. She felt sick, and it wasn't because of the hangover.

'She met my mum yesterday,' Mitch confessed.

'She met your mum?!' Rosie exploded. 'What, when? How?'

'Well, on FaceTime.' Mitch was lost with a dreamy expression on his face.

At least it wasn't in person, Rosie thought, but still. Mitch's mum loved Rosie, and the idea that Jenny might be about to usurp Rosie's position in his mum's affections was unthinkable.

'Isn't that a little soon?' Rosie asked sharply.

'It wasn't planned.' Mitch snapped out of his reverie. 'Mum FaceTimed and Jenny happened to be over. It just felt right, I guess.' He shrugged as if introducing his new girlfriend to his mother was an everyday occurrence. It really wasn't. Rosie couldn't remember him introducing anyone apart from her to his mother. She started to shiver.

'Are you OK?' Mitch asked, a look of concern on his face. 'You really are suffering today, aren't you?'

Rosie forced herself to laugh, 'Yeah, I need to remember that I cannot handle more than two drinks.'

A beep distracted him, and Mitch fumbled in his pocket for his phone. 'No, not me. Must have been yours.' He carried on staring at his phone and then realised Rosie hadn't moved.

'Rosie,' he said. 'Rosie?'

'Sorry, what?' Rosie had been staring into space.

'I think that was your phone,' he said, pointing at her bag. 'It wasn't mine,' he said. 'I'd been hoping it was a reply from Jenny. You see, I sent her—'

'Yes, yes, OK,' Rosie said loudly, fumbling in her bag desperate to stop him from telling her whatever it was he had sent to Jenny. She really didn't need to hear any more.

Her phone beeped again.

'You know you can turn off those multiple alerts?' Mitch said.

'What?' she asked as she looked at her phone seeing messages from both Jasmine and Nadia, 'Yes, I do know that, thank you very much. It was actually two messages.'

'Anyone interesting?' He craned his neck to look over at her screen having lost interest in his own phone.

'No,' she said, marking the message from Jasmine as read and reminding herself once again that she *really* needed to call her back. 'Unless you count either Jasmine or Nadia as interesting.'

'I count both of them as interesting,' Mitch said earnestly. 'How is Nadia, by the way? I haven't seen her for ages.'

Rosie put her phone back in her bag and realised that telling Mitch about Nadia might be a good way of distracting him from her love life.

'Actually, she's stressed.' Mitch looked at her quizzically. 'I know,' she said. 'It's unlike her. She's worried about the funding cuts she thinks are coming our way.'

Mitch leaned back against the bench, 'The Staverton report?' he asked.

'Yes,' Rosie confirmed. 'Actually, you must know all the

details. Maybe you can give her some reassurance?' she asked, suddenly eager.

Mitch sighed and stared up at the sky. 'I wish I could,' he said, 'but the report makes for pretty grim reading.' He looked back at Rosie, 'They're making cuts across the board, I bet it will have an impact on Nadia.' He gave a low whistle. 'I should have realised it might.'

'You knew?' Rosie spluttered. 'How long have you known for?'

'A few weeks – one of my contacts at the department gave me the outline of it.' He noticed the look on Rosie's face. 'But I didn't know the details until this week,' he said defensively.

'You could have warned me,' Rosie said a little crossly.

'I didn't think it would impact you,' Mitch protested, 'and it doesn't, right?'

'No, not really' she begrudgingly conceded. 'But it does impact one of my best friends.'

'Rosie,' Mitch said levelly, 'I get a lot of confidential information all the time, I can't tell you everything.'

Rosie knew she was being unreasonable. Of course her mood had nothing to do with the funding cuts and everything to do with Mitch and their plan and the Jenny-shaped spanner he had thrown into it.

'Rosie, I am sorry,' Mitch said reaching across to grab her arm. 'Let me talk to Nadia. I bet I can put in a word with some people and make sure her grant applications get seen by the right committees.'

'But it's not just her,' insisted Rosie, not quite ready to let this one go. 'Nico has already lost out on one of his applications, he's worried he's going to lose his job.' Mitch looked stricken.

'That's really terrible. I like Nico. Let me see if I can help. I'll talk to both of them, see if I can get any useful information for them.' He straightened up as if readying to stand up. 'But Rosie, it's really not my fault about the cuts.'

'Thank you,' she said in what she hoped came across as a conciliatory tone.

'Hey, before I forget, I'm going out with some work people a week Friday, want to come?' Mitch asked.

Rosie hadn't been out with Mitch's work crowd for ages. It was always good fun, journalists knew how to drink and if you were savvy with your own alcohol intake then you could get them to spill all sorts of gossip. Rosie was constantly amazed at the sort of tittle tattle that a supposedly respectable broadsheet journalist hunted down, only for it never to appear in their paper and to make a splash in a tabloid instead.

'It's all about understanding the market,' one of Mitch's colleagues had told her sagely when Rosie had asked her about it.

Maybe a night out with them would be just what she needed.

'Got any new single colleagues?' she asked.

Mitch gaped at her, 'Rosie! What's got into you? Looks like this online dating thing is starting to have an effect.' He put his hand on her arm. Rosie really wished he would stop touching her, it only made her realise the difference in sensation between his touch and Graham's. 'I am sorry about last night, though. I know online dating isn't your favourite thing to do and I'm really proud of you for putting yourself out there.'

Rosie grimaced at his patronising choice of words.

'And you can't fancy everyone,' he said wisely. 'Just because someone is perfect on paper it doesn't mean that sparks will fly. Look at me,' he said pointing at himself. 'I should know. The amount of dates I have been on with people I should fancy and yet...' He shrugged. 'Nothing happens.' He looked at her with puppy-dog sorrowful eyes.

Rosie laughed despite herself.

'But no, I don't have any new colleagues' he told her, 'just the same old crowd. But it will be fun!' Rosie found herself nodding. 'So you'll come?' he said eagerly, grabbing her hands; his enthusiasm was as ever infectious.

'Yes!' she agreed. 'I'll come.'

'This is great!' Mitch exclaimed, 'I'm so excited.' Rosie looked at him with a raised eyebrow.

'Oh, I forgot to mention the occasion,' he said, 'I'm introducing them all to Jenny!' Rosie felt her heart sink. 'This will be perfect, you can meet her at the same time.' He squeezed her hands tightly, 'you're going to love her, Rosie, I just know it.'

Rosie broke eye contact and looked out across the park. She felt nauseous at the thought of meeting Jenny, but knew she couldn't back out now without Mitch realising something was up.

Mitch was still talking and Rosie realised she had completely zoned out. He seemed to be telling her some long and complicated story about one of his colleagues, which Rosie would no doubt regret not listening to when called upon to discuss it at a later date. And then he stopped and noticed Rosie's expression. He followed her gaze.

'She's sweet,' he said, pointing to a mother and daughter.

'Sorry?' Rosie replied.

'The little girl? She's really sweet,' he said. 'How old do you think she is?'

Rosie deliberately looked in the opposite direction. 'I don't really know. I've never been good at telling.'

'It does make you want one though, doesn't it?' he continued. 'You know I've always been broody' he admitted, 'but I'm feeling it more than ever now.' He sighed.

'But I've got a good feeling,' he said, switching from his contemplative mood. 'I think you'll meet someone really soon now. And what with me and Jenny going so well I reckon you might escape having to use me as your fallback.' He laughed loudly, startling some pigeons which had crept closer to look for crumbs.

Rosie felt her tears start to brim again, and she pushed her sunglasses back up her nose. She felt like shouting, *Don't you understand? I don't want to be your fallback.* She wanted to tell him that she was terrified that he was falling for Jenny and that she would never get over him. But she didn't. Instead, she looked at her watch and made a decision. She *would* reply to Graham, and she *would* go on another date with him because she needed to do something to put Mitch and Jenny and his stupid plan out of her mind.

'I have to go,' she said, 'I've got a meeting at 2pm.'

Mitch looked at his watch, too. 'OK, I'll walk with you.'

'You don't have to,' she said, keen to escape both Mitch and her mood.

'But I want to,' he insisted, standing up and offering her his hand. Having no other option, she took it, grabbed her bag and stood up. 'It will do me good,' he said, 'I haven't been to the gym in ages.' Rosie gave him a sideways look; now she thought about it perhaps he had put on some weight. Maybe if he continued not going to the gym and she wore dark glasses all the time and squinted whenever she looked at him then she wouldn't find him quite so attractive.

'Been too busy with Jenny,' he said, giving her a wink. They walked arm in arm towards the gates of the park.

Rosie rolled her eyes and dragged him towards the road, completely forgetting that she still hadn't replied to Jasmine, whose last message had sounded urgent.

Chapter Thirteen

osie leaned into the mirror and poked a spot that had just appeared by her nose. It was typical; she hadn't had a spot in ages and today, just as she was about to meet Graham again, there it was. She was about to squeeze it, which would have been disastrous as she knew, when the door banged open and appearing as if the corridor was on fire, was Nadia.

'Hi,' Nadia exclaimed and rushed straight into one of the bathroom stalls, slamming it behind her. 'Sorry, need to wee!' she shouted through the closed door. 'I've drunk four cups of coffee this afternoon and haven't had a chance to go.'

'I can drink six before I need a wee,' Rosie said proudly and went back to inspecting her spot.

'Just you wait,' came the muffled response and then the sound of the toilet flushing. Nadia flung open the door. 'Just you wait,' she repeated, 'till you've had two children. Then let's discuss whether your pelvic floor can cope with the pitfalls of excess caffeine.'

Rosie held her hands up in protest. 'I wasn't suggesting my pelvic floor was any superior to your pelvic floor!'

'You look nice,' Nadia said, eyeing Rosie up in the mirror as she stood washing her hands.

'Do you think so?' Rosie asked, peering again at the spot and feeling grateful Nadia had saved her from squeezing it.

'Definitely,' Nadia said, nodding. 'I love those Converse, they look super cute with the black tights and that dress.'

Rosie had gone for a more casual look for the second date. She was wearing one of her favourite black dresses which had a ruffled hem and came in just on the decent side of her thighs. If she wore it with black tights and dressed it down with Converse she looked cool and chic and felt much more relaxed. And black tights meant she was much less likely to flash her pants at anyone. Unless it was planned.

'Are you going out tonight?' Nadia asked.

Rosie turned to her and grinned slyly. 'Second date with Graham.'

'Wow, that was fast.' Nadia grinned back.

Rosie had left Mitch after their lunch in the park and gone straight back to her office and messaged Graham. This time it was going to be different, she was determined. Graham was lovely and she was damn well sure she was going to make herself feel a spark next time they kissed. If Mitch could meet someone then she could, too. She wasn't going to let him win at this; she needed to move on.

Graham didn't seem interested in playing it cool at all and immediately asked Rosie when he could see her again, so here she was, in one of her favourite dresses, awesome trainers and a glint in her eye, ready to take her chances.

'Excited?' Nadia asked, practically feeling the energy radiating off Rosie.

'Yup. I've got a good feeling, Nadia!' Rosie ran over and wrapped her arms around Nadia, giving her a hug.

'It's so lovely to see you this happy.' Nadia hugged her back. 'Have you told Mitch?'

Rosie released Nadia and rummaged through her make-up bag, pretending to be suddenly very interested in applying more blusher.

'Erm, Rosie I think that's enough,' Nadia said in concern. 'You'll end up looking sunburned.'

Rosie stuck her tongue out in the mirror but she did put the brush down.

'No, I haven't told Mitch, he's too into the new girlfriend to care, though.'

'Oh,' said Nadia.

'What does that mean?' Rosie bristled.

'Nothing!' Nadia held her hands up. 'It means "oh" that's all.'

'Hmm.' Rosie continued to eye Nadia in the mirror as she applied mascara.

'I mean, I guess...' Nadia leaned against the wall in a nonchalant manner. 'I guess I just wondered whether Mitch had seemed jealous at all when you told him?'

'Jealous? Why would he be jealous?' Rosie put down the mascara wand in surprise and turned to look at Nadia.

'I don't know?' shrugged Nadia. 'I suppose I was just wondering if you were trying to make Mitch jealous and that was why you were going on a second date with someone you didn't like so much the first time around?'

'I did like him!' protested Rosie. 'I mean I *do* like him.'

'OK, sure. Well, you look super sexy,' Nadia said, walking up behind Rosie and putting her arms around her waist. 'I'd definitely do you if I wasn't married.'

'Good to know I've got a back-up option if you and Nico don't work out.'

'Sure thang,' Nadia said, winking at Rosie and giving her a

thumbs up as she headed out the door. 'Text me!' she shouted. 'And let me know if you get laid tonight!'

The door to the bathroom had swung shut, so Rosie only heard this as a muffled shout. Which meant that everyone outside in the corridor, everyone with their office doors open would have heard it loud and clear. Rosie hung her head in dismay and wondered just how long she would have to hide out in the bathroom before everyone had left for the evening and she could safely leave without anyone knowing that Nadia's comment had been directed at her.

Rosie stepped out into the evening, it was dark already and the lights were on in the buildings around the square her lab stood in. The rain that had poured down that morning had stopped but left behind large puddles which caught the headlights of passing buses and taxis.

'Rosie!'

Rosie turned to see Rachel back in the entrance hallway. She walked back towards her boss mentally running through a checklist of anything she could have done wrong, thinking that this really wasn't a healthy way to react each and every time her boss wanted to talk to her.

'Sorry to stop you on your way out, I wanted to know how you were getting on with the BioChem project?'

Rachel glanced around her as if concerned that BioChem's rivals might have spies camped out in the entrance lobby to their building.

'Good, I think,' Rosie said cautiously. 'I just want to look again at those test results they shared because I'm not sure they make sense. But I think I've got a plan of how to fix that and what we should do next.'

'They don't make sense, do they?' Rachel looked at Rosie. 'I thought that, too. Well, great that you've spotted that. Find some time in my diary tomorrow and we'll go through it.'

'Will do,' Rosie said, waiting to be dismissed.

'Going straight home tonight? Not off out?' Rachel asked, looking Rosie up and down.

Rosie felt paranoia wash over her before remembering that whatever she had chosen to wear for a second date wouldn't be what Rachel would wear. Not that superhumans like Rachel went on 'dates'. They had torrid love affairs, enjoyed trysts – they didn't meet for a drink in the pub.

Still, Rosie couldn't help but second guess her choice of outfit as she walked through the square to meet Graham. They'd arranged to meet at one of the pubs off Goodge Street and Rosie was walking quickly before slowing down as she realised how early she was going to be. She decided to go the long way round, crossing towards the north end of Tottenham Court Road rather than risking an early death by dodging the buses and running across.

Just north of Goodge Street station she stopped to cross a side street and found herself looking straight into the window of a pub on the other side of the road. There was a man sat at a table in the window who looked just like Graham. The green man flashed on the traffic lights and Rosie carefully crossed the street, realising as she got closer and closer that the man didn't just look like Graham, it *was* Graham.

Rosie glanced up at the name of the pub – she was fairly sure this wasn't the one they had arranged to meet in but perhaps she'd made a mistake? Or perhaps he was early and had decided to stop for a drink before meeting her? Before she could think through exactly what she was doing and why, and whether there were any more nefarious reasons for Graham sitting in a different pub, Rosie found herself walking into the pub and raising her hand in greeting. It was at that moment she realised that Graham wasn't sitting on his own in the pub. He was sitting across from a girl, one with rather striking red hair.

Rosie wondered if she could reverse, walk out, pretend she had never been there. But then what would she do? Ask him who he had been drinking with before their date? Check to see if he had met up with his sister recently? If he even had a sister. But given the body language going on at the table in front of her, Rosie was fairly sure that this wasn't Graham's sister, just as she was fairly sure that she couldn't leave now, because not only had Graham spotted her but he seemed to have gone rather pale.

The girl, noticing that something was wrong, spun around in her seat and looked up at Rosie.

'Who are you?' she demanded, immediately recognising that there was something wrong with this situation.

'Erm, Rosie?' Rosie now desperately wanted to stop time. She was mortified.

'Right,' the girl said, looking Rosie up and down. She turned back to look at Graham, 'Want to explain what's going on?' she asked.

Despite the fact that this girl looked like she would quite happily punch Rosie, or Graham, or perhaps both, Rosie couldn't help but admire her confidence. While Rosie shuffled awkwardly from one foot to the other in silence, this girl was asking questions and demanding answers.

Graham looked awkward but not as awkward as Rosie felt he ought to, given the fact it was looking more and more as if he had been caught arranging back-to-back dates with different girls on the same night. What was he going to do if this date had gone well? Just not turned up to meet Rosie? Rosie quickly felt herself getting just as angry as this other girl was.

'Yeah,' Rosie said, folding her arms, channeling the redhead. 'What exactly is going on, Graham?' Graham had the grace to swallow nervously. 'Because from where I'm standing it looks like this is a date, right?' Rosie looked down at the other girl whose lips were folded in a thin line as she nodded in agreement.

'And let me check?' Rosie looked at her watch, 'In thirteen minutes' time you're supposed to be meeting *me* for a date in a pub around the corner!'

'Un-fucking-believable,' the girl pushed her chair back, her eyes flashing in anger. 'Don't ever contact me again!' she shouted at Graham. 'You're welcome to him,' she practically spat at Rosie and stormed out of the pub.

'I don't want him!' Rosie called after her, wishing she too had turned on her heel and left already. Rosie turned to stare at Graham.

'Do you want a drink?' he asked a little pathetically.

'No!' she exclaimed. 'Of *course* I don't want a drink.'

'OK,' he replied, 'Don't get so angry.'

Rosie's face flushed. 'Don't get angry? You're telling me not to get angry? Seriously Graham what was that?'

'What was what?' he pleaded. 'Rosie, we've been on one date, it's not like we'd had any kind of conversation about being exclusive. I don't think it's so bad, don't overreact.'

Rosie's head almost exploded. 'No it's not that bad. What *is* bad is the way you went about it. Why would you arrange two dates on the same day, practically at the same time a couple of streets apart?'

Graham shrugged, 'It just worked out like that. I didn't plan it. You seemed really keen to see me and happened to be free this evening too.'

'I was *not* keen to see you!' Rosie fumed. 'To be honest, I really didn't feel like seeing you again at all.'

'But, then, why—' Graham looked confused.

'I thought I'd give you a chance, see whether there might be a spark second time around. Ugh!' Rosie stamped her foot in frustration. 'I didn't even fancy you in the first place!'

Rosie swung her bag onto her shoulder and stormed out of the pub leaving a wake of confused drinkers behind her.

'Oh, Rosie I'm so sorry.'

Rosie had done the only thing she knew would make her feel better, even though her mind was screaming at her not to. She had left Graham in the pub, called Mitch, asked him where he was and then gone to meet him in a different pub on the other side of town.

'But I thought you weren't going to see him again?' Mitch asked. 'What happened?'

'I don't know,' Rosie said glumly, kicking her foot against the table leg. 'I just thought I should give him a second go. I was only doing what you told me to do. Being more open minded.'

'I didn't mean you should date arseholes,' Mitch said, taking a sip of his pint.

'I didn't *know* he was an arsehole until just now, did I?'

'But you didn't fancy him, so why see him again?'

Rosie didn't reply. Mitch was right, infuriatingly so. But she couldn't tell him why it was so important that she see Graham again so she just said nothing.

'You know we're not all like that,' Mitch said, grabbing her hand.

'I know,' Rosie said, 'but sometimes it just feels like you are.'

'I'm not,' he said, stroking her hand with his thumb.

'Yeah, I know that Mitch,' she said pulling her hand back quickly. 'But I'm not dating you, am I? Jenny is.'

Mitch pulled a funny face, 'Yeah,' he said. He looked on the verge of saying something else, and then his phone beeped and he pulled it out of his pocket.

'Shit,' he said, looking at the message.

'Jenny?' Rosie asked, trying not to sound like a jealous and petulant child.

'Uh-huh.' He looked up at her.

'You've got to go?'

'Sorry Rosie, I said I'd meet her. Will you be OK?'

'Yes, sure absolutely,' she replied, not feeling sure or absolutely about anything. 'Totally fine, go!' She gave him a double thumbs up.

He stood and looked down at her as if unsure what to say or do next. 'I meant it,' he finally said, 'we're not all like that.' He bent down and kissed her on the cheek. 'You'll come next Friday?' he asked.

Rosie nodded and waved him off, hoping he would be out of the pub before her eyes filled with tears. And now what? Should she call Nadia or Jasmine and cry on their shoulders? She thought guiltily of the fact she still hadn't replied to Jasmine's messages. Or should she just go home and do a spot of doom-scrolling before crying into the void of Netflix?

Chapter Fourteen

Rosie adjusted her sunglasses and reached over to pick up her coffee. She'd taken an early lunch break and headed for the square in front of the British Museum, hoping to find a spot to soak up some sun before the tourists took up all the cafe tables.

She'd been in luck, grabbing the last free table just after the barista had handed her her flat white. Really she should be catching up on paperwork before her lab slot this afternoon, but this felt just as important. *This* being scrolling through dating websites and aimlessly taking photos of her surroundings. She was determined to put the Graham fiasco behind her, there must be someone out there who she half fancied and who wouldn't arrange two dates on the same night. Surely?

A shadow fell over her phone screen, seconds before two hands rested on her shoulder.

'Wotcha,' came a fake cockney accent over her left shoulder.

Rosie smiled. She'd know that terrible accent anywhere. Shifting in her seat she put one hand on her shoulder to touch the hand that rested there and swivelled round to smile up at Mitch.

'Fancy seeing you here!' she grinned.

'Amazing coincidence, isn't it?' he agreed. 'Whatcha doing?'

She held her screen up to him. 'Hate swiping.'

Mitch frowned. 'And that is?'

'It's where I find the least hateful person to swipe right on.'

Mitch laughed. 'You're so dark, Rosie.' He sat down on the chair next to her and without asking reached out and took her phone from her. 'Let me look.'

'How come you're not at work?' she asked as she stretched out in her seat.

'Could ask you the same question,' he replied, busily scrolling through her phone.

Rosie leaned into him, 'What about that one?' she asked, pointing at the screen.

Mitch gave her some serious side eye.

'What?' she protested.

'He's called Derek.'

'So? He can't help it. Presumably it's what his parents called him. We can't all have slightly *kooky* yet rather charming names like yours.'

'You think my name's *kooky*?'

Rosie dropped her sunglasses and looked over them at him. 'Mitch, we have had this conversation a million times.'

Mitch grinned at her, 'I know, but I like it when you say nice things about me.'

Rosie snorted. 'I think it says a lot about you when you think being called "kooky" constitutes flattery… Ooh what about him?'

Mitch peered at the phone screen. 'Hard no.'

'Why not?' protested Rosie.

'He's in IT.'

'And?'

'Boring.'

Rosie looked up at the sky, 'Mitch, come on, please tell me we can find one decent guy on there for me to go on a date with?'

Mitch continued scrolling.

'Him!' shouted Rosie, pointing at the phone.

There was a long pause while Mitch looked carefully at the profile picture. Rosie held her breath; it was like waiting for the final judgement, except with less hellfire and more damnation. 'Not him,' he finally declared and put Rosie's phone face down on the table.

Rosie sighed. 'What was wrong with that one?' She stared sadly down at her phone.

'Looks like he spends too much time in the gym and he definitely waxes his eyebrows.'

'You look like *you* wax your eyebrows!' Rosie said half playfully, half in frustration. She reached over and began pretending to pluck Mitch's eyebrows.

'Ow!' he protested, grabbing hold of her hand and then holding it firmly between his.

Rosie looked down, she hated it when Mitch held her hand like this. It sent all the wrong kinds of signals to her brain, not to mention other parts of her body. She quickly pulled it free and pretended to drink from her now empty cup of coffee.

'But seriously, Mitch, I'm trying to be less scientific about dating, going with the flow more? Do you really not think *any* of those guys are worth messaging.'

'No,' said Mitch emphatically.

Rosie exhaled. 'OK, help me out here, how *am* I going to find a boyfriend when none of them seem to live up to *your* exacting standards? I thought *I* was the picky one!'

'I'm just looking out for you,' Mitch replied. 'We don't want another Graham, do we?' he said sternly.

Rosie rolled her eyes and muttered something under her

breath. 'Anyway, you haven't explained why you're not at work,' she said, running her fingers through her hair and immediately regretting it when she found an obstinate tangle.

'Here,' Mitch said, turning her round slightly and teasing the tangle out himself. Rosie couldn't decide if this was more or less intimate than hand holding. Definitely more like monkey grooming. She smiled despite the awkwardness.

'There,' he said, turning her back to face the table. 'Funny thing about social media.'

Rosie frowned at him making him laugh out loud. 'Oh, Rosie, you posted a photo. I knew you were here. Thought I'd come say hi.'

Rosie's face brightened, remembering the picture she had snapped of the British Museum with the sunlight catching its roof, which she'd then posted to Instagram.

'I wanted to check you really were OK after the whole Graham thing?' Mitch looked at her with a concerned expression on his face.

Rosie shrugged. 'Just kind of cross with myself for giving him the time of day. Hey!' she exclaimed. 'Look at me, I'm getting so much better at handling rejection, aren't I!' She grinned at Mitch but this didn't stop him looking at her worriedly.

'You shouldn't have to deal with rejection Rosie,' he said softly, breaking his gaze and looking off towards Russell Square.

'Hmm, well I'm glad you came to check on me,' she said, reaching out and patting his arm. 'Even if all you've done is pour big buckets of scorn all over any potential dates.'

'You can do better than any of them,' Mitch said firmly.

'Really?' Rosie asked. 'Because I don't feel like I'm doing so well at this dating thing, Mitch.' She sighed.

He paused and looked down at his hands, fiddling with them in his lap. 'You'll meet the right person,' he said after a while.

'Ugh, I wish I had your confidence. I'm not sure I'd know Mr Right if he came up to me at this very moment and bought me coffee.'

Mitch's face twisted strangely at her words, his gaze fixed on his hands. Fearing she'd said something wrong, she continued quickly, 'I mean, it's hard to know exactly what I'm looking for, you know? It's OK for you.'

'What do you mean?' Mitch asked sharply, looking up from his hands into her eyes.

'Well you know exactly the type of girl you're looking for. Isn't that how you found Jenny?' Rosie flashed what she hoped came across as an I'm-super-comfortable-to-be-discussing-your-new-girlfriend smile at him. 'Didn't you just type in, cute, petite, blonde and the hits kept coming?'

Mitch didn't laugh. 'Something like that,' he said. 'Anyway, I should get back to work. Just glad you're doing OK.' He stood up quickly.

'Oh, OK,' Rosie replied, confused by his imminent abrupt departure. 'Well thanks for coming.' She stood too and they awkwardly hugged goodbye.

Rosie watched as Mitch walked off. She really wished he wasn't wearing those trousers today, her favourite ones, the ones that showed off his...

Oh, damn you, Mitch, she thought to herself. She was supposed to have been here angrily swiping left and right. Not getting all messed up in her head by Mitch's opinions on who was right for her and who was wrong. Fine for him to have such high standards for her, when he was already miles ahead in their plan. At this rate he'd be happily married to Jenny while she sat at home Miss Haversham-style, lacking even the being-jilted excuse to cry over.

Chapter Fifteen

The Duke of Cambridge wasn't your typical London pub. It didn't look like much from the outside: a brick building on a nondescript side street conveniently close to Mitch's flat. But the reason that Mitch managed to persuade people to travel across town to it was hidden behind the ordinary facade. Through the back door was hidden a huge (by London standards) beer garden, with tables nestled in wooden sections, cushions scattered across benches and fairy lights and bunting hung artfully between the trees. It was this that brought people to the pub, even in the depths of winter, when firepits were lit to provide warmth to the devoted drinkers.

Although it was edging deeper into autumn, the weather had been warm and the crowds in the garden provided enough heat that Rosie felt cosy in her jacket. She had put a scarf in her bag this morning when she left for work, but so far, she hadn't needed it.

Mitch had messaged her during the day, checking again that she really was OK about Graham and hadn't fallen into a pit of despair. But Rosie could read between the lines, he was really

187

checking that she was still planning to come tonight because he was obviously excited to introduce her to Jenny.

Rosie had half thought about cancelling, just to put a dent in his enthusiasm but she had to admit she was intrigued to meet this woman who had seemingly captured Mitch's heart when so many, herself included, had failed before.

Rosie had a plan; she would be friendly and polite but keep her distance. And she wouldn't stay long. If she knew Mitch's colleagues, none of them would be planning on consuming anything but alcohol and that could be disastrous for her, given the mood she was in. She'd stay for a drink, meet Jenny and then be on her way home to eat dinner by eight. She had a pizza with her name on it and a bottle of Sauvignon in the fridge – nicely chilled to take the edge off after meeting the new girlfriend.

But it was seven-fifteen already and still there was no sign of Mitch. Rosie was sat on one of the wooden benches between two of Mitch's colleagues, both of whom she had known for ages. On any other evening she would have been enjoying their banter but she was on edge, anxious to get this meeting out of the way and get home.

'Did Mitch not leave work with the rest of you?' she asked Lucy, who was sat next to her. Rosie had asked this question of several of Mitch's colleagues already but had not got a sensible answer so she decided to try Lucy who, of all Mitch's work friends, was probably the least likely to overcomplicate the answer to a straightforward question.

Lucy shook her head. 'No, he left early.'

'Early?' Rosie queried, confused by the reply. 'So why isn't he here yet?'

Lucy laughed. 'I think he went to meet Jenny from work and they were going to come on together. He was worried Jenny would be nervous about arriving on her own. It's so sweet, isn't it?'

Rosie mumbled something incomprehensible.

'He's really got it bad for this one, hasn't he? I haven't seen him like this before,' Lucy continued, obviously reveling in Mitch's newfound happiness. Mitch's happiness had the opposite effect on Rosie, who seemed to sink deeper into misery. 'But then, I suppose you know him much better than we do.'

Rosie shrugged miserably but didn't respond.

'Are you seeing anyone at the moment?' Lucy asked.

'Me?' Rosie replied in surprise, 'No.'

She didn't expand on this but Lucy obviously didn't take the hint that Rosie was not in the mood to discuss her love life.

'Does Jenny being on the scene mean you see Mitch less? I mean you two spend so much time together, we always joke that you're like a married couple.' Lucy laughed, 'It must be strange to share him with someone else, especially when you're still single.'

Rosie shot Lucy a look. Up until this point Lucy had been one of Rosie's favourites amongst Mitch's colleagues but she was rapidly reevaluating her judgement.

'Ben!' shouted Lucy.

Rosie winced; she should be pleased that Lucy was distracted from this topic of conversation but if Ben was providing the source of distraction then perhaps she shouldn't be so grateful.

Ben worked on the sports desk at Mitch's newspaper. He seemed to think this gave him carte blanche to behave like a premiership footballer, swaggering about the place and treating women as if they should be grateful he was blessing them with his attention.

If Lucy had been Rosie's favourite colleague of Mitch's, Ben consistently remained her least. Mitch felt the same, he constantly complained about Ben's behaviour, especially towards women.

Ben regularly boasted that he could have played for Arsenal but an injury ruined his chances. Mitch told Rosie that it was a well-known fact that Ben could barely kick a ball at all, far less play for a Premiership team.

The real problem with Ben was that he saw Rosie as some kind of challenge. Mitch had a theory that Rosie's complete lack of interest in Ben was a painful dent to his ego.

'Here,' said Lucy. 'We'll move up, you can sit next to us.'

Rosie frowned at her. She didn't think it was possible for Lucy to fall any further in her estimation.

'It's OK,' Rosie stood up, 'I'm going to the bar. You can sit here.'

'Excellent timing,' Ben grinned at her. 'I was going, too.'

Rosie fought the urge to sit back down. She didn't even want another drink; she was already two drinks in and with no food inside her was beginning to feel the effects. But she was cornered. Either she stayed and was trapped on the bench with Ben, who she had no doubt would forget his need for a drink if she stayed. Or she went to the bar with him. Rosie considered her options; at least with the latter she might bump into someone she knew on the way, or she could suddenly need the bathroom. Or just leave without telling anyone and run home to her pizza and wine.

Sighing, she made her way back through the other drinkers to the bar inside, constantly aware as she went of Ben behind her, his hand not quite touching her back but close enough to be guiding her through the crowds. At the bar, he waved away her purse in a patronising manner.

'These are on me,' he declared grandly.

Rosie said nothing. She wasn't above getting someone to buy her a drink, even if she didn't like them, especially when it was a drink she didn't really want.

'Fine,' she said, realising how unappreciative she sounded. 'I was drinking the Pinot Grigio, but just a small glass,' she said, before adding a grudging, 'please.'

Whether the last part of her order was lost in the hubbub at the bar, or more likely Ben completely ignored her, what she was presented with looked more like a bucket of wine than a small glass.

Hating herself for her very British inability to complain, Rosie even said, 'Thanks' through gritted teeth.

Back at the table, Rosie tried to escape Ben but it seemed his mission for the evening was to invade her personal space. Rosie kept shooting pleading looks at Lucy in the hope she would rescue her, but Lucy was now engaged in a deep conversation with someone Rosie didn't know. Tonight was really not going according to plan and there was still no sign of Mitch.

The garden got busier and louder and Rosie was reaching the end of her tether with Ben when she heard someone shout, 'Mitch!' in an excited tone. Ordinarily Rosie would have been thrilled to have been saved by his arrival, but this time it also meant she was about to meet Jenny.

Slowly, she looked around Ben, who still had her pinned into her space on the bench and there Mitch was, grinning and waving at his friends. He was wearing a dark grey jacket, which Rosie knew well. She had helped him choose it last winter on an exhausting shopping trip. Mitch had made her go into every shop on Regent Street before deciding that he wasn't interested in anything in any of them and making her trek back over to Bond Street, where he'd then bought the very first jacket he'd tried on in the very first shop they had been to.

Looking at him now, Rosie had to agree he looked amazing wearing it. Mitch had made it up to her by taking her for drinks on the roof terrace at Selfridges afterwards, where he had disappeared off to the bathroom at one point in the evening, reappearing wearing the jacket and with the number of a girl he had met on the way. And now here he was wearing that same jacket but with a different girl on his arm.

Rosie tried to forget the memories and turned her attention to Jenny. If Rosie had to describe in detail Mitch's ideal girl, she would have described Jenny; she was petite and looked all the more so tucked up close to Mitch's tall frame. She had a mass of blonde curls, which framed a pretty and expressive face. Rosie wasn't sure who looked more pleased with themselves, Mitch or Jenny. Both of them were beaming from ear to ear, so much for being too shy to come on her own, Rosie thought sourly.

If Rosie had been feeling especially catty she would also have commented on the length of Jenny's skirt but that would make her sound too much like her mother, so she settled instead for feeling extremely jealous of Jenny's jacket which Rosie could tell, even from this far away, was a beautifully soft leather one.

'There they are,' Ben said, turning back to fix Rosie with his gaze. 'Do you want me to move so you can go meet the new girl?'

Rosie had an uncomfortable feeling that Ben knew exactly what she was thinking. She broke eye contact and mumbled, 'No, it's OK, I'll go in a minute.'

Rosie watched over Ben's shoulder as Mitch was mobbed by his colleagues. He was always popular but tonight people were intrigued to meet the new girlfriend, about whom they had presumably heard so much already. Rosie knocked back her glass of wine and asked Ben to tell her again about the time he had almost made it at Arsenal.

The pub garden had begun to spin. Rosie had lost count of the amount of drinks she'd had but so far she had managed to stay out of sight of Mitch. Hiding behind his least favourite colleague had its advantages, she thought, even if it did mean that she had had to make conversation with Ben all evening. Rosie was just beginning to wonder if she could sneak out without Mitch ever having realised she was there and avoid having to meet Jenny.

'There you are!' Mitch said with surprise, finally spotting her in Ben's shadow, 'Everything OK?' he asked with concern as he noted Ben's hand on her knee. 'Mate,' he said, nodding quickly in acknowledgement at Ben before he reached over and pulled Rosie to her feet and away from him.

'Are you OK?' Mitch asked her again as he led her away from the table.

'I'm fine,' she replied, glad not to have to say much more as she was very aware that she was now in danger of slurring her words.

'I thought you hadn't come,' Mitch continued sounding put out. 'What were you doing with *him*?' he said, indicating his disapproval of Ben.

'I wasn't *doing* anything,' Rosie retorted, 'I was waiting for you. I've been here for hours.'

Mitch ignored the resentful tone in her voice. 'Come and meet Jenny,' he said enthusiastically, 'I've been looking forward to this all day.'

Rosie said nothing but wrinkled her nose with distaste.

'Jenny, Rosie; Rosie, Jenny,' Mitch said, switching his arm from around Rosie to pull Jenny in tight against his body. Rosie did her best to ignore the effect this had on her heart. Jenny beamed up at her.

'I've heard so much about you!' she said excitedly.

Rosie struggled to produce her best smile. 'Likewise!' There was an uncomfortable silence while Rosie and Jenny sized each other up and tried to pretend that they weren't.

'I need a drink,' Rosie said. 'Can I get either of you anything?' Not waiting for an answer she dived into the crowd, leaving Mitch watching her go in puzzlement.

Rosie stood outside the bathroom, leaning against the wall trying to get her bearings back. It was darker in the corridor here than in the main pub and she took advantage of the dim lighting to gather her thoughts. Tonight was not going well; she was drunk, she had failed to be polite and calm when meeting Jenny (although she hadn't actually seen the look on Mitch's face when she walked off, she could just imagine it). And she had spent far longer than she should have done in conversation with Ben.

This could all be fixed, she thought. Firstly she needed to stop drinking right now. Then she needed to get straight back to Jenny and Mitch and make polite conversation and, finally, she had to avoid Ben for the rest of the evening. She could do this.

'Rosie!' Rosie's head whipped round to look back towards the bar and she saw Mitch coming towards her.

'Where did you get to? Is everything OK?'

'I'm fine, Mitch. I was going to the bathroom.'

'Er, OK.' Mitch didn't look like he believed her. 'Look, I'll wait here and then we can go to the bar together. Jenny needs a drink, too.'

Rosie tried not to grind her teeth at the mention of Jenny's name. She merely nodded and went into the bathroom hoping that the queue might be so long that Mitch would lose patience and go back to find Jenny.

But that wasn't Mitch's style. If he said he was going to wait, he would wait. She stared at herself in the mirror, willing herself to wake up and find herself back in her own flat, out of this nightmare. But magic was not on her side tonight. Washing her hands in the cold water and playing for time by carefully drying them with a paper towel she made her way back out with a heavy heart and a churning sensation inside. Mitch grinned at her as she walked back out into the pub.

'What do you think of her?' Mitch asked as they stood waiting in the queue at the bar.

'Of who?' Rosie asked, aware of the stupidity of her response.

'Jenny, of course!' Mitch said in exasperation.

'Well, I haven't really spoken to her yet, but she seems nice enough.' There was a pause. 'Is it still going well then?' Rosie didn't want to ask the question but she had to know; perhaps bringing her out with his friends would make Mitch see Jenny in a different light. But Rosie knew this was a futile hope, she could tell by the expression on Mitch's face how smitten he was.

'It's going great!' he said enthusiastically. 'Better than great actually. I can't believe how different this feels to any other relationship.'

Rosie felt the alcohol churn in her stomach again.

'That's wonderful,' she managed to say through gritted teeth as they edged their way closer to the bar.

'I met her school friends last night,' Mitch said dreamily.

'You did?' Rosie said incredulously.

'Yeah, they're a really close bunch and she said it was important to her that I meet them soon.' Rosie stared at him. 'Apparently they all loved me, so I passed that test!'

Of course you did, thought Rosie. Apart from Ben, Rosie wasn't sure she had ever met someone who didn't love Mitch.

'You'll be meeting her family next!' she said with a fake laugh.

'I am!' beamed Mitch.

'What? I was joking!' she said, aghast.

'It's her dad's birthday on Sunday and they're having a party. She said she didn't want to go without me.' He shrugged as if meeting the family was nothing.

'Mitch,' Rosie said seriously. 'When was the last time you met someone's family?'

Mitch considered this for a moment, staring hard at the ceiling. 'I don't remember,' he eventually replied.

Rosie watched him, then after a while she said, 'You don't think you might be moving a bit quickly?'

'What?' he asked. 'No! I really like her, Rosie. She's funny and sweet and I think it's really nice that she wants me to meet her friends and family.' He paused. 'Why? Don't you think it's a good idea?'

He gave her a searching look. Rosie considered her reply, they were almost at the front of the queue now.

'I just don't want to see you get hurt,' she eventually replied, breaking eye contact. She realised this was a pathetic thing to say, there was no way Mitch was the one that was going to get hurt in this scenario.

'You're so sweet, Rosie, thanks for looking out for me.' Mitch put his arm around her and hugged her tight. 'But I'll be fine, this time it's different.'

Rosie let herself relax in Mitch's embrace. It felt good to be hugged by him, even if it was while he told her about how well things were going with his new girlfriend. Maybe the meeting with the parents would go badly wrong, maybe he would discover things about Jenny that he didn't like. Maybe...

'What do you want?'

Rosie's reverie was broken by their arrival at the front of the queue. Mitch was looking at her questioningly, waiting for her decision. For a brief moment she stared into his blue eyes and wished he wasn't asking about her choice of drink before replying, 'A vodka and tonic please.'

Rosie hadn't quite heard what Jenny's drink was but it looked disgustingly sweet and fizzy. It also came with a straw and an umbrella. Despite herself, this was another good reason not to like Jenny. Rosie shook herself and took a deep breath, giving herself the internal talking-to that she so needed to get her through the rest of the evening. A few more minutes of polite conversation and then she could go. Twenty minutes tops.

But Mitch had other plans. He'd left Jenny talking to some of his colleagues at one of the tables outside. There was one seat left and Rosie thought this might be her way out, surely Mitch would take it so he could sit next to Jenny, and Rosie could hang about awkwardly on the edge of the group for a few minutes and then quickly make her excuses to leave. But Rosie had underestimated Mitch's chivalrous nature that evening.

'Here, Rosie, you sit here next to Jenny.' Mitch hustled some of his colleagues along to make a space for Rosie.

'I should go and say hello to the rest of the gang,' he said, gesticulating deeper into the garden behind him. 'Jen, you'll be OK if I leave you with Rosie for a while, won't you?'

'Of course!' Jenny replied enthusiastically. 'It will give us a chance to get to know each other.'

Rosie shuddered slightly and watched as Mitch leaned in to kiss Jenny.

'I know you two are going to love each other!' he said as he headed off.

Don't bet on it, Rosie thought as she sat down reluctantly next to the smiling Jenny.

Rosie smiled awkwardly back at her. She had had plenty of conversations with Mitch's girlfriends over the years; mostly they seemed to be tearful encounters, with the girl in question begging Rosie's advice on how to keep Mitch interested. Rosie had become adept at managing these; she would be courteous and kind and offer a shoulder to cry on, safe in the knowledge that if it had got to this stage then she would almost certainly never see that girl again.

But she already knew it was different with Jenny. Mitch had told her so and what she had witnessed so far just confirmed it. He was relaxed and attentive around Jenny. Rosie gave her a sideways glance. Now that she was up close she could get a much better look at her and she realised how young Jenny was. Much younger than she had initially thought.

Had Mitch mentioned her age? Rosie didn't think so and she hadn't asked since she had kept her questions about Jenny deliberately limited, hoping it might quash Mitch's enthusiasm. Rosie wasn't surprised. She had long started accepting that Mitch's girlfriends were only going to get younger the older she got. When had that started? Guys her age dating girls in their early or mid-twenties? And did that mean that most men who would be interested in dating her would be in their forties? But Mitch had never been serious about settling down before and Jenny just seemed far too young to be thinking about that anytime soon.

Rosie realised she was staring and quickly picked her drink up from the table, taking a long gulp. Jenny looked at her expectantly.

Oh, Rosie thought to herself, *I've got to be the grown up here.* Reluctantly Rosie began wracking her brain for suitable openers. Suddenly all she could think about was asking Jenny how old she was. But that probably wasn't an acceptable way to start their conversation.

'So,' Rosie eventually started. Jenny looked at her like a puppy waiting for an instruction. 'Do you know this pub?'

'Oh no,' Jenny replied, 'I've never been here before but Mitch said it was somewhere he went a lot and I know it's close to his flat.' She laughed, the words tumbling out of her.

Was she nervous?

'So where do you live?' Rosie grabbing onto a conversation opener.

'I live with my parents,' Jenny replied.

Rosie had to stop herself gaping. She had realised Jenny was young but how young exactly was she to still be living with her parents?

'Oh!' she said out loud, with genuine surprise.

Jenny saw the look on her face, 'Only temporarily, it's just a stopgap. I moved back with them for a few months but I'm house hunting at the moment. There are four of us looking for a place together. Actually, I was hoping my friends might consider somewhere around here,' Jenny said, looking around the pub garden. 'It seems nice and then I'd be closer to Mitch. Unless—' she giggled again '—he asks me to move in with him!' Rosie did her best not to choke on her drink.

'You've known Mitch a while then?' Jenny asked.

'We've been friends for *years*,' Rosie said. 'We used to live together.'

It wasn't strictly necessary to tell Jenny this but Rosie wanted to emphasise just how close she and Mitch were. Hadn't Jenny said she had heard loads about her? Maybe not quite enough, Rosie thought.

Jenny looked suddenly awkward, twisting her hands in her lap, 'But nothing ever happened between you?' she looked up at Rosie shyly, 'I mean, in the romantic sense.'

Rosie paused. Jenny was obviously insecure about her, but it would be wrong to capitalise on that, wouldn't it?

'Nothing you need to worry about,' Rosie said cryptically. She could hear herself talking but no longer seemed to have any control over what she was saying. 'You sound quite serious about him, talking about moving in together.'

'I was joking!' Jenny spluttered. 'I know we've only been together a few weeks.'

'But you're introducing him to your family this weekend?' Rosie said pointedly.

Jenny glared at Rosie, her face beginning to flush. 'It's my dad's birthday, he's having a big party. I asked if Mitch would like to come because I'm fed up of going to those things on my own. So yes, he'll meet my family but it's no big deal. Why?' she carried on. 'Do you have a problem with him meeting my family?'

'No, no of course not,' Rosie replied. 'I was just saying how close you guys seem to be getting and so quickly. I'm really pleased for Mitch, I know how keen he is to settle down. I'm sure he's told you all about it.' Rosie glanced at Jenny trying to gauge her reaction.

'Erm, not really.' Jenny now looked slightly panicked.

'Oh, right,' Rosie replied with a fake look of confusion on her face. 'I just thought he would have told you all about his plans.'

'His plans?' queried Jenny.

Rosie made a split-second decision and before she could stop herself she found herself doing something that she would definitely come to regret, something which definitely wouldn't have been on Mitch's list of acceptable conversation topics for her and Jenny.

'Yeah, Mitch and I have this plan. We've had it for years. To be each other's fallback?' Rosie noticed the look of confusion on Jenny's face.

'Fallback?'

'Yeah, you know. If we don't meet someone by a certain age we'll have kids together. That kind of thing,' she said nonchalantly, feeling anything but nonchalant. Rosie could see a look of horror forming on Jenny's face but she still couldn't stop talking.

'You...you...you've talked about this?' Jenny spluttered incredulously, 'About having kids together?'

Rosie nodded; she knew this was the wrong thing to do. She knew that Mitch would hear about it and it wouldn't end well. And even though she didn't really like Jenny, it went against everything in Rosie's nature to deliberately hurt her – or Mitch – which was what she was obviously doing. But she suddenly had a desperate feeling that she must break Jenny and Mitch up, to keep him for herself at all costs.

Jenny looked like she might cry. 'I...I don't understand,' she faltered.

'Oh, don't worry,' Rosie said smoothly, or as smoothly as she could while slurring her words. 'I don't think he'll need me, now that he's met you.' She put what she imagined was a comforting hand on Jenny's arm. Jenny looked down at it as if Rosie had thrown up on her. 'Now that you and Mitch are together, I'm sure it won't be long before you two are settling down and having babies together.'

Jenny shook her arm free of Rosie's hand, giving her a look of anger and disgust as she stood up from the table quickly.

'Is this seat free?'

Jenny turned to look at Ben who was pointing at her chair.

'Yes, take it,' she said bitterly. 'I think this conversation is over.' And she stormed off.

'What's up with her?' Ben asked as he smoothly sank into the seat.

'No idea,' replied Rosie, trying to ignore the churning sensation in her stomach.

'I have to say,' Ben said, 'I'm surprised that Mitch seems so into her.'

'You are?' Rosie wasn't sure if it was the alcohol talking but she suddenly felt warmer towards Ben than she had ever done before.

'Yeah,' he exclaimed. 'She's too young and really not that interesting.'

It was all Rosie could do not to kiss Ben. But she was also aware that Jenny had found her way over to Mitch on the other side of the beer garden. Through the crowds Rosie could definitely make out a heated exchange taking place between them and some gesticulations in her direction.

'Hey,' she said, grabbing Ben's arm, 'Do you fancy going for a drink somewhere else?'

Ben's eyes lit up, like he couldn't believe his luck. 'Sure! Let me just finish this drink.'

Rosie took the glass out of his hand. 'No,' she said, standing up and putting his glass rather too firmly on the table, 'let's go now.'

Rosie put her hand out for Ben to take and pulled him up out of his seat and in the direction of the exit.

Chapter Sixteen

The pounding in Rosie's head seemed to be getting worse, not only was it now behind her eyes and up inside the base of her skull but it was operating in surround sound, coming at her from all angles.

Blearily, she raised her head and immediately regretted it as the room span around her. Twice now – twice in the last couple of weeks – she had woken up swearing off alcohol with a terrible hangover, although her current state felt closer to death than just a common or garden hangover. What had she been thinking?

Rosie closed her eyes again only to blink them wide open a second later as she realised the pounding wasn't just in her head, it was actually coming from an external source. Her front door. Stumbling for her dressing gown and not daring to look around at the detritus in her bedroom, she gingerly picked her way out of the room and crept down the corridor to the front door of her flat.

'Hello?' she said pressing the button on the intercom and with her other hand steadying herself against the wall.

Just how much had she had to drink last night? She remembered agreeing to another drink with Ben. Then Mitch and

Jenny arriving and her trying to avoid them. But Mitch had tracked her down hadn't he, and left her to get to know Jenny?

Oh, she thought to herself and then *ouch* as her head pounded again.

The memories started flooding back, just as the alcohol she had drunk threatened to come flooding out of her mouth. That conversation, what she had said to Jenny and the way Jenny had immediately sought out Mitch and so Rosie had... What had she done? It was something bad, wasn't it? Something she was going to regret? After that, it had all got a bit blurry.

'Rosie!' barked the intercom.

Rosie could hear the fury in Mitch's voice, coming full throttle at her. She stared at the intercom and groaned, images of last night kept flashing in her mind.

'Er, hi, Mitch.' She tried to sound upbeat.

'Don't even try, Rosie,' he almost growled. 'Don't pretend you don't know why I'm here.' There was a crackle on the line, possibly the sound of Mitch exploding with fury. 'You know perfectly well what I want to talk to you about,' he shouted.

Rosie paused. Should she invite him up? She really, *really* didn't want him in her flat. She looked down at her dressing gown and her slightly shaky hands. But then she didn't want to have this conversation stood on the pavement in her dressing gown, either.

'Are you going to let me up?' he demanded, before she could make a decision about what to do.

Reluctantly, she pressed the buzzer that unlocked the door downstairs. Within seconds he was stood on her doorstep glowering at her.

'Well?' he said. 'What have you got to say for yourself?'

'Mitch,' she said imploringly. 'I really don't know what you're talking about.'

'Right,' he replied. 'I know you were drunk last night but don't try to tell me that you were so drunk that you don't remember the conversation you had with Jenny.'

'I was not *that* drunk,' Rosie replied wearily, forgetting for a moment where this conversation was headed.

'Then you will remember exactly what you said and why I am *furious* with you,' Mitch said in an icy tone. Rosie couldn't think of a decent response. 'How could you?' he hissed. 'What were you thinking?'

Rosie tried to rouse her fighting spirit, which was currently curled up in a corner wishing that alcohol had never been invented. She decided to go for an apology, hoping that might calm Mitch down.

'I'm sorry, Mitch, OK?' she started. 'I don't really think I did anything wrong, though.'

Seeing the fire in Mitch's eyes, she realised that perhaps that caveat wasn't the wisest follow-up to her apology. And it's not like she didn't already know that last night wasn't her finest moment, but still.

'You told her that we were going to have a baby together!' he shouted.

Rosie desperately hoped her neighbours were out. She had managed to be the perfect neighbour for years now, never creating a mess, never making noise. This was going to completely ruin that.

'Why would you do that?' he continued.

'Er, because it's true?' she queried. 'Don't you remember your plan? The one I thought was ridiculous and would all end in tears?' Her fighting spirit was finally putting in an appearance, although its arrival was not helping her headache.

'But you told my new girlfriend!' Mitch was now a worrying shade of red. 'How do you think she felt?'

'I'm not sure, Mitch, but I did think that you might have had a conversation with her about all this, seeing as how you seemed so keen on her. Perhaps it's a good thing she knows how serious you are about settling down, before you got too involved with her!' Rosie was starting to get angry herself now, too.

'It wasn't your job to have that conversation with her, and it's not your decision to make whether I do or not!' Mitch retorted.

'Sorry,' Rosie snapped. 'I just didn't know that it was top secret. Perhaps you should have prepped me before you left me to babysit your new girlfriend!'

Mitch took a breath and stared at her. 'What *exactly* are you saying?' he said in a dangerous new tone.

'What I am saying, Mitch, is that she's a *child*. She's what? All of twenty-two, maybe twenty-three? It's just ridiculous.'

'She's twenty-four, actually,' snapped back Mitch.

'Exactly! She's years younger than us! You talk about wanting to settle down, you talk about being desperate to have children, you come up with some kind of hare-brained scheme that takes absolutely no account of my feelings, and then you introduce me to your new *twenty-four*-year-old girlfriend! Do you remember what we were doing at twenty-four?'

Mitch was silent.

'No!' Rosie shouted. 'Neither do I, but I can assure you that we weren't thinking of getting married and having kids! You're making a fool of yourself, Mitch.'

There was a long silence while they stared at each other. Eventually, Mitch broke the silence. 'I don't think my relationship with Jenny is any of your business, Rosie.'

'What?' she asked incredulously. 'It *is* my business when you drag me into one of your insane plans and then leave me high and dry when a better offer comes along. And anyway, it's OK for you to have all these opinions about who I should date? No, not that one, he has a silly name, no not him he's too well groomed. But it's not OK for me to have the opinion that your new girlfriend *is just too young for you!*'

Mitch stared at her speechlessly.

'She's barely out of uni, Mitch. Think about it. Do you really think she's interested in having kids anytime soon? She looked completely horrified when I brought up the subject.'

'Well maybe you shouldn't have brought it up then?' Mitch shouted back.

A noise in the corridor behind Rosie startled them both. Mitch peered around her.

'Is someone here?' he asked. 'Did you spend the night with someone?' Mitch's tone switched completely from anger to interest.

'What?' Rosie said, that queasy feeling rising up inside her again. 'No, don't be silly, it's just…' but her voice tailed off. There was a reason she didn't want Mitch in her flat, there was a reason she was reluctant to let him in, and Rosie was fairly sure that the reason was still fast asleep on her sofa, or had been, but was now probably wide awake and listening to every word. Something bad was about to happen, something that no amount of explanation would smooth over. And there was absolutely nothing she could do to stop the disaster that was just this moment making its way down the corridor towards them.

'Morning, Mitch!' Ben said with a swagger as he stepped out from behind Rosie and put his arm playfully around her neck. Rosie closed her eyes and shuddered.

Mitch said nothing, just stared at Ben with his mouth wide open. Ben looked from Rosie whose gaze was now fixed on the ground, a blush creeping up her neck and into her cheeks, to Mitch who continued to stare speechlessly.

'Right,' Ben said confidently. 'Well, it sounds like you two are having an interesting discussion. Don't let me interrupt. I'll leave you to it.' He dipped his head to kiss Rosie on the cheek but she flinched and moved away.

'OK, well I'll see you soon,' he said, moving past her and out into the corridor. 'Mitch.' He nodded and walked off. Rosie and Mitch both watched him go.

There was a long silence.

'You spent the night with him?' Mitch eventually said in a strangled voice. 'You spent the night with Ben? *What were you thinking?*'

Rosie said nothing and went back to staring at the ground.

'Seriously Rosie, I don't get it? You hate Ben, you've always hated Ben.'

Rosie continued to stand in silence. She could have told Mitch that it was because she was drunk, because she was lonely, because Mitch had Jenny, because Rosie was running away from the drama she had created and Ben was a useful decoy, because she had wanted to annoy Mitch and this seemed like the best way to do that? None of those excuses seemed like they would help defuse the tension. They all sounded so stupid in the clear light of day, stood in her hallway in her dressing gown, with a hangover. Mitch was right, what had she been thinking?

Rosie shrugged. 'I don't know, Mitch, it just sort of happened.'

'I can't believe you,' Mitch said angrily. 'You lecture me on inappropriate relationships, telling me how Jenny isn't right for me, that she's too young, and all the while you're sleeping with Ben!'

'We're not sleeping together,' Rosie said weakly, wishing she had the strength to explain. Mitch had seen what he had seen and was going to read whatever he wanted into it and she was going to allow him to because she couldn't face telling him the truth.

'Whatever Rosie,' he said scornfully. 'I'm not interested.

Whatever you want to do, that's your business. I really don't understand you anymore. The Rosie I know wouldn't have slept with Ben and she certainly wouldn't have set out to sabotage my relationship.' He glared at her and took a deep breath. 'Look, I am sorry that things didn't work out with Graham, I know you were disappointed. But please don't think that means you can ruin things for me, OK?'

Rosie had never seen him look at her like that before; he had such scorn and distaste in his eyes. He turned around and started walking back down the corridor.

'Mitch, wait,' she called. 'Where are you going?'

Without turning around, he shouted, 'To try and make it up to Jenny, if she will listen.'

'I'm sorry, OK?' Rosie called, desperate for him not to leave on this note.

Mitch turned to look at her one last time, 'No, you're not. For some reason you want to split me and Jenny up, and until you tell me why, I'd rather you just stay away from me.'

Rosie thought of running after him, trying to get him to stay and talk but she didn't have the energy. She watched him walk away without turning back, then she closed her front door, slid down the inside of it and sobbed.

Chapter Seventeen

By the time Rosie dragged herself to work on Monday morning she had cried herself out. Her eyes were swollen and red and she had a constant headache from dehydration. She had spent the weekend calling and texting Mitch, who never replied, and avoiding calls from Ben. Every time his name flashed up, she shuddered.

Rosie was grateful that she had a day planned in the lab on Monday. Rachel had made it quite clear that she wanted to see some results on the BioChem project soon and Rosie had put her off but she knew she could only do that for so long. Rachel was not the sort of person to take heartbreak as a legitimate excuse. Rosie thought it might be touch and go as to whether Rachel would take heart *failure* as a legitimate excuse.

Once Rosie had her lab coat and safety goggles on, perhaps no one would notice she had been crying and she might even manage to go the whole day without speaking to anyone. The only person she wanted to speak to was Mitch. Every time she replayed Saturday morning, she felt sick. She had never seen him so angry, especially not with her. Of course they had had fights over the years, but the fights were about whose turn it was to do the washing up, or which one of them had forgotten to book a restaurant table. Not about ruining each other's relationships.

Rosie tried to make herself smile when she recalled one of those more recent fights. Mitch had had a promotion at work and wanted to go out to celebrate. He had booked them a table at a restaurant he had been going on about for weeks; it had been described as London's culinary event of the year and had a waitlist of months. But Mitch being Mitch, he had managed to get them a booking, or he thought he had.

THEN

Mitch looked down at his phone in confusion. The hostess looked like she was about to lose her patience with him which was an unusual situation for Mitch to find himself in.

'Are you sure you don't have us down on your list?' he asked once again. 'Because look,' he held his phone up to her, 'I've got the email right here.'

The hostess politely smiled at the people in the queue behind Rosie and Mitch. Her smile said, 'please excuse the delay while I deal with these morons, I will have them killed later'. Rosie shuddered slightly, she hated making a scene, she'd much rather have just left and found somewhere else to eat. But Mitch was determined.

The hostess leaned forward to study Mitch's phone and then took it from him – with one hand she swiped at the screen, with the other made a small but important adjustment to her asymmetrical bob. Without thinking, Rosie's hand went to her hair, too, subconsciously wondering what she would look like with half her head shaved. Definitely not as hot as this hostess, that was for sure.

A small smirk played on the girl's lips. 'Sir,' she said, 'your reservation is for *next year.*'

'What?' exclaimed Mitch, grabbing the phone back from her.

Rosie caught the girl's eye and tried not to laugh. Seeing Mitch flummoxed like this was both hilarious and adorable. He ran his hand through his hair in a state of distressed confusion.

'Would you mind stepping to the side so I can seat people who have a reservation for *this* year?' she asked somewhat snarkily.

Rosie grabbed Mitch's arm. 'Come on,' she whispered, 'let's get out of here.'

Mitch allowed himself to be pulled out onto Dean Street and by the time the cold night air hit him he had regained his composure and mustered his ire.

'Why didn't you check?'

'I'm sorry, what?' Rosie asked turning in surprise.

'I sent you the confirmation email. Why didn't you check the year?'

Rosie laughed, thinking he was joking before quickly realising he wasn't. 'Mitch? Seriously? I read the date and put it in my diary, I didn't check the *year!*'

'Well, you should have done,' he said mutinously and turned to look in the direction of Soho Square.

Rosie wished, not for the first time, that she could read his mind. It was just dinner. Yes, it was to celebrate his promotion but, really, did it matter? It was the two of them, why did it matter where they celebrated?

'Mitch?' Rosie put a hand on his arm. He jerked it away and continued to ignore her. 'Come on,' she nudged him gently. 'At least we know where we'll be in a year's time?'

Her attempt to make a joke seemed to thaw him a little.

'I just wanted tonight to be special,' he said, continuing to stare in the opposite direction from Rosie but his body language was softening.

'I know,' Rosie said consolingly, putting her hand back on his arm. 'But we can celebrate anywhere. Come on, let's go find somewhere for a drink.'

Mitch allowed himself to be pulled towards Oxford Street. 'I'm sorry, Rosie,' he said taking her hand. 'I just had other plans for tonight, I really wanted to take you somewhere special.'

That fight had been ridiculous yet brief, and they had made up over drinks and burgers in a grotty pub the other side of Oxford Street where the draft beer was so undrinkable Mitch had relented for once and drunk wine with Rosie. Afterwards, as they wandered the streets of Soho laughing, they had both admitted that they had probably had far more fun drinking in the pub than they would have had in a stuffy, upmarket restaurant.

NOW

Rosie felt her eyes welling up as she recalled telling Mitch that they would be back at that restaurant in a year's time. It was probably almost a year since then and Rosie didn't dare to hope that Mitch would remember and invite her. He'd probably take Jenny, she thought bitterly. In fact, Rosie wondered whether Mitch would ever forgive her enough to spend even just an evening in a grotty pub with her again.

Rosie's safety goggles were now misted up and with her lab gloves on she was finding it hard to remove them to wipe her eyes, so her tears collected on the bottom rim of her goggles and the fog began rising higher and higher. It was a good thing no one was there to witness the state she was in.

Usually, Rosie managed to lose herself in the lab, concentrating carefully on each of her actions, the focus being so intense to ensure that no mistakes were made. But that morning she found herself repeating standard steps as she forgot to keep track of where she was in the process. By lunch she had only managed a tiny portion of what she needed to get done and Rachel was not going to be pleased. Frustrated, Rosie shrugged off her lab coat and safety equipment and went to shut herself away in her office.

The light on her office phone was flashing, alerting her to an answerphone message which she knew she ought to listen to, but she really *really* couldn't be bothered. Instead, she put her head down on her desk, always grateful that she had the space to do so, unlike Nadia, who would presumably have to put her head down on a pile of lab reports – if she ever allowed herself to get into the kind of state where she would need to stick her head down on her desk and ignore the world, which Rosie doubted.

Rosie closed her eyes only for her office phone to immediately begin ringing. Without lifting her head, she pulled the receiver to her ear and gingerly balanced it there. She said nothing, hoping that perhaps it was a spam call. Eventually a voice on the other end spoke.

'Hello? Rosie? Are you there?'

Rosie sat upright. Her brother never rang her, he certainly never rang her at *work*. She couldn't remember the last time she had actually *spoken* to him on the phone. They'd occasionally exchange brief text messages to discuss practicalities but most of their mutual plans were arranged between Rosie and Jasmine. Jasmine's name elicited a jolt of guilt in Rosie. She'd read her messages, she knew Jasmine wanted to talk but Rosie hadn't called her back. still hadn't returned her messages.

'Chris?' she said, 'Is everything alright?'

In a split second Rosie had run through all the awful possibilities in her mind: her mother was hurt, one of the kids had been in an accident – she even considered briefly that something had happened to their dad and that for some strange reason, her and Chris were being alerted as next of kin.

'Rosie, where have you been? I've been trying to reach you.'

Rosie looked at her watch. 'I've been in the lab, Chris, you know I can't take my phone in there.'

'For twenty-four hours?' Chris asked incredulously. 'You've been in the lab for twenty-four hours?'

Rosie reached for her mobile and remembered that not only had she been ignoring Jasmine's messages, but that yesterday she'd missed some calls from an unknown number, which, given Chris' tone was probably their landline, and she didn't have that saved because who actually used a landline anymore? Thinking about all the reasons he could be calling, Rosie suddenly felt terrible for passing judgement on the landline, but not as terrible as she felt for ignoring the calls.

'Chris, what's happened?' she asked again.

Chris sighed, 'I'm at the hospital, Rosie. No, no...' he said as she tried to interrupt him, 'it's not the kids and it's not Mum. It's Jasmine.'

'Jasmine? What's wrong?' Rosie felt a sense of ominous dread seep through her, made worse by the fact she knew she had been ignoring Jasmine.

'She had a miscarriage yesterday,' Chris replied, a catch in his throat. Rosie knew him well enough to realise that he was trying not to cry.

'A miscarriage?' Rosie asked in confusion. 'But...but I didn't even know she was pregnant?'

'Well, that is a long story,' he sighed, 'and I'm sure she'll tell you it at some point. But I thought you would want to know.' Chris paused. 'Rosie, she's really not in a good way. The doctors say she'll be fine physically, but she seems really fragile. Rosie, I don't know how to help her.' His voice went deep and muffled and Rosie just knew that he was crying properly now.

'Oh, Chris. I'm so sorry. What can I do? Can I come get the kids?'

'No, it's fine, Mum's looking after them. She's been great.'

Rosie knew he didn't mean to compare them, but she was already feeling terrible about not helping out. Not even answering the phone because she was too busy crying over Mitch.

'I'll come to the hospital,' she said firmly, keen to be doing something. 'Which one is it?'

Chris gave her the name and then stopped. 'But Rosie, I don't know what's happened between you two but she's said she doesn't want to see you right now.'

Rosie made a small noise as a strangled sob and gasp escaped her.

'She's really tired, Rosie and she's very upset. I'm sure it's just a combination of the two.' Chris said consolingly, Rosie knew that she should have been the one consoling him. She found herself vigorously nodding, hoping that Chris was right and that Jasmine's refusal to see her had nothing to do with the fact Rosie hadn't returned her calls.

'Look,' he said in a comforting tone, 'we should be allowed home tonight. Give her some time to recover and then let's see if you can come and visit in a few days?'

Rosie barely trusted herself to speak. 'OK,' she said in a small voice. 'Can you let me know when you're home?'

'Yes, of course,' Chris agreed.

'And Chris?' Rosie asked. 'I'm really sorry about not being there.'

'It's fine Rosie, OK? I'm sure you don't believe me but I do remember what weekends were like when you're single and don't have kids. I'm sure you had better things to do than keep tabs on your phone. But next time, if you get two missed calls from us, can we agree that you'll consider it serious enough to call us back?'

Weakly, Rosie nodded, before remembering she was on the phone and whispered, 'Yes.' Chris's interpretation of what her weekend had been like was so far removed from the reality that she felt disorientated. She hadn't been off having fun, living her best single life and all that; when Jasmine had been lying in the hospital Rosie was too busy feeling sorry for herself over her fight with Mitch that she hadn't even bothered to answer the phone. She put down the receiver and put her head back down on her desk. The report that Rachel was desperate for Rosie to send to the execs at BioChem would just have to wait.

––––––––––––

Late that night, Chris messaged Rosie to tell her they were home. Jasmine was still very tired and had gone to bed, he said. He promised to keep her updated. Rosie had spent the afternoon in constant contact with her mother who was too busy being run ragged by her grandchildren to engage in any discussion about why Rosie had not been in touch or even whether either of them had known about Jasmine's pregnancy.

Rosie couldn't sleep that night. Her mind whirled with thoughts of Jasmine and what she had been going through. She felt so guilty that she hadn't spoken to her properly in ages. Jasmine had obviously been trying to talk to her, but Rosie had been so caught up in her own drama with Mitch that she hadn't made time to call her back.

At least all this had put him from her mind, she thought wryly to herself as she turned her pillow yet again in an attempt to drift off. Rosie knew that at some point she would have to work out what to do about Mitch, but for the moment she needed to focus on Jasmine and Chris and what they needed. Finally, she fell asleep, certain of what she should do in the morning.

———————

Rosie woke early, her mind surprisingly sharp and focused given the amount of sleep she hadn't had. It was a little after eight-thirty when she rang the doorbell at Jasmine and Chris's house. Rosie wasn't sure whether her mother had stayed, but knowing Susan, she had left soon after Chris and Jasmine returned from the hospital, sensitive about giving them their space. And it was very likely that Chris had taken the boys to school and would be out when she arrived. Part of her felt guilty about surprising Jasmine like this, and she promised herself that should Jasmine tell her to leave she would do so without complaint. But Rosie felt she had to see her, had to apologise and to try to make it up to her. And Chris had said maybe in a few days, hadn't he? Did the next day count as a few?

Rosie stood on the doorstep for quite some time. All was quiet behind the front door. She was just starting to think about putting the flowers she had brought on the doorstep and leaving when she heard the latch click. The door swung open and Jasmine stood in the doorway wearing her pajamas and looking pale and drawn. For a moment neither of them said anything until finally Rosie held out the flowers she was carrying and asked:

'Can I come in?'

Jasmine looked at Rosie but said nothing. She let the door fall open and stood to the side to let Rosie through. Stepping into the hallway, Rosie couldn't help but notice the silence in the house. She was so used to being here when the family was there, amid all the mayhem that wrought. Jasmine waved her hand at the coat rack, indicating that Rosie should hang hers up. Carefully Rosie closed the door behind her, shrugged off her coat and then stood facing Jasmine.

'Jasmine,' Rosie started, 'I'm so *so* sorry.'

Jasmine didn't say anything, just continued to stare at Rosie. 'You've been ignoring me,' she eventually said in an uncharacteristically quiet voice.

'It's not like that,' said Rosie before realising that actually, it was *exactly* like that. 'Can I give you a hug?' she asked tentatively. Jasmine raised her shoulders noncommittally and although she didn't hug back she allowed Rosie to wrap her arms around her as they stood awkwardly in the hallway. After a moment Rosie stepped back and looked at Jasmine.

'Can I make you tea?' Rosie asked. 'You should come and sit down.' Jasmine allowed herself to be led into the sitting room. Once again Rosie wished they had one of those sofas that enveloped you, rather than the hip achingly modern one which made you feel guilty about sitting on it for too long.

'I'll be right back,' Rosie said, leaving Jasmine sat with her legs curled up under her staring at the wall opposite.

Rosie knew her way around their kitchen. She busied herself with making tea, Jasmine probably wouldn't care right now how it was made but Rosie knew how picky she normally was. Carefully, she carried the mugs back into the sitting room and placed one on the coffee table in front of Jasmine. For a moment Rosie wondered where to sit, Jasmine hadn't exactly welcomed her in but it seemed too awkward to take a chair on the opposite side of the room. Gingerly, she sat on the sofa a little way away from Jasmine, clutching her mug.

'I'm so sorry,' Rosie said again. 'For everything,' she continued. 'I've been a rubbish friend, a terrible sister-in-law. I should have known something was wrong.'

Jasmine continued to stare ahead without saying anything. After a moment's silence, Rosie started again.

'I've been so caught up in my own world that I wasn't there for you when you needed me. Jasmine, I'm so sorry. Is there anything I can do?' she pleaded.

Eventually, Jasmine sighed and reached forward for her tea. 'I know,' she said, still not looking at Rosie. 'I know you've been busy and I know you've got a lot to think about with Mitch and everything.' Rosie felt herself shiver involuntarily. 'But I don't think you stopped for a minute to think that you're not the only one with things going on in their life.'

Rosie stared ahead. It wasn't going to be comfortable listening to what Jasmine had to say, but maybe she was right and maybe Rosie needed to hear some home truths.

'You're so caught up in your own world at the moment, it's been all you can talk about – Mitch, dating...' Jasmine paused. 'It's not like I don't care, Rosie, and of *course* I'm interested but to be honest it's all been about you. When was the last time you asked me a question about my life?' Jasmine looked at Rosie, who tried to meet her eye. 'You act as if just because I've got Chris and the kids, it's OK to ignore me. But things might not be as perfect as you *seem* to think, and you *never* bother to ask.' Jasmine sounded bitter and close to tears.

'You're right. I do think your life is perfect.' Rosie waved her arm around the immaculate living room. 'You always seem to have everything so sorted: gorgeous kids, a successful career, beautiful house...' She paused, wondering whether to risk a joke. 'Husband might be the weak link if you don't mind me saying.'

Luckily, Jasmine smiled wryly. 'He's not so bad,' she said, finally, 'especially after what I've put him through.'

Rosie warned herself to tread warily, she didn't want to push her luck and ask outright what was going on, but she saw an opening in what Jasmine had said, a softening towards her, perhaps a desire to talk.

'Do you want to talk about it?' she ventured.

Jasmine gripped her mug tighter and seem to shrink in on herself a little. Rosie reached over and rubbed her arm. Jasmine didn't flinch, which was a good start.

'We'd been fighting,' Jasmine eventually said. Rosie kept her hand on Jasmine's arm but said nothing. 'Not constantly, but on and off for a while.'

Rosie let the silence lie for a minute and then asked, 'Was it about anything in particular?' Jasmine said nothing. 'Or just lots of different things?'

Jasmine turned to look at her, her eyes filled with tears, 'It was always the same thing,' she said in a thick voice. 'I wanted another baby, and Chris, well, Chris didn't.'

For a moment Rosie didn't know what to say, she had never imagined Chris and Jasmine having a fight, they seemed so calm and civilised all the time. And she certainly had never thought that Jasmine would want another baby; two children had always seemed like their plan. But then she realised that she had never asked them what their plan was, she had just presumed.

'Oh, Jas. I'm sorry, I never realised you wanted another baby.'

Jasmine put her mug down and pulled a crumpled wad of tissues out of her pocket and wiped her nose on them.

'I never thought I would, either. Two was always my plan. But then Rory turned three and my plan didn't seem to work anymore.'

'Hang on,' said Rosie. 'Rory turned three two years ago. You mean you've been feeling this way for two years?' Jasmine nodded miserably.

'Jasmine,' Rosie said and scooted closer to her on the sofa, putting her arm around Jasmine's shoulders. 'When did you tell Chris this?' she asked.

'Two years ago,' Jasmine said through her soggy tissues.

'Two years!' exclaimed Rosie, 'You've been fighting about this for two years?'

'Not at first, it started out as a bit of a joke. I would just refer to it every time someone made a comment about how big Rory was getting, or when he passed certain milestones. But the more I tried to make it a joke the more I became certain I wanted another baby.'

'And Chris didn't?' Rosie questioned.

Jasmine shook her head. 'Definitely not,' she said. 'He said we had always discussed two, we'd just got past the nappy stage, life was getting easier, if we had another one we would have to move, get a new car.' She sighed. 'All the usual things people say when they're trying to talk themselves out of having another baby.'

Jasmine pulled her knees up to her chest. 'He told me to be practical, that he was used to me being the rational one. But the problem is that there's nothing rational about wanting a baby and he just didn't understand that.'

She began sobbing and laid her head down in Rosie's lap. Rosie stroked her hair and felt her own heart tug. It wasn't the same, but Rosie could empathise. Jasmine was right, there was nothing logical or practical about wanting babies or not wanting babies. It was the most illogical thing in the world when you thought about it, yet people did it all the time.

'I'm so sorry, Jas,' Rosie said again. 'He's such an idiot.'

Jasmine jerked away, sitting up. 'No, he's not!' she said vehemently. 'He's right, it *is* impractical, it *isn't* rational and life *was* getting easier. We had always planned on two, so what gives me the right to throw a spanner in our plans and change that?'

Rosie let her arm fall back into her lap. 'I just meant that I would have hoped Chris would have been more supportive and more understanding.'

'He was, Rosie,' Jasmine said adamantly, 'but he was also sure that he didn't want another baby. And one of us was going to lose that fight.'

Rosie sat and stared at her now cold cup of tea. She didn't know what to say. Jasmine was right, either she or Chris were going to lose this fight, and neither one had the right to force the other to live their life in a different way. Rosie looked at all the beautifully framed photographs on the shelves and mantelpiece opposite her, each one of them a testament to the life that Chris and Jasmine had created together. There were newborn photos of Rory and Joe, first day of school photos, family holidays and other occasions. In every one of them they were all smiling. From the outside they had seemed so happy.

Rosie couldn't imagine what life had been like for the last two years for Jasmine or for Chris; both of them knowing that the more they dug their heels in, the unhappier they were making the other. It made Rosie think about her own choices. All she wanted was for Mitch to be happy, and if Jenny made him happy then maybe she had to swallow her own misery and be happy for him. Even if that meant giving up on the idea of having a baby – a baby she hadn't even thought she wanted until a few weeks ago. She just needed to get him to talk to her again. She could live without the romance, but she didn't think she could live without his friendship.

Rosie was aware Jasmine was looking at her, expecting her to say something. 'So, aren't you going to ask me?' Jasmine said.

'Ask you what?' Rosie replied, suddenly conscious that once again she was thinking of Mitch and not of her grieving friend.

'What happened,' Jasmine said flatly. 'How we got from

fighting about another baby to losing this one?' Fresh tears began to run down her cheeks.

'Right,' said Rosie, realising that so far she only had half the story. 'So, what happened?'

'A few months back I had a stomach bug,' Jasmine started.

'I remember!' exclaimed Rosie. 'We were supposed to be going to the new exhibition at the Royal Academy and you had to cancel.'

'Yep, well it turns out that even after twenty years of careful birth control I still forgot that being ill might make the pill less effective. And then...' she paused, 'then I discovered a few weeks later that I was pregnant.'

Rosie felt her heart contract. Poor Jasmine. After all that debate with Chris, to then get pregnant by mistake. Jasmine turned to her with an earnest expression on her face.

'It was an accident, Rosie, honestly.' She grabbed Rosie hands and gripped them tightly.

'Of course,' Rosie said with confusion, feeling she was missing something.

'It's just...' Jasmine paused. 'I'm not sure Chris completely believes me.'

Rosie's stomach sank. Right, because it would be all too easy for it not to have been an accident. She looked at Jasmine's desperate face and believed her with absolute certainty.

'Jas, I believe you and I'm sure Chris does, too.'

Jasmine shook her head sadly. 'He's never said anything and I don't think he ever would, but I'm sure he sometimes wonders.'

Rosie thought of her brother; his honesty and openness had always been an essential part of his character, but even so, after such a lengthy and bitter argument, Rosie could imagine that there might be some small part of him that every so often questioned whether the stomach bug was entirely responsible.

'What did he say when you found out you were pregnant?' Rosie ventured.

'I didn't tell him at first.' Jasmine's voice quavered. 'I was so worried that he would think I had done it deliberately, but then of course it looked like I hadn't told him because I wanted us to have less time to make an alternative decision.'

She clenched and unclenched her hands in her lap. 'But when I did finally tell him he was lovely,' she said earnestly, looking at Rosie, desperate for her not to think ill of Chris. 'He said it was a surprise, of course, but that we would make the best of it.'

'Jas, I'm sure he doesn't think it was deliberate.'

'I don't know,' sighed Jasmine. 'Wouldn't you, though? Just a small part of you?' Rosie said nothing. She knew what Jasmine meant.

'And now of course there's nothing left to fight over, anyway.' Jasmine's face contorted as a fresh wave of grief hit her. Rosie caught her in her arms and shushed her. 'And I can't help feeling angry at Chris, even after everything,' Jasmine admitted. Rosie tried to catch up with Jasmine's thought process.

'What do you mean?' Rosie asked carefully.

'That he never wanted the baby, anyway and now he's got his own way. And that makes me a terrible person because of course it's not his fault!' she wailed.

'You're grieving,' Rosie said firmly. 'It's OK to feel all sorts of terrible things but you're right, it's not Chris's fault. It's not anyone's fault.' She squeezed Jasmine tight. 'And when I spoke to Chris he sounded devastated. I know he's grieving as well, even if having another baby wasn't something he had planned.'

Jasmine put her head on Rosie's shoulder and nodded. 'I know,' she said softly, 'I know he is.'

They sat side by side in silence for a while. The house still felt empty to Rosie without Rory and Joe racing about. Their absence seemed even more noticeable when she considered the reason she was sat with Jasmine on the sofa.

'I'm a bit jealous of you, you know,' Jasmine eventually said.

Rosie edged away in surprise. 'Of me? Why?'

'Because you've got all the baby years ahead of you.'

Rosie grimaced. 'I wouldn't be so sure of that,' she said darkly. 'I'd have to find someone who wanted to have babies with me first. And I'd want to be sure I wanted them, too,' she followed up swiftly.

'What about Mitch?' Jasmine looked at her. 'What's the latest on your plan? Have you discussed it again?'

Rosie leaned forward and pretended to be considering drinking the cold tea. The milk had gone filmy on top which made her feel a bit sick. She couldn't bring herself to drink it even if it meant she couldn't hide from Jasmine behind her mug.

'Shall I make us another tea?' she suggested, holding her mug up at Jasmine. Jasmine frowned at her.

'Anyone would think you were avoiding my question,' she said sternly.

'Hmm, yeah, well maybe I am,' Rosie admitted. 'It's complicated.'

'Complicated how?' asked Jasmine, 'You and Mitch have always been able to talk about things.'

'Yeah, well maybe this was something we should never have discussed in the first place,' said Rosie tautly. 'It's tricky.'

'Go on, then,' said Jasmine, reaching forward and passing her cup to Rosie. 'You can make me another tea but only because I didn't drink the last one. And don't think that we won't be discussing Mitch as soon as you're back.'

Reluctantly Rosie took the cup from Jasmine. Now that it was no longer a means of avoidance, she had lost her desire for one.

But if Jasmine wanted a tea she would make her a cup. Rosie felt it was the least she could do for her poor friend.

'Be right back,' she said as she made her way through into the kitchen.

Rosie was reaching into the cupboard to find the tea bags when she heard Jasmine behind her say, 'I felt like a change of scenery.'

'You made me jump!' Rosie said accusingly, turning to see Jasmine sat on a bar stool staring at her.

'I've been sat on that sofa most of the night, at least if I'm sat in here when Chris gets back, he might worry less.'

Rosie looked at her watch. 'When will he be back?' she asked, suddenly aware that although she and Jasmine might be finding their way back to an even keel, her brother might not take too kindly to finding that Rosie had taken the morning off, and was in his house when he had specifically asked her to give Jasmine some space.

'Not for a while,' Jasmine answered. 'I told him to go to the shops after he had dropped the boys off. I wanted some space. No, no it's fine,' she said as Rosie began to apologise for her presence. 'It will do him good, he's been cooped up at the hospital and then fussing around after me. And besides, you make better tea than he does,' she added, as Rosie pushed a fresh mug across the island at her.

'Well, that's true,' said Rosie smiling at the thought of Jasmine, despite everything, still refusing to drink the weak tea that Chris always made.

'So,' said Jasmine. 'Mitch.'

Rosie leaned against the island across from her and pulled a face.

'Bad?' said Jasmine in response.

'Very bad,' said Rosie nodding.

'Ok bring me up to speed. I'll stop you when you become too self-involved, OK?'

Rosie smiled. 'I'm not sure where to start,' she said, taking a sip of her tea and wincing at the heat.

'Well,' said Jasmine, 'the last I heard you had accepted his proposal. So what happened? Did you change your mind?' Rosie shook her head. 'Did he?' asked Jasmine in surprise.

'Yes I suppose he did,' Rosie said sadly, 'in a manner of speaking.' Jasmine looked at her quizzically. 'And if he hadn't been having second thoughts before, then he certainly will be having them now.'

'OK,' said Jasmine firmly, 'you need to explain, I don't follow.'

'He's got himself a new girlfriend,' Rosie began. 'Jenny.' She hated herself for the tone of scorn she had poured into the poor girl's name.

'Oh,' Jasmine pulled a face. 'Well, what's new? I suppose that gets you off the hook, though, doesn't it? I mean you weren't keen on the whole thing to start with.'

Rosie put her head in her hands. 'No, well I wasn't. But then it got me thinking.' Rosie moved her hands and stared down at her tea instead, thinking about Mitch and about how quickly this disaster had enveloped them. She picked up her cup and took a sip of her tea and then took a deep breath.

'I started to think that maybe I did want a baby. And that maybe Mitch wasn't a bad choice for me to have a baby with.' Rosie looked up and saw the look of surprise on Jasmine's face. Perhaps this was enough honesty for one day. 'In the absence of an alternative father!' she said quickly.

Jasmine leaned back on her bar stool. 'Well, I wouldn't worry too much about it,' she started. 'Mitch always has a new girlfriend and they never last so I expect your plan will be back on before long.'

Jasmine looked at Rosie. 'Oh. Is this one different?' Rosie nodded slowly. 'Right, I see,' said Jasmine. 'What's she like?'

Rosie shrugged. 'Small, blonde, petite. Complete opposite of me.' Jasmine looked at her curiously.

'Oh and she hates me,' blurted Rosie. Jasmine looked surprised.

'Hates you? Why?' She took a sip of her tea. 'She's not one of those possessive jealous girlfriends, is she? She'll never last with Mitch if that's the case, don't worry.'

'No, it's not that,' said Rosie, fiddling with the rings on her fingers awkwardly. 'I might have done something to make her hate me,' she said slowly.

Jasmine moved from looking surprised to downright startled. 'People never hate you!' she said adamantly. 'What happened?'

Rosie braced herself against the island. 'I may have told her about mine and Mitch's plan.'

Jasmine was trying to suppress a smile. 'Yeah, I guess that might put her off you.' She picked up her tea again struggling not to laugh.

'And I might have told her that Mitch was desperate to settle down and have kids.' Rosie looked sheepishly at Jasmine, who could no longer contain herself and let out a loud cackle of laughter.

'Oh, Rosie, that's brilliant. How old is this girl?'

Rosie shook her head. 'Twenty-four?'

Jasmine laughed again. 'When did this happen?' she asked.

'Friday night,' Rosie replied. 'In the pub. With all of Mitch's colleagues there.'

A moment of dawning realisation came over Jasmine's face.

'Does Mitch know?'

'Yes, he arrived at my flat on Saturday morning and we had a massive row about it all.'

'And that's why you were MIA all weekend?' said Jasmine. Rosie nodded her head sadly.

'I'm so sorry about that, Jas.'

Jasmine waved her hand away, 'It's forgiven, you're starting to make up for it with this story.' Rosie's eyes started to well up.

'It's not funny, Jas,' she protested.

'Oh, Rosie I'm sorry, I didn't mean to make fun of you. But really, I don't think you need to worry, Mitch will come round.'

'I don't know,' said Rosie, 'it's a bit more complicated than that. He was really angry with me and…and I might have taken Ben, one of Mitch's colleagues, home with me on Friday night.'

Jasmine's eyes lit up. 'Good for you! But why should Mitch care?'

'Because he hates Ben. And I wasn't so keen on him, either.'

Jasmine looked baffled. 'So why did you…?'

Rosie sighed. 'I don't know. I was drunk. I was angry at Mitch and I thought this would be a good way of getting back at him.'

'And now?' asked Jasmine.

'Now I think it was stupid, because I don't want to see Ben again and it didn't get back at Mitch, it's just made him more angry with me than before. I didn't sleep with Ben!' Rosie clarified. 'Nothing actually happened. He needed somewhere to stay and I let him spend the night, that's all.'

Jasmine was looking at her curiously. 'I don't think it matters if you did sleep with him,' she said. 'But I *am* wondering why you wanted to get back at Mitch? I know you've got this plan with him but you didn't seem so invested in it before. It seems strange to me you should be so angry with Mitch for getting a new girlfriend.' Jasmine paused. 'Unless there's something I'm missing?'

There was a long silence.

'You can tell me anything Rosie, you know that,' Jasmine said earnestly.

Rosie turned away from her and looked out into the garden, immaculate as always, despite the autumnal gloom.

'I think,' Rosie began turning quickly back around, 'to be honest Jas...' Rosie took a deep breath getting herself ready to rip the plaster off.

'Go on,' encouraged Jasmine.

'Maybe I'm a little bit in love with Mitch,' Rosie blurted out, her face flushing dramatically.

Jasmine's face remained unreadable, and breathing hard, Rosie then stared down at the beautifully smooth marble surface of the kitchen island. She could hear the clock ticking in the hallway, cars hooting on the main road, and somewhere at a distance a siren set up a wail. But inside the kitchen, everything was silent. Eventually, realising that Jasmine still hadn't acknowledged her outburst, Rosie looked up.

'Well?' she asked. 'Aren't you going to say anything?'

'I'm not going to lie and pretend this is a surprise,' Jasmine eventually said, coolly.

'What?' exclaimed Rosie, 'I've never said anything before.'

'You didn't need to. I always wondered whether there was something between the two of you,' Jasmine said. 'I mean, you've always been so close and I thought there might be something more.'

'Well, there isn't,' Rosie said indignantly. 'Not on his part, anyway.'

'Really?' said Jasmine.

'No!' exploded Rosie. 'Really, no. You didn't see him Jasmine, he was so angry at me for ruining things with Jenny.'

'Maybe,' shrugged Jasmine. 'Or maybe he's desperately been

trying to put you from his mind and is mad because he's realised his latest girlfriend isn't going to do the trick.'

'I think you're reading too much into this,' Rosie said flatly. 'If he did have feelings for me, why hasn't he said anything before now?'

'Like you have, you mean?' said Jasmine, half laughing.

Rosie crossed her arms across her chest and scowled at her.

'Look,' Jasmine said, 'maybe I'm wrong, it's not like I've been single for a long time. But it does seem to me that you two are as close as two people can be without sleeping together. Neither of you has had a successful relationship since you've been friends. And this plan of yours has thrown up all sorts of complicated feelings for both of you that have resulted in this fall out.' Jasmine held her hands up as Rosie continued to frown at her. 'Like I say, maybe I'm wrong. I mean it's not like anything has ever happened between the two of you. Oh!' Jasmine exclaimed, seeing the change in expression on Rosie's face. 'It has! It totally has! When? How? Why am I only hearing about this now?!'

Rosie looked uncomfortable. 'It was ages ago. Right when we first moved in together.' She said nothing more.

'And?' pressed Jasmine. 'You have to tell me everything now!'

'Honestly it was nothing, almost nothing,' she said. 'We kissed. Once,' she added firmly.

'That's it?' said Jasmine, with disappointment.

'That's it,' confirmed Rosie.

'Nothing else?' Jasmine queried.

'Nothing else,' Rosie confirmed again and then realising that Jasmine was going to keep questioning her she continued, 'We'd been out, we were both drunk, we ended up kissing. I thought it was probably a bad idea to be kissing my new housemate, but in the end, he fell asleep anyway and I went to bed. The next day he pretended nothing had happened and we've never mentioned it since.'

'Never?' said Jasmine in disbelief.

Rosie shook her head. 'Never,' she said. 'He obviously either completely regretted it and decided not to mention it, or he was so drunk he didn't remember it.'

'Or,' proposed Jasmine, 'the fact *you* never mentioned it made him think you weren't interested.'

Rosie raised an eyebrow at Jasmine. 'I don't think so,' she said firmly.

There was a long silence. 'Oh, maybe you're right.' Jasmine looked thoughtful. 'I know this won't be what you want to hear, but given how close you two are, I'd have thought he might have tried it on with you again before now, if he was really interested.'

Rosie felt the sting of Jasmine's assessment. She was right, of course, and Rosie had thought the same thing in the past, but it still hurt to hear Jasmine say it out loud. They both drank the rest of their tea in silence, Rosie wondering how many more people she was going to confess her feelings about Mitch to in the next few days. At this rate she might as well tell him, too.

'I'm sorry, Rosie, this really sucks. I wish I could wave a magic wand and make you meet someone amazing to take your mind off him.'

'Yeah, me, too,' Rosie replied. 'Where's your magic wand when you need it?'

There was a long pause.

'When he first proposed it, Nadia suggested I go ahead with the plan anyway, although she doesn't know the latest drama.'

'Nadia knows?' Jasmine said in rather a high-pitched voice. Rosie looked awkward, she knew Jasmine wouldn't take kindly to Nadia knowing Rosie's secrets, especially not before Jasmine knew them.

'Yes, she knew about our plan,' Rosie said carefully.

'Did she know about you being in love with him?' demanded Jasmine.

'Well, yes, but she guessed, I didn't actually tell her,' Rosie protested. 'She doesn't know about our argument, though!' she added, eagerly, keen to give Jasmine an exclusive on one part of the story.

Jasmine looked huffily at Rosie, 'Fine, but I'm not sure why you would tell her before you told me,' she said sulkily.

Rosie laughed. 'Jas, you sound like a child. Honestly it doesn't matter who knew what before whom. I'm asking for *your* advice now, not Nadia's.'

'Well, OK,' Jasmine said reluctantly. 'I think we need to get you over Mitch and on with your life. You know what they say about getting over someone...'

Rosie rolled her eyes. 'Jasmine! I can't even find someone I want to go on a date with, let alone find someone who will replace Mitch. I just want him back in my life as a friend, Jas. That's all I'm asking for.'

'Hmm, devil's advocate here, but I'm not sure that's the best option. I don't think you're going to get on with your life if he's still in it.'

Rosie felt herself go cold. This definitely wasn't what she wanted to hear. Where was Nadia and her loopy theories when you needed her?

Jasmine reached across the island to squeeze Rosie's hand. 'We'll work this out, don't worry.'

They heard the door click and seconds later Chris walked into the kitchen holding a small shopping bag. Rosie glanced at her watch and then back at the small bag Chris was holding and came to the conclusion that given the amount of time he had been gone he had managed to do very little shopping.

'Rosie,' he said as he bent to kiss the top of Jasmine's head. 'I wasn't expecting you.' He eyed her and his wife warily, unsure of what he had walked in on.

Jasmine twisted and squeezed his arm. 'It's OK,' she reassured him, 'Rosie came to see how I was. I'm pleased she did,' she said and smiled across at Rosie.

Rosie smiled back. 'But I should get going and leave you to rest.'

Rosie walked round the kitchen and hugged Chris. 'I'm really sorry Chris,' she said and then pulled away so she could see Jasmine, too, 'Both of you.'

'Thanks Rosie,' Jasmine looked tearful again. 'We appreciate it, don't we Chris? And we'll be fine, we'll get through this.' Chris looked from his sister down to Jasmine and pulled his wife close to him.

'I'm glad you two have sorted things out,' he said.

'Call me if you need anything,' Rosie said as she picked up her bag from near the kitchen door. 'I'm sure Jasmine will fill you in on everything,' she said as she walked to the front door. 'Or maybe not *all* of it, Jas,' she called back over her shoulder. If she had looked back she would have seen Jasmine smiling to herself as Chris enveloped her in a hug.

Chapter Eighteen

R osie was having a toxic love-hate tussle with her phone, and the phone was winning. She knew she'd been lucky to salvage things with Jasmine and Chris, and she was determined to be as responsive and supportive as possible. But at the same time this meant she was constantly checking her phone, which was beginning to drive her completely crazy.

She couldn't even escape to the lab as Rachel had put a pause on all her experiments after sending Rosie an extremely terse email late at night telling her, in no uncertain terms, to do nothing further on the BioChem project until Rachel told her that she could.

Rosie's head was so awash with thoughts about Jasmine and Chris, Mitch and Jenny, *her* and Mitch, that she didn't have the headspace to think too much about Rachel's email. Rachel could be a control freak at times and given the magnitude of the BioChem deal it was hardly a surprise that Rachel had intervened. Whatever was going on with the project, Rosie just hoped it would be fine, because honestly, she had other things to worry about at the moment.

Currently top of her list of things to sort out was the unpleasant sensation she experienced in the pit of her stomach every time her phone made a noise, and whether there was a way of ensuring she never had to experience it again. The hope – and ensuing disappointment – that Mitch might be replying to one of her many messages was making her feel sick. Since their argument she had texted him, WhatsApped him, and overcome her aversion to speaking on the phone and left him voice notes. She had even gone completely old-school and written him a letter, which she had hand delivered to his apartment one evening after work. Rosie had hovered by the entrance to his apartment block and considered ringing the doorbell, before deciding that it was bad enough for him to ignore her messages, but to be rejected face to face would be unbearable. She didn't think she could handle that. She had stood for a long time wondering what to do, but in the end she had posted her letter through his letterbox and walked back to the tube station with yet another ache inside her, and although she wasn't an expert in anatomy, she was pretty sure this one was close to her heart. That letter, too, had gone unanswered, and now Rosie really didn't know what to do next. Every time she thought about Mitch, she felt tears forming in her eyes and a lump in her throat. Life without him in it felt flat and miserable.

It was in just such a bleak mood that she left her office one evening. Everything was beginning to feel like it was stacking up against her. Rachel still hadn't come back on BioChem and Rosie was starting to feel uneasy about her silence. Without the lab to escape into things had been slow at work. Rosie hated not being in the lab at the best of times, and this was very far from the best of times.

Paperwork was all very well when you could intersperse it with fun stuff like messing around with new lab supplies, but Rosie thought she might scream if she spent any longer reviewing undergraduate papers or end up causing some serious trauma to the students on the receiving end of her red pen. She'd become so desperate for some diversion, that she had started preparing a lecture that she gave once a year for a Women in STEM event. She had six months before she needed to deliver it, it should have been easy; she had her notes from the previous years, yet every time she sat down to work on it, the words wouldn't come and everything ended up sounding clunky and boring. She was going for inspirational and interesting but it was just not happening.

Nadia had been no help; Rosie had barely seen her all week. Her office door had been shut, and the only time Rosie had seen it open was when Nadia flew out of it as Rosie was passing, speaking quickly and fiercely into her mobile and waving distractedly at Rosie as she passed. Rosie wasn't sure if she was pleased to miss Nadia or not; she was worried about her and Nico, but she was also worried that Nadia might ask her how things were going with Mitch, and that wouldn't be good. Falling out with Mitch had not been on the plan that Nadia had formulated for her.

The one bright spot in the week had been Jasmine and Chris. Their shared grief seemed to have brought them together and Rosie was trying to feel some comfort that they were working together to face their future. Rosie had had several tearful conversations with Jasmine, whose grief was still very raw but each time they spoke, Jasmine had sounded stronger and more positive than she had seemed when Rosie had seen her the previous weekend. Physically, she was mending, but mentally it would take a lot longer. Rosie was grateful that she had Chris with her to support her through this. She was also grateful that currently Jasmine was rightly concentrating on getting well again, not on having an opinion on Rosie's life.

Rosie was thinking about her conversation with Jasmine about

Mitch as she made her way out of the building. It was not improving her mood. Neither were the Christmas lights that had started to go up across the square from her lab; Christmas still felt a long way off but the shops had put out their festive displays and all the cafes were promoting their seasonal coffees for a hugely inflated price, considering it was exactly the same coffee but with a small amount of ginger and spice. Twilight had fallen across London, although it was hard to tell with the bright lights of the streetlights and cars. It had been drizzling on and off all day, a fine mist settling on clothes and hair whenever one ventured outside, but it had cleared up now that dusk was here. Rosie had decided to walk home since she had no plans that evening and so it didn't matter what time she got home. It also put off the inevitability of yet another evening at home on her own.

She realised how much her life revolved around Mitch and that without him it suddenly seemed very empty. Even her flat, which had always been a bolthole of calm, was too quiet and still for her and her jumble of confused thoughts. Glumly, Rosie pulled her coat around her and set off. She was stood waiting to cross Oxford Street when her phone rang. Pulling it from her pocket, her heart skipped a beat when she saw Mitch's name flash up on the screen. For a split second she thought about hitting decline; she wasn't sure she could concentrate on fighting for their friendship when she was trying to dodge traffic. But had he got her messages? Was he ready to forgive her? And if he wasn't, was she even brave enough to hear what he had to say? But curiosity and a desperation to hear Mitch's voice again overcame her misgivings and as the pedestrian light flashed to green, she answered his call.

'Mitch?' she said warily, pressing the phone to one ear and putting her finger in the other, desperate not to miss anything he said because of the noise of the street around her.

'Hi.' Rosie couldn't fail to miss the note of weariness in Mitch's voice. 'Can we talk?' he asked.

'Yes, yes of course,' she quickly replied. 'I'm on Oxford Street, though, so there's a lot of background noise. Should I call you back when I'm somewhere quieter?'

'No,' he said firmly. 'This won't take long.'

That didn't sound good. Rosie's stomach sank, she allowed herself to be carried across the road by the swell of commuters as she waited for Mitch to continue.

'I got your messages,' he said in a flat voice.

'Mitch,' she said, 'I meant everything, I'm an idiot and I'm so sorry. I didn't mean to mess things up with Jenny.'

'Well, you did,' he replied, sounding more resigned than furious.

'Is she, are you guys…' Rosie didn't know how to frame her question. Of course she wanted to know what had happened, and part of her hoped that they were no longer together, but she also knew that if they weren't it was because of what she had done and that the chance of Mitch forgiving her would reduce to a big fat zero.

'I don't know.'

'I'm so sorry, Mitch,' she whispered into her phone. 'Can I do anything? Maybe if I spoke to her?' she said hopefully.

'I really don't think that's going to help, Rosie. I think you've said enough.' There was a pause. 'In fact, I was calling to say that I'd rather you stop contacting me.'

'What?' Rosie wailed. 'Mitch no, don't say that. I said I'm sorry. What can I do to make it better?'

'You can't do anything, Rosie,' Mitch said in an irritated tone. 'I'm so angry and confused at the moment and you're not making things easier.'

Rosie's eyes filled with tears as she stood on the street corner and listened to Mitch vent his anger. 'Mitch, please,' she begged as the tears began to roll down her cheeks.

'No, Rosie, I'm sorry. I just don't understand you at the moment,' he continued.

'But I can explain!' she said in anguish.

'Can you? OK, try me,' he said confrontationally. 'I'm listening.'

There was a long silence while Rosie contemplated this. Could she explain? How would she even begin to go about telling him *why* she had sabotaged his relationship with Jenny? What would he think, knowing that she had entered into their agreement under false pretences? He might think she had been trying to trap him into a relationship with her by getting pregnant, which was unthinkable. But he would also think their entire friendship had been a sham. That all the time she had been working out how to make a move on him, that she was never interested in his friendship and had only been trying to work out how to get him into bed. And nothing was further from the truth, she thought with anguish.

If it was a choice between a friendship with Mitch and nothing more, or a failed romance, which ended up destroying everything, she knew which one she would choose every time. And hadn't she shown that by the way she had behaved during the long years of their friendship? But would he ever accept and believe that if she told the truth? A car horn beeped nearby and a commuter bumped into her.

'So I guess that's a no, then? You can't explain,' she heard Mitch say down the phone. 'Yeah,' he laughed bitterly to himself. 'It is pretty hard to explain why you would want to break your best friend's relationship up. Unless you secretly hate me, of course.'

'No, Mitch!' Rosie exclaimed, aghast that he would jump to this conclusion.

'Really, Rosie? Because it seems that way to me. Which is funny, because I thought we were really good friends, the kind of friends that had even discussed having children together.'

Rosie's heart gave a lurch. 'Mitch, it's not like that,' she said weakly.

'Well, I don't see what way it is like,' he replied.

Rosie could hear the distress in his tone. She knew he was pressing her for an explanation. But she didn't feel strong enough to offer him the truth.

'So you see, Rosie, this is why I would rather you just leave me alone for the moment? I think we both need space and time to think.'

Rosie opened her mouth to say something, but as she did, she realised he had put the phone down.

'Mitch? Mitch?' she said frantically into her phone.

She tried to call him back but it went straight to voicemail. Rosie swallowed down a howl of grief and frustration, and bent to catch her breath in a shop doorway. Just at that moment she felt a hand on her back. Looking up, she saw a woman, older than she was, asking her if she was OK. Incapable of saying anything, Rosie just shook her head, not even caring whether she was saying yes or no to the woman.

'Can I do anything?' the woman asked. Rosie continued to shake her head. For a moment the woman kept her hand on Rosie's back and then she reached into her bag and brought out a packet of tissues.

'Here,' she said, 'at least take these.'

Overwhelmed by the small act of kindness, Rosie took the tissues with a shaking hand and straightened up.

'Thank you,' she said in a tiny voice.

The woman smiled at her. 'No need,' she said. 'I hope whoever he is, that he's worth it.'

Weakly, Rosie tried to smile back, thinking to herself that her friendship with Mitch was worth everything she had to offer, all the emotions that she could endure. But that she might just have ruined it all forever.

Chapter Nineteen

'Rosie? Rosie? Are you even listening to me?'

'Of course I'm listening to you' Rosie snapped back in irritation at Nadia.

Rosie hadn't been listening, if you had asked her whether she'd noticed Nadia was even in her office, she wouldn't have been able to give you an answer. But she wasn't a million miles away either, she was about three streets away, in the direction of Oxford Circus, reliving the conversation she'd had with Mitch and wondering, not for the first time, where it had all gone wrong and whether she should just have kissed him again all those years ago. At least if it hadn't worked out between them, she wouldn't be in this nightmare scenario now. She had ended up losing him, anyway. Maybe it would have been better never to have really had him.

'OK, so what have I been saying?'

Rosie's attention snapped back into the room. Nadia was staring at her with the kind of look that Rosie could imagine her using on one of her children when they had been caught doing something they shouldn't have been and were trying to finagle their way out of it. Momentarily, Rosie quailed before remembering that Nadia was not her mother.

'Alright,' she confessed holding her hands up. 'I have absolutely no idea what you have been talking to me about. Was it about funding?' she asked hopefully, although she had no real desire to revisit that thorny issue right now.

'No, it wasn't,' Nadia said firmly. 'It was about the disaster that seems to be unfurling under your nose and which you don't even seem to be aware of.'

'I am quite aware of it, thank you,' Rosie said crossly, while simultaneously wondering how Nadia had found out about the fact Mitch was no longer talking to her. Realisation dawned gradually.

'Oh,' Rosie said. 'You're not talking about Mitch, are you?'

It was Nadia's turn to snap. 'No I'm not talking about Mitch,' she replied. 'Why would I be talking about Mitch?' she asked in confusion.

'Er, no reason,' Rosie replied, keen to move Nadia off the subject before she had to explain.

'So, we were talking about...?' Rosie queried.

'BioChem!' Nadia exclaimed in exasperation.

'Oh, right, right of course.' Rosie pretended she understood. 'Hold on, you know about the project?'

'Know about it?' Nadia exploded. 'Of course I know about it. Rachel has been going on about what a brilliant project it is. And if you're not careful it *will* be solely Rachel's project and not yours anymore.'

Nadia started playing with the pens on Rosie's desk and grumbled, 'Honestly, I don't know what's got into you, Rosie? It's amazing you've been offered this opportunity. The Women in STEM fanatics are going to go crazy with excitement when they find out that it's your research that's behind all this. How good is it going to look for them? It's fantastic for their profile. Fantastic for women in science full stop.' She pointed the pen threateningly at Rosie.

Rosie felt her heart lift, wondering exactly where the problem lay in all of this, and then Nadia said, 'And what do you go and do?'

Rosie shook her head, waiting to be enlightened.

'You fuck it up! That's what you do.' Nadia threw the pen at the wall in frustration.

Carefully Rosie reached over to retrieve the pen from the floor and wheeled her office chair back to her desk, placing the pen out of reach of Nadia. It was one of her favourite pens and she didn't think it deserved to be treated like that just because of something Rosie had allegedly done...

'Hang on, what have I done? How have I fucked this up? I don't fuck things up!' Rosie was indignant. She *didn't* make mistakes, she *never* fucked things up.

'No, you don't!' countered Nadia. 'And this is exactly why I am so cross with you! Where is your brain right now?' Nadia tapped the side of her own head.

Rosie didn't like to tell her where her brain was right at that moment; given Nadia's mood she didn't think admitting the truth would help the situation.

'Your data,' Nadia continued, 'it's all over the place, it's a mess! I can't believe you had the nerve to even show it to Rachel, let alone expect her to accept it.'

Rosie tried to unscramble her brain. It was true, she hadn't been paying the close attention in the lab that she usually did, but surely it wasn't all that bad? And then she remembered that she hadn't even checked the latest results before she sent them off to Rachel and to the BioChem execs.

'Shit.' Rosie's face drained of colour. 'What have I done? What have you heard Nadia? Was it really that bad?'

'Really that bad,' confirmed Nadia, examining her bitten nails. Now that she had Rosie's attention, she seemed to have calmed down considerably. She looked up at Rosie. 'And I am here as your friend to warn you of that. Rosie, does any of this ring *any* bells with you?' she asked.

'No, I mean, yes. I mean, I didn't know it was that bad,' said Rosie, spreading her hands out in front of her.

Nadia shook her head. 'Have you even spoken to Rachel?' she asked.

'Well, not exactly. She sent me an email, in fact.' Rosie swivelled in her chair to turn to face her computer, tapping the keyboard to bring the screen to life. 'She might have sent me more than one,' she admitted, turning back to face Nadia with a look of horror on her face.

'Did you read *any* of them?' asked Nadia incredulously.

'I read the first one,' Rosie replied defensively.

Nadia sighed. 'Rosie,' she said, 'has nobody ever told you that when you get an email from your boss you should read it immediately? Come on, this isn't like you.'

Rosie was scanning the contents of Rachel's emails, terms like *suspension, cancellation, diligent investigation* jumped out at her.

'God, Nadia, I think I'm about to be fired.'

'No, you're not.' Nadia said pragmatically. 'Honestly Rosie we've all been there, you're not going to get fired, but you do have a lot of work to do to make this right. Rachel's mainly furious because you haven't responded to her already. Once you do, she'll calm down.'

Rosie felt a panicked flush creep up her cheeks. 'What should I do?' she asked Nadia in anguish.

Nadia rolled her eyes. 'What you should have done

immediately, as soon as you read her first email,' Nadia replied in a no-nonsense manner. 'Reply, apologise for the delay, make up a decent excuse and ask her for an appointment to discuss it.'

'Yes, yes you're quite right,' Rosie said noticing how much her hands were shaking as she typed out Nadia's suggested response.

'What were you saying about Mitch?' Nadia nonchalantly asked, pretending to go back to inspecting her nails, as Rosie finished her email.

'What?' Rosie replied looking up from her screen. 'Oh, er nothing, it's fine.'

'Well, it obviously isn't,' said Nadia looking at Rosie over her nails. 'What's he done now?'

'He hasn't done anything,' Rosie replied defensively. Even when she and Mitch weren't on speaking terms she couldn't help but leap to his protection.

'Interesting,' said Nadia. 'OK, what have *you* done now?'

Rosie groaned, 'I thought we were trying to fix this mess I've made with the BioChem project?'

'Oh, sure,' agreed Nadia. 'But you've emailed Rachel. She's not in yet, by the way, I checked on my way over here. So, we've got time to kill before you're summoned. Tell me what it is you've done.' Nadia sounded suspiciously like she was enjoying herself now.

Keen to do anything to take her mind off her impending meeting with Rachel, Rosie confessed, 'I did something really bad.'

Nadia stopped attempting to conceal her interest. 'What?' she said, excitement now written clearly across her face. 'Rosie you never do anything bad! I mean, except this monumental fuck-up with BioChem.'

'Yeah, well, I've obviously gone for the double this time,' Rosie said flatly.

'Oh, wow!' exclaimed Nadia. 'You haven't got yourself pregnant already have you?! That's why you're all over the place!' She clapped her hands with excitement.

'No, I have not,' snapped Rosie indignantly. 'And it's now looking very unlikely that that will happen anyway.'

'Tell me what happened?' Nadia practically begged.

Rosie leaned her chin in her hands and looked across her desk at Nadia before beginning the whole sorry tale. Nadia listened patiently before reaching across to cover Rosie's hands with her own.

'Rosie,' she said firmly, 'I agree, it's not great, but really it's not the end of the world. You and Mitch have been friends for years; how long has he been seeing this Jenny girl?'

'A few weeks,' mumbled Rosie.

'Exactly, a few weeks. I really don't think the two compare. And anyway, he would probably have got bored of her in a month or so, had you not said anything.'

'But I did say something, Nadia,' insisted Rosie, 'and whether he would have got bored with her or not is irrelevant, because now he'll never find out and I will always be the so-called friend who ruined his relationship.' She felt the ever-present tears prickle behind her eyes.

Nadia looked at her pityingly. 'Have you ever thought of telling him the truth?' she asked.

'No!' exclaimed Rosie. 'It's already bad enough without me making it worse by admitting why I sabotaged his relationship.'

'Is it?' questioned Nadia. 'Because from where I'm sitting, I'm not sure you've got a lot to lose at the moment and potentially a whole lot to gain.' She paused. 'Think about it,' she said, holding her hands up at Rosie. 'He's not talking to you, anyway. If you tell him and he hates you for it, nothing has changed. But if you tell him and he feels the same way, then you've gained a whole lot.'

Rosie shook her head crossly. 'He doesn't feel the same way, Nadia, I've told you this before.'

'But do you know? I mean *really* know?' insisted Nadia. 'Because you've never asked him, have you? Or told him how you feel? Maybe he was trying to get you to admit it during that conversation when he asked why you had done it.'

'But then, why wouldn't he say something?' asked Rosie.

'For exactly the same reason you're not saying something!' said Nadia, throwing her hands up in frustration. 'Maybe he has spent all this time being in love with you. Maybe,' she continued, 'that's the reason he never manages to keep a girlfriend longer than a few weeks because they never measure up to you. Maybe that's the real reason he asked you to be his fallback.'

Rosie looked at her friend. She couldn't deny that these suggestions were incredibly attractive to her, but logically they couldn't be true, could they? She didn't even dare to hope that they might be. And then the sound of her inbox pinging brought them both back down to earth.

'Check it,' Nadia said pointing at Rosie's computer. 'Then go to the bathroom, pull yourself together, and go and grovel to Rachel like you should have done to begin with.'

Nadia stood up out of her chair and walked towards Rosie's door. She turned at the last minute and said, 'Rosie, it will be OK, you know? You've got this.'

Rosie wasn't sure whether Nadia was talking about the Mitch situation or the Rachel situation but she knew which one was more pressing right at this moment. Rosie had always got on well with Rachel, but apart from the Christmas party, they observed a professional distance. Rosie was a diligent and conscientious employee and she prayed that all of that would help her out of this mess as she stood outside Rachel's office door and nervously ran her sweaty palms down her trousers. It felt like she was stood outside the headmistress's office, not that Rosie had ever done anything even approaching naughty enough to be sent to the headmistress' office. Come to think of it, this might be the first time she had ever been in real trouble at work or school. It did not make for a comfortable experience.

'Hold on a moment.' Rachel held one finger up to Rosie and continued to read her computer screen.

Although it could only have been a matter of seconds, to Rosie it felt like hours, but finally Rachel turned from her computer, swept her glasses off her nose and gazed coolly across her desk at Rosie. She beckoned Rosie in.

'I have to say, this is unexpected,' Rachel began.

Rosie stared at the floor, feeling more and more like a naughty schoolgirl. 'I'm sorry Rachel,' she mumbled.

Rachel continued to watch her, her elegant hands now folded on the desk in front of her. 'Do you want to explain to me what happened?' she asked Rosie. 'Actually I'm going to rephrase that. Tell me what the *hell* happened.'

Rosie shuffled her feet and said nothing.

'We have a real problem, Rosie. That data you sent me? That data that you sent *directly to BioChem*? It's worthless. Completely useless!' Rachel threw her hands up in the air. 'What were you doing in the lab? It was you, wasn't it?' She narrowed her eyes at Rosie, 'You're not covering up for some useless student, are you?'

Rosie shook her head, 'No, it was me,' she mumbled.

'Did you even look at the results before you emailed them?'

Rosie shook her head again miserably.

'Unbelievable.' Rachel sighed deeply. 'It's bad enough to send it to me without checking but to send it to BioChem?' She gestured towards the door, as though there was a long line of BioChem executives waiting outside in the corridor to come in and join this shaming session.

'They trusted us with this project,' Rachel continued. 'They asked for you in particular, and I backed you, I vouched for you and you've let me down.' She shook her head. 'They must think we're idiots.'

She smoothed down her crisp white shirt. Academics got a bad press as far as fashion was concerned, all worn T-shirts and ratty jeans under their lab coats. But Rachel had never gone in for the Mad Professor look and Rosie had always admired her for undermining the stereotype.

'This was supposed to look good for the department, the VC was so impressed with us, with *you*.'

Rosie felt a wave of nausea wash over her. The Vice Chancellor knew about this? What was he going to think when he heard how she had messed it all up?

'The university are obsessed with diversity, with getting more women into STEM and you were the perfect poster girl.'

Rosie hung her head again.

'Luckily, the VC doesn't need to know about this.' A small surge of optimism ran through Rosie. 'Yet,' said Rachel, warningly, 'I can keep it from him for the time being while we sort this out.'

Rosie didn't like to think how Rachel was planning to distract the VC from finding out about this. Perhaps their affair wasn't quite as dead in the water as Nadia had told her it was.

'I'm really disappointed in you.'

Rosie digested those words. For a people-pleasing overachiever, this statement was like a dagger to her heart.

'I'm really sorry, Rachel.' She looked up from her shoes and risked looking at Rachel who glared back at her.

'It's so frustrating. I mean look at this,' Rachel waved her hand over a pile of papers on her desk. Rosie couldn't read the details from this far away but she presumed, given Rachel's distain, that these were the offending data sets.

'Completely useless data, two weeks' wasted lab time, BioChem think we're idiots and can't deliver and I haven't even begun to look at the financial impact yet.'

Rosie felt tears prickling in her eyes. There was a pause and it seemed Rachel realised how close to crying Rosie was because she suddenly changed tack.

She exhaled deeply. 'It's OK, we can fix it. I've already spoken to BioChem and explained that it was an error on our end, that we sent them an erroneous report by mistake and that we would have some new data for them by the end of next week. That's doable, isn't it?'

Rosie didn't consider this a question, it was an order. And it didn't matter how doable it was, she would put in as many hours as she needed to get it done.

'Yes, absolutely Rachel,' she confirmed.

'But the thing I find most worrying about it all...' Rosie had momentarily relaxed, but now found herself braced once again for what Rachel was about to say. '...is that this is so out of character. In all the time you have worked for me, I have *never* had to pull you up like this,' Rachel looked pointedly at Rosie. 'In fact, quite the opposite. You're the one I have relied on to check *my* results and to point out issues in other experiments.'

Rosie rocked from foot to foot.

'So, the thing I'm asking is, what's going on with you?'

Rosie saw that, interestingly, Rachel's expression wasn't one of fury. In fact, it had more of a look of intellectual curiosity about it. Rosie felt like a lab rat.

Rachel sighed. 'Can you sit down now, please?' she asked Rosie. 'You're making me nervous shuffling back and forth like that.'

Slowly Rosie pulled one of the chairs towards her and sat down in it across from Rachel who ran her hand slowly and carefully through her perfectly smooth bob. When Rosie had first met Rachel, she had had jet-black hair. Ten years later, it was now peppered with grey. But the sharp edges of the bob endured and what might look aging on other women just added to Rachel's gravitas, and general air of intimidation.

She continued to watch Rosie, rather as one might look at an interesting exhibit in a museum. 'So, what is it?' she finally demanded.

'I'm not quite sure what you mean,' Rosie replied falteringly.

'What is it,' Rachel said now in an exasperated tone, 'that is distracting you from work?' Rosie said nothing.

'OK. Let me ask you something else. What's your plan, Rosie?' Rachel leaned back comfortably in her chair. Being head of department meant she had a rather more luxurious chair than the one Rosie had, which was held together with duct tape.

'Oh, I see,' replied Rosie, feeling herself on more comfortable terrain now that they could discuss her career plans. 'Right, well I thought with a couple more years leading this lab I might be on the right track for tenure.'

She paused, waiting to see if Rachel would laugh at her confidence, but she didn't and so Rosie went on. 'And if that progresses smoothly, then I'd look for external funding to expand my lab and take on more collaborations. If you and the university agreed, of course,' she said quickly, keen not to presume too much.

'I didn't mean with this,' Rachel said tersely, waving her arms about her wood-panelled office. 'This isn't an interview where you try to wow me with your ambition while also treading a delicate line and trying not to sound too arrogant. I meant your life plans.' Rachel sat forward again. 'Because make no mistake, Rosie, this,' again she indicated her office, 'is not a life. It's a job. Maybe even a fulfilling career. But it is not and it shouldn't be your life. So, what is your plan?' she pressed Rosie.

Rosie visibly deflated. In all the time she had worked here, Rachel had never shown any interest in her personal life beyond offering her a choice between champagne and martinis at a party. So why now? Why when everything was going wrong with Rosie's life did Rachel suddenly seem to care?

'I don't know,' she said in a quiet voice, deciding to go for the honest approach.

'Ah.' Rachel regarded her, kindlier than before. 'I see. Remind me,' she asked, 'how long have we worked together for?'

'Over ten years,' replied Rosie.

'And in that time,' Rachel went on, 'how many times have you called in sick?'

'A few maybe?' responded Rosie.

'How many times have you come in hungover?'

'Hardly ever,' Rosie replied more reluctantly, choosing to ignore the morning after her dismal date with Graham.

'And how many times have I caught you in the bathroom crying?'

'Erm…' Rosie thought for a moment. 'Maybe once, that time one of the students broke the lab equipment and we lost a week's worth of work in a split second.'

'A perfectly good reason for some tears.' Rachel nodded wisely. 'But I think that might be the problem,' she said. 'You've been so busy being a good colleague, an excellent scientist…' she fixed Rosie with a steely glare as if daring her to disagree '…that you've forgotten to go out and live your life.'

Rosie considered this for a moment before replying, 'Maybe you're right but to be honest, if living my life means calling in sick or turning up hungover and crying in the bathroom then I think

I'm OK with my life choices so far.' She smiled at Rachel who rolled her eyes.

'Yes, fair point,' Rachel said. 'But you get my meaning? And the thing is, after this mess...' Evidently Rosie was not going to be let off the hook anytime soon. 'Perhaps it is time to look at what else is going on in your life and whether it's affecting your work.'

Rosie began to apologise again but Rachel batted her away.

'I have two theories when someone takes their eye off the ball at work. The first one being that they've met someone.' She studied Rosie's face for some kind of reaction. 'And the second being that they've had their heart broken.'

Rosie wondered if she was supposed to tick the box that applied to her and couldn't work out which one she would choose. Because yes, she had met someone but she had also had her heart broken. Not in a single sharp snap, but with a slow tearing apart over several years.

'Now,' Rachel said, tidying up the papers on her desk. 'I'm your boss so I don't expect you to want to talk to me about any of this. And frankly I'd rather you didn't. But you do need to talk to someone and work out what's going on before you mess up any more of my collaborations, OK?'

'OK,' Rosie agreed.

'Maybe try your friend.' She waved her hand at Rosie. 'The one who used to work here? Mitch?' Rachel suddenly looked pleased with herself that she had recalled the name of one of her more disappointing students. 'He wasn't up to much as a scientist,' she said, 'but I hear he's gone on to good things as a journalist. Presumably putting his good looks and charm to work for him.' Rachel chuckled to herself. 'You're still friends, aren't you? I mean you bring him to every party?'

'Er, yes,' confirmed Rosie, not really feeling like explaining that the fact that she and Mitch were currently not on speaking terms was exactly the issue which was distracting her from work.

'Well, good. Try him. But for goodness' sake, do it soon, I can't have any more messes to clear up.'

Rosie nodded dumbly. Perhaps if she told Mitch that Rachel had instructed him to listen to her, he would have to stop ignoring her?

'Right,' Rachel clapped her hands together. 'BioChem. You'll get back to work in the lab? And I need to work on this press release.'

'Press release?' Rosie asked, feeling she had missed a step.

'Yes, press release. You know, one of those things we send out to the newspapers when we have something to announce?' Evidently touchy-feely time with Rachel was over.

'Erm, what are we announcing exactly?'

'The collaboration!' Rachel snapped.

'Oh,' Rosie looked confused. 'I thought it was confidential?'

Rachel sighed, 'Do try to keep up, Rosie. Yes, it was. Now it isn't. BioChem want to announce this project and get out ahead of one of their competitors.'

'OK,' Rosie said, sounding very unsure of the situation.

Rachel sighed again and stared hard at her. 'I'm drafting it. BioChem will check it and then I will send it to you to circulate.'

'Me?' Rosie asked sounding terrified.

'Yes!' Rachel sounded increasingly irritated by Rosie's questions. 'You're the lead scientist on it, it should come from you. You're the poster girl remember?'

Rosie didn't feel like talking to the press or being the poster girl for anything right now, but she knew she couldn't argue with Rachel.

'OK, right.'

'I'll send it to you as soon as it's finalised.' Rachel waved Rosie off towards the door.

Rosie quickly stood up from her chair, eager to get out of Rachel's office before any other terrifying instructions came her way.

'Oh, and Rosie?'

Rosie turned back to look at Rachel.

'I promised the comms team at *The Post* that they could have a short exclusive on our next press release. I owe the director there a favour.'

Rosie didn't like to ask what kind of favour Rachel might owe and anyway she was already feeling sick enough at hearing the name of Mitch's newspaper.

'So, once it's ready, we'll give them a twenty-four-hour exclusive, OK?'

'OK.' Rosie wanted to sound more confident than she was. Press releases and journalists (who weren't Mitch) were not her thing. But it was a simple instruction, wasn't it? Forward on the document that Rachel would send to her. How hard could that be?

Rosie walked back to her office feeling like she'd narrowly avoided being hit by a bus. For some reason Rachel had forgiven her so Rosie needed to double down and get this lab work done extra quickly and extra carefully. And then she needed to run the gauntlet of contacting Mitch's press department who would undoubtedly put her straight in touch with him. He was the science correspondent after all, who else would be interested in this press release but him?

Rosie had gone straight off to book the first available slots of lab time and then walked past Nadia's office to update her on how it had gone with Rachel. Nadia was on the phone, but Rosie had managed to give her a thumbs-up and a smile. Nadia had grinned back and mouthed, 'Told you it would be fine.'

Rosie wasn't so sure that Rachel had fully forgiven her but she was determined to try and make it up to her. It was bad enough not having Mitch in her corner, but without Rachel she would feel completely alone. Lost in thought, she ran out at lunchtime to grab a sandwich and ran straight into Ben, the absolute last person she wanted to see, ever.

'What are you doing here?' she said accusingly.

'Nice to see you, too, Rosie.' He laughed. 'You weren't answering my calls or texts so I thought I'd try and catch you in person.'

Rosie eyed him warily. She didn't like being caught off-guard, especially not by someone she was actively trying to avoid.

'Come for a drink with me?' he asked.

'No,' she said firmly. 'It's midday. I'm not going to the pub.'

'Later?' he asked.

Realising her mistake, she clarified, 'I'm not going to the pub with you *ever*, OK?'

'Please?' he asked.

'I don't know, Ben, I don't think it's a good idea given everything that's happened and anyway I've got stuff to do.'

'I promise I won't try and kiss you,' he said, holding his hands up in front of him.

Rosie looked sceptical and glanced down at her watch. She actually had almost two hours until the lab would be free and eating one sandwich wasn't going to take all that time.

'All right.' She sighed. 'But I'm not drinking at lunchtime, OK? I need to clear up a mess, not make another one.' She mentally ran through everything she needed to get done in the lab that afternoon.

'Why, what's happened?' Ben asked suddenly curious.

'Nothing you need to know about,' she said dismissively, shoving her hands into her pockets and second-guessing her decision to say yes.

'Where do you guys drink around here?' he asked, looking back over his shoulder at the busy street.

Rosie shrugged. 'There's the pub round the corner but that will be packed with students. If you're happy to walk five minutes, there's a quieter place just down the road.' Rosie had no desire to bump into anyone from work with Ben in tow. Imagine having to explain who he was and why she was with him.

Ben nodded. 'Sounds good,' he said. 'You lead the way.'

Rosie kept glancing at Ben as they walked round Russell Square. She was aiming for a pub she knew near Tavistock Place. It would hopefully have no students and no faculty in there but be busy enough that Ben wouldn't try anything on.

She *had* been avoiding him, that much was true; she hadn't seen him since he left her flat the morning of her argument with Mitch, but he had sent her enough messages that she knew he was trying to get her attention and she also knew he must have heard some of what was said but she didn't know how much or what he had subsequently guessed to be true.

The pub was practically empty. There were two men drinking at the bar and a couple sat in one corner. Rosie looked around and hoped this was enough people to make Ben keep his hands to himself. This was where Rosie came with Nadia when they had something to discuss after work, mainly because it was always quiet and the students either hadn't discovered it yet or it wasn't cool enough for them. It was also somewhere that she had never been with Mitch, which made it feel like neutral territory. Ben followed her in looking around as he went.

'Is this OK?' she asked, noticing that he hadn't immediately gone to the bar as she was expecting him to.

'Yes, it's fine,' he said. 'Can I get you a drink?'

Rosie noticed his hesitancy. The Ben she had encountered before would have gone straight to the bar, ordered himself a drink along with whatever he thought Rosie might want.

'A white wine, please,' she replied, deciding that any conversation with Ben did, after all, require alcohol. 'A small one' she added.

Rosie noted the small glass of wine that Ben carefully placed in front of her, minutes later. She looked at him suspiciously as he sat down across from her, removing his jacket.

'OK,' she said. 'Who are you and what have you done with the real Ben?'

Ben looked around from hanging his jacket on the back of his chair.

'What?' he asked, confused.

'You just seem different, that's all,' Rosie said. She decided she didn't know him well enough to insult him openly so she left it at that.

Luckily, Ben laughed. 'Less arrogant?' he asked.

Rosie demurred before nodding her head ever so slightly.

'Well, let's just say I've been doing some soul searching,' he said before taking a sip of his beer.

'Right,' Rosie said nervously. 'Look Ben, if it's about the other night I thought I had made it clear, I'm not interested in dating you. Or sleeping with you!' she quickly followed up with, in case her first statement had lacked clarity.

Ben waved his hand at her to make her stop. 'I know, OK? You did make it clear. You're not interested in me and that's fine.'

He took another sip of his beer. 'We had a fun night and I appreciate you letting me crash at yours, even if your sofa is really uncomfortable. I'm glad I didn't have to wake my sister and her husband. She can be really awful if you disturb her sleep.'

'Are they still staying?' Rosie asked.

'Just till the weekend,' he replied, 'and then I can have my flat back and not have to sleep on the sofa of girls who won't even let me kiss them.' He gave her a sheepish grin and Rosie blushed. 'Anyway,' he said, 'I wasn't seriously trying to kiss you, I value my life too much.'

'What do you mean?' Rosie asked.

'Mitch,' he said. 'He would kill me if I tried anything on with you.'

Rosie laughed disbelievingly, 'It doesn't seem to have stopped you before.'

Ben looked at her. 'I'm not stupid,' he said, 'I know exactly what he thinks of me. And anyway, he'd be mad at anyone who tried to kiss you. It's pretty hard to watch someone you fancy with someone else. Just like you felt seeing him with Jenny.'

Rosie's blush became more furious and she took a long drink of her wine. They watched each other across the table and eventually Ben leaned forward and said, 'So, I overheard some interesting things the other morning between you and Mitch.'

Rosie groaned. 'I don't want to talk about it, OK?' she begged. Ben ignored her.

'Have you two really got some sort of plan to have a baby together?' he asked.

'Not anymore,' said Rosie, picking up her glass again and wishing she'd actually asked for a larger one.

'But you did, right? You two had agreed to be each other's fallback if you didn't meet anyone else?'

Rosie nodded slowly. 'Yeah,' she agreed. 'It was Mitch's idea and I sort of went along with it. But now he's met Jenny, and anyway he's not talking to me so I don't think that plan will be top of his list of priorities at the moment.'

Ben didn't say anything for a while.

'It was a smart move,' he said eventually.

'I'm sorry?' she asked.

'Well, it's a good way of putting the moves on someone you like without actually admitting to them that that's what you're doing,' he said.

'I told you,' Rosie replied, 'it was Mitch's idea not mine.'

'That's what I meant,' Ben said. 'It was smart of Mitch.' Rosie shook her head.

'What do you mean?' she said in confusion.

'Well, it's obvious you two are in love with each other, but neither of you can admit it,' he said.

'Not you, as well?' Rosie said, looking up at the ceiling.

'What?' asked Ben, looking confused.

'Nothing,' replied Rosie. 'You were saying?'

'To be honest, it's what made me want to flirt with you. Because it made Mitch so mad and I enjoyed winding him up.' Then seeing the look on Rosie's face, he added, 'And obviously, because you're really attractive and I would have been delighted if you'd been interested in me.'

'Obviously,' she deadpanned. 'Go on, then, explain your version of this seemingly popular theory.'

Ben looked at her in confusion again before regaining his composure and leaning back in his chair as if he was about to unveil a great secret to Rosie. 'So, Mitch is always meeting new girls, isn't he? And none of them last long.' She nodded. 'Jenny just happens to be the most recent. But what I think is this: he likes her, sure, I think that's obvious, but he's also hoping that if he pretends he *really* likes her then it might push you into admitting that you want to follow through on this plan for real, not as a fallback option.'

Rosie resisted the urge to tell Ben that he wasn't the first person to give her this theory, not even the second. And that he was bottom of the list in terms of people she would normally trust. But he *was* the first person who had no skin in the game, he had no interest in pandering to Rosie, or trying to cheer her up, so maybe, ironically, he was the one she should actually hear.

'Remember, I heard quite a lot of your row with Mitch, Rosie, and what I heard was someone trying to get you to admit to your feelings for him.'

'What's in this for you?' she asked.

Ben shook his head. 'What do you mean?' he replied.

'I mean,' she said, 'why are you telling me this? Why are you even here? No offence, Ben, but based on your past behaviour this seems a little out of character.' Rosie searched his face for sign of a reaction. 'You've just told me that you enjoyed winding Mitch up. So why tell me this? What's in it for you?'

Ben sighed and pulled a face then picked up his beer, swirling the dregs of it around the bottom of the glass. 'I said I had been doing some soul searching,' he finally said. 'I wasn't trying to eavesdrop on your argument. I couldn't help but hear, I think most of your neighbours heard as well.' Rosie winced at that. 'But seeing you two so worked up over each other, made me realise that I would quite like to find someone that I felt so worked up over, rather than...' here he looked down at the table sheepishly '...hitting on girls who aren't interested.'

Rosie raised her eyebrows.

'OK,' she said, 'but I still don't see why coming here to tell me your theory helps your soul searching?' She fixed him with a stare, willing him to look up from the table, which he did.

'Call it karma?' he said, shrugging his shoulders. 'I realised how sad it would be if the two of you lost each other because of stupidity or cowardice.' Rosie opened her mouth to argue but he stopped her. 'And I thought if I could help you both see sense then maybe the universe might repay me the favour and introduce me to the girl of my dreams.'

He looked at Rosie and grinned. 'Also, Mitch has been an absolute nightmare at work since that argument. He thinks you and I are sleeping together and nothing I can say or do will make him change his mind.'

Rosie began to protest.

'I know, I've tried everything,' Ben said, 'but he has a huge bee in his bonnet about seeing me at your flat that morning, even though I've told him absolutely nothing happened and you were just being kind and letting me sleep on your sofa. And to top it all off we're supposed to be working on a project together and I need him to start talking to me and pulling his weight because I don't want to end up doing all the work on this.'

Rosie smiled. 'OK, now we get to the truth, it's making life awkward for you at work and you need to get it sorted?' She cocked her head to the side and gave Ben a thin smile.

'That, as well,' he confirmed and drained the rest of his pint.

'Well, I appreciate you coming to tell me your theory, Ben,' Rosie said. 'I'm not sure it stands up to scrutiny. And also I'm not sure I can help you straighten things out with Mitch as he's not talking to me at the moment either.'

Ben looked distraught. 'Please, Rosie, you must be able to do something,' he begged, 'I can't stand this atmosphere any longer.'

'I'll tell you what,' she said, 'I'll think about what you said, and as and when Mitch decides to start talking to me again, I'll tell him straight out that nothing happened.' And she fixed him with a look. 'And nothing ever will, OK?'

Ben nodded enthusiastically. 'Thanks, Rosie,' he said, 'I

appreciate anything you can do to help. Also,' he continued, 'now that I am a reformed character and not just on the lookout for one-night stands, if you've got any single friends to set me up with then that would be great.'

'Enough!' Rosie protested, trying not to laugh at his cheek. 'Look, I appreciate the drink and the "advice",' she made air quotes, 'but I really do have to go.' She stood and picked her coat and bag up. Waving to Ben as she left, she headed back out into the street and towards the sandwich that she now needed to soak up the wine and the nonsense that Ben had been spouting.

Chapter Twenty

R osie's mind raced as she laid out her equipment on the lab bench. She was supposed to be concentrating on this experiment, with getting the right data for Rachel this time. Not on dissecting the ramblings of Ben. So what if he had a theory about her and Mitch? It wasn't as if he was some kind of expert on romantic engagements; his track record with relationships was about as strong as hers.

She tried to put Ben from her mind; she couldn't afford to mess this experiment up again. Her plan was to email Rachel before she left for the day and give her an update on how things were looking. Also, she could check in on whether Rachel had sent her that press release yet. Rosie was dreading having to deal with it but at least once she had it, she could send it off and get it over and done with.

As she walked back into her office several hours later, her phone rang, Jasmine's name flashing on the screen.

'Hey!' Rosie said as she picked up, 'How are you doing?'

'Yeah, OK, I'm getting there,' Jasmine said. 'Work want me to take more time off but I'm itching to get back, I need some distraction.'

'I get it,' said Rosie and she really did. 'But please promise me you'll take it easy? You've been through a lot and rushing back to work isn't necessary.'

Jasmine said nothing. Rosie knew that there was no way Jasmine would be listening to anyone but herself on this matter.

'So, erm, what's up?' Rosie asked.

'Well I was ringing to see if you're OK, after Mitch's post?' Jasmine said carefully.

'What post?' Rosie said, her interest suddenly piqued, 'Is everything OK?'

'Yeeesss,' said Jasmine cautiously. 'Have you been on Instagram recently?'

Rosie felt her stomach fall, she knew from Jasmine's tone that she was about to hear something that she didn't want to.

'Not today. What are you trying to tell me?' Rosie asked in a flat tone. She knew – just knew – what was coming.

'Well…' hesitated Jasmine, 'there's a picture of him and a girl.'

Rosie waited for her to continue.

'Oh,' said Rosie as the air went out of her, she knew it was coming but that didn't make it any easier to hear. 'Jenny, I presume?'

'Mm-hmm,' confirmed Jasmine. 'I presume so.'

'What did it say? His post?'

There was an even longer pause, 'She's kissing the side of his face…'

'OK. But does it say anything?'

'*To all the haters out there…*' Jasmine said reluctantly, tailing off.

'Wow. Right.'

'I'm sorry, Rosie, you know you shouldn't read too much into it, OK?'

Rosie laughed hollowly. 'I don't know, Jas. I think his message is pretty clear. Hang on, let me look.'

Rosie took the phone from her ear and swiped. Opening Instagram, she searched for Mitch.

'Rosie?' said Jasmine. 'Rosie, are you still there?'

'I don't understand,' said Rosie putting the phone back to her ear. 'He's gone!'

'Gone?' said Jasmine in confusion. 'what do you mean, *gone*?'

'I mean just that,' Rosie said insistently. 'He's disappeared, gone, I can't see his profile anymore.'

There was a very long pause.

'Jas,' Rosie eventually breathed, 'He's blocked me, hasn't he?' She gave a low laugh. 'I feel so stupid even saying that. Why am I so surprised? He's blocked me in real life already so why wouldn't he block me online?'

'Rosie, I'm so sorry, are you OK?' Jasmine asked, concerned.

Rosie felt her voice catch. 'It just feels really public, Jas,' she whispered. 'Now everyone will know he's not talking to me.'

'They won't,' Jasmine replied in her most matter-of-fact tone. 'How will they know? In fact, who even goes on Instagram anymore?'

'We do,' said Rosie, flatly.

'Well, yes,' agreed Jasmine, 'but I couldn't see he had blocked you, could I?'

Rosie said nothing.

'Has he posted anything else recently?' Rosie asked, desperate for more information even though she feared hearing it would hurt.

There was a long pause, Rosie could hear her nephews in the background, it made her long for some familiarity and comfort.

'Is there anything else?' she said again, more insistently. 'Jasmine, I need to know.'

'He's posted some more photos of him and Jenny,' Jasmine said in a rush.

'Where are they taken?' Rosie asked, more out of something to say than because she really cared. The fact he had posted the photos was enough.

'Some look like they're taken in a bar. Some with the river behind them and one of them looks like they're cuddled up on a sofa. At his flat, by the looks of it.'

Rosie was quiet again. As far as she could remember, Mitch had never posted photos of girlfriends before.

'Rosie, are you OK?' asked Jasmine.

'I'm fine,' she replied tersely. 'Isn't this what you wanted, anyway?'

'Sorry?'

'You thought I should cut Mitch out of my life, and it looks like he's done it for me!'

'Rosie, I'm sorry.' Jasmine pleaded. 'I thought it would help you move on. I never wanted it to happen like this. Or for you to get hurt. Do you want to come over? We're just going to eat pasta and watch TV. We'd love to have you.'

Rosie shook her head. 'No, I'm fine, I just want to go home.' She failed to add, *and cry desperate tears of sadness into my pillow.*

'I hate the thought of you being on your own, Rosie,' Jasmine said desperately. 'I can come to yours as soon as Chris gets in?'

'Jasmine, it's fine,' Rosie insisted. 'I'm completely fine being on my own, which is good, because it looks like I will have to get used to it.'

She hated the tone she was using with Jasmine but she couldn't help herself. She knew Jasmine was right. She needed to get over Mitch. And she knew now that Nadia and Ben's theory was wrong, that it was just them telling Rosie what she wanted to hear. Mitch had never given her any reason to believe he might like her romantically. And now she was so frustrated that she had allowed herself to get carried away in the daydream, even just for a moment.

'I've got to go. I'm getting on the tube,' she lied. 'I'll call you later.' And she ended the call, knowing that she wouldn't be calling Jasmine back that night.

Furiously, Rosie woke her computer and started angry-typing an update to Rachel, whose reply was instantaneous and curt.

'Good,' it read. 'Press release coming your way now. It's been approved by BioChem and the VC. Have it ready to send to *The Post* when I tell you.'

Rosie stretched her arms over her head and waited for the press release to land in her inbox. She'd read it through, update her electronic lab notebook with today's results, then go home, where she would switch her phone off to prevent her doing some idiotic internet-stalk of Jenny. Then take a long bath and attempt to numb her sadness with pizza and Netflix.

Right on time, the email from Rachel arrived. The press release was in the body of the email, which would make it simple enough just to forward when Rosie was told to. She scanned it, hoping her name wouldn't be mentioned too many times, if at all. But it was extremely vanilla which gave her hope that the news desk at *The Post* would ignore it and Mitch might never even hear about it.

But then an attachment at the bottom of the email caught her eye. Idly wondering whether it was the press release as a PDF, Rosie clicked it open before realising three things in quick succession: firstly this was not a PDF, it was an email chain, secondly that it was an email chain between Rachel and the VC, which was definitely not for Rosie's eyes, and thirdly, Rachel would be apoplectic if she ever found out that Rosie had seen it.

Rosie shut it down but not before she had received far too much information about how Rachel and the VC had spent their recreational time at a recent conference. Horrified, Rosie picked her phone up and dialled Nadia's extension, hoping against hope that tonight was a night that Nico was picking the kids up and that Nadia would still be around.

Her wishes were granted.

'Hello?' came Nadia's curt response.

'Nadia,' whispered Rosie. 'You have to come to my office right now.'

'Er, OK. Why?'

'I can't tell you. You have to come and see something on my computer.'

There was a sigh.

'Can't you just email it to me?'

'No!' Rosie whisper shrieked. 'You have to come and see it.'

'Why are we whispering?'

'Just get down here now.'

Three minutes later, an out of breath Nadia appeared in Rosie's office doorway. In those three minutes Rosie had not moved, in fact she had barely breathed and was staring at her computer as if it was a poisonous snake that was ready to strike should she make one false move.

'Show me,' demanded Nadia.

'Shut the door!' barked Rosie. 'Is Rachel still here?'

'I don't know. Why?'

'Just shut it and then come look at this.'

Rosie nudged her mouse and then shut her eyes, allowing Nadia to revel in the full glory of their boss's extracurricular activities. It took some time, the emails were extensive.

There was a long silence as Nadia digested all the information.

'Wow,' she said eventually. 'So, I guess they are still at it then?'

Rosie gazed up at Nadia who was still bent over Rosie's desk.

'That's it? That's all you've got to say?'

'Well, yeah,' Nadia said looking back at Rosie in confusion. 'What do you want me to say? They're consenting adults, neither of them are married. I mean, I guess I would prefer not to know how the VC gets his kicks, but each to their own. Everyone has their little quirks.'

'Nadia,' Rosie said with a quiver of panic in her voice. 'Are you not going to ask me why this is on my computer?'

'Oh, right!' Realisation dawned on Nadia. 'Yeah, what's the deal there?'

'It's attached to the BioChem press release that Rachel just sent me,' Rosie said in a panicked voice.

'That's weird,' Nadia scrunched her nose up. 'Firstly, why would you save your filthy emails as a PDF? And second, why would she have attached *it* and sent it to *you*?' she asked as she wandered over to one of Rosie's office chairs and flung herself into it.

'Well, Nadia,' Rosie said scathingly, 'I am guessing it was an accident and she didn't mean to send it.'

Nadia started laughing, 'Yeah, I suppose so. I mean, would you want your students knowing that what you really like in bed is—'

'Nadia!' screamed Rosie, closing her eyes and holding her hands up. 'Please. There are things in there that I now can't get out of my head, I do not need you repeating them, thank you.'

Nadia carried on sniggering. 'Still doesn't explain why she saved them in the first place.'

'Oh, I don't know Nadia.' Rosie tried to stem her irritation that Nadia seemed to be completely missing the point here. 'Maybe she keeps a stash of them? Maybe she saves all her dirty messages?'

Nadia's face brightened with understanding. 'Like a personal porn collection?'

'Yes. Just like that. But what do I do?' Rosie asked.

'Do? What do you mean?'

'Well, do I tell Rachel she sent this to me by accident?'

'Good god, no!' exclaimed Nadia sitting bolt upright. 'Are you mad? Rachel might fire you out of embarrassment when she finds out that you've read she gets turned on by—'

'Enough!' screeched Rosie again and she glared at Nadia who simply grinned back at her, seemingly unperturbed by this new, unexpected and unpleasant insight they now had into their boss's sex life.

'Don't you think it will be worse when she realises she's sent it to me and I never said anything?' asked Rosie.

'Rosie,' Nadia said levelly, 'how often do you go back and look at your sent emails?'

Rosie considered whether Nadia wanted the real answer, which was actually quite often because she liked to file them away by date and subject matter should she need to refer to them at a later date. She decided that Nadia might think that was strange so opted for a white lie instead.

'Rarely?'

'Exactly. She'll probably never know she's sent it to you.'

'But isn't that like—'

'No,' said Nadia firmly. 'Because if you tell her you know, then she will always know that you know and then she'll be forced to act irrationally.'

'Such as?' Rosie asked weakly.

'Firing you,' Nadia shot back. 'I'm joking!' she said quickly seeing the look of panic on Rosie's face. 'As if Rachel has ever been irrational. She can't fire you simply because she sent you an email outlining her sexual proclivities in eye-watering detail. Imagine what HR would say if she tried.'

Rosie groaned at the thought.

'But I think it's much better to say nothing and let it all drift off into the ether. Except when you see Rachel and the VC in the same room, and it all comes flooding back to you.' Nadia cackled evilly and Rosie rolled her eyes.

'Just don't end up doing something stupid and forwarding that to anyone.' Nadia pointed her finger at Rosie.

Rosie rolled her eyes again. 'I know?' she said. 'That's why I got you here to look at it rather than sending it on to you.'

'Very wise,' replied Nadia leaping suddenly from her chair. 'Right, I have to go. I have a pressing engagement with Year Two maths homework.' She mimed shooting herself in the head and wandered out of Rosie's office.

Rosie still hadn't managed to get certain images out of her mind by the time she got home that evening. She'd tried listening to Miley Cyrus at top volume which hadn't helped but had got her dirty looks from the Clapham Mummies on the Northern line. She'd downloaded an incredibly boring podcast on genome editing, which had begun to have the required brain-numbing effect until Rachel was mentioned as an upcoming guest and immediately an image of the VC naked from the waist down had sprung into her mind. Obviously, these images were drawn entirely from descriptions in the email and not from Rosie's first-hand experience, but that made them no less real and she shuddered nonetheless.

Now not only did she have to worry about Mitch and BioChem, but also not accidentally exposing her boss's illicit *and* explicit affair with the Vice Chancellor. Her list of things to be anxious about was growing daily. She slumped into one of her kitchen chairs and stared morosely out of the window wondering how long she could waste deciding on what to order on

Deliveroo, and hoping that the same driver who had delivered the last three nights would be on a different route for the evening. She was all out of the ability to deal with judgement right now.

Her laptop pinged at her. It was sat at the far side of her kitchen table and she half-heartedly pulled it towards her. The previous week, driven completely insane by the constant traffic, she had turned the dating notifications off on her phone but she hadn't yet done so on her laptop. Rosie hadn't looked at them in days, her mind on Mitch instead, but something tonight caught her eye: a familiar name.

Quickly, she pulled the laptop closer to her, her breath catching in her throat. She must be mistaken, her mind playing tricks on her. How much excess stress and anxiety did one have to experience in order to hallucinate? Or maybe there were two of them? One of them on this dating app sending her a message, and the other her ex-boyfriend, the one who had stolen her heart when he'd left for America all those years ago. Because surely it couldn't be the same Connor Ryan who was now messaging her, could it?

Her attention was now fully snared as she clicked open the message, only pausing momentarily to consider how the sight of Connor's name could still have an effect on her all these years later. She was intrigued to know what this alter ego of Connor's was like and she allowed herself a smile to think how funny it would be if she ended up going on a date with him. She just imagined the teasing that Mitch would subject her to, before she stopped and reminded herself that they weren't even on speaking terms, let alone teasing terms.

Opening her messages, she gave an involuntary gasp; just from the opening lines she could tell that this wasn't an alter ego. This was him, *her* Connor Ryan, the one who had left her heartbroken at Heathrow when he had moved to Washington to pursue his dream of reenacting *All The President's Men* and winning a Pulitzer for his efforts.

Hi Rosie

After months of procrastination, I finally succumbed to the pressure to join the online dating world. I had resisted because I couldn't believe that I would find the one on here. My friends called me a snob and perhaps they were right. Because the first person I saw on here was you. Some would call this a blast from the past, I would prefer to call it fate.

I'm in London and would love to meet for a drink if that's not an inappropriate thing to ask? If it is, I apologise and you can tell me, or just block me, whichever you prefer. I couldn't ignore the feeling that it was destiny that led me back to you on here.

Connor

Rosie sat back in her chair and stared at her screen. What were the chances? That after all these years, Connor would be back in London, single, and that the algorithms had aligned and thrown them together? For a moment she thought she might be dreaming. This sort of thing didn't happen in real life, did it? If Mitch had been speaking to her, she would have picked her phone up immediately to discuss it with him. But he wasn't and so she didn't. She considered calling Jasmine but she was worried Jas would say something less than constructive, such as pointing out that getting over Mitch by getting under her ex was not especially healthy.

Rosie recognised Connor immediately from the tone of his message. Well-written and to the point, confident but self-effacing too. It brought up so many memories of their time together and despite herself she smiled, momentarily forgetting all the other rubbish stuff that was going on in her life.

Rosie's hands hovered over her keyboard... Was this a good idea? Even to meet him for a drink might open a whole can of worms. She had successfully erased him from her life for a reason.

But there was also a part of her that wondered if maybe he was right, and this was fate. And, silencing Jasmine's imaginary voice, maybe this was the answer to her heartache over Mitch. If anyone could make her forget about Mitch, it would be Connor Ryan.

Before she could over-analyse everything that had led her to this point, and where her decision might take her next, she typed a reply. It was no good trying to be clever with language, Connor would see straight through that. He made wordplay into an art form. Rosie kept her reply brief although she was dying to ask him so many questions: about where he had been, how long he had been back in London for, and most importantly, how many girlfriends he'd had over the years.

It suddenly struck her that he could have been married or had children for all she knew. But something more than hope told her he hadn't. She had always told herself that Connor was too much of a free spirit to put down roots, and that's why things hadn't worked out between them. The star-crossed lovers narrative would have to have been rewritten if all it took was a different girl on a different continent to persuade him to settle down.

Hey, stranger, what are the chances? Lovely to see your name pop up. Let me know when you're free. Rosie x

---

Connor suggested they meet for a coffee near her work the very next day. He had wasted no time in replying with both a time and a place, presuming that Rosie would be free. For half a second, she had thought about playing it cool and pretending to be busy, but given she hadn't seen him in over a decade, was desperate to find out everything he had been up to and he had picked a place right around the corner from her work, she decided against it and messaged him back to agree. She knew she was going against every rule in the dating handbook by appearing too available and keen, but it wasn't like the dating handbook had firm guidance for what to do when your ex turned up out of the blue, offering to meet you at an incredibly convenient location *and* you were trying to get over the heartbreak of falling out with your best friend who you had secretly been in love with for a decade. When they updated it to include that guidance, Rosie would follow it. Until then she would live by her own rules.

Still, her heart was in her mouth when she walked into the coffee shop the following morning. She was dying to ask all those questions about what his life had been like since they had last seen each other, in tears, in an airport departure hall. Just thinking about that day made her emotional. But first she needed to get through ordering a coffee and drinking some of it, and presumably making polite small talk for a few minutes as well. These weren't the kind of questions one could launch straight into.

The window of the coffee shop was misted up. It had been cold overnight, and frost had settled in small patches on the ground. Rosie hadn't been able to look inside and see if she could catch a glimpse of Connor before she walked in. Inside it was busy, the combination of hot coffee and chattering commuters adding to the misted windows. But as soon as she walked in she saw him, stood at the far end of the coffee counter, evidently waiting for her before he placed his order. He had his back to her but even after all these years she recognised his slim frame. She had spent the previous twenty-four hours wondering how he had changed physically. There wasn't much to go on in his profile, just a head shot which she recognised from a time she had accidentally caught site of his byline on a news story before speedily closing the tab.

Rosie gave herself a moment to compose herself and observe him. He looked at ease, comfortably leaning against the counter studying his phone. She didn't get long – something caught his eye and he looked up, spotting her moments later in the doorway. His face broke into a smile and he walked towards her, his arms open wide in order to hug her. Rosie felt her breath catch in her throat as his arms encircled her. The years seemed to drop away and they could have been those young graduates, enjoying those halcyon summer days before the reality of working all hours for the man had kicked in.

'You haven't changed a bit!' he said as he led her back to where he had been standing in line.

'Neither have you!' she replied, although now, close up, she could see those years marked in various places. His eyes were slightly more hooded than they had been when she had last seen him. The smile lines around them that she had loved were more clearly defined. His hair was shorter, and he had a sprinkling of grey at his temples. But none of this detracted from his classic good looks, and anyway, the accepted response to his comment was to demur and say likewise. Unused as she was to meeting up with ex-boyfriends, Rosie recognised that commenting on ageing would have made things awkward and weird. And maybe he was noticing changes about her, too. But whatever he saw, it wasn't stopping the smile he had pasted on his face since she had walked in.

'What can I get you?' he asked as they found themselves at the front of the queue. While Rosie wavered between tea and coffee, eventually settling on coffee, Connor turned to the barista and said, 'This is the girl who broke my heart; we haven't seen each other in years.'

'Name?' asked the barista, who couldn't have looked less interested in their reunion. Connor gallantly waved away Rosie's attempts at paying.

'He was friendly,' Connor said as they stood and waited for their coffees.

Rosie looked at him and laughed, 'Well, you probably embarrassed him.'

'How?' He looked at her in surprise.

'Telling him that I broke your heart!' she said, she felt a blush creeping up her chest as she said it. 'And anyway, it's not true.'

'Totally is,' he said, picking their coffees up and ushering her to a free table in the window.

Rosie smiled to herself; this was the Connor she remembered, magnanimous and charming. And with a journalist's ability to completely rewrite history.

'It's really great to see you,' he said pulling out a chair for her to sit on. 'I'm glad you didn't think a message from me was too strange.' He sat down opposite her. 'I couldn't believe it when I saw your profile. I thought it must be some mistake because I couldn't believe you'd be single. You *are* single, aren't you?' he said, leaning forward across the table as if to check. He picked up her left hand and studied it carefully to check for the indentation of a hastily removed ring.

Rosie laughed and tried not to be too flattered by Connor's irreverent charm. But it was hard not to be. With everything else going on in her life right now, Connor lavishing attention on her was pretty difficult to resist.

'Well,' he continued, putting her hand down, 'even if you're not, I'm glad you agreed to meet me.' He took a sip of his coffee and grimaced.

'Not good?' she asked, pleased to be able to move the subject away from her love life.

'I guess when you've drunk coffee in some of the places where they actually grow the beans it sort of ruins it when you drink it anywhere else.'

Rosie had so many questions, like when was the last time he was in a coffee-growing region? Where? Surely he had had to endure many cafe chain coffees as a journalist, and were they really that bad? And finally, did he realise that he came across as just a tiny bit pompous? But she kept those questions to herself, and generously decided that he was perhaps nervous and showing off.

'I was surprised to see your name, definitely,' Rosie replied, choosing not to engage him in any more coffee-drinking posturing. 'But I didn't think it was strange to get your message. I liked it.' She bit back a smile.

'Surprised?' he asked. 'Why?'

'Oh, just surprised you were back in London. And I guess I didn't think dating apps would be your thing.'

Connor laughed. 'Well as I said in my message, they're not, but my friends persuaded me to give them a try and I'm glad I did. I'm also glad that you haven't changed, Rosie, still asking incisive questions.'

Rosie frowned and turned to look out of the window, which was still as misted up as it had been when she had entered. Did she ask incisive questions? Sometimes she felt like she didn't ask enough questions, but maybe Connor remembered a different side to her, a more confident side. One that hadn't been beaten down by London dating and heartbreak over the years. Maybe he brought out her best side.

'Now, tell me why,' Rosie turned to look back at Connor as he spoke. 'Tell me why it's so strange that *I* should be on a dating app?' he asked, the sound of amusement clear in his voice.

Rosie considered this. She watched his face which she had once known so well, she heard the carefully combative tone which she recalled him using often, always managing to fall on the right side of what was considered polite. She didn't want to confess to him that she had built him up in her mind to be a mythical creature, the kind of person who couldn't exist in real-life London, and who certainly wouldn't be found dead on a dating app.

Instead she shrugged and said, 'Honestly? I thought you'd find it soulless.'

'Interesting.' He took another drink and this time he didn't pull a face. 'Although I would have said exactly the same about you.'

Rosie looked at him curiously. 'Really?' she asked.

'Really' he insisted. 'You were always so vibrant, so in tune with people. I couldn't imagine you needing dating apps to meet someone. Everyone always loved you. At least I always did.'

Rosie felt herself blush. She remembered how consuming it was when Connor turned his full attention on you. She chose to ignore the suggestion that using a dating app was a sign of desperation, or of her having lost the charm of her younger years.

'Tell me about you?' he continued, either not noticing or not caring about the effect he was having on her. 'Still in academia? I saw you got your PhD. I was really proud of you when I heard.'

Rosie felt a ripple of pleasure thrill through her; had he been keeping tabs on her all these years? 'I was one of the fastest in my year to graduate.' There was just something about Connor that made her want to impress him.

'I'm not surprised,' he said, 'you were always the smartest girl I knew.'

They smiled at each other across the table, their eyes locked, Rosie's stomach doing cartwheels. She was back in her early twenties, thinking about those memories she had shared with Connor and everything that had happened to her since.

'But now, my clever girl, I'm afraid I have to go.' He drained his coffee cup.

'You do?' Rosie asked in confusion. She glanced at her watch and tried to ignore the uncomfortable sensation that she was being both brushed off and patronised at the same time. She wasn't sure she was *his* anything, yet. And the way he said 'clever girl' made her skin tingle, and not in the good way.

'Yep. I'm on deadline. Need to get an interview done before I lose this contract.'

'Oh, OK.' Rosie tried to hide the disappointment in her voice. Was this a brush off? His way of saying 'hi but bye'? He'd completed this walk down memory lane and it had not lived up to his expectations?

'But...' He leaned over the table and grabbed her hands. 'Can I see you again?'

'Oh!'

'Only if you're *sure* you're single?' he said teasingly.

'Definitely single,' she managed to say.

'I'll call you, 'he said and stood up. He leaned down and brushed his lips against her cheek. Damn, he smelt good. Sort of woody but citrusy at the same time. And his lips on her cheek pushed all her negative thoughts to one side, causing instead a long-forgotten sensation in parts of her anatomy which she had begun to fear had gone into permanent hibernation.

He took one of her hands in his and looked down into her eyes. 'It's really great to see you, Rosie, it's made me realise how much I've missed you, how much I've missed out on.'

Rosie tried to come up with a witty response, but she ended up sounding more like a frog in distress. Not that Connor seemed to notice.

'I want to take you out, somewhere special. Would that be OK?'

She nodded, not trusting her voice to come out in a normal pitch. The last thing she wanted was to scare him off by sounding like a foghorn again.

He grinned, kissed her hand and then he was gone. Rosie looked around. No one else seemed to recognise the momentous occasion that had just occurred under their very noses. The barista looked as bored and disinterested in the path of true love as he had been half an hour ago. But Rosie tried not to care. Connor was back, he was just as she remembered him and he was definitely interested in her. Not that it had been a date, but it was the best non-date she had been on in a long time, and she still had a proper date with him to look forward to.

The next two days passed in a blur for Rosie. The press release had yet to be approved so she was still waiting for the go ahead from Rachel to send it. Which meant she could park that particular anxiety for the moment. She was busy in the lab, getting the assays done for BioChem. Nadia had offered to help, but Rosie knew she was busy herself, trying to get new funding in place for her projects. And anyway, Nadia had never had the steadiest hands when it came to pipettes, and Rosie didn't want to risk more muck-ups. Mitch still wasn't talking to her, and Rosie had taken Jasmine's advice and hadn't tried to contact him again. She felt a dull ache when she thought about him so she tried not to, and for the most part it worked. And at least she now had Connor to take her mind off Mitch. So whenever her mind drifted to thoughts of him, she tried to think of Connor instead. If Mitch was going to ignore her then maybe she could do the same? Perhaps Connor was right, perhaps this was fate and this was how it was all meant to be.

And Connor hadn't given her much chance not to be thinking of him; within an hour of leaving the coffee shop he had messaged telling her that his interview was a waste of time and that he wished he had stayed with her instead. Before she had had a chance to reply, he asked her if she was free in two nights' time and when she told him she was he sent her reservation details at the Cafe Royal. Rosie smiled to herself when she saw the address; she remembered the conversation she and Connor had had before he left for America. He told her that when he came back he'd take her somewhere fancy with his first pay cheque, somewhere like the Cafe Royal. At least he'd kept his word, even if it was over a decade late.

He'd told her to meet him in the hotel bar at 7pm so Rosie found herself on Regent Street pushing through the tourists and the Christmas shoppers. It was bedlam; buses were backed up along Regent Street and Piccadilly Circus, horns were blaring, pedestrians were spilling dangerously out into the street and oblivious tourists were causing chaos by stopping to take photos of the Christmas lights. So much for peace and goodwill, Rosie thought, as a man in a suit shouted angrily at a bunch of kids who had inadvertently tripped him up with their Hamleys bags.

Against all this, the Cafe Royal was a haven of contemporary class amongst the tourist attractions of central London. The Christmas festivities hadn't yet infiltrated this achingly cool bar and Rosie was relieved to see that Connor was already there and waiting for her, leaning against the bar in the corner. As if he could sense her arrival, he looked up and grinned when he saw her, and Rosie felt her stomach swoop. After all these years, it was nice to experience it with someone other than Mitch.

She walked over and he wrapped his arm around her waist, bringing her up against him and kissing her on the lips. She felt lightheaded with anticipation of what the evening might bring. *This* was the date she had been waiting for all these years, and *this* was the guy who was supposed to sweep her off her feet. She just knew it. And if the start of the evening was anything to go by then perhaps it would make up for the lost years and all that time they had spent apart.

Connor waved to the barman and turned to ask Rosie, 'Would you like champagne?'

Rosie glanced around her, taking in the crystal chandeliers, the sparkling cocktail shakers and the whispered conversations of the other patrons and decided that yes, yes she would very much like champagne, thank you.

'You look amazing,' Connor said, looking Rosie up and down in such a way that made her feel that frankly it had been unnecessary to have spent so long deciding on what to wear. Most of her wardrobe lay discarded on the floor of her bedroom, but she had finally settled on skintight, jet-black jeans, stiletto boots and a floral blouse that she sometimes worried made her look like Henry VIII but tonight was obviously working for her, unless Connor had developed a Tudor fetish in the intervening years. She also congratulated herself on choosing good underwear, too. If Connor was looking at her like this now, who knew where the night might end? She enjoyed the fizzing sensation inside her and sipped her champagne.

'So, the interview was a waste of time?' she asked. 'You're not going to run out on me again?'

Connor took her hand. 'I promise,' he said, 'I wish I hadn't run out on you for America.' He let his statement stand for a second. 'And yes, the interview was a complete waste of time.' He shook his head. 'I don't know why these people agree to be interviewed and then refuse to say anything.'

'Can I ask who you were interviewing?'

Connor leaned forward and put his hand on her thigh, then he whispered into her ear, 'You can, but I'd have to test your ability to keep a secret under pressure first.'

Rosie bit her lip and looked up into his face. He was staring

287

down at her mouth, looking at her as if *he* wanted to be the one biting her lip.

She cleared her throat, unsure of how to respond. She turned to the bar, picking up her glass of champagne in an attempt to clear her head. Connor took the hint and leaned back but he kept his hand right where it was on her thigh. Dangerously close to being inappropriate for a public place.

'So,' Rosie said, wondering how on earth she was supposed to make polite conversation with Connor, who looked like he just wanted to undress her there and then. Actually it was making her feel uncomfortable rather than desired. 'What brought you back to London, then?' She played nervously with the stem of her champagne flute.

'This and that,' Connor said non-committally, leaning back and finally taking his hand off her thigh. Rosie felt a sigh of relief, she was beginning to think her entire lower body would go numb with the effort of sitting still to prevent his hand from creeping any higher.

'Actually,' he said after a pause, 'there's been a spate of weddings and you know what it's like. You start getting all the standard questions about when you might settle down, whether it might be you next. You know, the usual.' He smiled at her knowingly. 'But I suppose it started me thinking about what I *do* want and whether I did want to be next or not.'

Rosie nodded in agreement. 'There's nothing worse than being the only single person at a wedding,' she laughed. 'All those well-meaning comments about it being your turn next, that you just haven't met the right person. I always want to shout something inappropriate like maybe I don't want to get married, or maybe I have met the right person but...' She felt herself blush again, knowing she was on the verge of saying too much. 'But it's not the right time,' she said quickly. Connor gave her a curious look.

They both took a drink. 'So did it feel strange to leave Washington?' she asked.

Connor looked momentarily confused. 'Oh, I haven't been in DC for years.'

'Really?' she asked. 'I imagined you getting into the political scene there and never wanting to leave,' Rosie laughed.

'Yeah but the real DC is not like *Veep* or *The West Wing*, you know. There aren't loads of incredibly smart, good-looking and essentially well-intentioned people walking the corridors, talking quickly. It's real life, not TV,' he said archly.

'So more *Designated Survivor*?' quipped Rosie before noticing the look of disdain on Connor's face. Perhaps she had misremembered and Connor wasn't much one for the banter? Maybe it was Mitch that'd had the thing about Kiefer Sutherland? 'I mean, of course not,' she quickly continued. 'I just thought, you know, you seemed so keen to go.'

Neither of them said anything for a moment, Rosie was thinking back to the painful conversations that had consumed them when Connor had first been offered that job. How dedicated he had been to the political cause, how driven he had been by his career. And how supportive and undemanding Rosie had been even when she had been desperate for him to show as much dedication and drive towards their relationship instead. Connor meanwhile was studying the whiskey menu.

Rosie felt panicked. Was she really about to lose him over an ill-judged joke about a rubbish Kiefer Sutherland series? 'So, where else have you been working?' Rosie picked her champagne up again, put it back down, readjusted the fancy napkin that the barman had placed underneath it. All the while she was hoping she could move their conversation away from American political TV series and back into something less challenging, like how uncomfortable it was to be the only single person at a wedding.

'Oh,' he said, looking up from the whiskey menu. 'I basically get moved each time there's a new political event to cover. I've been all over the world.' He stretched back on his bar stool, giving Rosie a glimpse of his stomach which was definitely flabbier than she recalled it being. She looked quickly away, keen not to let the spell break entirely.

'I think the longest I've stayed in one place was six months and that was partly because I got sick and spent three months recuperating.'

'I'm sorry,' Rosie said with sympathy, 'that must have been tough to be away and be sick.'

'It comes with the territory,' he said, 'one of the drawbacks of the career I chose.' He nodded sagely. 'Or perhaps,' he continued, starting to laugh at his own joke, 'the career that chose me. I think I was fated to be a journalist.'

There it was again, Connor's use of the word fate. Did he really believe in fate? Or was it a useful phrase that he used to convey the magic and mystery of being Connor Ryan. Was it really fate that had led him back to Rosie or something else? She didn't know what to say. Despite her best endeavours to reignite those feelings she had felt for Connor back in the day, and the excitement she was desperate to feel ever since his dramatic arrival back into her life, it was all starting to feel a little like a damp squib. One more smug comment and all her feels for him might disappear forever.

He was definitely different to the boy she remembered. More self-absorbed and dare she say it, arrogant? But Rosie had spent enough time around high-achieving men to consider putting this down to bravado. Maybe he was nervous about seeing her again? Just as she was nervous about seeing him.

'So, where's the best place you've been? What's your favourite location?' she asked, bending over backwards to lighten the tone and to get him to relax.

'That,' he said, reaching over to pick his whiskey tumbler up and roll the remaining liquid over the melting ice cubes, 'is an easy question to ask.'

'And to answer?' Rosie asked bluntly. She was becoming frustrated with doing all the heavy lifting in this conversation.

But he didn't get the chance to answer, because just at that moment Rosie's stool was knocked from behind, and her glass flew out of her hand, throwing what was left of her champagne all over Connor's neatly pressed shirt.

'What the—!' he exclaimed, throwing his hands up in anger.

'I'm so sorry!' the person behind Rosie said.

Rosie whipped round, stunned to hear that voice. 'Mitch?'

'Rosie!' 'Are you OK?' Mitch asked with both surprise and concern. 'I'm so sorry, the person the other side of me knocked into me. I didn't know it was you.' He looked down at her, both of them sensing the awkwardness that was heading their way.

'You two know each other?' asked Connor.

Neither Rosie nor Mitch said anything.

'What are you doing here?' asked Rosie eventually, ignoring Connor's question.

'Erm, early Christmas drinks with some work people,' Mitch replied, nodding towards the corner of the bar where a group of people were sat.

Connor was now stood up with a small dark, damp stain spreading across his shirt. 'I'm sorry, who are you?' he said confrontationally to Mitch.

Rosie stood, too. 'Mitch this is Connor, an old friend.' Rosie saw the gleam of recognition in Mitch's eye. Even now he would remember who Connor was, who he had been to Rosie. But he said nothing and politely allowed Rosie to finish the incredibly painful introductions.

'Connor, this is Mitch...' Her voice tailed off. She didn't really know how to describe Mitch. Could she get away with still calling him a friend? She certainly wasn't going to go with, 'Oh, hey this is Mitch, the guy I've been in love with for years and who I was hoping you, Connor, would help me get over.' She raised her eyes to the ceiling, wishing she was anywhere but stood between these two men.

Luckily, Mitch saved her by extending his hand towards Connor. 'I'm really sorry about your shirt,' he said, 'but pleased to meet you anyway.'

Rosie could tell he sensed how awkward this was for everyone. Mitch hated to put anyone in an uncomfortable position and he didn't want to be rude but at the same time it was obvious that he too would rather be anywhere else than stood at that bar right now.

Connor said nothing for a moment leaving Mitch looking increasingly uncomfortable. 'Can I get you another drink? Some napkins?' he offered. He picked up some napkins that the barman, seeing what had happened, had discreetly placed on the bar. 'So, you're the Connor that Rosie was at uni with, right?'

It was obvious to Rosie that Mitch was floundering, too. He didn't know what to say to this person he had never met but had heard so much about, and whose date with his ex-best friend he appeared to have crashed.

Connor's chest seemed to swell with pride at being recognised. 'I am,' he confirmed. 'Although I have absolutely no idea who *you* are,' he added laughing.

Rosie winced at his tone. Mitch looked at Rosie as if to confirm what he should say, but she had no advice to offer. Her eyes widened in panic.

'Rosie and I used to work together,' Mitch finally said neutrally.

'Oh, right, so you're an academic as well,' Connor said dismissively, as if being an academic was one of the most boring professions in the world.

'Actually, no, I'm a journalist, I'm the science correspondent for *The Post*.' Mitch paused. 'You're a journalist, too, aren't you? Who is it you work for?'

For the first time Connor looked awkward. 'I'm freelance,' he blustered. Mitch looked baffled before turning to Rosie.

'You're OK?' he asked, 'I didn't hurt you? Can I get *you* another drink?' Rosie shook her head, mutely refusing to meet Mitch's eye.

'Of course she's OK,' Connor said somewhat aggressively, 'I'm the one who got the drink poured down my front.'

Mitch turned back and looked Connor up and down calmly before saying, 'As I said, I'm sorry, but I'm sure you'll live. Bye Rosie.' And he picked up his drink from the bar, turned on his heel and walked away.

Rosie watched him go, her heart pounding as he went. He threaded his way through the bar to a table in the corner, directly in her line of sight. She watched as he gave a tight smile to the people sat at the table. Two of them stood up to let him pass and he sat. As he put down his glass he looked up and caught Rosie's eye. His expression was completely unreadable.

'What an incredibly arrogant guy,' Connor said.

'Excuse me?' said Rosie, startled out of her observances of Mitch.

'That guy,' Connor replied, jerking his head over his shoulder in the direction of Mitch. 'He seemed incredibly arrogant. I bet you're pleased you don't have to work with him anymore.'

Rosie said nothing. She realised how little Connor actually

knew or understood her, and how much she was starting to wish, despite her very best endeavours, that she was sitting here with Mitch and not with Connor.

She wondered how on earth she was supposed to salvage the evening. Connor seemed even more self-absorbed now that he was covered in champagne. He kept stretching up to look at himself in the mirror behind the bar and was constantly patting down the front of his shirt and then looking over his shoulder, presumably to see if anyone else had noticed what had happened.

'So, how are you finding life now you're back in London?' she asked again, her tone flat, her thoughts back on Mitch and wondering whether he felt as confused and sad as she was now feeling.

'Hmm? Oh, it's OK. For the moment.'

'For the moment?' Rosie repeated. 'I don't understand. I thought you were back for good? You know, wanting to settle down etc? The pressure of weddings?'

Connor laughed. 'Oh, god no,' he said. 'I can't imagine anything more depressing than conforming to *that* traditional stereotype: falling in love, a big white wedding, two kids, moving to suburbia.'

Rosie looked at him in surprise. She didn't want a big white wedding, she wasn't sure if she wanted one kid let alone two, and she couldn't imagine anything worse than moving to suburbia. But the way he said all of this, with such bitterness and scorn, left her cold.

'That was one of the reasons that I looked you up,' Connor was saying.

'Excuse me?' Rosie replied. 'Looked me up? I thought you came across me by accident? You know, fate?'

Connor waved his hands as if her question was an irrelevance. 'Yes, yes, what I meant was that was one of the reasons I was keen to see you again. To see if you still had the same level of disdain for tradition that we always shared.'

Rosie's confusion only increased. Had she been so disdainful? She remembered her and Connor having long, philosophical discussions about the institution of marriage. Perhaps she had even said she didn't believe in it back then, she couldn't recall, it *was* a long time ago and they *were* only at university. But she didn't remember being as cynical as Connor was making her out to be.

'I don't remember being so sure of my future back when I was twenty-one,' she said tactfully.

She looked over Connor's shoulder as she said this and became sharply aware that Mitch was watching her. How long he had been doing so she didn't know, but he quickly looked down at his drink when she caught his eye.

Connor laughed at her reply. 'Yes well, quite,' he said, 'we were kids then, weren't we?'

Rosie wasn't really sure what he was getting at. The evening was taking an unexpected turn. Connor was not the person she had recalled and Mitch's arrival had thrown her composure completely.

'But you must be planning to be back in London for a while if you've signed up to dating apps?' she asked.

'Actually I have them in most of the countries I spend any time in,' Connor said.

'What?' she asked incredulously. 'Firstly that must be incredibly time-consuming; and secondly, what's the point if you're only around for a brief period of time?'

Connor raised his eyebrow at her. He probably thought he was being mysterious, she thought and she was quickly growing weary of him.

'Are you really asking me why I'm on them?' he joked. 'I

disable them when I'm out of the country and reactivate them when I get in. So they don't distract me.' He sounded so smug. Rosie wanted to punch him.

'I don't understand?' she said, her tone hardening. 'Aren't there apps for random hookups? Why aren't you on those?'

'Because, Rosie,' he said condescendingly, 'there is a certain type of girl who goes on those apps and they're not the kind of girl I'm interested in.'

Rosie felt a furious flush creep up her neck, and this time not because Connor was making her blush, this was a flush born out of pure fury. 'You mean the female equivalent of you? Girls who are interested in one-night stands?' she challenged him. 'And before you start,' she continued, 'this is not some moral judgement on my part, I'm not saying there is anything wrong with that, but what I am saying is that it seems morally dubious to be using these apps under false pretences. Pretending to be interested in a relationship when you're just interested in sex.'

She practically spat the final word. She was aware that their conversation was becoming more heated and it was drawing attention. She knew Mitch was watching her again and something about the chivalry he had displayed to her earlier on in the evening, compared to the cavalier attitude of Connor, fired her up even more.

'Oh, come off it, Rosie,' protested Connor. 'It's not like I'm tricking girls. I tell them I'm not in town for long and not interested in a long-term relationship.'

'Do you tell them this before or after you sleep with them?' she challenged. 'Because there is a big difference, Connor.' Her eyes flashed with anger. Connor merely smiled; it was no different to his usual smile but now it made him look sleazy.

'I get it,' he said at last.

'Get what?' she snapped back.

'I thought you wouldn't have changed, but I guess you have. It seems to happen to most *girls*.'

'Please don't patronise me by calling me a girl. I'm a grown woman Connor.'

'Sorry,' he held his hands up, 'I didn't mean to offend. But that's what I'm talking about. Most *women*,' he said with emphasis, 'pretend that they're anti-establishment, not interested in settling down and getting married and having babies. But as soon as they hit thirty and their friends start doing it, they can't trap you into it fast enough. I've had it happen so many times,' he said somewhat sadly.

'Excuse me?' Rosie said, now practically incandescent with rage. 'You think women trick you? Don't you think you're the one tricking them into sleeping with you? And why is it not OK to change your mind? Why are we supposed to want and feel the same things in our thirties that we wanted at twenty? It's called growing up, Connor, maturing, which is something you obviously haven't yet done.'

It was as if a mask had fallen from his face. The Connor she had known was indeed the same one as the person sat in front of her now. But what had seemed charming and alternative when she was younger was now sad and bitter and downright misogynistic.

Maybe he had always been like this but she had been too young and naïve to recognise it? And as the mask slipped, so it felt too that a curtain had fallen from her memory. For too long she had thought of Connor as the one who had got away, the person who might have saved her from falling in love with Mitch. But she now saw that this simply wasn't the case.

Yes, it was inspiring that he had been passionate about his job and the move to America but she now realised that not for one moment had he considered that their relationship might have been worth fighting for. That they could have made it work if he had been a little less interested in himself and a little more interested in her. And that had the job offer in America not come up, then their relationship would have floundered anyway as she discovered what kind of man he really was. She would have met Mitch at work and perhaps he would have been the one to have made her realise the idiot that Connor was. Maybe it would have been Mitch all along anyway.

Movement caught her eye. Mitch had stood up and was saying something to his friends. One of them caught his arm as if to stop Mitch from leaving, but Mitch shook his head and picked his jacket up. The others quickly started doing the same, finishing drinks and picking up bags. Rosie watched them move towards the door as a group.

Before she could second guess herself, she hopped down from her bar stool. 'Excuse me,' she said to Connor, grabbed her purse and turned to follow them.

Baffled, Connor asked, 'What are you doing?'

Rosie turned back to him. 'I would say this has been a lovely trip down memory lane but that would be a lie. I'll say it's been a useful one.'

'Rosie, come on. Don't be so dramatic.' He tried to put his arm out to stop her but she shook him off. 'Where are you going?' he asked.

'To grow up, to be an adult, to take a risk that I should have taken a long time ago,' she shot back at him as she headed for the exit. She left him, stood at the bar, open-mouthed, and was happy she hadn't offered to split the bill.

Rosie pushed through the doors of the bar and looked both ways down the busy street. It was crowded and at first, she couldn't see Mitch, but then a flash of red caught her eye, the red coat of one of his friends. Quickly she headed in that direction, pushing past fellow Londoners on her way. No one batted an eyelid, they were all used to being pushed and pulled by the London crowds.

'Mitch!' she shouted as she saw them draw close to the stairs heading down into the underground at Piccadilly Circus.

She saw him start, wondering if he had heard his name called.

'Mitch!' she called again and this time he stopped and turned, almost being swept off his feet by the crowd as he did so. He spotted her.

'Rosie?' he called back. 'Are you OK?'

Even after everything, after the fights and the sabotaged relationships, after their fallback plan lay in tatters, the first thing Mitch did was to ask if she was all right. Rosie felt her heart soar in a much needed way after the bitterness and unpleasantness that had been her date with Connor. Mitch's friends stood hesitating on the top of the steps.

'I'll meet you there,' he said to them as he stood to one side and waited for Rosie.

Rosie hesitated. The crowd was only getting thicker but the distance between her and Mitch was closing. Two more steps and she would be close enough to touch him. Taking a deep breath, she took those two steps and looked up at him.

'Mitch, I...' she began, unsure of what she had planned to say.

Mitch looked down at her. He seemed hesitant, too, waiting for her to say something, almost willing her to do so. She felt herself totter on the brink of something major, this was the moment to tell him, to admit her feelings for him. If she didn't, she knew she would regret it, but again she had that small voice of doubt telling her that it could ruin everything.

But she had listened to that voice too many times, and what was there left to ruin? Mitch wasn't talking to her, anyway. And really, how could she tell him in words what she really felt? Surely there must be some truth that actions speak louder than words? Before Rosie could allow her stupid voice of caution to open its mouth and destroy any confidence she had, she stepped up on her tiptoes and kissed Mitch on the lips.

Around them the commuter crowd surged, Rosie felt herself losing her balance, but not before she had opened her eyes to see Mitch's wide-eyed look of surprise. Her lips felt charged by an electric current and she toppled slightly to the side. Mitch put his arm out to catch her but at that moment a loud group of men pushed through, pulling Mitch in one direction down the steps and Rosie in the other. Rosie could just see the top of Mitch's head over the crowd before it disappeared down the steps.

'Mitch!' she shouted again in desperation. She didn't know what that look had been on his face but she knew that he must have felt something to look so surprised.

'You OK, love?' a man asked as she felt herself propelled to the edge of the crowd.

Rosie put her hand out to steady herself against the brick wall of the building and nodded. He looked concerned, but then plunged into the crowd himself – concerned maybe, but not concerned enough to miss his train home. Rosie tried to catch her breath but her mind was racing. Part of her was punching the air in delight at having had the courage to kiss Mitch, *she'd done it!* But now she needed to find out what that look on his face meant.

She looked for an opening in the press of commuters and stepped back into the path, racing quickly down the steps into the ticket hall of Piccadilly Circus. London rush hour was not for the faint-hearted. People were rushing this way and that, swiping their cards and phones with precision over the readers before disappearing off down the escalators leading to the tube trains.

Desperately Rosie tried to scan the crowd but she couldn't see Mitch anywhere. Hadn't he waited for her? Known that she would come down the stairs and look for him? Couldn't he feel that? For a moment she thought about getting the tube over to his apartment, she could talk to him face to face there. Make him understand. Maybe even kiss him again... Her heart squeezed tightly at the memory. But he had been heading somewhere with friends, hadn't he? That was obvious. So he might not be back home for hours. Pulling her phone out, she tried to call him, but it went straight to voicemail as it would if he had got on the tube. She didn't leave a message, because what was the right thing to say to your best friend who you had just kissed?

Rosie walked around the ticket hall several times, hoping against hope that she would find Mitch waiting for her somewhere. On her third lap round, she finally accepted defeat. He wasn't here, he hadn't waited for her, he hadn't come back up to find her and he hadn't called her. That was what the expression on his face had meant, and it wasn't the answer to her kiss that she had been hoping for.

Her shoes felt like lead. All she wanted to do was to talk to Mitch but she now felt further away from him than ever. Resigned, she pulled her card out of her bag and headed for the tube herself. Her heart was heavy but she wasn't angry at herself for kissing Mitch. Quite the opposite. For the first time in a long time, Rosie felt she was living her life and taking some risks. It wasn't the answer she wanted, but she had an answer. Maybe it would be the end of her friendship with Mitch but at least she would now know and could follow Jasmine's advice. It was the last thing Rosie wanted, but maybe she was strong enough for a fresh start, maybe she could begin looking to the future and to start planning what the rest of her life might look like if Mitch wasn't in it.

Chapter Twenty-One

Rosie woke to several missed calls on her phone, none of which were from Mitch, and a pillow streaked with tears and mascara. The high from the previous night had dissipated quickly and she rolled over and bleakly observed the pile of clothes on her floor, left over from her date preparation. Although nothing materially had changed in her room since then, the excitement she had felt last night while she got ready, was in stark contrast to the nauseated despair she now felt. Damn men and their ability to ruin a perfectly good evening. She should have stayed in, ordered takeout and mainlined a box set. None of these had so far reduced her to tears in the way men had.

Two of the calls were from Connor who had left her a voicemail, which Rosie quickly consigned to oblivion by deleting it. Whatever that idiot had to say to her was not going to be worth listening to. Rosie wondered if there was a way of getting him barred from all dating apps before deciding that if the people who ran dating apps were at all interested in policing the behaviors of toxic men, the apps wouldn't exist in the first place.

The last call was from her mother and Rosie knew she needed to return it. She was just summoning up the mental resilience that would be needed to speak to anyone when her mother beat her to it.

'Mum,' Rosie said in as bright a voice as she could muster, 'I was just about to call you. Is everything OK?'

'Everything is fine, darling, don't worry. I was just calling to tell you I was going to be in town today and to ask if you would like to meet for lunch or a coffee? If you're not too busy.'

Rosie hesitated and her mind raced forward to her day ahead. She knew she had a ton of work to do in the lab, but her spot wasn't reserved until late morning. If she sat at her desk for too long, her mind would replay that kiss with Mitch over and over again. She needed something to distract her.

'Can we make it coffee?' she asked. 'I'm due in the lab at eleven but I can meet you before then?'

'Of course,' her mother replied enthusiastically. 'You can tell me all about how work is going, I want to hear everything.'

Everything. That was a broad ask, Rosie had a lot going on at work, what with BioChem and her suspect lab results and *those* emails of Rachel's she had seen. Maybe her mother didn't need to know *everything* about work. Perhaps those emails could be filed away with the copy of Rosie's PhD thesis that her mother had proudly insisted on having, but which had, as far as Rosie was aware, sat on a shelf gathering dust ever since.

'Can we meet at that place on Russell Square?' her mother asked.

Rosie frowned. 'You mean the place where the baristas are always rude and the coffee is terrible?'

'That's the one,' her mother confirmed brightly.

'Why?' asked Rosie in confusion.

'They have those delicious little macaroons that the boys love and I thought I'd take them a box tonight. I'm babysitting,' Susan said by way of explanation.

Rosie paused for a moment; it would be easier just to say yes and to deal with the rudeness and the subpar coffee but actually today she thought she deserved kindness and good coffee and damn it if she wasn't going to treat herself.

'How about this?' Rosie suggested. 'Why don't I get you a box of those macaroons on my way in this morning and you meet me at Cafe Driade, you know the one two doors down from my lab? The coffee is a lot better there,' she said by way of explanation.

'Do you have time to do that?' her mother queried.

'Sure,' Rosie lied. She didn't really have time for any of this, she ought to be in the lab already checking on her results, but she had seen who had reserved lab space ahead of her and no crisis was worth crossing paths with Handsy Pete.

'Well, that would be lovely, and the coffee really is terrible in that place,' her mother agreed. 'Tell me what time suits you.'

———

Susan was already waiting when Rosie arrived at the cafe. She was stood on the pavement in a powder-blue coat and fuchsia scarf which Rosie hadn't seen before. She exuded maternal warmth and stability on a grey London pavement. Along with coffee, it was just what Rosie needed.

'You look lovely, Mum,' Rosie said kissing her on the cheek and finding her eyes welling up for no apparent reason. Evidently, she could no longer greet her own mother without crying. *Thanks Mitch, thanks men of the world*, she thought bitterly.

'Oh, thank you darling, do you like my new coat? It was an

early Christmas present to myself,' Susan asked, doing a little twirl.

'I love it,' Rosie said, squeezing her mum's arm, 'it brings out the blue in your eyes.'

Susan looked at Rosie with an expression of concern. 'You look tired,' she said in a worried tone as they walked through the door of the cafe.

'Busy at work Mum,' Rosie said by way of explanation and handed over the box of macaroons as a diversion technique.

'Oh, lovely! Thank you,' her mother exclaimed. 'Did they have the strawberry ones?' she asked peering into the box with concern. 'Those are Joe's favorites although he will deny it till he's blue in the face. Apparently, it's not "cool" for boys his age to eat pink food,' Susan said. 'But they still seem to disappear when I'm not looking.'

Rosie laughed. 'Yes they did and I got several of those. It's funny how quickly he is growing up isn't it?' she said to her mother.

'I'll get the coffees,' Susan said, pulling out her purse. 'You go and find us a seat. What would you like?'

'Just a flat white, thanks,' Rosie said and headed straight to the far corner of the cafe where she could see two seats free. It wasn't that she was doing anything wrong, she wasn't skipping out on work, but she also didn't want to advertise the fact she was enjoying coffee with her mother should any of the students or her colleagues walk past the window. Or have to introduce her mother to any of her colleagues. She wasn't sure who would embarrass her more.

'So, you're going to Chris and Jasmine's tonight, are you?' she asked as her mother returned with the coffees. 'How do they seem?' Rosie didn't want to pry but she knew her mother would give her a straight answer.

'I think they seem good actually,' Susan replied.

'Good?' Rosie asked in surprise. It seemed a strange statement to make given the circumstances.

'Sorry, that sounds crass,' her mother conceded. 'They're obviously still very sad about the miscarriage. But I think this has brought them a little closer than they were before. I have to admit I was a bit worried about both of them before this happened.'

Rosie stared at her mother in astonishment. Susan showed amazing insight for someone who seemed to have a very hands-off approach to the private lives of her children. How did Susan know so much about Jasmine and Chris' marriage? Briefly she wondered whether her mother had secretly had her and Chris tagged in order to monitor them. And then she shuddered just thinking of what her mother would have discovered about Rosie in the last few weeks.

'Did you know about any of it?' Rosie asked. 'I mean about them trying or not trying for a baby?'

'I knew it was a source of tension between them.'

'You did?' Rosie gaped again. Did her mother know *everything?* 'I didn't even know they had been considering a third baby. Did they tell you?'

'It's amazing what you pick up on when you spend a lot of time babysitting for a couple,' her mother said sagely. 'But yes, Jasmine did tell me that she had been wanting another baby for some time.'

'And Chris told you he didn't?' Rosie asked.

'Well, not in so many words,' her mother said. 'But I could tell that it wasn't something he was completely sure about.'

'But you think they're going to be OK?' asked Rosie, feeling like a small child who desperately wanted her mother's reassurance.

'I think,' Susan began carefully, 'I think this has given them a chance to talk to each other. And I think Chris has been surprised by how sad he has been about the baby. Not that he wasn't terribly upset about Jasmine, of course,' she said hastily. 'But I do think it has made him wonder whether he does in fact want another child.'

'You think they'll try again?' Rosie asked, silently cursing herself for her constant tone of surprise.

Her mother tilted her head to one side considering Rosie's question. 'I'm not sure,' she said. 'I think that ironically it has made Chris more keen and Jasmine less so.'

Rosie shook her head. 'Yikes,' she said. 'I don't envy them trying to sort that one out.' But she really hoped that they would, because she had realised how fundamentally important it was to her that Jasmine and Chris were OK. If they couldn't make a relationship work then she may as well just give up now. It wasn't as if she had a lot of other positive personal experiences to draw on.

'I think they will be fine,' Susan said emphatically. 'They love and care deeply about each other and that's the most important thing. I think they will both wait and see what happens, and if they get pregnant they'll be delighted, but I don't think Jasmine will be devastated if they don't. Anyway, talking about couples, it's sweet news about Mitch,' Susan said as she took another sip of her coffee.

'What do you mean?' Rosie said, narrowing her eyes. Why was it that Mitch seemed to figure in *all* of her conversations at the moment, no matter how much effort she put into trying not to think of him?

'His new girlfriend,' Susan said, smiling. 'She looks...' he paused for a moment and Rosie wondered what she was about to say. 'Lovely,' Susan continued blandly, to Rosie's disappointment who hoped her mum might say something catty. 'She does look rather young, though,' Susan concluded, which cheered Rosie up no end. She knew she could rely on her mother to say the right thing.

'But how do you know about her?' Rosie asked in consternation.

'Instagram, of course,' Susan said cheerfully. 'I saw he had updated it with some lovely pictures of them both. Have you met her?'

Rosie confirmed that yes, she had indeed met her and took a large gulp of her coffee, relieved that it had cooled down enough for her to do this. 'You follow Mitch on Instagram?' she asked her mother.

'Oh, we've been following each other for years,' Susan confirmed. 'I sent him a request when I joined. In fact, he accepted my request before you did,' she said a little pointedly.

Rosie blushed; it wasn't that she really ever had anything to hide from her mother but the follow request had felt like such a massive invasion of her privacy. The type of thing that had made Rosie go through her entire past activity just to check she wasn't about to be shamed.

'In fact,' Susan continued, 'I often find out what you've been up to from Mitch's posts.'

'I'm not "up to" anything, Mother,' Rosie said defensively.

Susan looked up sharply at Rosie. 'I just meant he posts more often than you do.'

'Hmm,' Rosie grudgingly conceded. She knew it wasn't her mother's fault that she and Mitch had fallen out and it certainly wasn't Susan's fault that he had blocked her, but there was something incredibly irksome about the fact that her Mum knew about Mitch's new girlfriend. And that if Instagram was anything to go by, their kiss last night hadn't resulted in him immediately ending things with Jenny. Rosie knew she was being silly, but there was a tiny part of her that had been hoping Jasmine would call her today with the news that online at least, Mitch suddenly appeared to be single again.

'Mum,' Rosie asked, hoping to change the subject, 'do you remember Connor?'

Susan looked baffled. 'Remind me?' she asked.

'Connor, Connor Ryan, he moved to Washington the autumn after we graduated?'

Susan's face cleared. 'Oh, Connor, of course! I remember you were quite upset when he moved away, weren't you?'

Rosie felt relieved at her mother's understatement. Whenever she thought of that summer all she could remember were long and painful conversations with Connor in London parks and an embarrassing amount of tears after he had left. Which felt even more embarrassing now that she'd grasped what an idiot he actually was.

'I saw him last night,' Rosie told her mother.

'You did? How lovely. So, he's not still in Washington?'

'No, Mother, he's not still in Washington' Rosie replied tersely. 'How could I have seen him last night if he was still in Washington?'

Susan smiled sweetly over her coffee cup. 'You know what I meant, darling.' She pretended not to hear her daughter's barbed tone.

'Actually, it was really strange,' Rosie said. 'It sounds silly now but I pined for him so much after he left. I spent so long wondering what my life would have been like had he stayed.'

'Really?' Susan said, putting down her coffee cup, her turn to be surprised.

'Yes, Mum, really,' Rosie said, irritated that her mother had interrupted her midway through her confession.

'I'm just a little surprised, that's all.'

'Why?' asked Rosie, suddenly intrigued by what her mother might say next.

'Oh, well it's not like I knew him,' Susan said in an off-handed manner.

'But?' prompted Rosie. 'What were you going to say?'

'Well, I only met him the once, remember, at your graduation, but he seemed, how shall I put this?' Susan paused and looked thoughtful. 'A little self-obsessed, shall we say?'

Rosie gaped at her mother. 'Did you really think so?'

Rosie wished she had talked to her mother about this at the time, perhaps if she had, her history might have been totally different? Although probably not; Rosie would have just been annoyed at her mother's assessment of Connor and it would have done nothing to stop Rosie falling for Mitch.

'Absolutely,' Susan said firmly. 'I just remember that everything we did that day was because *he* wanted to do it. Even down to what time we went for dinner. And I just felt sorry for his mother who looked as if she knew she had raised a monster!'

Rosie stifled a giggle. 'Hmm, yes but she was incredibly uptight herself. It's funny though, Mum. I never realised that about him then. And then suddenly last night it was as if I was meeting him for the first time. He just wasn't the person I remembered.'

'Well, that can happen when you haven't seen someone for a long time,' her mother said teasingly.

'Ha, bloody, ha,' Rosie retorted. 'You know what I mean.' They both sipped their coffee in silence.

Susan broke it, musing, 'It's funny you talking about Connor like that. I don't think I knew at the time how serious you must have been about him.'

'Mum,' said Rosie sharply. 'I was moving to bloody London to be with him!'

Susan gave her a look. Rosie knew she didn't appreciate the language. It wasn't that Susan necessarily disapproved of swearing, she had just always told Rosie only to use it when it was strictly necessary. And apparently it wasn't deemed necessary while in a cafe with your mother.

'I suppose I never saw him as being the person you would end up with,' Susan said obliquely.

Rosie took a deep breath. 'Right.' She paused. 'So are you going to tell me who the sort of person you thought I would end up with might be?'

Although she couldn't keep the irritation out of her voice, she was also intrigued by what her mother's answer would be; Susan did have annoyingly perceptive insight as Rosie had established during the course of this coffee date.

'I don't think that's my place to say,' Susan replied, chancing the wrath of her daughter who looked to be completely out of patience. But then, being incapable of leaving it there, Susan continued, 'I always thought and hoped that you would end up with someone kind. You're so good at looking after yourself, you always have been, but I hope that one day you'll find someone who will be just as good at looking after you. Someone who is a good friend to you.'

Rosie's mind inexorably drew to Mitch. He was someone kind, he was someone who was good at looking after her. But when she thought of Mitch now, she thought of the kiss and the look on his face afterwards. She shook her head, trying to shake loose these images and hoping her mother wouldn't notice her doing so and start asking probing questions. Rosie's phone pinged and she reached into her pocket. 'Shit!' she exclaimed.

'Rosie!' Susan admonished, looking around as if hoping that no one had heard her daughter's expletive.

Rosie didn't have the heart to explain that it was probably a given that ninety-nine per cent of the clientele and staff in this cafe had heard much *much* worse already that morning. She also didn't have the time to explain this, because her phone was alerting her to a text message from Rachel telling Rosie that she needed to be sending that press release *right now* if she valued her career in academia.

'Sorry, Mum,' she said typing a quick response to Rachel. 'I've got something really urgent to send.'

Susan frowned but seemed to accept the explanation. 'I should let you go anyway,' she said. 'You need to get on with work.' Susan stood up from the table and handed Rosie her bag. 'But I will say that I've always thought the best basis for a relationship is friendship,' Susan said, starting to pull on her coat. 'All that passion...'

'I'm sorry?' Rosie said in surprise looking up from her phone where she had been looking for the press release email that she had carefully saved, and wondering what she had missed and why her mother was now harping on about passion.

'I was saying,' Susan said, now handing Rosie her coat, 'all that passion, it wears off after a while; you can't always be at it.'

'Oh, Mum, please!' Rosie begged, snatching her coat. She did not want to have this conversation with her mother *ever*, and especially not in a public place and when she was distracted by an urgent email to send. Rosie held her phone in one hand, scrolling down to the email with the press release as she and Susan walked to the door of the cafe.

'So, you'll give my congratulations to Mitch, won't you?'

Susan said. 'Tell him I'm looking forward to meeting his new girlfriend.

Rosie gritted her teeth and nodded grimly as she hit send on her email. She kissed her mother goodbye, grateful to have got her off the topic of Mitch and passion, and to have sent that stupid press release out. Now she just had to hope it would disappear into the overflowing inbox of the press department at *The Post* and never be seen again.

Chapter Twenty-Two

I t was good to be in the lab. Rosie's happy place. The place where she didn't need to think about press releases, kisses, exes or ex best friends. All she had to do was to get this micro plate onto the reader without any mistakes. Why was it so hard? Who had designed these things anyway? She took a deep breath and steadied her hand. She couldn't afford to spill anything.

Very, *very* carefully she placed the film cover over the top and eased it safely into the machine, exhaling deeply as she did so. There was something powerful about the quiet and the calm of the lab, the methodical nature of what she did and all the tiny meticulous steps she took in each experiment that could add up to something massively life changing for so many people.

But she was now exhausted and a little sweaty and concerned that her hands had started shaking from adrenaline which was a less than optimal state to be in when she needed to measure things so carefully. She pushed her safety goggles up to her forehead and sat down on the stool by her lab bench.

Weary from concentrating, she rubbed her eyes, it was a good job she hadn't put any mascara on that morning; fears about crying over Mitch had the happy benefit that she could now rub her tired eyes and not worry about looking like a panda. Her stomach growled and she felt a pang of regret at not having bought an extra box of those macaroons when she was buying one for her mother. She was starving and could do with the sugar rush. Rosie smiled to herself thinking how crazy her nephews would be after they had consumed the box. It would be just her mother's style to drop a macaroon bomb and then make an exit, leaving Jasmine and Chris with a sugar-fuelled battle at bedtime.

The lab phone rang, startling her from her moment of reflection. No one ever called the lab phone, it was there for emergencies, when a colleague needed to reach one of them or a family member urgently needed to contact whoever was working in there that day. Rosie reached for it quickly, hoping there might be some good news at the end of the line. Perhaps Rachel was ringing to thank Rosie for sending the press release, or to tell her that BioChem had decided that actually their last results weren't all that bad. Or—

'Rosie, it's Nadia,' came the voice from the other end.

'Er, hi? Everything OK?' asked Rosie.

'Yes, it's fine, but do you never look up? I've been trying to catch your attention.'

Rosie swivelled round on her lab stool and looked over at the glass screen which separated the lab from the corridor of the main building. Nadia was stood looking irritated, holding her phone with one hand and waving at Rosie with the other. Rosie couldn't help but giggle.

'How long have you been stood there?' she asked.

'Long enough to wonder if you were going to fall asleep on that stool,' Nadia replied shortly.

'Sorry, I'm exhausted,' Rosie said.

'Yes, well you'll need to find a bit of extra energy.'

'What? Why?'

'Just come back to my office and you can see for yourself.'

Rosie groaned in protest. 'Can't you just tell me?'

'No,' came the reply and Rosie watched as Nadia firmly ended the call and stalked off back down the corridor.

Without bothering to take her lab coat and goggles off, Rosie made her way out of the lab and down the corridor to Nadia's office, hoping that Rachel hadn't sent any more emails by mistake. The door was closed and Rosie pushed it open wondering what situation she was going to have to discuss with Nadia now. She loved her friend and she knew she was having a tough time but, honestly, Rosie just didn't have the energy to deal with another rant over the idiocy of the government's science-funding programme. Or a discussion over whether it was acceptable to tell the PTA to 'sod off' and stop making completely unreasonable demands of parents such as, 'Can you please shamelessly ask anyone and everyone you have ever met to sponsor your child for the annual bounce-a-thon?' On reflection, Rosie had advised that there might be more constructive ways for Nadia to get her point across to the PTA. All Rosie really wanted to do now was finish up in the lab, go home, find whatever was easiest to eat and have a hot bath. And try to find something that would take her mind off constantly running replays of her kiss with Mitch and the look on his face afterwards.

'Mitch!' Rosie exclaimed in surprise. Mitch stood and smiled shyly at her. His tall frame dwarfed Nadia who was hovering near her desk looking both nervous and excited, hopping from one foot to the other and grinning at Rosie.

'What are you doing here?' Rosie asked in confusion.

'I had some things I needed to talk to Nadia about,' he said. Rosie looked between him and Nadia, her confusion only deepening. She was very aware that the last time she had seen

Mitch was up close, lips touching. And now he was stood in her friend's office and she had no idea why.

'Yes, well erm, I should get going,' said Nadia as if she would much rather grab some popcorn, pull up a chair and see for herself what kind of showdown was about to happen. Instead, she picked up her bag from the floor near her desk and, shoving some piles of paper into it haphazardly, she made for the door. Rosie shuddered to imagine what kind of important raw data was being desecrated in such a manner but she held her tongue and stood to one side to let her friend pass. She was too confused to ask exactly what was going on, why Mitch was in Nadia's office and what he and Nadia had been discussing together.

'I'll leave you two to it,' Nadia said cheerfully, gave them a thumbs-up and slammed the door a little too hard behind her as she left.

Mitch now looked nervous. He was fiddling with the cuffs on the sleeve of the jumper he was wearing. Rosie realised with a pang that she didn't recognise it. There would have been a time when she knew every single item of clothing in his wardrobe, down to the embarrassing T-shirts he had had as a teenager and now couldn't bear to part with. Mitch still maintained that if he kept his Babyshambles T-shirt long enough it might be worth some money. Given his suspect taste in music Rosie wasn't even sure he really knew who Babyshambles actually were. But this jumper was one that he had obviously bought without her and just made her realise how far they had drifted from each other. He looked good in it, though, she thought. It showed off his shoulders and the blue brought out the colour in his eyes. He fixed them on her now.

'I thought we should talk,' he said simply.

Rosie felt her stomach sour. Actually, the last thing she wanted to be doing was 'talking' to Mitch. Talking would involve meeting his eye, talking might involve him telling her about Jenny. It might also involve Mitch telling her to leave him and Jenny alone and to stop chasing after him in the street and kissing him or he would be forced to take out a restraining order against his crazy ex-best friend. But Rosie took the path of least resistance and nodded in agreement. He was right. They should talk. She should listen to what he had to say, take it on board and then finally move on. And then she stopped and reframed her inner monologue, she started shaking her head instead.

'Here?' she asked looking up at him incredulously. 'You thought we should talk here? At my work? In my colleague's office?' Mitch couldn't help but laugh at the expression on her face but Rosie didn't smile back. In fact, her frown intensified. Mitch was right, they should talk, but why now and on his terms? Why did he not want to talk all those times that *she* tried to talk to him? The unfairness of it all washed over her. Here he was, stood in *her* workplace, talking to *her* friends, interrupting *her* experiments.

'I have been trying to talk to you for weeks!' she exclaimed. 'I've called you, I've messaged you, I even wrote you a letter although you probably couldn't read my terrible handwriting.' She took a deep exasperated breath. 'And you have ignored me *every-single-time.*' Her eyes flashed in anger. 'And then you think it's OK to march in here, into *my* space and expect me to be ready to talk?'

Her anger took her by surprise, but she was done with all of this, done with wondering what Mitch was thinking/doing/wearing. She had spent so long worrying about Mitch and about her feelings for him and now she had just had enough.

'I'm sorry about Jenny, I really am,' she continued. 'I shouldn't have told her. But I have apologised enough, and I don't see what you showing up here expecting yet another apology is going to achieve.'

'I didn't know,' Mitch said softly.

'What do you mean?' Rosie barked, 'I left you enough messages, surely you must have realised I was sorry?'

'No, no, I meant I didn't know why,' Mitch said. He was slowly walking towards her. Rosie looked at him in confusion, wondering just what he was going to say or do next. Why did this all have to be so confusing? Couldn't he just have accepted her apology weeks ago? She could have been now peaceably sat in the lab, waiting for some good results.

'I *had* hoped. I'd hoped for years to be honest, but I didn't *know* for sure why you told Jenny,' he said.

Rosie, weary of another telling-off from Mitch, barely heard what he said. She wiped her hand across her face.

'Well,' she said flatly. 'Well, now you do.'

At least she didn't have to explain. At least Mitch finally understood how she felt about him and maybe he would take that as a suitable apology, although they could never go back to the way things had been. Every time they hung out Mitch might worry she was about to jump him. And she was sure as hell that Jenny would never condone them being friends anymore. But at least the feeling of constant dread of Mitch discovering how she actually felt about him would finally be lifted from Rosie. It would be awkward and sad but in time they might be able to bear being in the same room. Although they would have to remain at a safe distance, and Rosie would have to make sure she never drank when he was there so that she didn't have to run out halfway through and weep and beat her breast at the enduring tragedy of all she had lost; of the friendship they had once had and could no longer go back to, at the sadness of falling hopelessly in love with someone who would never love her back...

'Hang on,' she said, her thoughts stalling mid-spiral as she recalled more of what he'd said just now. She looked up into his face which was now alarmingly close to hers. 'Why would you be hoping?' There was a long pause. Her heartbeat was hammering in her ears, drowning out all logical thought, because he couldn't mean... Could he?

'I feel the same,' he said, reaching out and taking her hand.

Rosie looked down in surprise and then back up at him, her mouth now hanging open. For a moment she said nothing, not comprehending why her hand was in Mitch's. What he was saying to her, what he was even doing in Nadia's office with her. 'I'm sorry, I...I don't understand,' she eventually stammered, sounding about as clueless as she thought it was possible for someone who possessed a top-class PhD to sound.

'I feel the same, Rosie,' Mitch continued. 'About you.'

Rosie's head buzzed. None of this made sense to her. 'What?' she asked again. 'You can't feel the same,' she continued. 'Because... How? Why?'

Mitch reached out with his other hand and gently cupped her chin. Rosie's heartbeat was now racing as fast as it had when she had kissed him last night. He was as close to her now as he had been then. One hand still cupping her face, the other moved from holding her hand to rest on her waist, gently, insistently, pulling her even closer. Rosie felt her stomach swoop as his lips touched hers. Her lips felt electric as the pressure from his lips intensified and their kiss grew increasingly passionate. Mitch made a moaning sound that she'd never heard him make before and which seemed to vibrate through her. For a moment Rosie thought her legs might give way, and then, instead of enjoying it, of course her brain went into overdrive. Her fear about falling over quickly gave way to the realisation of the state she was in. Sweaty, make-up-free, still in her lab coat and with her goggles pushed up onto her head – absolutely *not* how she imagined she'd look if this ever happened. Suddenly reality, and her shouty intrusive thoughts, intervened and she pulled away.

'Mitch I'm…' She gesticulated to her face and clothing. She immediately desperately cared what she looked like to Mitch. Now that he miraculously seemed keen on kissing her she had become self-conscious over every single part of her body; her face was too shiny, her hair too tangled, her hands strangely sweaty. Just every part of her felt too much. Much, much too much.

'I don't care,' he said, his face a study of seriousness. 'I've seen you in every state, Rosie. I've seen you dressed up for a party, I've seen you in your pyjamas, I've seen you hungover, I've held back your hair for you, held your hand for you. And every single Rosie I have seen I've thought was perfect and I've wanted to kiss.'

Hearing Mitch say these words to her was more than she had ever dared to dream, her breath caught in her throat, and for one terrifying moment she thought she might have to add 'choking to death in front of Mitch', to her list of bodily functions to be anxious about.

'Can I kiss you again? Please?'

Rosie didn't trust herself to speak, and honestly? She was trying to focus on breathing again, his lips on hers was the softest yet most intense feeling she had ever experienced. It was messy and delicious and frankly terrifying.

'Hang on.' Rosie put her hand on Mitch's chest and tried not to get distracted by how good it felt to let it rest there. 'What about Jenny?'

Mitch looked confused for a second. 'What about Jenny?'

Rosie pushed him further away, giving him a stern look. 'I think you'll find it's generally considered unacceptable to kiss someone else when you have a girlfriend.'

'I'm not kissing anyone else,' Mitch murmured and reached for her again.

'OK, you're not kissing me right now,' she said, fending him off, 'I meant, I think we should stop and talk about this a bit more.'

'You're right,' he said, pretending to look chastened. 'Lots to talk about, but isn't this more fun than talking?' He gave her a grin which made her want to pull him back towards her and feel his lips on hers again. But she held firm. 'Mitch,' she protested, 'Jenny. I want to know what's going on.'

'There's nothing going on,' Mitch said. 'I know this makes me a bad feminist but honestly? Jenny was only ever a way of distracting me from my feelings for you. They all were,' he said earnestly, his thumb running across her cheek bone in an intensely distracting way.

It was Rosie's turn to look confused. 'But what about your posts? On Instagram?'

'What are you talking about? I hardly ever post.'

'Well, that's what surprised me,' Rosie confessed. 'So I thought it must be serious if you were posting photos of Jenny. And I guess…even more serious to block me.'

Mitch pulled away from her and reached for his phone in his pocket. 'I don't understand,' he said. 'I haven't posted anything, or blocked you!' He scrolled through his phone, colour draining from his face.

'She must have done this,' he stammered, 'her or one of her friends.' He was silent for a moment and then he groaned. 'Oh, god, I remember now. It was the last time I saw her, I told her the truth, that I couldn't be with her anymore and that I had to sort out my feelings for you.' Despite Mitch's obvious distress, Rosie allowed herself a small self-satisfied smile at his confession. 'We were out with her friends, it was awful, I felt so old when I was with them.' Rosie didn't even try to hide her smile now. 'Yes, yes you were right,' he said, seeing the look on her face. 'Anyway, we had had this conversation and she was pretty upset, I lent her my phone to book a cab home and I guess instead of using it to book a cab she must have decided to sabotage my social media accounts.

Rosie didn't know whether to laugh or cry. She remembered the cold hard feeling that had settled in her stomach when she believed it was Mitch who had updated his profiles and him that had blocked her. But Mitch looked so pitiful and she could just imagine him trying to do the right thing.

'You're an idiot,' she said, swatting him with her hand.

'What was I supposed to do?' he said, holding his hands up. 'She was upset and I wanted to make sure she got home safely. I'm not a monster, you know.'

'You shouldn't be so trusting,' Rosie said, knowing that this was one of the reasons she loved him so much. 'Maybe next time you should book the cab yourself, or not leave apps open on your phone?' she suggested.

'I'm hoping there won't be a next time,' he replied, taking her hands in his and pressing them between his two. He leaned forward and kissed her, but she was now smiling so much that he ended up kissing her teeth. 'Mmm, sexy,' he murmured in an amused tone, slipping one hand to the back of her head and kissing her harder this time.

'Hold on,' she said, stopping him in his tracks.

He groaned. 'Now what?'

'You haven't told me what you are doing in Nadia's office? If you were coming to see me why didn't you just wait for me in mine? She said you had some things to discuss.'

'We did,' he said matter-of-factly. 'Work things.'

Rosie cocked her eyebrow at this, 'Explain.'

Mitch sighed. 'I'd much rather be kissing you,' he said and

then seeing the look on her face he added quickly, 'OK, I'll explain. You told me she was worried about funding after the latest cuts?' Rosie nodded. 'So, I spoke to a few contacts and I've put her in touch with someone who runs a fund operating in this area, it looks like they will sponsor her research with funding for at least the next two years. And then after that, who knows? If she gets good results, I expect they'll want to continue.'

Rosie's chin dropped. 'You did that?'

Mitch shrugged as if it was nothing. 'I wanted to help, I knew how worried you were about her.'

Rosie pushed him back into the chair behind him, straddled him and kissed him firmly on the lips as she did so. It was amazing how natural it felt, how easily she could slip from friend zone to straddle zone.

'Wow!' he said. 'I'm extra glad I helped now.'

Rosie pretended to look nonchalant. 'Just thanking you on behalf of Nadia.'

'Thanks, I'm glad it's you thanking me and not Nadia. But…' He ran his fingers down her spine giving her a delicious thrill. 'I'm extra keen to find out what you'll do when I tell you that I helped Nico find a new job.'

'What?' shrieked Rosie, she struck his chest with one of her hands. 'You didn't?'

Mitch looked smug as he held her hand tightly. 'I did.'

'Mitch, you're amazing.' She reached her head up and kissed him on his jaw line which seemed to make him shudder underneath her.

'I confess that I may have had an ulterior motive,' he said, looking her straight in the eye. Rosie looked back at him. 'I hoped that it would make you like me again,' he said shyly.

'Do you mean like you, like you or *like* you like you?' Rosie said, biting her lip and smiling.

'Like me enough to let me do this,' he said and kissed her neck, wrapping his arms tightly around her waist.

'It definitely worked,' she murmured into his hair. 'But hang on...'

Mitch growled, 'Seriously, Rosie? What could possibly be more important than this?' He bit her lower lip.

Just managing not to lose her mind with desire, Rosie stuttered, 'Where did you go?'

'Go?'

'Yes, last night? Where did you go after I kissed you? I tried to find you and I tried to call you.' Her voice went very small. 'I presumed you weren't interested.'

She looked up and saw Mitch. He looked like he might be about to cry. 'Oh, Rosie, I'm so sorry.'

'It's OK,' she replied, meaning of course that it really wasn't OK and could he now explain why she had spent the last twelve hours believing it was all over between them only to end up sat in his lap in Nadia's office.

'No, it's not,' Mitch said firmly. 'I am sorry. I just... To be honest my head was all over the place. Seeing you there with Connor, the way it made me feel...and then you racing after me and kissing me. I didn't know what to make of it.' He grimaced. 'My mates were waiting for me down by the ticket barriers and I was too shocked to do anything but just let them take me on to this club we were supposed to be going to. Which was awful by the way, underground, so I had no reception, too loud to think straight so I couldn't make sense of what had just happened. But I should have come to find you Rosie. I'm so sorry. I should do better, I *will* do better I promise?'

Rosie grabbed his face between her hands. 'Mitch, it's OK,' she said firmly. 'I get it. It's a lot. But hey, we've waited, how many years? I could handle another twelve hours of misery. I'm kidding,' she protested, seeing the pained look on Mitch's face. 'But what now?' she asked.

'Well, I was thinking we could risk staying here a bit longer? If I remember rightly the cleaners won't disturb us for a while,' he grinned suggestively at her.

'No, Mitch I meant what now as in, what now for us?' Rosie looked at him earnestly. 'Don't get me wrong, I'm really enjoying this,' she said, seeing the look of concern on his face. 'But I think we should talk.'

Mitch leaned his head back on the wall in frustration. 'Do we have to?' he said, 'I'd much rather we just did this instead.' Rosie attempted to clamber off him but he pulled her back and held her tight, kissing her again. She gave in and enjoyed the new but familiar sensation of being this close to Mitch. But then she pushed him away and stood up, straightening her clothes as she did so.

'I'm serious, Mitch. We've been friends for a long time, we came up with a crazy plan to have a baby together which resulted in you getting a new girlfriend and us having a massive fight, we haven't spoken to each other in weeks and now this happens? I think we need to talk about things before we go any further.'

Mitch grinned up at her. 'Any further?' he questioned. She felt her stomach drop, that grin, that question.

'Stop it!' she said but she laughed. 'Yes, any further.'

Mitch groaned. 'OK,' he relented. 'Where would you like to do this talking? Your place or mine?'

'Mitch!' she exclaimed, 'That's a terrible pick up. I'm beginning to think you're not as charming as I thought you were. Is this how you treat all your girls?'

'No,' he said taking her hand, 'just the ones I really, really like.'

Chapter Twenty-Three

Rosie lay resolutely still, refusing to open her eyes and shatter the dream she had been enjoying. She wriggled one arm free and edged her hand across the sheets which were definitely not her Egyptian cotton, reaching for something to reassure her that it *hadn't* all been a dream. And there it was, or more accurately, there *he* was. Rosie opened her eyes and looked across the bed to where Mitch lay. He was wide awake and smiling at her.

'Come here,' he said and pulled her against him, curling himself around her from behind.

'Mmm. Not a dream then?' she asked. Mitch laughed and kissed the back of her neck gently, her toes curled with delight and a sleepy smile spread across her face.

'I don't normally do this,' she said a little anxiously.

'I should hope not.' Mitch's reply was muffled as his lips found the edge of her hairline. 'I'm hoping you're not sleeping with any of your other best friends,' he said jokingly.

'Mitch!' she protested lazily. 'You know what I mean!'

Rosie pushed herself up to sitting, wrapping Mitch's sheets

around her as she did so. Despite everything that had happened last night she was suddenly shy of him seeing her in the morning light. Mitch groaned, 'Can we not just stay here all morning?'

'I wish.' Rosie sighed.

Mitch sat up next to her, running his hand through his hair and yawning. He picked his phone up from by the bed. 'Sadly, you're right,' he said looking at the time. 'I need to be at morning conference, I'm presenting to the editor so I can't be late, but...' He pulled Rosie against him and wrapped his arm tight around her resting his chin on her head. 'You can have me for precisely half an hour more and then I have to go. Do you think we have time to...'

Rosie sighed. Truthfully, there was nothing she would like more than to pin Mitch back down on the bed and waste the day away with him. But he had to leave, and she had work to do too. And they really needed to discuss some things before this went any further. They'd got a bit distracted when they got back to Mitch's last night.

'Mitch,' she said tentatively, 'can we talk?'

'If we're not going to spend the next thirty minutes doing what I really really want to be doing then yes, OK, we can talk instead,' he conceded. She twisted round in his arms so she was facing him and could see he was smiling. She pulled her knees up, wrapping her arms around them and resting her chin on them.

'This whole baby thing for a start?' She looked carefully at his face, waiting to see what his reaction might be. 'I know how important it is to you, I know it's always been your plan, but for me?' she hesitated 'I'm not sure how I feel about it.'

A small frown started to appear on Mitch's forehead. Rosie panicked, this was meant to be a clear the air chat, not a last-night-was-amazing-but-we're-totally-incompatible chat. She needed to turn this around quickly.

'I'm not saying I don't ever want one, I'm just not sure,' she gabbled. 'And also, all of this?' She gesticulated to the space between them, which seemed to be growing with every word that came out of her mouth. 'It's all so new. I think we need some time to figure it out, don't you think?'

Mitch looked down at his hands. 'You seemed so keen, though,' he said eventually.

'I am keen!' she protested. 'Oh Mitch, you have no idea how keen I am on you!' She smiled at him, putting her hand out on his chest.

'No, I meant about our plan.'

'Oh!' Rosie exclaimed.

'Well, I thought you were. I mean, you did agree to it, after all.'

She could hear a note of uncertainty creeping into his voice.

'Yeees,' she said hesitantly, 'I did, but only because I was scared of losing you.'

Mitch looked up at her sharply. 'What?'

Rosie immediately regretted what she had just said. 'No, I didn't mean it like that. I just...'

Mitch frowned at her.

'It brought up a lot of feelings for me and one of those was the fact I was scared of losing you.'

Mitch looked at her confounded. 'So you thought you'd say yes to having a baby with me?'

Rosie attempted a laugh, 'Yeah, it does sound a bit crazy when you put it like that.'

Mitch didn't laugh in response. 'It does.'

'I don't want to put pressure on us,' she tried to explain.

'I didn't realise I was putting pressure on you.' A hard tone had entered his voice.

'I didn't mean you had!' Rosie exclaimed, feeling desperately that the situation was running away from her. 'I just want to take things slowly and enjoy this.' She grabbed his hand and they both stared at each other, neither of them sure what to say next.

Mitch broke the silence, 'We should get ready for work.' He turned and swung his legs out of bed. Rosie wasn't sure where to look. Was it OK to see your best friend naked the morning after you'd slept together? Was it OK to see them naked when it seemed like you'd just messed the whole thing up?

Apparently not. Mitch pulled on his boxers and a T-shirt over his head and went to take a shower.

———

Rosie got off the tube with Mitch at his stop, deciding she'd walk from there to her lab. It might give her time to clear her head, or buy coffee, or maybe some new pants. She looked at her watch and made a mental calculation as to whether Marks & Spencer's would be open yet and then made a little strangled noise in her throat that she was having these thoughts after having *spent the night with Mitch*. Part of her wanted to blush with embarrassment but the bigger part wanted to do a little dance in the street and tell everyone she knew that her and Mitch were together. Or sort of together. Or they would be if she could just find a way through this latest situational quagmire.

The atmosphere had really shifted after their conversation, although Mitch still reached out to hold her hand tightly as they walked towards his work. Rosie suddenly felt shy as if everyone would be staring at them, but nobody seemed to even notice them. She couldn't believe that her world had shifted so radically on its axis, and yet all around her people were carrying on as if this was just a standard morning rush hour; nothing to see here.

'Mitch, we do need to talk.' She said as they reached his building.

'Yeah, I get it. But I'm late.' Mitch looked at his watch. 'And you'll be late, too.'

Rosie couldn't shake the feeling that he was trying to get rid of her.

'I'll call you later?' Mitch put his hands on her waist, looking down into her eyes. She didn't think she'd ever get bored of seeing him in this new light, at this new angle which screamed boyfriend/girlfriend rather than just two friends. Mitch bent to kiss her. And she definitely wasn't ever going to get bored of what kissing him did to her insides.

'Mitch?' she said as they pulled apart. 'We'll figure it out, won't we?'

Mitch gave her a smile, but there was tension around his mouth and his eyes. 'Of course,' he said. 'Trust me.'

Rosie walked away, pulling her phone from her pocket to work out the closest M&S. She didn't want to say goodbye to Mitch. Despite his assurances she knew they weren't on the same wavelength. She desperately wanted to talk to him about everything, to make him understand, because she had a horrible feeling that her happy ever after wasn't just slipping away but was making a mad dash for the nearest exit.

'Morning!' came a loud and irritatingly familiar voice.

Ben, of course. Of course, she would bump into Ben outside Mitch's work, on the morning after she and Mitch had spent the night together and immediately after Rosie had probably destroyed the whole thing. How many times had she stood waiting for Mitch outside his building and she had never once bumped into Ben. She looked up at the heavens and wondered why someone had it in for her.

Ben had obviously spotted her from a distance and had run towards her. He stopped as he reached her, slightly out of breath.

'Er, that looked cosy.' His eyes went past Rosie to the entrance to *The Post* which Mitch had just gone through. Ben winked at Rosie and she sighed in response. 'Funny because I was just thinking about you.'

Rosie blanched. *Please, god, could this not be happening*, she thought to herself. Whatever sleazy thing Ben was going to say, could he keep it to himself? Maybe he could be struck temporarily mute or, better still, make it permanent. Maybe a minor but seemingly dramatic traffic accident could occur right this instance and prevent him from uttering whatever horror was about to issue from his mouth. Or maybe a wormhole could just swallow her up and spit her back out into Mitch's bedroom where she would never have started the stupid baby conversation this morning, and saved it for a later date, or maybe never. And then she could have got the damn tube straight to her work and dealt with wearing the same pants two days in a row. Really any of these things would be fine right now.

'Yeah,' Ben continued, grinning, 'I was out with the comms team last night. One of them showed me that email you sent over yesterday.'

'And?' asked Rosie in confusion.

'I'm guessing you didn't mean to leave that attachment on the press release.' Ben was openly laughing now.

The colour immediately poured from Rosie's face. Her stomach soured and she felt her knees go. 'Oh, god.' She put her hand out to steady herself against the wall. 'Oh, god. Oh, fuck. Oh, no, this can't be happening.'

She looked up at Ben, who at least had the decency to look slightly concerned about her. She put her hands on her knees and bent over as if she was about to be sick, her head was pounding in panic. She hadn't? She couldn't have? Could she? She thought back to the day before, to Rachel's urgent message telling her to send the damn press release. To her scrolling through her emails, half listening to her mother, to find the version she had saved to forward. She couldn't have sent the wrong one? Could she? And then she realised how easy it was to mix up the two, to have forwarded the press release that had Rachel's private email correspondence attached at the bottom. She really could have, and it really looked like she had.

'I've really messed up.' She looked desperately up at Ben. 'Rachel's going to kill me when she finds out. What am I going to do?' she asked, not expecting Ben to come up with any kind of useful response.

'I guess you could ask Mitch if he can help?' Ben reached up and scratched the back of his neck thoughtfully. 'Although he's probably got enough on his plate with his upcoming transfer. He might not have time to ask for any favours.'

'What?' asked Rosie, beginning to straighten up.

There was a long, tense pause. Rosie felt yet another weight drop out of her stomach. It wasn't even 9am and it looked like yet another nausea-inducing revelation was headed her way.

'What do you mean, Ben?' she eventually asked in a strangled tone.

Ben looked at her almost apologetically, and took a deep breath. 'He hasn't told you about his transfer?' he asked quietly.

'Transfer?' asked Rosie turning to look back in the direction Mitch had gone, hoping he might magically reappear and be able to rescue her from what was now becoming a nightmare. 'Ben, are you going to tell me what you mean?' she demanded.

'I just, I thought,' stammered Ben, 'I thought Mitch would have told you.'

'Told me what!' Rosie stamped her foot.

'That he put in a transfer for work, and it got accepted yesterday.'

'What?' Rosie asked weakly.

'I'm sorry, Rosie. I heard the announcement at work and I just presumed you knew.'

Rosie shook her head numbly. Ben looked nervously at her, starting to regret his meddling. 'I mean, it's not insurmountable,' he said in what he hoped was an encouraging tone. 'Plenty of people do long distance.'

Rosie said nothing, her head spinning from this new revelation.

'You just need to plan things a bit better. Work out a travel budget and things.'

'A travel budget?' Rosie asked weakly.

'Yeah, if you book them far enough in advance, transatlantic flights can be really affordable…' Ben's voice tailed off as he saw the look on Rosie's face.

'Transatlantic?' she questioned. 'Where exactly is he being transferred to?'

There was a long pause. 'New York,' he confirmed reluctantly.

Distantly, she heard him calling her name repeatedly as she ran down the street away from this mess. Her mind was racing as fast as her heart was pumping. She couldn't do this. It was just like Connor all over again, except this time it was Mitch and Mitch was ten times the guy that Connor had been. Or was he? She began to reevaluate. When had Mitch put in this request and why hadn't he told her? What exactly was his plan? Why had he let last night happen without telling her any of this? And what the hell was she going to do about that email? She was about to lose her career along with her best friend. For a moment she thought she might be about to lose her breakfast, too. And if she was going to be sick and Mitch wasn't around to hold back her hair, she knew where she would go.

Chapter Twenty-Four

Bloody Christmas shoppers thought Rosie as she tearfully pushed her way through the crowds on the tube. She looked forlornly at the woman with the half a dozen Hamleys bags and tried not to cry. When Rosie was a kid, her mum would take her and Chris to Hamleys at Christmas and they would be allowed to pick one thing out as a treat.

And then Rosie remembered more recent Christmases: going up to Regent Street with Mitch to see the Christmas lights, drinking mulled wine in cosy pubs. Last-minute dashes to the shops because Mitch had forgotten yet another Christmas present that he desperately needed. The year he bought her the most beautiful cashmere jumper he found in Liberty's which she was gutted as it turned out to be completely the wrong size and he had then surprised her at her flat, whisking her off in a cab to exchange it for the right size instead. She remembered shopping in Hamleys with him for presents for Rory and Joe; he was always so much better at picking out the things they would love. And then she suddenly felt a weird longing to take her own children to Hamleys one day. And let them pick out a toy, just as she had done as a child. Rosie felt the tears welling up in her eyes again and turned quickly away only to end up looking straight at a couple who were wearing matching Christmas hats and staring soppily into each other's eyes. The only explanation being that they were celebrating their first Christmas together.

Rosie fought those tears; it wasn't as if she was even sure she had wanted kids before bloody Mitch had put the idea in her head. And now she was imagining taking them to Hamleys! And she was a hundred per cent certain that she had never wanted to wear matching festive hats with anyone, even with Mitch. She made a solemn vow to herself that if she was ever, ever lucky enough to get over Mitch and to find someone else then they would never, ever wear any kind of matching clothing. The girl in the hat turned and caught Rosie's eye and smiled at her, in the way someone does when they're happy and all is right in their world. But the girl's smile faltered when she saw the tears on Rosie's cheeks.

As soon as her tube came above ground, she dialled Nadia's number frantically. She knew she should have done this before disappearing into the underground but she was so panicked by Ben's revelations that she just wanted to disappear.

'You have to tell me everything!' Nadia demanded.

'What?' Rosie asked.

'You and Mitch!' Nadia shouted excitedly down the phone. 'What happened? Did he declare his undying love for you? I *knew* he would,' she continued, not giving Rosie a chance to interject. 'Is he coming to the party with you? As in properly *with* you this year? I'm so excited.'

'Party?' Rosie said dumbly.

'The party?' Nadia replied. 'Rachel's party?'

Rosie shook her head, Rachel's party, which was coming up in a couple of days' time, was the furthest thing from her mind. If

Rachel had found out about Rosie's errant email she doubted she would still be welcome.

'Is Mitch coming with you? What are you wearing, by the way? Actually, don't tell me, I don't have time to discuss wardrobe choices right now, that marvellous Mitch of yours has got me so many contacts to follow up with. I bloody love him.'

Rosie's response came in the form of a strangled noise. Right now, she didn't really feel like celebrating Mitch's marvellousness, bloody or otherwise.

'Nadia, something really bad has happened.'

'What is it?'

'Remember that email chain I showed you?' Rosie asked. 'The one with Rachel and the VC and the…'

Nadia started chuckling down the phone. 'How could I forget?' she laughed. 'I think about it every time I catch a glimpse of either of them.'

'Yes, right. Well, you know you said not to do anything stupid like forwarding it on to someone…' Rosie let that hang there. There was an audibly dramatic intake of breath from the other end of the phone line.

'Oh, god, Rosie. No!'

'Yep,' confirmed Rosie grimly.

'Who to?'

'I accidentally sent it to *The Post*'s communications team on the bottom of the press release.'

Rosie held her phone away from her ear. Either this was a terrible connection or Nadia was struggling to contain her laughter.

'It's not funny!' wailed Rosie. 'What am I going to do? Rachel is going to kill me!'

'Can't you ask Mitch?' Nadia asked matter-of-factly. 'Can't he just go see his comms team and get them to delete it?'

Rosie ran her hand over her face. If only it was that easy. If only she'd realised this had happened before she'd found out about Mitch's plan to move to New York. Or better still, it hadn't happened at all and she could be happily in her lab, messing about with petri dishes.

'I don't really think I can,' Rosie's voice broke.

'Why?' Nadia suddenly sounded full of concern. 'Rosie, what's happened?'

'It's complicated...we slept together.'

'What!!!!' Nadia exploded down the phone. 'You did? Last night? Oh, my god, Rosie you have so much to tell me! How did it happen?'

'Erm, do you need a diagram?'

'No,' Nadia said firmly, 'just assure me it was *nothing* like the contents of those emails.'

Rosie's mind wandered back to the night before. No, it had been nothing like that. Despite everything that had happened since, she felt her cheeks blush at the memory.

'Anyway, it doesn't matter because it's not going to happen again,' she said as firmly as she could with a massively wobbly lower lip.

'Oh, Rosie. Are you OK?'

'No, not really.' Rosie's voice joined in the collective wobbling. 'I just found out from one of his colleagues that he's put in a transfer at work and he's moving to New York.'

'Wow. That's...a lot. And he didn't tell you this?'

'No,' Rosie's voice sounded reedy and thin. 'Not before or after we slept together. Who does that, Nadia? I mean if it had been a random one-night stand then fine. But this is Mitch. There's nothing random about us. I can't believe he wouldn't tell me.' Rosie was now fully sobbing. 'I've lost Mitch and I'm scared I'm going to lose my job, Nadia.'

'OK, Rosie, you need to calm down,' Nadia now had her best I-can-fix-anything voice on, which immediately slowed Rosie's racing heart down. 'Yes, Rachel is going to be cross about this when she finds out but I don't think she can actually fire you for it.'

'You don't think so?' asked Rosie weakly, in-between hiccupping sobs.

'No' insisted Nadia. 'You didn't write those emails, it's not your fault that she sent them to you. Yes it's unfortunate that you forwarded them on...'

'Unfortunate is one way of putting it,' Rosie said bleakly.

'We can just pretend you never opened the attachment. Didn't know what was in it but just presumed it was the press release in another format. Yes that's it!' Nadia sounded remarkably pleased with herself.

'Nadia I don't think that's going to work,' Rosie said slowly. 'Yeah, OK, technically she can't fire me. But think about how miserable she can make my life here.'

There was a silence on the other end of the line.

'I actually quite like working here,' Rosie continued in a small voice. 'I like working with you. I like working for Rachel when I'm not terrified of her.'

'Aren't we all terrified of her, like all the time?' asked Nadia.

'Yes, but I respect her. I *want* to keep working here. I don't want to fuck up my career, I've done enough damage to my personal life.'

There was another long pause.

'Leave it with me,' Nadia said eventually. 'I don't know if I can help with Mitch but I'll do my best on the work front.'

'Thank you, Nadia. You're amazing, I hope you know that. Will you let me know if you get the sense that Rachel knows about it already?' Rosie begged. 'You know, if she seems really tetchy or cross...'

'Isn't that how she normally seems?' Nadia queried.

Rosie smiled despite herself. 'True.'

'Where are you now?' Nadia asked. 'Are you coming in?'

'No!' exclaimed Rosie. 'I can't. What if she knows?'

'Rosie, you can't hide from this, and if she *can't* fire you over the email she *can* probably justify firing you for not coming into work.'

'I can't face it, Nadia. Work, Mitch, it's all just such a mess.'

Nadia sighed. 'OK, take today. We can pretend you're not feeling well. But that's all I'm giving you, one day, maybe two tops,' she said firmly. 'Promise me you'll call me if you need anything? And I'll ring you later OK?'

It was Chris who answered the front door. 'Hi!' he said enthusiastically and then immediately looked confused. 'Er, were we...' He tailed off.

Poor Chris was obviously silently panicked that he had forgotten his sister was coming over, and what with both his wife and mother in the kitchen behind him he was about to get something horribly wrong. Rosie didn't have the resources to reassure him right now.

'I just needed somewhere to go...' The rest of her sentence was lost in a sob. Chris, now quite clearly panicking, grabbed his sister by the arm and pulled her inside.

'Jasmine!' he shouted over his shoulder. 'Could you please come here?' By this time, Rosie had her face buried in his sweater, a damp patch spreading across his front. He patted her gently on the back and looked back in the hope that his wife was on her way to rescue him.

'Rosie?' said Jasmine with concern, peeling Rosie from Chris's front with one hand and handing him his coat with the other.

Chris looked over Rosie's head at Jasmine. 'Should I stay?' he asked.

Jasmine shook her head. 'I'll call you later, OK?' She shooed him to the front door.

'Erm right, OK.' Chris tentatively patted Rosie on the back again, before heading out to work.

'What's happened?' Jasmine asked in her usual, commanding tone. She took Rosie's coat and bag and put them on the bottom stair and ushered Rosie into the kitchen. Susan was sat at the island with a mug of coffee looking shocked at the sudden, dramatic entrance of her daughter.

'Hi, Mum,' managed Rosie before she started sobbing again.

Susan pulled her in for a hug.

'Did you have plans today?' hiccupped Rosie into her mother's shoulder.

'Oh, just our Christmas shopping. We can postpone.'

'I'm sorry!' wailed Rosie. 'I've ruined your day!'

'Don't be silly,' Jasmine frowned at Susan. 'I wanted to do it online anyway.'

'Sweetheart,' said Susan when Rosie had composed herself a little, 'come and sit down.' She led her to one of the stools and Jasmine smoothly slid a cup of coffee in front of her.

'So,' said Jasmine, leaning against the sink on the far side of the kitchen. 'Let me guess: Mitch, right? What happened?'

'Mitch?' said Susan sharply. 'What about Mitch?'

Rosie did a speedy evaluation of how much her mother knew and how much she might have guessed. Jasmine caught her eye and mouthed, 'Does she know?' Rosie shook her head imperceptibly and Jasmine grimaced in sympathy.

Rosie took a deep breath. 'It's OK, Jas, I think she needs to know.'

'So let me get this straight,' Susan said after Rosie had tried to explain everything, with a few clarifications and interruptions from Jasmine thrown in. 'You and Mitch cooked up a plan to have a baby together?' Rosie nodded. 'Then Mitch went and got a new girlfriend?' Rosie nodded again. 'And you got jealous and told the girlfriend about your pact?' Rosie said nothing but looked shamefacedly down at her coffee.

'So, the two of you fell out. But then Mitch confessed he has feelings for you and then... Where are we now?' Susan looked at Jasmine in confusion.

Rosie caught Jasmine's eye again and realised that Jasmine had guessed exactly what had gone down last night. Rosie shook her head. Susan did *not* need to know that Rosie was wearing the same pair of pants as yesterday.

'I'm guessing you didn't take my advice about not seeing Mitch?' Jasmine asked dryly, raising an eyebrow at Rosie. Rosie glared Jasmine into silence, allowing Susan the time to process the surprising information she had just been made a party to.

'I didn't think you wanted children?' she eventually said.

Rosie's head snapped up to look at her mother. 'After everything I've just told you, *that's* the thing you focus on!' she exclaimed. Susan looked surprised. 'And why does everyone keep saying that!' Rosie shouted.

Jasmine and Susan exchanged a look, which conveyed a silent 'after you, no after you, I insist,' conversation.

Rosie noticed and looked tearfully at both of them. 'First, *you* presume I don't want kids,' she said, pointing at Jasmine, 'and now you're doing the same.' She turned to her mother. Neither of them said anything.

'I'm not sure, OK?' said Rosie eventually. 'I'm not sure I do want kids but stupid Mitch started me thinking about it and now I can't stop!'

Susan clapped her hands brightly. 'Well that's lovely, darling. I have to say I'm surprised but I think you and Mitch would make wonderful parents. He's so kind and caring, I think he'll be a great dad.'

Rosie stared at her mother. 'Care to add anything about how I would make a great mother?'

'Of course you'd be a great mother!' Jasmine jumped in and said soothingly. All three of them shared awkward glances.

'Anyway, it's completely irrelevant,' said Rosie, breaking the silence, 'as he's moving to America. Just like Connor!' she said with a dramatic sob.

'Who?' asked Jasmine loudly as Susan pushed a box of tissues across the island to Rosie.

Susan rolled her eyes. 'Don't ask,' she said. Jasmine looked quizzically at Rosie who explained between sobs.

'Connor? Connor Ryan? Remember, my boyfriend who moved to Washington?'

'Yessss, I remember him,' said Jasmine in confusion, 'I just wondered why we're talking about him?'

Before Rosie could say anything her mother interjected, 'Because Rosie seems to have got it into her head that he was her one great love, the one who got away and she's been pining for him for years when all along it looks like she should have just been copping off with Mitch!'

'Mother!' said Rosie in shock at the same moment as Jasmine

exploded with laughter. It wasn't clear whether Jasmine was laughing at what Susan had just said or the thought of Rosie pining after Connor all these years.

'Connor?!' Jasmine asked. 'You thought that idiot was the one? Oh, good grief!' she said and took a large sip of her coffee.

Rosie didn't know whether to laugh or cry. 'I haven't been *pining* for him,' she said stiffly. 'But it was a difficult break-up, you know,' she said defensively.

'Yeah, OK whatever,' said Jasmine. 'I mean I only met him a couple of times but he was incredibly self-obsessed.'

'Exactly!' exclaimed Susan. 'That's just what I said!' They clinked their coffee cups together in a celebratory fashion. Rosie dramatically dropped her head in her hands.

'But I still don't understand why we're talking about him?' said Jasmine again.

'Because,' sighed Rosie, 'he left me to move to America and broke my heart, remember?' She noticed another look passing between Jasmine and Susan and chose to ignore it.

'And now,' she said dramatically, 'exactly the same thing is happening with Mitch! We just got together and now he's leaving me to move to America! AND I'm about to lose my job,' she wailed.

'What?' they both demanded.

Rosie pulled a face. 'I've messed up. I sent an email by mistake and now Rachel is going to kill me, straight after she fires me.'

Jasmine was immediately all business. 'We'll recall it,' she said briskly.

Rosie fixed her with a look. 'You do know that doesn't actually work right?'

'OK,' conceded Jasmine. 'But it was a mistake, everyone sends emails by mistake. There was the time—'

'Have you ever sent an email which outlined, in eye watering details, what your boss's sexual proclivities are?' Jasmine's jaw dropped. 'Or that they would like to fulfill said proclivities with *their* boss, the Vice Chancellor of an internationally recognised university?'

'Oh my,' said Susan.

'Exactly' Rosie said grimly, staring at Jasmine. 'How do you suggest we fix that?'

'Right, well that might be a little more complicated.' Jasmine tapped her fingers on the work surface. 'Can I ask how you happened to have this and who you sent it to?'

Rosie sighed. 'Rachel sent them by accident to me, and I forwarded them *by accident* to the comms team at *The Post*.'

'Where Mitch works?' Jasmine snapped to attention. Rosie nodded.

'So, we ask Mitch for help?' Susan suggested.

'Oh, god!' exclaimed Rosie. 'Have neither of you been listening? I can't ask Mitch for anything right now! He's moving to America, remember? And I am *really* upset about it?'

'Well, actually,' said Jasmine, 'that's not strictly true, you *could* ask him if you wanted to. But you don't want to, right?' She clarified, seeing the look on Rosie's face.

There was a long silence while Jasmine and Susan reflected on the situation.

'Remind me how you know about all this? About Mitch's move?' asked Jasmine after a while.

'Ben told me,' Rosie said morosely.

'Ben, as in Ben who has a thing for you?' Jasmine asked.

Susan's ears pricked up. 'Who's Ben?'

'No one, Mum,' Rosie said wearily, not wanting to throw another red herring into this already complex situation. 'And he doesn't have a thing for me,' she directed at Jasmine.

Jasmine shrugged but looked unconvinced. 'I'm just saying

that maybe you should consider talking to Mitch? Get his side of the story? And ask for his help deleting that email while you're at it.'

'No,' said Rosie definitively.

'Rosie,' began Susan, 'I really think you should.' Rosie said nothing, which just encouraged Susan, so she continued. 'Come on, Rosie, this isn't like you. You're normally so logical. I do think hearing him out might give you the clarity you need.'

'I'm fed up with being logical!' she exclaimed. 'It's got me nowhere. I don't want to hear his side, Mum! And I don't want to ask him for help!' she began to wail. 'I don't want to get hurt again!' Tears leaked down her face.

'Oh, Rosie,' Susan said and grabbed Rosie's hand. 'None of us want to see you get hurt, either!'

'For a fleeting moment, I thought everything was going to be OK between me and Mitch,' Rosie said, looking at her mum. 'I felt happy, really happy, like life had finally worked out the way it was supposed to work out. The way I had always *wanted* it to work out.'

Susan made comforting shushing noises while Jasmine looked thoughtful.

'Does Mitch know you know about New York?' she asked eventually.

'I don't know,' replied Rosie sniffling a little, 'I'm not sure.'

'Has he tried to contact you since you saw Ben?'

Rosie shook her head.

Jasmine looked surprised. 'He hasn't called? Messaged?' Rosie shook her head again. 'You have got your phone turned on, right?' Jasmine asked, her eyes narrowed.

Rosie balled up the tissue she was holding. 'No' she said in a small voice.

'Rosie!' said both her mother and Jasmine in unison.

'I don't want to talk to him, OK? I don't care what he tries to tell me. I don't understand how he gets from let's have a baby together and declaring he has feelings for me, to leaving the country and moving to America.' Tears continued rolling down her cheeks. 'I'm so hurt and scared. I finally thought we'd worked things out, that maybe he *was* the one, and now it turns out he's not. He can't feel the same way as I do.'

'I just think you should hear his side,' said Jasmine tentatively. 'Susan?' she asked, looking for backup.

'I agree, sweetheart,' said Susan putting her arm around Rosie's shoulder. 'But maybe when you're ready?' she said consolingly.

Rosie still wasn't ready the next morning after having spent the night at Jasmine and Chris's. The day before, she had eventually persuaded Jasmine and her mum to go and do their Christmas shopping. Assuring them that she would be fine without them and promising not to do anything stupid. Like sending intimate details of her boss's private life to the national newspapers again.

Rosie gagged every time she thought about it. So far, Rachel didn't seem to know and hadn't noticed that Rosie wasn't in work. Nadia was keeping Rosie updated from her vantage point in the lab. She said that every time she had seen Rachel, she had been uncharacteristically chatty and friendly, even going so far as to ask Nadia how her kids were.

'Definitely not the sign of someone who knows that their sex tape has been leaked.'

'It's not a sex tape!' Rosie protested.

'Same thing,' Nadia said in a manner that made Rosie suspect she was not taking this situation as seriously as Rosie had hoped.

'I brought a spare jacket from home and draped it over the back of your chair, and I turn the light on and off and open the door and stuff each time I walk past. It's quite fun!'

She then proceeded to tell Rosie a long and involved story about a man who had fooled all his colleagues this way for months, while all the time he had, in reality, been lying dead in his flat instead.

'So, he wasn't actually trying to fool them?' Rosie asked. 'He was *actually* dead?' She sighed. 'Nadia, remind me how that story is supposed to make me feel better?'

'Never mind. The point is you're OK for the moment but you need to come back to work soon or Rachel *is* going to notice.'

Rosie knew Nadia was right, but until she'd figured out how she was going to handle the whole situation she couldn't countenance going in. Imagine coming face to face with Rachel and realising that she had discovered what Rosie had done? Rosie would prefer to be fired for absenteeism and had already mentally worked out what personal possessions she would need Nadia to fetch from her office when that happened.

But despite this career Armageddon hanging over her, Rosie couldn't stop thinking about Mitch. It didn't help that every time Nadia messaged, she would mention something about how amazing Mitch was and how he had saved her job. And every time Rosie would reply with gritted teeth, hating Mitch for meddling in Nadia's life but also grateful that he had sorted things out for her.

'Has he called you?' Nadia asked. Rosie had been screening her calls but decided that Nadia didn't need to know that.

'I'm still not ready,' Rosie said defiantly, as Jasmine carefully placed a cup of tea on the table next to the sofa. Rosie was wrapped up in a blanket, wearing Jasmine's pyjamas and watching daytime TV. Her nephews had begged to be allowed to stay home and do the same, but Chris had wrestled them out of the door about an hour ago to take them to school.

'I didn't say anything,' said Jasmine, sitting down on the sofa next to Rosie.

'You didn't have to,' Rosie said flatly. 'I can tell by the look on your face that you think I should talk to him.'

Jasmine raised her eyebrows. 'Actually, I think he's behaved like a shit, to tell the truth.' Rosie looked over at Jasmine in surprise. 'I've been thinking it over and you're right, if he asked for a transfer at the same time that he asked you to have his baby, then I think we can agree that's shitty behaviour.'

'You think?' said Rosie who had begun to think that actually she didn't honestly know when Mitch applied for the transfer. And that maybe everyone was right and she should return one of his calls and hear him out. And that he really probably was the best person to help her out with this email fiasco and that she should swallow her pride and just pick up the phone…

'Yes, I do,' confirmed Jasmine, 'And I also think that you need to make a decision. Either you talk to him, hear him out, or you move on with your life.'

Rosie felt her eyes well up at Jasmine's words. She didn't want to hear it.

'Rosie, I know this is hard, but you two have been messing about in each other's lives for over a decade, during which time nothing romantic has happened – until now. Both of you have put your lives on hold. And then as soon as something does happen, it all goes wrong!' Jasmine put her hand on Rosie's arm and gave her a gentle squeeze. 'You really need to talk to him, see if you can figure things out. And if you can't, well then at least you'll know. I'm only saying this because I care about you, I hate seeing you like this, and I hate the thought that you've wasted all this time waiting for Mitch.'

Rosie inched herself closer to Jasmine and rested her head on her shoulder. She didn't want to hear her words, but she did want the comfort of Jasmine's hugs. As if reading her thoughts Jasmine put her arm around Rosie and squeezed her.

'I still think you should hear him out. Get some closure and then you can move on.'

'Really? I was sort of hoping I could hide here forever and pretend none of this had ever happened.'

'I'm going to pretend you're joking,' Jasmine said with a raised eyebrow. 'You *need* to hear his explanation, for your sake, not for his.'.

'Shouldn't you be at work?' Rosie asked, changing the subject.

'Slow morning,' Jasmine said.

Rosie looked at her pointedly. 'You never have slow anytime.'

'Yeah, well I wanted to check that you weren't going to sit here and wallow all day. I want those pyjamas back at some point.'

Rosie pointed towards the TV and then her cup of tea. 'I'm not wallowing. This is medicinal.'

Jasmine rolled her eyes. 'Right, whatever. But if you're not going to listen to my advice on Mitch you need to listen to my advice on work. Do you have a plan?' Rosie reluctantly shook her head.

'OK,' continued Jasmine, 'well you need to get one. Because it's not acceptable that you throw away your career sitting around moping over some boy.'

'I'm not moping!' protested Rosie.

'You are,' insisted Jasmine. 'You need to work out what you're going to do. Either you fess up to Rachel before she finds out from someone else, because that –' Jasmine pointed at Rosie forcefully '– would be *so* much worse. Or you need to work out how to get that email back. Which brings me back to the fact that you need to talk to Mitch.'

'All right, all right,' Rosie said grumpily. 'I'll do something. Nadia said she would help.'

Jasmine stood up. 'Well make sure she does.'

'Are you going now?' demanded Rosie.

Jasmine walked towards the door stopping to give Rosie's shoulder a squeeze. 'By the way, Chris said you can stay as long as you like!'

'He did?' said Rosie, looking up at Jasmine in surprise.

'Well no, not exactly. But he did say you could stay for a night or two.'

Chapter Twenty-Five

'D rop us here, and then you can go and find somewhere to park,' Nadia commanded imperiously. Rosie muttered a thank you to the ever patient Nico who was evidently used to being treated worse than a Uber driver.

'Don't you need to tip him?' Rosie asked with a wink as they stood together on the pavement outside Rachel's beautiful Highgate house and watched Nico pull away from the curb.

'What? No. Don't be silly. He doesn't mind. He's not one for parties anyway, so he'd probably rather be searching for a parking spot for half the night.' Nadia paused. 'At least I think that's the case?' She suddenly looked less sure about the way she had just treated her husband and glanced distractedly over her shoulder as if wondering whether to call him back and offer to park the car herself. Or perhaps to tip him. Rosie smiled at Nadia's confused face.

'Come on,' said Rosie, grabbing her friend. 'Let's get this over with. The sooner we're in, the sooner we can get out.'

'Not the attitude!' Nadia replied, having regained her composure. 'It's a party, Rosie, we're here to have fun. Remember what that is?' Rosie raised her eyebrow at Nadia and they walked up the steps together.

Earlier that evening Nadia had arrived, uninvited, at Jasmine and Chris's house and staged a one-woman intervention. She was halfway through a rousing speech when Rosie had held her hands up and said, 'I get it, I know. I need to go to the party. I don't want to.' She paused. 'I'm scared of seeing Rachel and Mitch. But I know I need to face up to this. And talk to Mitch, listen to what he has to say. And work up the courage to ask him if he can help with that email.' She shuddered.

'Great!' Nadia had said. 'But, don't take this the wrong way, you look bloody awful.'

Seeing Rosie's face, Jasmine had rushed to her side. 'You look great, Rosie. Nothing a shower and some make-up won't fix. Come on, you can raid my wardrobe.'

Not one to look a gift horse in the mouth Rosie had allowed herself to be led upstairs where Jasmine and Nadia had bonded over her makeover. So here she was now, stood in front of Rachel's house, knowing she needed to deal with whatever the evening held. And hoping that the (incredibly expensive) clothes she had borrowed from Jasmine would form some kind of protective armour around her.

Rachel's front door was decked in a beautiful Christmas wreath, the sounds of the party could be heard out on the street and the windows were stylishly lit from within by candlelight.

The party was already in full flow. They were met at the door by a waiter carrying a tray of champagne and another one who took their coats. Rosie craned her neck to see where he had taken them in case she needed to make a speedy exit later. If it had been a coat of hers, she might have cut her losses and run, but it was Jasmine's and Rosie valued her life too much.

Rosie suspiciously eyed the tray being proffered but Nadia had grabbed two glasses and swept her through the door before she had a chance to ask if sparkling water was an option – alcohol had *not* been her friend recently. They made their way through the crowd of guests on the ground floor. There was not a lab coat to be seen, everyone was in glamorous dresses, chic suits or a combination of the two. Rosie saw one girl, who she knew she had met at a previous party but couldn't remember the name of, who was wearing the most incredible corset top – all black silk and boning and with feathers down the back. It was cut so low that Rosie felt flushed just trying not to stare. She was downing a glass of champagne and laughing loudly at something the man next to her was saying. Catching Rosie's eye, the girl raised her glass and smiled. Rosie lifted her eyes away from where they had been resting a moment before and smiled back, before feeling herself propelled forward by Nadia.

They had yet to see Rachel, although they discovered lots of their colleagues congregated in the basement kitchen. Rosie found herself sipping her glass of champagne slowly, propped against a table in the corner of the room.

'Do you need another one?' Nadia shouted over the increasingly loud conversation, evidently having downed hers quite quickly.

'No, I'm fine,' Rosie replied.

'Sorry, what?' Nadia shouted back. Rosie held up her glass and pointed to it while shaking her head.

'OK! I do. I'll meet you back down here,' Nadia said and turned to go back upstairs in search of another drink. She turned back at the bottom of the stairs. 'Don't do a runner!' she warned, fixing Rosie with a stare.

Rosie smiled at her sweetly. 'I wouldn't dream of it.'

But it was hot and loud and no one was paying her any attention so she edged towards the double doors that led out into the courtyard garden. She had half a mind on getting some fresh air and the other half on wondering whether this might be a possible escape route. She could always claim that she fell through the doors, accidentally locking herself out of the party, and then as she couldn't find the front door, she went home, and put her sweatpants on and never left her house again.

Rosie felt for the handle behind her. It turned easily and she slipped out into the darkness of the garden. Very quietly, she closed the door behind her and immediately the sounds of the party became muffled and distant. She took a deep breath, feeling the cold air burn in her lungs. She exhaled and stared up at the sky. Not that she could see much, it was London and most of the stars were blocked out by light pollution. As if she needed another reminder of her urban surroundings, a car horn blared nearby followed soon afterwards by the siren of an emergency vehicle. On the next road over she could hear the sounds of drunk revellers; Christmas party season was in full force.

Despite the streetlights it was still dark in the garden, high walls ran all the way around it and ivy crept up some of them adding to the feeling of enclosure. Rosie had been here before, though, and was fairly sure there was a small round metal table in the far corner with chairs surrounding it. She edged her way carefully towards it, feeling with her feet over the slightly uneven ground. A large London plane tree shaded that part of the garden and the table was hard to make out. Rosie felt the leg of the table and next to it a chair. Carefully placing her glass on the table, she gingerly sat down where she thought the chair might be and screamed.

Instead of coming into contact with cold metal, she felt the warmth of two limbs and quickly realised someone else had had the same idea and was sat in the exact chair that she had chosen.

'This one is taken,' came a voice as her scream echoed away.

'Mitch?' Rosie had stood back up by this point and was staring at where the voice had come from. She was just beginning to make out the tall, lanky frame of Mitch sat at the table. 'What are you doing here?' she demanded.

'Same thing as you I should imagine. Trying to avoid the party, wondering what I was thinking coming here,' he said. 'Avoiding *you*. Ironic really, isn't it?' he said after a pause. She could see he had cocked his head to one side.

'Right,' said Rosie, 'well, I don't want to ruin your evening. I'll leave you to it.' She turned and walked more quickly this time back towards the door to the kitchen. But as she drew closer she heard a very distinctive sound, the sound of a key turning in a lock. Looking up she saw Nadia stood in the glass doorway holding up a key.

'What are you doing?' Rosie yelped.

Nadia grinned and pretended not to be able to hear. She cupped her hand behind her ear and continued to smile.

'I said, *what are you doing*?' Rosie raised her voice.

'I can't hear you!' came the muffled reply. Rosie frowned and put her hands on her hips and then watched as Nadia turned and handed the key to Rachel, who Rosie could now see was stood behind Nadia. Rosie looked up at the starless sky and wished she had bailed out of Nico's car when he had stalled at those lights south of the river. She cursed herself for not being brave enough and worrying about trifling concerns such as traffic accidents.

'Nadia told me you two needed to talk?' Rachel shouted through the glass, pointing over Rosie's shoulder into the dark corner where Mitch sat. With her other hand she reached for a switch on the wall of the kitchen and suddenly fairy lights lit up over the walled garden, bathing everything in a soft, romantic glow.

Rosie glared at Rachel and Nadia who waved happily at her.

Rachel pulled the curtain over the back door and presumably slipped back off into the party. Rosie spun round to face Mitch who she could now see more clearly. He had stood up, his hands in the pockets of his jeans.

'Did you plan this?' she demanded.

'What? Of course not!' he scoffed at her. 'I haven't even seen Rachel yet; I had been lurking on the edges of the party wondering when I could politely leave.'

Despite herself Rosie smiled. 'Join the club. So, what do we do now?' she asked. 'Is there a gate round to the front somewhere?'

Mitch looked around the garden. 'Doesn't look like it,' he said after studying the walls. 'It looks like the only way in or out is through that,' he said, pointing back at the still locked door. 'Unless you feel like scaling one of these walls and ending up in a neighbour's garden?'

Rosie glanced nervously at the walls, for a moment sizing up whether it might be possible to do so and then remembering that she was wearing Jasmine's clothes. Being stuck in a garden in the middle of winter with Mitch seemed preferable to risking the wrath of Jasmine should Rosie return her clothes with rips in them.

'Maybe not,' she said.

Mitch looked over at her. 'Jasmine's clothes?' he questioned. Rosie nodded, feeling a sudden pang that Mitch knew her wardrobe well enough to identify her sister-in-law's clothes and recognising that it meant wall-climbing was off the agenda.

'That's where you've been hiding out?'

'I wasn't hiding out!'

'Hmm, what would you call it?' He looked at her questioningly. 'You certainly haven't been at your flat because I've been staking it out.'

'You have?'

357

'And maybe it's just my calls you've been screening, or perhaps you don't turn your phone on for anyone anymore?'

Rosie stared down at the ground twisting her hands; this was beginning to get awkward. She didn't know who she was more frustrated by: Rachel for locking them out here, Jasmine and Nadia for making her come to the stupid party in the first place, or Mitch for making life so unbearably difficult and painful. She looked back at the house, hoping to miraculously spot an open door.

'It's still locked,' Mitch confirmed, watching her nervous glances. 'We might as well sit down. Presumably at some point someone will let us in.' He sat back down at the table and pointed to the chair opposite him.

'And if you don't want to talk to me then we can always use this to pass the time.' He reached under his chair and pulled out an almost full bottle of champagne. He offered it towards Rosie. Almost imperceptibly she nodded, and he filled her glass up.

'Where did you swipe that from?' she asked as she tentatively sat down opposite him.

'One of the waiters.' He topped up his own glass. 'It seemed like a good idea to bring it outside with me. Rather glad I did now.'

They both sat in silence sipping their champagne. Rosie tried to screw up the courage to ask for Mitch's help. She knew she had come here specifically to ask him, but now that she was sat here, she didn't know what to say. Eventually she blurted out, 'Mitch? I need your help.'

Mitch cocked his head. 'That email?'

Rosie looked confused. 'How did you know?'

'Ben told me.'

'Ben?' Rosie asked in astonishment.

'Yup. Kind of funny that. He came to see me straight after that conversation you had with him. I guess he felt guilty.'

'Oh, so you know?'

'Uh-huh. And it's sorted.'

'*What*? How?'

'I just went to see the girl in the comms team who had shown the email to Ben. Turns out she was feeling dreadful about even having shown it to him so she was only too happy to delete it.'

'Oh, wow. I don't know what to say.'

'Thanks would cover it,' Mitch said dryly.

'And she hadn't forwarded it to anyone else?' Rosie still couldn't quite believe that Mitch had sorted it out so easily.

'Nope. As I said, she was feeling bad enough about showing it to Ben. And by the way? Your non-X-rated press release will be going out tomorrow.'

So that was that. So simple. Rosie felt a weight lift off her shoulders. She wasn't about to get fired. Rachel never need know how badly she had cocked up. She could forget the whole thing ever happened, and she had Mitch to thank. 'Well, thank you.'

'It was nothing.' Mitch shrugged.

'Not for me it wasn't. It was a stupid thing for me to do.'

'Rosie,' he said patiently, 'we all make mistakes, you simply forwarded an email. It was Rachel's mistake in the first place.'

'Ha!' laughed Rosie bitterly. 'Do you really think she'd have seen it that way?'

'Yeah, OK, maybe not. Anyway, it was easy enough to fix. I just wondered why you didn't ask me yourself?' He paused. 'We said goodbye outside my work and the logical Rosie I've always known seemed to do a vanishing act. It's kind of funny. For years I've told you not to be so analytical about stuff, and as soon as I want you to be, you're not.' He shook his head.

Rosie looked across at him, her expression deadpan. 'I've come to the conclusion that sometimes logic doesn't apply to real life.'

Mitch smiled at her. 'Eureka!' he said softly. 'So do you want to explain why you vanished?'

'*Me* explain?' spluttered Rosie. 'Don't you think *you* ought to explain about New York?!'

Mitch sighed. 'I've been trying to explain Rosie, that's why I've been calling you, that's why I've been hanging around your flat. By the way, it's a miracle your neighbours haven't called the police on me yet.' Rosie watched him warily. 'I thought maybe you'd like to explain why *you've* been avoiding *me*. Why *you* wouldn't take *my* calls? And why on earth you would listen to Ben's version of events and not ask *me* what was going on?'

Rosie shook her head. 'He's not that bad, Mitch.' Mitch laughed. 'No, really,' she insisted. 'You do believe me when I tell you nothing happened between us don't you?'

Mitch shrugged his shoulders. 'Yeah, I know that.'

'Good,' she exhaled in relief.

'I know he's not all bad, after all he did come and find me to tell me what he'd told you. But that still doesn't explain why you would listen to his story and not mine?' he said sadly.

Rosie sighed. 'OK, I agree that I shouldn't have listened to him. But he wasn't lying, was he? I had to hear about New York from him, not from you.'

'Yes, but it's not like that,' Mitch protested, 'I've been trying to explain it to you.'

Rosie looked at him cautiously. She reminded herself that this was *her* Mitch, *her* best friend, who up until recently had never done anything to hurt her. 'OK, I'm listening. But Mitch, you have to understand,' she said, tears beginning to well in her eyes, 'from my point of view I felt you had persuaded me that you wanted to have a baby together and then ditched me as soon as you got a better offer.' Mitch opened his mouth to protest but Rosie held her hand up, asking that he allow her to continue. "Then you got me to confess that I'm actually *in love with you, you* pretend that you have feelings for me, too, but all along you'd been planning to leave the country!'

'I wasn't pretending!' Mitch blurted out. 'Of course I have feelings for you, Rosie. I always have done. Ever since we first met.'

'So why didn't you say something sooner?'

'Why didn't you?' he countered, both of them starting to sound like petulant children. 'And anyway,' he said, 'you're the one who ran away when I kissed you in our flat.' Mitch slumped back in his chair.

'You remember that?' Rosie said in shock.

'Of course I remember that,' Mitch sighed. 'It was one of the best and worst nights of my life.' Rosie stared at him. 'I'd wanted to kiss you ever since we first met in that awful pub,' he smiled sadly, 'and I finally got to do it, but then you obviously weren't interested so it quickly became the worst night of my life.'

'You fell asleep!' Rosie protested.

Mitch looked embarrassed. 'I was drunk! And when I woke up the next morning, I wanted to kiss you again, but you never mentioned it so I thought you wished it had never happened.'

'Because you never mentioned it!' she protested. 'And anyway, we were housemates!'

'So?' Mitch asked.

'So, it would have been a terrible idea.'

'Why? Why would it have been a terrible idea?'

Rosie sat for a moment and thought. Why had she *really* not said anything that morning? Why had she been so sure it wouldn't have worked? She was always looking for the practical approach; she didn't want to take the risk, get swept off her feet

361

and it all end in heartbreak, but why had she been so sure that it would have ended that way? The thought of trying to explain all of that in an articulate way made her head spin. So, she simply said, 'Well, *you* never mentioned it and you never tried to kiss me again!' She folded her arms across her chest defensively.

Mitch groaned in frustration. 'Because you made it so damn clear that you didn't want to talk about it, you pretended it had never happened! And anyway, I tried loads of times to talk to you about it, but every time I did something would conspire against me.'

'Like when?'

'Like…' Mitch paused for a second, thinking. 'Like in Italy!' he said triumphantly. 'I was about to talk to you and then we got the phone call about my mum.'

Rosie remembered that night so clearly. She had thought Mitch was about to tell her to back off, and now it turned out he had been going to say the opposite? 'But why didn't you say anything about it when we got back to London?'

'Because my mum was really sick, Rosie! Because I was tired and frightened she might not make it and I couldn't risk losing you as a friend because I needed you so much to help me through all that. I don't know what I would have done without you! And that night,' he continued, 'a year ago. When I got that promotion? When I had booked that table at that fancy restaurant but I got the wrong date?'

'You mean the wrong year,' she said, a smile starting to play about her lips.

'Yeah, OK, whatever, the wrong year. I was planning to tell you then at dinner. And then I messed up.'

'But why didn't you tell me in the pub? Why did it have to be in that restaurant?'

'Because I had it all planned out, exactly how it was all going to be, and then it didn't work and I was so mad at myself, and I took it out on you, and it all felt wrong to be telling you that night.'

Rosie looked at him across the table, cross with him for missing the opportunities, cross with herself for apparently missing the signs. To hell with keeping a clear head, she thought, and drained her glass of champagne. Ever the gentleman, Mitch reached over to refill her glass.

'You still haven't explained New York.'

Mitch put his head in his hands and rubbed his face. 'I thought it would help me get over you.' His voice came out muffled between his fingers.

'Get over me? You suggested we have a baby together!'

Mitch groaned again, 'It was all such a mess.'

'Explain' demanded Rosie tapping the table. Mitch looked down at his hands, then up at the sky, then he too picked up his glass of champagne and drained it.

Eventually he said, 'I've always been in love with you, Rosie. It's always been you. Ever since you answered my advert for a roommate. I still remember what you were wearing that day.' He smiled at her sadly. 'Do you remember?' Rosie didn't move. 'You had on a grey T-shirt, black combat trousers and seemed to be carrying the rest of your worldly goods in that enormous rucksack you used to lug around with you.'

Rosie remembered, of course she remembered. She was nervous about moving to London on her own, Connor had recently left for Washington and all the plans she thought she had made were up in the air.

'You said you were anxious about moving to London for the first time, but you seemed anything but anxious. You were so quietly confident, so self-assured, I thought you could do anything you wanted to do. I still do,' he insisted.

Rosie just remembered feeling like a mess. She hadn't worn make-up, those combat pants were a real fashion faux pas and she actually did have most of her things in that rucksack. She just desperately wanted to make sure she had somewhere to live sorted before her PhD started. Rosie never would have imagined that the person she would end up living with would have been Mitch, or that he would remember their first meeting just as clearly as she did.

'I couldn't believe it when you said yes to moving in. I remember thinking that this is what it felt like to win the lottery. But all the time I was telling myself to calm down.' Rosie looked at him quizzically. 'Because while I was getting to live with the girl of my dreams, you might not feel the same way. And that's what I feared when we kissed that night.'

Rosie blushed at the memory; it still made her stomach somersault. 'I was hurt, I thought you either didn't remember or wanted to forget,' she protested, 'and I worried that it would ruin our friendship if I brought it up and then you rejected me, you already meant so much to me, even by that point, Mitch.' They stared at each other across the table for a moment, lost in memories.

Mitch smiled ruefully. 'Well, that was a lost opportunity.'

'But what about all the other girls?' Rosie pressed him.

'What about them?' he asked. 'None of them lasted, none of them ever measured up to you.'

'But none of them looked anything like me!' she exclaimed. 'If you could pick the polar opposite of me, you seemed to do so each and every time which just reinforced my belief that you couldn't have been interested in me because I wasn't your type.'

'Don't you think there's a different reason?' Mitch asked. 'That maybe I was trying to escape my feelings for you? That if I just dated girls that looked like you then I would end up thinking about you instead of them? And anyway, wouldn't it have seemed a little creepy if all my girlfriends looked like you?' Rosie bit her lip, trying to hold in a smile at this thought.

'I did date one girl who looked like you,' Mitch said.

'I remember!' exclaimed Rosie. 'I liked her!'

'Of course you did!' Mitch smiled. 'She was like a carbon copy of you. I ended it after a few weeks when I accidentally called her Rosie.'

'You didn't!' Rosie gasped. 'You never told me that!'

'Was I likely to?' he asked in amusement. 'I realised that the reason I was attracted to her was because she reminded me of you. That was an awkward break-up.' He grimaced at the thought.

The sound of shattering glass came from inside the house, and both of them looked around startled. 'Sounds like the party is really getting started now!' said Mitch and he turned back to look at Rosie. 'You know, all these years I lived in terror of you meeting someone else and me getting my heart broken. But you never did,' he said. 'And then I started to dare to hope that maybe you and I would grow old together, even just as best friends.'

'Now that does sound creepy,' said Rosie. Mitch laughed.

'It gets creepier. I saw all our friends starting to settle down, get married and have kids. I always said that's what I wanted. But really, I only ever wanted it with you. And so, then I got this hare-brained scheme in my head that maybe I could suggest we be each other's fallback. That we should have a baby together and that way, we could make a life together.'

Rosie looked at him. 'Yeah, you're right, that is more creepy. And it's exactly what Nadia suggested I do.'

Mitch laughed. 'Nadia knew? I should have guessed that. Anyone else?'

Rosie contemplated this for a moment. 'Jasmine,' she

confirmed, 'and so I guess Chris knows too. Probably my nephews. My mum.'

'*Susan* knows?!' exclaimed Mitch, 'What did she have to say about it?'

Rosie laughed. 'Well, she wasn't fazed by it, as I'm sure you can imagine, even when I told her we had discussed having a baby together. In fact, she thinks you'd make a really good dad. She had less to say about whether I would make a good mother.'

Mitch blushed. 'I love your mum,' he said.

'Feeling's mutual,' Rosie replied. 'But you know,' she said after a pause, 'this is what I wanted to talk about the other day, Mitch. I've never been sure about kids. It's not as if I knew I *didn't* want them, but they've never been something I have been certain I *did* want.'

'I know,' said Mitch quietly, 'and that's when I realised I had messed up. I really thought that this silly idea might bring us together, maybe it would give me the confidence to confess my true feelings. Or even...' He stared back down at his hands. 'I dared to hope it might make you realise you had feelings for me, too. But it didn't work out like that.' He shook his head and leaned back to look up into the sky. 'I knew I was following my own dreams, not yours. And I felt really guilty. I felt like I'd put pressure on you to do something you didn't want to do, and that's when I panicked, put in an application for an international transfer and started dating Jenny.'

'O-kaaay,' Rosie screwed her nose up. 'That's an interesting train of events,' she said dryly. 'I'm not sure I quite follow.'

Mitch sighed and picked up his empty glass, toying with it. 'When I realised you weren't about to declare your true feelings for me, and when it became clear that you weren't keen on our plan, and I'd basically strong-armed you into it, I worried that you *would* meet someone. That I had forced you into dating again. And if you were dating then you might finally meet someone you actually liked. And that it wouldn't be me.'

Mitch put his glass down and leaned forward in his chair, his elbows on his knees, his chin resting in his hands. 'You're so great, Rosie. You're beautiful and clever and funny. And I knew that the reason you hadn't met anyone yet is because you never seemed that bothered. And that if you started dating properly it wouldn't be long before someone fell in love with you, and you might fall in love with them, too. And I couldn't sit back and watch that happen, *especially* when I knew it was really all my fault for forcing you into this stupid fallback plan in the first place. So then when my boss started asking me about career plans and said that they were putting together a new list for international assignments, I agreed to put my name down. I thought if I couldn't be with you, then I needed to be as far away from you as possible,' he explained.

Rosie exhaled. 'Mitch you're an idiot. Could you not have explained this to me?'

'I tried to!' He reached forward and took her hand. 'I've been trying to. I even wanted to talk to you about it at the time... but then I got worried that you might think it was a great idea for me to move and then I really would have known there was no hope for me and you.'

'I'm sorry, Mitch.' Rosie hesitated before reaching over and taking his hand. 'I should have given you the chance to explain but I was hurt and confused and scared.' She paused, figuring out how to put into words what she wanted to tell him. 'I had wrapped my heart up so carefully for so many years and then after all this time, I had you, and you were about to break it anyway.' She felt tears rolling down her cheeks.

Mitch stood up so quickly, he rocked the table. Rosie grabbed it to stop the glasses toppling over. 'I would never break your heart,' he said, coming round to her side of the table pulling her to her feet. 'I will *never* break your heart.' She looked up into his face, he gently wiped her cheek with his thumb.

'It took me years to tell you how I felt,' he said, pulling her closer to him. 'I just needed you to give me a few minutes to explain what a mess I had made of it all. You have to believe me, I would never deliberately hurt you,' he said earnestly. He clasped his hands around hers as they stood staring into each other's eyes. Rosie was suddenly aware of how fast she was breathing, how loud her heartbeat seemed to be and how no matter how romantic the situation, if you were outside in London at night, you would invariably hear foxes mating.

'So, what now?' she asked. 'I mean, for us?'

'Always with the questions!' he exclaimed. 'Can't we just live happily ever after?' he asked smiling down at her.

'Mitch! Don't be an idiot. I meant what now, what about New York? What about babies? It's all so complicated.'

'Oh, I don't know.' Mitch looked thoughtful. 'Why don't you just come to New York with me and have my babies? I'm joking! Joking!' he protested, seeing the look of panic on her face.

'I don't have to take the New York job,' he said. 'It doesn't matter.'

'You'd turn it down for me?' she asked incredulously.

'Rosie,' he said sternly, 'I only applied for it because of you. If you're not about to break my heart, and you're telling me that you want to be with me, then the first thing I'm going to do is turn it down.'

'But won't you get into trouble?' Rosie asked with concern.

'You're always so worried about doing the right thing,' Mitch smiled. 'It's *my* life, *my* career, they can't make me go. And even if it does make things awkward for a while at work that's fine, I can find another job. I did get Nico one after all!' Rosie still looked worried, 'Will you stop worrying,' he insisted. 'It will be fine.'

'And what about the other thing?' she asked. 'You know, babies?'

'I know how you feel about babies,' he said, 'and frankly I couldn't care less. If I have you, I don't care whether we have them or not. My dream for the future has only ever involved you, Rosie, and I want our life to be whatever *you* want it to be. I don't think I can build the life I want without you in it.'

Rosie looked keenly into his eyes, searching for something. Eventually, she said, 'I don't want to scare you off, but I've started thinking, and I'm not saying now, but maybe in the future, after we've dated for a long time and we've worked out whether we're compatible, and that it seems like the right time, and I've convinced my mother that I would be a good parent, then maybe, *maybe* we can talk about it.' She paused. 'And not just as co-parents.' Mitch laughed. 'But I'm making no promises,' she insisted, the words tumbling out of her mouth.

Mitch squeezed her waist, and smiled. 'I agree. Maybe when we have fulfilled all your criteria to make our lives a perfectly planned scientific experiment, we can discuss it.'

Rosie frowned at him. 'You're making fun of me,' she said.

'Yes', he said, 'I am. It's what makes our relationship so special. I don't plan to stop, is that OK?'

Rosie wrinkled her nose, 'So we're in a relationship now, are we?'

'We always have been, Rosie,' Mitch said, grinning at her.

'I'm not just your fallback plan?' she asked shyly.

'Rosie, you were never *ever* my fallback,' he said sincerely. 'Was I ever yours?'

'Never,' she replied. One of his arms was behind her, holding her body, with his other hand he caught her chin and kissed her. His lips on hers, warm and soft yet insistent.

A cheer rang out from the backdoor of the house. Mitch and Rosie broke away and both turned to look. The curtains which Rachel had firmly pulled across the door were now open and framed against the light they could see Rachel, Nadia and Nico lifting their glasses towards them and clapping. Rosie felt herself blush. Mitch took her hand and gripped it tightly.

'Now what?' she said out of the corner of her mouth.

'Let's smile and wave,' he replied.

'What?' She looked up at him. 'We're not the royal family!'

'Let's pretend we are, just without the divorce and the unhappiness and the illegal activity, OK?' Bemused, Rosie followed his lead and started laughing as Mitch snaked his hand around her waist pulling her tight against him while waving manically at her friends.

'And now?' she asked, as their friends lost interest and went back to the party. She could finally have Mitch properly to herself.

'Now, we're going to do something we should have done years ago. Rosie.' He pulled her round so she was facing him again, putting both hands on her waist. 'We're going to go back to that pub on the Strand.' She looked up at him in confusion. He laughed at the expression on her face. 'We're going back to where this started, and I'm asking you this time, not to be my flatmate, never *ever* to be my fallback, but Rosie...' He looked earnestly into her eyes, leaned in until his lips were touching hers, and whispered against them. 'Will you go on a date with me?'

Acknowledgments

To my brilliant agent Becky Thomas, the first one to say 'let's do this' and to whom I actually listened. Thank you for your belief and support and for being my agent of the year, every year.

To Charlotte Ledger, my amazing editor and publisher, who fell in love with Rosie and Mitch and who only made their story stronger. And to the whole team at One More Chapter and HarperCollins (because I know how much work goes in to telling stories,) in particular to Lucy Bennett, Arsalan Isa, Dushi Horti, Chloe Cummings, Emily Thomas and Chloe Quinn.

To my girl crew; Anna Kalsi, Helen Abnett, Lauren Fortune, Louise Denning & Nicola Wood. You might be 1000s of miles away but you're always right with me in my heart.

To Tara Hiatt and Mary Thompson who steadfastly refuse to believe that we no longer share an office and who keep the deskmate vibes going despite an actual, physical ocean between us.

To Jamie Credland and Will Parkhouse; thanks for all the love and literary succour, you clustered up clever kids.

To my family and especially my Mum and Dad, for never thinking that spending an afternoon in a bookshop was wasted time. To Christine for all her love and support.

To Nancy and Edie; my brilliant, funny, smart girls. I love how excited you are about this book!

But mostly this is for Charlie; who was never my fallback,

always my one. Thank you for everything in general and for being mine in particular.

ONE MORE CHAPTER

The author and One More Chapter would like to thank everyone
who contributed to the publication of this story...

Analytics
Abigail Fryer
Maria Osa

Audio
Fionnuala Barrett
Ciara Briggs

Contracts
Sasha Duszynska
Lewis
Florence Shepherd

Design
Lucy Bennett
Fiona Greenway
Holly Macdonald
Liane Payne
Dean Russell

Digital Sales
Lydia Grainge
Emily Scorer
Georgina Ugen

Editorial
Kate Elton
Dushi Horti
Arsalan Isa
Charlotte Ledger
Bonnie Macleod
Jennie Rothwell
Emily Thomas

International Sales
Bethan Moore

Marketing & Publicity
Chloe Cummings
Emma Petfield

Operations
Melissa Okusanya
Hannah Stamp

Production
Emily Chan
Denis Manson
Francesca Tuzzeo

Rights
Lana Beckwith
Rachel McCarron
Agnes Rigou
Hany Sheikh
Mohamed
Zoe Shine
Aisling Smyth

**The HarperCollins
Distribution Team**

**The HarperCollins
Finance & Royalties
Team**

**The HarperCollins
Legal Team**

**The HarperCollins
Technology Team**

Trade Marketing
Ben Hurd
Eleanor Slater

UK Sales
Laura Carpenter
Isabel Coburn
Jay Cochrane
Tom Dunstan
Sabina Lewis
Holly Martin
Erin White
Harriet Williams
Leah Woods

**And every other
essential link in the
chain from delivery
drivers to booksellers
to librarians and
beyond!**

ONE MORE CHAPTER

One More Chapter is an
award-winning global
division of HarperCollins.

Subscribe to our newsletter to get our
latest eBook deals and stay up to date
with all our new releases!

signup.harpercollins.co.uk/
join/signup-omc

Meet the team at
www.onemorechapter.com

Follow us!
 @OneMoreChapter_
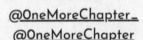 @OneMoreChapter
 @onemorechapterhc

Do you write unputdownable fiction?
We love to hear from new voices.
Find out how to submit your novel at
www.onemorechapter.com/submissions